"THE BAD MAN! THE BAD MAN!"

Somewhere in the darkness, Vicki was screaming. Josh groped around until he found her. The little girl was thrashing about on the bed, arms waving wildly.

"The bad man!"

"Vicki, wake up," Josh commanded his sister. As if his words were magic, she snapped awake, then sobbed loudly in the darkness.

"Where are we?" Vicki asked. "Did the bad man hurt Daddy? Where's Mommy? I *want Mommy!*"

Untangling himself from his sister, Josh got up and walked slowly, hands outstretched in front of him, until he found a wall. Feeling his way along the wall, he found a light switch and flipped it up. His eyes squinted shut at the bright overhead light.

The children were in a windowless room that seemed to be a cellar. Josh spotted a door at the back of the big room. He hurried over and tried to open it. And tried again. And again.

They were locked in.

Tor books by Clare McNally

Somebody Come and Play

There He Keeps Them Very Well

CLARE MCNALLY

A TOM DOHERTY ASSOCIATES BOOK
NEW YORK

THERE HE KEEPS THEM VERY WELL

Copyright © 1994 by Clare McNally

Cover art by Paul E. Stinson
Inside cover photograph by Doug Fornuff Studios, Inc.

A Tor Book
Published by Tom Doherty Associates, Inc.
175 Fifth Avenue
New York, N.Y. 10010

Tor ® is a registered trademark of Tom Doherty Associates, Inc.

ISBN: 0-812-53525-1

First edition: July 1994

Printed in the United States of America

0 9 8 7 6 5 4 3 2 1

This book is dedicated with love to my Aunt, Mary Hoffer, for rides in the country, great ice cream, creative fun and secret dollar bills!

PROLOGUE

Christy Burnett picked up a tray in the school cafeteria, anticipating the taste of hot chicken noodle soup. She hadn't had breakfast that morning, and the delicious smell was making the seven-year-old feel faint with hunger.

"Move it, will you, Creepy Christy?" a little boy said.

Christy moved along compliantly, keeping her eyes on the metal bars that lined the serving area.

"Why don't *you* move, you dumb jerk?" another child said.

Eda Crispin pushed ahead of the offending boy and started to fill her own tray. She grabbed a bowl of Jell-O, a hot dog, corn, French fries and a container of chocolate milk. Christy's brown eyes grew wider with each acquisition.

"Gosh, you must be hungry," she said.

"Guess so," Eda said, poking through a tray of fresh

fruit. She chose a banana. "I got my allowance today. Five dollars."

Five dollars! To Christy, it might as well have been a million.

"I'll share with you, okay?" Eda said.

"Thanks," Christy said with a shy smile.

Eda had just come to Chandler Elementary School a month ago. Mrs. Mincini had told the class she was from Chicago. At recess, all the girls had flocked around the pretty newcomer, anxious to be her friend. Only Christy had remained far off, knowing she wasn't welcome. She had wiggled idly back and forth in a swing, watching.

It hadn't taken the girls long to realize Eda wasn't like them—quiet and well-behaved in starched crinolines and pigtails. She got into a wrestling match with one of the boys and had to stand in the corner on her very first day at Chandler. Soon, the other girls were whispering that Eda was a *tomboy*. They wanted nothing to do with her. But Christy was full of admiration. She couldn't imagine anyone being as brave as Eda, who stood up to bigger kids and always did what she wanted to do. She also couldn't figure out why Eda wanted to be her friend, when no one else did.

As she waited her turn at the soup kettle, Christy watched her friend. She thought Eda Crispin was just about the prettiest kid she'd ever met. Gosh, she had these fat, yellowy curls just like Shirley Temple. Her eyes were big and blue. Her parents bought her the most beautiful clothes. It didn't matter that fidgeting at her desk had wrinkled Eda's dress and pulled her ribbons loose, or that she'd scuffed up the toes of her saddle shoes. Christy thought she looked just like a doll.

The two girls carried their lunch trays—one plentiful, one meager—to a table across the room. They sat apart from the others, unwelcome within the cliques that had already formed at that young age. Eda really didn't care about the other kids, but Christy couldn't help wishing they liked her, too.

A little girl in neatly coiled pigtails and a plaid dress came up to the table. She handed Eda a small pink envelope.

"It's for my birthday party," Tiffany Simmons said. Eda thought she sounded as stuck-up as a princess handing out royal invitations. "My mother met your mother at the Civic Association meeting, and she says I have to invite you."

She gave Christy a disapproving once-over.

"Of course, only *special* kids come to my parties," Tiffany said.

Christy stared down at her soup bowl, taking the insult in silence. She knew that "special" meant "rich."

"I don't want to come to your stupid party," Eda said. "I've got better things to do."

"Gee, too bad," Tiffany said, her high voice squealy with sarcasm.

She skipped off, pigtails and skirt bouncing in unison.

"What a dope," Eda said. "I hate snots like that. And she acted like you weren't even here!"

Christy shrugged. "Most of the girls don't like me."

"Then they're all dopes," Eda said.

She peeled the banana and gave Christy half.

"You wanna ride bikes after school?"

"Okay," Christy said. "But I hafta change out of my school clothes. We have a big rule at my house about that."

Probably the biggest rule *of all*, she thought as she ate the banana. Her mother, Sarah, had spent an entire paycheck on school clothes for Christy and her brother, Harvey. Her father, Harvey Sr., had gotten so mad he beat Sarah up for it. Now those clothes had to last as long as

possible. So a rule had been established—change out of
school clothes or risk their father's wrath.

Christy and Eda finished their lunch and went outside
on the playground. Eda's father had given her a new box
of colored chalk, and they drew pictures on the blacktop.
Christy's depicted a mountain lioness with her cubs.

"That's so good," Eda said. "I wish I could draw like
you, Christy."

Christy smiled her thanks. Soon, a bell beckoned them
inside for afternoon lessons. When at last the day was
over, Eda was the first to race from the classroom.

"Walk, Eda!" Miss Mincini called.

Eda came to an abrupt halt, but hopped from one foot
to the other. A few of the girls in her class looked at her
with distaste, and one commented on what a tomboy she
was. Eda stuck out her tongue.

Christy caught up to her, clutching her bookbag tightly.

"Come on, let's get our bikes," Eda said.

Eda's bike was safely chained as she had left it that
morning. The girls walked out of the school yard, heading
across the street to Christy's home, an apartment over a
pizzeria. It was situated on the corner of Skye and Central
streets, the last of a row of pretty, whitewashed storefronts
that made up downtown Aberdeen. The little town was situated in the midst of Big Sky Country, a vast stretch of
flat land that belied the name of Montana. It was hundreds
of miles to the nearest mountain.

When they reached the pizzeria, Eda stayed on the sidewalk while Christy walked inside.

"Hi, Mr. Venetto," Christy said. "Can I have the key to
the garage? I want to get my bike."

"Of course you can," the broad-shouldered man said.
He looked at the equally broad-shouldered woman behind
the counter, and an expression of sadness came over both
their faces.

Christy had seen that look before, but she didn't understand it.

"Wait, *bambina*," Mrs. Venetto said. She produced two freshly made zeppoles. "For you and your little friend."

"Thank you!" Christy said, delighted.

She followed Mr. Venetto from the store. His wife watched her, shaking her head. She had heard the screams from upstairs, had seen the bruises on Christy's body. If only there was something more she could do than just give the child a treat once in a while!

And such a pretty child, too, Mrs. Venetto thought, despite the almost boylike shortness of her brown hair. She was like a frail flower, so delicate she might have been painted with an artist's finest brush.

Outside, Mr. Venetto rolled Christy's bike from the garage.

"Thanks, Mr. Venetto," Christy said.

"You have fun, *bambina*."

Christy's bike was a rusty, squeaky contraption she'd inherited when Harvey outgrew it. She felt shy bringing it alongside Eda's. *Her* bike was brand-new, with the words PINK LADY stenciled across the bar in fancy script. Eda didn't seem to notice, but Christy was sure she did.

"Wait here," Christy said. "I've got to go upstairs and get out of my school clothes."

To her surprise, she found a note taped onto the locked door. She read it, frowned, and went back downstairs.

"I can't go with you," she moped, sitting down on the steps. "Mommy forgot Harvey had a dentist appointment. She says I have to stay here until she gets back, and that won't be until five. She didn't have time to get someone to watch me."

Eda made a face, her freckled nose crinkling. "That's so boring! You mean you're just gonna sit here on the stairs for two hours?"

"What else can I do?"

Eda thought a moment, then smiled.

"The dentist's office is only around the corner," she said. "Let's find your mom. We'll tell her you want to come to my house."

Christy frowned, unsure what to do.

"Please, Christy?" Eda begged. "We could play with my chemistry set. I have a box of Red Hots candies, too. I'll share."

"Well . . ."

Christy looked back at the dimly lit staircase, where her mother expected her to spend the next hour or so. She compared this with the thought of a nice bike ride into Old Winter Hills, Eda's part of town. She wasn't so sure about the chemistry set—that sounded dangerous—but a mouthful of burny, hot cinnamon candies sure sounded good.

She nodded.

"Okay," she said. "I'll tell her."

They rode through the main part of Aberdeen to the small brick medical building. Christy hopped off her bike.

"You wait here," she said. "I'll go inside and ask Mommy if it's okay."

"I'll come in, too," Eda said.

"No!" Christy cried.

Eda frowned at her. Christy felt herself grow warm. How could she tell Eda she didn't want her friend to see her mother? Christy knew what Sarah would be doing in that waiting room. She'd be staring at the wall, her lips moving quickly as if in conversation with someone no one else could see. If Eda saw Sarah like that, maybe she'd turn against Christy as the other girls had done.

"I—I mean, you need to watch the bikes," Christy stammered.

"Okay," Eda said, still looking puzzled.

Christy pushed her way into the dentist's waiting room.

The air was filled with a funny odor, and the chilling sound of a drill permeated the closed door of the examination room.

"What are you doing here?" Harvey asked, coming up to her.

Harvey was fifteen years old, a kid with a perpetual scowl on his face. Christy pushed past him, refusing to let him start a fight.

"Hi, Mommy," she said, bending down to kiss the woman's cheek.

Sarah did not respond. Her lips were moving, and Christy knew she was hearing her voices again.

"Forget it," Harvey said. "She's freaked out again. Too bad she wasn't freaked out enough to forget my appointment."

"Harvey, could you do me a favor?"

"Okay, but you'll owe me," he said grudgingly.

Christy frowned. "I guess so. Harvey, could you tell Mommy I went to Eda Crispin's house? I'll be back before dinnertime, before it gets dark, okay? Can you tell her that?"

"Sure," Harvey said.

"You won't forget?"

"I said 'Sure,' didn't I?" Harvey snapped.

Christy hurried from the building before he could change his mind.

"I can go," she said. "But I have to be back before dark, and I can't do *anything* to get my clothes dirty."

"We'll be careful, Christy," Eda said. She knew how strict Christy's father was.

For the next hour and a half, Christy had a great time. Eda had more toys than Christy had ever seen, and she was always willing to share. When it was finally time to go home, Christy felt sad.

"I wish you could stay for dinner," Eda said. "I think the cook is making roast chicken."

Christy wondered for a moment what it would be like to have decent meals every night, let alone a cook to prepare them.

"Maybe another time," she said.

After saying good-bye, Christy mounted her bike and sped home. She whizzed by fine brick homes, pink and white azalea bushes no more than flashes to her eyes. These gave way to smaller homes on acre tracts. Christy went by a sump, the drainage from yesterday's storm sending up musty smells. The half block beyond it was solely occupied by a huge gray house. Its front corners were rounded into towers, and old ivy with branches as thick as a man's finger clawed up the rough stone facade.

Christy had always thought the house was haunted. The shades were usually drawn, as if to say "You are not welcome here." She knew a crazy family lived there. She'd heard grown-ups talking about the Gammels. Christy remembered one time when the mother had been arrested for dumping a bagful of newborn kittens in the middle of Lake Aberdeen. Kittens! Christy wondered how anyone could be so cruel!

She picked up speed as she approached the house, wanting to be past it as quickly as possible. But as she was speeding by, the front door crashed open, startling Christy so much that she slammed on her brakes. She slid off the seat, balancing on her toes, as a woman came running towards her, screaming.

"His head! He took off his head!"

Her eyes were wide and crazy, her apron covered with patches of blood. Terrified, Christy fumbled to get herself mounted again. She wondered frantically if this was Irene Gammel, kitten murderer. The woman grabbed Christy's blouse and screamed:

"Help me! Please! They took off his head!"

"Lemme Go!" Christy shouted, pushing the woman with all her might.

The woman went screaming down the street. Shaking all over, Christy got up on her seat. She turned to be on her way, and nearly crashed into a man. He glared at her in a strange way, his eyes full of accusation. Christy felt faint for a moment, fear threatening to black out everything around her.

She blinked and the man was gone. Other neighbors had come out to see what was happening. Christy finally found the strength to pedal away. Her heart pounded so wildly it seemed ready to burst right through her small chest. But the fear she experienced from her encounter wasn't near as intense as the horror of seeing bloodstains on her white blouse, the blouse she was never, ever, to get dirty.

She came to a halt at the corner of Skye and Central, and only then did she feel the sticky warmth against her chest. The blood had soaked right through her slip and undershirt. It was all over the blouse, like a red flag a toreador would wave at a bull. It would have that effect on her father, she was certain. He would accuse her of breaking the rules, and Christy would be severely punished.

As she approached the door that led up to her apartment, something felt hot in her lower abdomen. She might as well have been a prisoner on death row, heading towards the gas chamber, her young mind was that full of terror. Christy was sure that if she opened the door and walked up the stairs, she'd wet her pants. Then she'd be whipped twice as hard for doing such a baby thing.

Without much thought, Christy turned away from the door, got on the bike again, and pedaled down the road. She really didn't know where she was going, only that she had to find some way to make the blouse right again. Ruining an eight-dollar blouse (oh, how many times had

her mother quoted that figure) would result in a beating so
harsh she'd be wearing long sleeves and dark tights for
weeks.

She was so blinded by tears that she could hardly see
where she was going, and it might have been Divine Guid-
ance that kept her from being killed in rush-hour traffic
along Central Street. One pickup truck just missed her, the
driver shouting something Christy couldn't hear.

The old bike bounced up onto the next curb, rattling
down the uneven sidewalk. The town hall sat on this
block, a big square brick building with the words ABER-
DEEN, EST. 1881 carved into the stone lintel above the door.
It was more than a town hall, housing the civic center, police station and library as well. It was from this latter that
a nine-year-old named Lucille Brigham was exiting at the
very moment Christy came flying down the street. Just as
Christy was blinded by fear, Lucille was completely ab-
sorbed by the Dr. Seuss book in her hands. She was just
about to read what happened next on Mulberry Street
when she was knocked flat by Christy's speeding bike.

Lucille's pile of books went flying in all directions. She
landed on the sidewalk with a scream, long legs poking
out from her blue corduroy skirt in a big V. Her black hair
hung over her shoulders like a cape. Christy, entangled in
the bike, began to sob even louder and harder. And then,
in a moment of anger, she began to rip at the blouse. It
was a hateful thing now, the cause of so much trouble.

Lucille, startled but not really hurt, was amazed at the
smaller girl's tantrum. Somehow, when she saw the blood,
Lucille gained the presence of mind to reach out and grab
Christy's arm before the child ripped at yet another button.

"Stop that!" Lucille cried. "Just stop!"

Christy, still bawling, ignored her. But Lucille was big
for her age (some people guessed it closer to thirteen than
nine), and she quickly overpowered the younger child.

"You'll get in trouble if you do that!" she said.

The words were so ironic that they cut through Christy's fury. She sniffled hard and blabbered:

"I'm—I'm already in t-t-trouble!"

Lucille stood up, brushing dirt and grass from her outfit. She looked down at Christy, wide-eyed. Then she carefully pulled the bike from her.

"You got hurt," she said. "You should go into the library and let Miss Greenstrom help you."

"N-no," Christy choked.

"But you're all covered with blood!"

"Not mine," the second-grader replied. "A crazy lady did it to me. She had b-blood on her hands and she wiped them on my blouse and now I'm gonna get a . . . get a . . . whip . . . whipping!"

"Oh, of course you won't," Lucille said. "It wasn't your fault. Your mom and dad can't be that mean, can they?"

The look on Christy's tearful face told the older girl that they very well could be. Lucille sighed. She gathered up the fallen books, then helped Christy to her feet.

"I live just around the corner," she said. "You can come to my house and we'll wash the blouse."

"But that'll take forever," Christy said.

"You can say you fell off the bike," Lucille said. A story was forming in her mind. In it, this little girl with the big brown eyes and boylike brown hair was a princess, held captive by evil people pretending to be her parents. It was up to Lucille to save her—at least this once.

"Yeah," she said, a gleam in her eyes. "You could say you fell off your bike and got knocked unconscious. Maybe you'll still be in trouble, but maybe your mom will be so glad you weren't really hurt that she won't beat you."

Christy sighed, considering this. It was unbelievable

even to her young ears, but this other girl was so much *older* and *bigger* that it had to be a good idea. She nodded.

"Okay," she said.

She and Lucille began to walk together, the bike between them.

"What's your name?"

"Christy Burnett. I'm seven and a half."

"My name's Lucille Brigham. I'm in the fourth grade and I'm head of Student Council."

That didn't mean much to Christy, but she oohhed appropriately.

"Tell me about the lady with the blood on her hands," Lucille requested.

Christy related the story as best as she could, although much of it was a blur. Lucille's eyes went round with fascination.

"I bet she murdered somebody," she said with something akin to glee. "Everyone in town knows that whole Gammel family is nuts. She said something about a head, didn't she? I bet she decapitated someone!"

"Decapi—what?"

"Means she chopped off someone's head," Lucille said, proud to know the big word. "Can you show me the house tomorrow? Can you?"

"I—I don't think I'll be going out tomorrow," Christy said.

They reached a farm, where a yellow house stood back from the road.

"This is my house," Lucille said, leading her along the gravel path. "Come on in, and I'll wash your blouse."

They entered the front door, and Christy's eyes were immediately drawn past the dining room entrance to the sliding glass doors at the back of the house. They offered a view of a large yard. Christy froze for a moment, staring at a horse that ran about a paddock.

"Isn't she cute?" Lucille asked. "She's my mom's, but I'm allowed to ride her if I'm especially good. Like when I help Daddy with the sugar beets. We grow sugar beets, you know. Daddy's the most important sugar beet farmer in the country."

"Wow," was all Christy could say.

"Come on," Lucille said. "The washing machine is downstairs. I know how to use it, too. I help Mother with the wash all the time!"

They descended the wooden staircase to the basement, entering a dark and damp cellar that smelled a lot like turpentine. It was just a jumble of paint cans and tool benches and old clothes boxes to Christy. All she really saw was the gleaming white knight that was the washing machine.

"I know how to use this," Lucille said with pride that made her seem even taller than she was. "Your blouse will be as good as new."

She thought a moment.

"Except for the button."

The button wasn't the worst of it. Christy could live with that.

"You sure are nice," she said.

Lucille smiled. "Thanks."

It was a strange start to a lifelong friendship. Christy didn't go home again for over an hour, and when she did, Harvey Jr. was waiting on the stairs with an evil grin spread across his face.

"Boy, are you gonna get it," he said.

"I—I fell off my bike," Christy lied. "A nice girl took me in to help me, and . . ."

"Save it," Harvey said. "You were supposed to be waiting here on the steps when we got home."

Christy's eyes went round.

"Why didn't you tell Mommy I was at Eda's place? You said you would!"

"Did I say that?" Harvey was completely guileless.

"You stupid drip," Christy said. "I really hate you."

She pushed by him roughly.

"Daddy's got the paddle out," Harvey sneered.

Christy's heart skipped a beat. She wanted to run away again, but this time there was no escape. Trembling all over, her head hanging, she went in to face her punishment.

Harvey Burnett, Sr., was a massively big man, and the sight of him towering over his frail seven-year-old daughter would have been ludicrous if it wasn't so terrifying.

"Where the hell have you been?" he demanded.

"Daddy, Harvey was supposed to tell—"

"Don't make excuses!" Harvey Sr. roared. "You made your mother half sick with worry! She's got enough problems!"

"But, I—"

"Enough talk," her father said. "Get in your room. I'll be there in a minute."

Christy did as she was told. She sat on the edge of her bed, crying, terrified of the punishment she was about to receive. She had no idea that there was a much greater threat hanging over her, something more deadly than her father's wrath.

The woman who had wiped blood all over her had just run from the scene of a gruesome murder. As Christy had suspected, she was Irene Gammel, and the murder victim had been her husband, Darren. The blood had come from the open pipe of his neck, where his head had been just a few minutes earlier.

The crazed expression Christy had seen was probably the most animated Irene had been in years. She was a painfully introverted woman who rarely left her house, and certainly never had anyone to visit. Her neighbors all whispered about the Gammel family and how strange they were. Sometimes, they spoke with pity of Irene and Darren's children, ten-year-old Teddy and four-year-old Adrian.

But that evening, the boys were the subject of an intensive search. They had disappeared without a trace, perhaps kidnapped by the same person who had murdered their father.

"I'll bet the old bitch did something to those kids," Harvey Sr. speculated as he lounged in front of the TV set.

"You think she killed them, too?" Harvey Jr. asked with gory fascination.

"Chopped their friggin' little heads right off!"

Both father and son laughed out loud.

Christy heard the conversation from her bedroom, where she had stayed after the beating her father gave her. She tried to cover her ears, but her mind kept replaying her father's words. Irene had chopped off her little boys' heads. Some grown-ups beat their kids, some grown-ups chopped off heads. She fell asleep thinking those horrible thoughts and began to dream.

In the dream, her father was chasing her with the biggest Ping-Pong paddle she'd ever seen. It was bigger than a tennis racket and covered with spikes! Christy ran as fast as she could, but she didn't go anywhere. She took a great leap, her legs scrambling in midair, but she couldn't land. Panic filled her as she desperately tried to make contact with the sidewalk below her. Somehow, in the dream, the inside of the apartment had turned to the street where the Gammel family lived.

Something grabbed her. Christy screamed soundlessly as her father swung her around. But it wasn't her father anymore. It was a complete stranger, who pulled her up close to his face and glared at her with the cruel, ugly green eyes of a devil.

"Keep your mouth shut, girl," he breathed. He pushed a knife right up to her face, the blade gleaming in light from an unseen source. "Keep it shut or I'll rip your face right off!"

Christy woke up screaming. Her father ran in to her, called her a hysterical little bitch because she'd interrupted his TV program, and threatened her with another beating if she didn't shut up.

Christy shut up.

But it was hours before she fell asleep again.

ONE

Thirty Years Later

INDEPENDENCE DAY WAS almost over, but the grand finale, the fireworks, had yet to come. A slight figure in a sleeveless white dress sat on the grass that sloped down to Lake Aberdeen, just one of hundreds who had come to the festival. A little girl sat in the hammock her skirt made over her crossed legs. Christine Wander kissed the top of her daughter Victoria's head. It smelled of bubble gum shampoo, a reminder of the bath the five-year-old had taken under extreme protest. Vicki wriggled.

"When's Daddy and Joshua coming back?" she asked.

"There are a lot of people here," Chris told her. "There must have been a long line at the snack vendor's."

"I'm hungry! I want a Sno-Kone!" Vicki said.

She jumped from her mother's lap and shot off into the crowd. Chris was on her feet at once.

"Victoria!"

Vicki ignored her. Lucille, who sat beside Christine, shook her head with a smile.

"Oh, let her run," she said.

Chris frowned, craning her neck to see through the groups of families.

"I just don't like her out of my sight," she said.

"You worry too much," Lucille replied.

She uncrossed her legs and got up to stand beside her friend. Lucille was dressed in jeans, her black French braid perfectly aligned with the pleat down the back of her Liz Claiborne shirt.

"Must be great to feel so free," she said. "I'm not sure if I ever ran around like that."

"Oh, sure you did," Chris said. "You weren't as wild as Eda, but you had your fun."

"Have you heard from Eda lately?"

"Just talked to her on the phone last week," Chris replied. "And her partner, Tim Becker, sent a clipping from *New York Newsday*. Eda received a citation for saving a man's life!"

"And she didn't tell us herself," Lucille said. "That figures."

"You know Eda," Chris replied. "She hates a fuss."

As the women spoke, Vicki made her way through the crowd. She had spotted her father in the group a few yards away. She could tell it was her daddy even from this far away. Her daddy had red hair just like she did, and everyone would say: "Where did you get that red hair?" Vicki thought that was a dumb question. She'd *always* had red hair. Did they think she went to the store to buy it?

She jumped at her father, hugging him from behind.

"Hi, Daddy!" she squealed, delighted that she'd snuck up without being heard.

Her father grunted and turned around. Instantly, Vicki saw that it wasn't her father at all. This man had red hair, but he wasn't Daddy. The man glared down at her, freezing her with a look. Even in the fading light, Vicki could see that his eyes were rimmed with red and full of meanness. She felt something congeal in the pit of her stomach.

"Girl . . ."

The man's voice was as deep as a bullfrog's croak, spoken through thick lips that split a stubbed face. He reached out to grab Vicki's arm. But the child was like a cricket, jumping at the slightest touch. She ran back to her mother as fast as she could. Vicki threw herself against Chris, practically knocking her down.

"Victoria Wander, don't run away from me!" Chris said, her voice sharply edged with anger. "Don't you ever do that again!"

"Mommy, there was this really creepy man over there!" Vicki said, pointing. Safe with her mother, she turned to look where the man had been. The spot was empty. "He tried to grab me!"

"Are you sure, honey?" Lucille said, thinking of her own eleven-year-old son, Jerry, off to buy a treat for himself.

"Sure, I'm sure! He had mean eyes and he sounded like a lion, and . . ."

But the sentence was lost in the sound of her brother's voice.

"They didn't have any cherry ones," Joshua said, one thin arm stretched out with a paper cone full of flavored ice. "I got you grape."

Vicki took the Sno-Kone, forgetting all about the fright she'd had.

"I got one, too, Mom," a blond-haired boy with large brown eyes said to Lucille. "Mr. Wander paid for it."

"That was nice, Jerry," Lucille said. She looked at Brian. "You didn't have to do that."

"No big deal," Brian said.

Lucille considered the handsome man her friend had married twelve years earlier. Brian's auburn hair was neatly trimmed, his eyes the most incredible emerald green behind his glasses. He was handsome, and he was also one of the nicest guys Lucille had ever met. If her husband had been one iota as nice as Brian, she might not have divorced him two years earlier.

"What about you, Josh?" Chris asked her son. "Where's your Sno-Kone?"

"I don't like grape," Josh said. He held a huge pretzel up to his face, peering through it with round, dark eyes. "So I got one of these."

"Looks like they're almost ready," Brian said, pointing to the barge in the middle of the lake.

The fireworks began with a rendition of the National Anthem. Over the next half hour, the sky above the lake was filled with color, and the cries of the pleased crowd were second only to the massive booms that followed an occasional dud. Vicki kept her hands over her ears. At last, the final Roman candle was set off. Families gathered together and made their way to the parking lot. Brian went ahead, carrying Vicki. She seemed ready to fall asleep. Josh and Jerry ran circles around them.

"Are you busy tomorrow?" Chris asked Lucille. "I thought we could go to the mall for the big sales. We could make a day of it. You know, leave the boys at the video arcade? I wouldn't have to rush home, because Brian's heading out on a business trip."

"Another one?" Lucille asked, a hint of disapproval in her voice.

But Chris wouldn't argue with her. Yes, Brian left her alone for long stretches of time. That was part of being head buyer at Brenley's, the area's biggest department store. Lucille worried too much about her—had been worrying about her ever since that day Chris had crashed her bike. Sometimes, Chris had to remind her friend that she was no longer in the second grade.

"Well, it's only overnight this time," she said.

"It's just too bad he has to go away so frequently," Lucille said. "If you need anything while he's gone . . ."

Chris smiled at her. They'd reached the parking lot, where Lucille's teenaged sons were waiting.

"Hi, Mrs. Wander," the fifteen-year-old twins said in unison.

"Hi, Eric," Chris said. "Hi, Robby."

The families parted company then. But Lucille's words stayed with Chris, and she was thoughtful during the drive home. Brian *did* go away a lot these days. He'd only held his position for six months, so she supposed it would take her a while to get used to it. But, still . . .

"I wish you didn't have to leave tomorrow," she said to him. "It would have been nice to have a long weekend together."

Brian shrugged. "Business, honey. I have to work my tail off to prove myself to my employers. Eventually, I hope to have enough clout to send someone else in my place once in a while."

He pulled into the driveway and stopped the car. Then he looked at her.

"Are you okay?"

"I guess so," she said. "It's just that I love you so much, and I really miss you when you're away."

"I love you, too, honey."

"Save it for later!" Josh cried, stopping their kiss before they even got near each other. "Ick!"

"Oh, Josh." Chris sighed. To the ten-year-old, any display of affection was "ick."

She opened her door. "Brian, carry Vicki in. She's out like a light."

Even in her sleep, Vicki cuddled lovingly against her fa-

ther's shoulder. Chris smiled, feeling warm inside. That
was the way a father was supposed to treat a daughter. Not
the way her father had; the only times he had touched her
was to hurt her.

She followed them up the stairs and helped tuck the little girl into bed. Then, impulsively, she turned and gave
her husband a big kiss.

Brian smiled and whispered:

"What brought that on?"

Chris shrugged. "I guess it's just seeing how sweet you
are with the kids."

Brian put an arm around her and led her from the room.
As they got ready for bed, Chris remembered the strange
man Vicki had seen. She told Brian about him.

"Probably just a weirdo," Brian said. "But I'm glad
nothing happened. Vicki's just too friendly, if you ask me.
You've got to have a talk with her about strangers."

"I've done that," Chris said. "It doesn't sink in. But remember, she's only five."

They climbed into bed. Chris slid close to her husband,
resting her head against his chest. She started massaging
him.

"I had such a good time tonight," she said.

"Me, too," Brian said.

He kissed the top of her head.

"You'll probably dream about red-white-and-blue
sparks," he said.

Chris was silent for a moment. Thinking she had fallen
asleep, Brian started to pull away from her. But her arm
went across his waist and she held him tightly.

"You know I don't dream, Brian," she said. "At least,
not any more."

Brian was glad that she no longer dreamed, because her
dreams had always been horrible. For the first two years of
their marriage, she'd woken up many nights screaming in

terror. Brian would have to hold her and assure her again and again that nothing was going to hurt her.

"I guess you stopped dreaming about the time Josh was born," Brian said.

About the time she was able to trade the memory of her own childhood for the happy childhood of her son. Even if she lived it vicariously, she got great pleasure from seeing Josh's normal, well-adjusted upbringing. She hadn't had a nightmare in over ten years.

"Can you hold me until I fall asleep?" she asked.

"Sure," Brian said. "Mind if I ask why? I mean, you usually seem more comfortable over on your stomach, with room to stretch your legs."

"Guess I need a little loving," Chris said. "That man tonight, the one Vicki saw, frightened me. Do you remember when we first met? How that weirdo had been following me?"

"Coincidence," Brian insisted. "Put it out of your mind and get some sleep, babe. You'll probably never see that man again."

"God, I hope not," Chris said. "I don't know what I'd do if . . ."

She yawned.

". . . anything happened to the kids."

"Nothing's gonna happen," Brian swore. "I always tell you that, don't I? Nothing will happen so long as I'm around to keep you safe. I love you so much, Chris, that I . . ."

The arm that had been hugging him so tightly suddenly went limp. This time, Chris really was asleep. Brian moved her arm and turned to settle in himself. But he didn't fall asleep right away. He wouldn't admit it to Chris, because he had always been the rock she leaned on for support, but the thought of Vicki talking to a stranger made him nervous, too. He was almost tempted to cancel the trip he was taking in the morning. But he thought better of it. It was important, and he couldn't put off going.

Still, he couldn't fall asleep right away. He lay there gazing at his wife, her face softly illuminated by the moonlight pouring in through the curtains. Brian thought she was as beautiful now as she'd been the day he met her. Maybe even more so—back then, she'd been the pallid, dark-circled-eyed product of an abusive childhood. When he'd seen how that man had been following her, tormenting her, he'd wanted to kill him. More than that, he wanted to keep Christine Burnett with him forever, to protect her as one might protect a delicate work of art.

Slowly, he reached through the dim light and stroked the outline of her face. Her cheeks had filled out a bit in the last decade, but she had needed the added weight. Brian knew that even real family love, combined with many hours in a therapist's office, couldn't completely eradicate what her father had done to her. Sometimes things would happen that would bring out the fearful child she'd been. Like the man in the park tonight. Brian wondered who he might be, and finally fell asleep with a growing sense of worry that promised bad dreams.

The next morning, Chris and the kids stood in front of the house, waiting with Brian for the taxi that would take him to the airport. He kissed them all warmly, and Chris gave him a tighter hug than usual. Brian wanted to warn her to watch out for strangers, but he knew he didn't need to do that. Chris was a naturally wary person.

After he had gone, Chris met Lucille and headed for Longacre Mall. They left Josh and Jerry with a supply of quarters at the video parlor, but Chris insisted Vicki was too young.

"I am not!" Vicki cried. "I can stay by myself!"

"No way," Chris said, thinking how easily Vicki had

spoken to the stranger at the fireworks. "But tell you what—I'll treat you to an ice cream, okay?"

Vicki considered this, then nodded.

"Okay," she said. "But I can *still* stay by myself."

After buying Vicki a cone, Chris and Lucille headed to Brenley's, the big department store where Brian worked as head buyer. His discount card, combined with the sales, helped Chris fill a huge shopping bag without spending too much. The day sped by, and it seemed Chris didn't think about Brian even once.

But that night, when she was lying alone in their bed, she couldn't help missing him.

"Silly," she told herself, rolling over to his side of the bed. His pillow smelled faintly of after-shave. "He'll be back tomorrow."

Chris fell asleep, breathing in the aroma of her husband's after-shave.

Sometime near four A.M., she was awakened by the barking of the dogs next door. For a moment, she lay there with her eyes wide open, her heart pounding. She listened as the dogs' owner came out to shut them up, but even after it became quiet again she couldn't fall asleep.

She had a strange feeling that something was wrong.

For a long time she lay there, listening to the quiet of the house. When the silence was suddenly interrupted by the sound of Josh coughing, Chris was filled with an overwhelming desire to make certain her kids were okay. She didn't know why she felt nervous, but she pushed her covers aside and went down the hall.

Both Josh and Vicki were sleeping like angels. She adjusted Vicki's covers, tucking the yellow unicorn close to her. Then she checked to be certain Josh's breathing was okay. Maybe the cough had been caused by the dry air, but she hoped he wasn't coming down with a cold.

She was about to go back to bed when she suddenly understood why the barking had put her off. Those dogs never barked at night! Even if they'd done it before, it hadn't been enough to wake her up.

What had they heard? Had someone been out there?

She thought about the stranger at the Fourth of July festival and her panic began to rise. Had he come to find Vicki?

"Oh, Brian," she said. "I wish you were here!"

She hated being alone, especially with two children. The nervous pounding of her heart made it impossible for her to try to sleep again. Instead, she became somewhat manic, rushing from window to door to be certain every lock was secure. The dogs were completely silent now, but she listened intently for any odd noises.

Sometimes, she wished that Brian would let her have a gun.

She sat on the couch and listened, waiting. . . .

TWO

▼

Chris woke up on the couch the next morning. Bright daylight chased away all her fears, and everything seemed all right again. She ate a quick breakfast and immediately worked on straightening up the house for Brian's homecoming. She got so busy that she completely forgot the previous night's scare. She put on a nice outfit and pulled her hair back with a matching headband. Brian had only been gone overnight, but Chris wanted to look her best for him when he returned.

The kids were playing out front with their friends when the taxi pulled up. Vicki and Josh raced each other into the house to announce their father's arrival. With a smile on her face, Chris hurried out to greet him. Her heart sank when she saw a scowl on his face. His eyes were darkly circled as if he hadn't slept that night.

"Oh, honey," Chris said, "it looks like you had a bad time."

"Terrible," Brian said simply.

He gave her a perfunctory kiss, and barely acknowledged the children. Chris saw the disappointed looks on their faces and said:

"Your father's tired out. You go on and play and we'll call you in later."

She walked into the house with her husband.

"Was it a difficult trip?"

"The worst," Brian said. "The client was a real pain in the ass. It took all my effort to convince him I didn't want every single item in his line."

"Oh, Brian." Chris sighed. "Is the hassle worth it?"

"For a forty-five-thousand-dollar per annum salary it is," Brain snapped. The tone of voice was so unlike him that Chris took a step back. He spoke more softly. "I'm sorry. I shouldn't take this out on you. If I'm to continue being the head buyer for one of Montana's biggest department store chains, I have to get used to hard work. And the occasional annoying supplier."

He rubbed his eyes. Bloodshot from lack of sleep, they seemed a duller green than usual.

"I don't want to talk about this now, Chris," he said. "I just want to take a nap."

"Okay," Chris said. "I'll make sure the house is quiet."

She watched him drag up the stairs, his head hanging from exhaustion. It wasn't the first time he'd come home from a trip this way, and the stress was aging him. There were times when Chris wished he'd never gotten that promotion.

Alone in their room, Brian stared at his reflection and hated what he saw there: a liar. Not just a liar, but a man who told falsehoods to the most important, most cherished person in his life.

"I have to do it," he said. "I have to do it until everything is straightened out, or terrible things will happen to my family."

Nothing bad must ever happen to Chris and the kids. He'd worked too hard to win her, and the children had been a wonderful added prize. Thoughts of his competitor reminded him how weary he was. He lay down on the bed and closed his eyes, thinking that Chris must never learn the identity of that competitor for her affections. Soon, he was fast asleep.

When he came down two hours later, the change was miraculous. He was smiling, his eyes bright.

"Let's take the kids to Burger Barn," he suggested.

"Brian, are you sure you're up to it?" Chris asked worriedly.

"I'm fine," Brian insisted. "Let's enjoy the rest of the day together."

Brian seemed to be his old self. He opened the front door and called out to the crowd of kids playing dodgeball in the street.

"Josh! Vicki!"

Two small heads, one raven-haired, one fiery red, turned to him. Brian suggested a trip to Burger Barn, and they came running. They piled into the backseat of the car, and the family was on its way.

"Can I have a PeeWee Pack?" Vicki asked.

"Sure," Brian said. "Why not? Do you want one, Josh?"

Josh rolled his eyes as if to show he was too sophisticated for the specials kids' meal.

"The prizes are always dumb," he said.

"I like them," Vicki insisted.

Chris rested an arm on the back of her seat and turned to look at the kids.

"Why don't we pick lunch up at the drive-in window?" she suggested. "Then we can take it down to Lake Aberdeen and eat there."

"Primo!" Josh cried.

"Royal!" Vicki cried.

"Groovy!" Brian said with a big grin.

Bewildered looks crossed the children's faces. Chris began to laugh, and she gave Brian's thigh a little squeeze.

"You kids aren't the only ones with a language of your own," she said. "We used to say 'groovy' when something was great."

Josh and Vicki giggled.

"What other silly things did you say?"

Brian straightened himself up with mock indignation.

"I beg your pardon," he drawled. "We did not say silly things."

"Not too silly," Chris said. "Stuff like 'Right on' and 'Out of sight.' "

" 'Right arm,' " Brian said, holding up his arm. "And 'Out of state.' "

This, the children decided, was *definitely* silly. They burst into gales of laughter, falling over on the backseat.

"What's so funny?" Chris asked her husband. "That we talked like that?"

"That we were really kids once," Brian said.

Chris looked back at her rambunctious children with a smile. But Brian could see it was a melancholy smile, and he wondered if she was thinking of her own childhood. Had she ever laughed like that? He doubted it.

They had reached Burger Barn. Brian pulled up to the outdoor menu and shouted his order for lunch. Twenty minutes later, they were sitting at a picnic table on the banks of Lake Aberdeen. It was a particularly gorgeous summer day, and other families had come to enjoy the lush green grass and trees and the sparkling water. There was no evidence at all of the festival that had taken place a few days before, not a bent firecracker or an empty pretzel bag.

"They do a good job on this place," Brian said.

"It's a lovely park," Chris agreed.

Vicki pushed a mysterious pile of brightly colored plastic at her father.

"Put this together?" she asked.

Brian took a look at the pieces, then quickly snapped them into a little bear with wheels.

"Burger Bear!" Vicki cried. She wheeled it around the painted green surface of the table with one hand while eating her cheeseburger with the other.

"It *was* a dumb prize," Josh mumbled.

Nobody paid attention to him. When they finished their lunch, they cleaned up their mess. Then Josh and Vicki ran off to play while Brian and Chris took a hand-in-hand walk along the lake.

"I'm glad we did this," Chris said. "It's too bad you don't have more days off from work. I love spending time together as a family."

"Me, too," Brian said. "I know it sounds old-fashioned, but sometimes I just can't believe what a good life we have. I'm really very happy, Chris."

"You can't believe it?" Chris said, dubious. "There are mornings I still wake up and wonder if this is all a dream. Those nine years I spent in therapy cleaning up the mess my father made of my childhood never quite convinced me things could really be wonderful."

Brian gave her hand a squeeze.

"But you are happy," he said. "I promised you that the day I asked you to marry me. Now things are starting to change, even for the better. I have my eyes on a bigger house."

"Oh, Brian!"

"Well, it's just an idea," Brian said. "A nice place across town on several acres. It has five bedrooms."

"Why do we need five bedrooms?"

"I don't know," Brian said absently. He stopped to stare

across the lake at a sailboat. "It isn't that our family isn't complete with a boy and a girl, but . . ."

Chris laughed. "My goodness, you're just full of interesting ideas today. Are you saying you want to try for another baby?"

"Maybe." Brian was thoughtful for a few minutes. "I think it's good for kids to have lots of siblings. That way, they can protect each other."

"From what?" Chris asked. "You really don't know much about siblings, do you? When I was growing up, my brother spent half his time tormenting me."

Brian nodded, a sad look of understanding coming over his face.

"I'm willing to go for number three," Chris said. "But just remember that Vicki was the pregnancy from hell. You really want to put up with my crazy emotions and aches and pains for nine months?"

Brian stopped and took her into his arms.

"Do you?" he asked.

He didn't wait for an answer, but gave her a kiss warmer than the sunshine washing over them.

"Well, at least our kids are pretty decent to each other," Chris said as they started to walk back. "I mean, Josh complains that Vicki bothers him all the time, but they're never actually cruel to each other."

"Siblings should always get along," Brian said.

"It isn't always like that in the real world," Chris reminded him.

The children came running up to them.

"Can we go for a hike?" Josh asked.

"Great idea," Chris said.

"Royal idea," Brian amended.

Vicki laughed, "Say 'Groovy.' "

Brian pulled her up into his arms and danced around with her, singing a song from the late sixties.

The woods surrounding the lake were huge, and it was easy to get lost in them. For this reason, the Parks Department supplied a free trail map. They obtained one in the fat little brick building that housed the park's administration. For the next two hours, they hiked through the woods, admiring different trees and flowers. Vicki often raced ahead, but a quick word from Brian brought her back again.

At last, Vicki ran out of steam. Brian carried her piggyback as they traced their path out of the woods. They were in the parking lot when Vicki pointed back at the trees and shouted:

"Mommy! Daddy! There's that man!"

Chris turned to the edge of the trees. Although he stood clear across a large parking lot, she could easily make out a man in scraggly clothes. Her heart jumped into her throat.

"What man?" Josh asked.

"I don't see anyone," Brian said as he set Vicki down on the ground.

Chris saw that the figure had moved back into the shadows of the trees. The chill she felt made no sense on this hot summer day.

Brian must have recalled the creepy man Vicki had run into at the fireworks, because with a serious look on his face, he kept his eyes on Chris while he ushered the kids into the back of the car. Once the doors were closed, he felt he could speak.

"What are you thinking?" he asked.

"I don't understand what you mean," Chris said weakly.

"Yes, you do," Brian said. "I'm the man who loves you most, remember? Something about the man Vicki saw upset you. Please tell me what bothers you."

Chris looked at him with imploring eyes.

"That he's back again," she said. "That the man who terrorized me long ago is back again. Only now, he wants my children."

"Chris, that's impossible," Brian insisted. "It's been thirty years!"

"He followed me when I was seven," Chris said, "and later, when I was nine."

"But you didn't have me those times," Brian said.

"I'm just so afraid of—"

Brian cut her off. "If you're nervous, why don't you give Dr. Romano a call?"

"My therapist?" Chris said. "I haven't seen her in three years. I don't need her anymore, Brian. I need to know that man isn't the same one who was after me."

Brian was about to say something, but Josh cracked the window a bit and called out impatiently:

"Some of us are roasting like turkeys!"

"Oh, Josh, I'm sorry!" Chris said. "It must be beastly in that car! Open the windows!"

Brian climbed in on the driver's side. He turned on the engine and flipped the air-conditioner control to MAX. Josh began to study a collection of small rocks he'd stored in his pocket. Vicki retrieved a bright yellow unicorn, her favorite toy, from the car floor and began to march it across the back of the seat. The subject of the stranger was dropped in their proximity, but Chris hoped to bring it up again when they got home. She needed more reassurance. But when they arrived, the phone was ringing. Brian went off to do some yard work while Chris answered it.

"Hello?"

Silence.

"Hello?" Chris pressed.

"Wrong number," a gruff voice replied, and the line went dead.

Chris stared at the receiver. She tried to feel annoyed at the caller's rudeness, but instead a feeling of trepidation filled her. Maybe it was just residual nervousness after seeing that strange man in the park, but . . .

. . . but there was a strange and frightening familiarity in that deep voice.

THREE

▼

A WEEK LATER Brian came home to find Chris was barbecuing chicken for dinner. She stood on the patio, tongs in one hand, portable phone in the other. She was wearing a pair of red-and-white gingham shorts and a red tank top, her hair pulled into a high ponytail. Brian gave her a kiss on the cheek.

"It's Eda on the phone," Chris said. "She just called to say hi."

"Hi, Eda!" Brian called into the phone. He heard her voice return the greeting.

After a few minutes, Chris said good-bye to her friend and hung up.

"Doesn't Eda know long-distance is cheaper on weekends?" Brian asked. "Or do New York City cops make that much money?"

"Eda never cared about money," Chris said. "And she's always been a spur-of-the-moment person. She felt like calling, and she did. It was nice to hear from her."

There was a rolling bar on the patio, set up with plastic tumblers, an ice bucket, and soft drinks. Brian poured himself a ginger ale, then said:

"Is she planning to come back to Montana soon?"

"No." Chris sighed. She really missed her friend, whom she hadn't seen in nearly a year. "Eda's working extra time towards her detective's shield. She's hoping to be promoted by the end of the year."

She began turning the chicken. Brian inspected an aluminum package on the back of the grill, gingerly pulling back a hot corner with two fingers. The smell of garlic wafted toward him.

"Garlic potatoes and barbecued chicken," he said. "My favorite dinner. We're eating early, babe. How come?"

They usually sat down to the table around seven.

"Did you forget?" Chris asked. "I'm teaching at the adult ed center."

Brian nodded. "That's right. Your art class starts tonight."

Chris had worked part-time in the local art supplies store for years. Her boss had pointed out her talent for drawing as a potential money-maker, and had offered to display some of her work in exchange for her teaching a class. She'd agreed readily, and had been surprised how quickly her drawings had sold.

Josh came into the yard then, dressed in his bathing suit. His hair was wet; water dripped down his tanned face. He took the towel from his shoulders and wiped the drops away.

"Hi," he said. "We're eating early?"

"Mom's teaching tonight," Brian said. "Where's your sister?"

"Vicki's playing with Nicole," Josh said, referring to a four-year-old who lived two doors down the block.

He rested a bare knee on the picnic bench and snatched a carrot from the top of the salad.

"Go on and get her," Chris said. "We'll be eating soon."

A short time later, the four Wanders sat around the picnic table, enjoying a wonderful summer dinner. The corn on the cob was sweet; the tomatoes, sent over from Lucille's garden, were like candy. Vicki made loud noises sucking barbecue sauce off her fingers, setting Josh off to say what a pig she was. But it was good-natured teasing, and the blueberry pie Chris had made for dessert put everyone in a good mood.

An hour later, Brian, Vicki and Josh settled in front of the TV set. Chris came into the den to say good-bye. Brian was manning one of the controls to their Sega Genesis system, Josh had the other. Two alienlike creatures moved about the screen to a fast-paced tune.

"Don't be playing that to all hours," Chris warned. "You know how riled up Vicki gets."

"Oh, we won't," Brian promised, not taking his eyes from the screen. A strange being disappeared in an explosion of stars.

A triumphal tune played.

"Wow! We beat the fifth level boss!" Josh said.

"My turn! My turn!" Vicki insisted.

"Brian, I mean it," Chris said.

Brian handed Vicki his controller.

"Only one more level," he reassured her. "I promise."

Chris gave them each a kiss, leaving the house with the knowledge that one level might take an hour. Well, if Vicki was too excited to fall asleep at a normal time, Brian would have to deal with her himself.

She enjoyed her first painting class. The students were blessed with a mix of talents, and they all seemed to learn something from her. As she drove home, she was already making plans for the next class.

When she pulled her car in behind Brian's, she noticed the house was unusually dark. Brian hadn't left the outside light on for her.

"Bulb probably went out," she told herself without worry.

But a funny feeling came over her as she entered the house. She had to stop inside the door to get her bearings, to understand why an old feeling of dread had come back again. She'd felt it the other night, when the dogs awakened her.

She hadn't felt it before that since . . .

Chris quickly realized what had set her instincts on edge. It was just a little thing, but so *wrong*: one of Vicki's favorite toys, a bright pink horse with flowers painted all over, was on the steps. Brian would never have permitted it to remain there, unless . . .

"Oh, don't be silly," she told herself.

The command didn't work. She felt trouble in the air as thickly as if it was pouring out of the vents. Chris picked up the horse. Something wet came off on her hands. It was blood.

"Brian?" she called, quietly, nervously. Vicki must have cut herself, that was all.

She waited to hear him call her from the den. When he didn't, she told herself he had probably fallen asleep in front of the TV.

There was a streak of blood on the corridor wall.

"Brian?" A little louder now. Her heart was beginning to pound.

She raced into the den. The TV screen was dark gray, silent. A bowl of popcorn Brian had shared with the kids had been knocked onto the floor, small pieces scattered everywhere. Brian would never have left such a mess.

Her heart beating wildly with fear now, Chris ran for the stairs.

"Brian!"

She burst into their bedroom and threw on the light switch. When she saw his red hair peeking out from the upper edge of the bedspread, she let out a cry of relief that was half laughter, half whimper.

"Oh, Brian," she said in a shaking voice. "You won't believe the crazy thoughts that just went through my head!"

Brian didn't move. Chris moved closer to the bed.

Poor guy. These past few days really wore him out.

"Brian?" she whispered. Her voice was still trembling. She sat on the edge of the bed.

"Brian, wake up!" she cried, desperate for an explanation of the chaos downstairs. She had a feeling he was awake by now, but too tired to respond. "Please, honey? I just had a terrible fright."

The feeling of trouble was starting to surface again. Chris shifted position on the bed, kneeling beside her sleeping husband. The movement rocked the mattress, and Brian's head turned. There, Chris thought with relief. He's waking up now.

Then she noticed Brian's head had rolled a little too far; his head, but not his body. His neck was even now with the outline of his right shoulder.

But that was impossible. . . .

Chris jumped from the bed. This time, she did not cry out tentatively. She screamed with all her might:

"Brian! Brian! BRIIIAAANNN!"

In a moment of fear and fury, she grabbed for the bedspread and jerked it away. The Oriental pattern had hidden the horror beneath: the blanket was soaked with blood. Shaking all over, but unable to stop herself, Chris peeled away the blanket, then the top sheet. Then she stopped screaming. The shock of what she saw stifled any noise she could make.

Brian was lying on his stomach, dressed only in his briefs. A thick but perfectly even line of blood ran down the valley in the middle of his back, where his muscles joined at his spine. There was a huge puddle of blood on the pillow, just above his neck.

He had been decapitated. His head lay on its side, jiggled a good eight inches from his neck in her frenzied stripping of the bed. His face, half turned into the mattress, pointed away from her.

Oh, no, this can't be happening! Chris tried hard to deny what she was seeing. *I'm having nightmares again! I'm having a bad dream and I'm going to wake up and Brian's going to be okay and . . .*

In the midst of her panic, something in Brian's clenched hand caught Chris's eye. Sobbing, begging herself to wake up, she bent and peered closer.

It was a hank of hair from the mane of Vicki's toy horse.

The children! Overwhelming terror gripped Chris as she ran from the room, calling to her children in a voice that could have been heard across the street.

"Josh! Vicki! VICTORIAAAAA!"

Their beds were empty, never slept in.

"WHERE ARE YOU?"

Chris ran through the house, yelling at the top of her lungs. There was no sign of the children.

She was cruelly aware that this was no nightmare. This was hell.

But she'd lived through hell already, all through her childhood!

"How can this be happening?" Chris wailed, stumbling towards the front door on feet that seemed made of rubber.

She ran outside and crossed the darkened street to

Lucille's house. Her friend answered the wild pounding on her front door within moments, the twins standing groggily behind her.

The sight of Chris's wild animal eyes were enough to snap Lucille completely awake. She took hold of her friend and steered her into the house.

"Chris! What's wrong? What's happening?" she demanded.

Chris grabbed Lucille by the arms and left blood on her skin.

"Someone's killed Brian," she gasped. "Someone's cut off his head and taken my babies—Oh, God. Oh, God . . . !"

She fell into the taller woman's arms, sobbing.

"Who would want to hurt my family?"

"Chris, what are you talking about?" Lucille demanded.

"Brian is dead," Chris choked. "I just found him upstairs in our room. He's dead, and the children are gone."

Lucille was stunned by Chris's statement. Brian was dead? The kids gone? It didn't make sense!

"Help me, please," Chris whimpered. She had screamed herself hoarse.

"Okay, okay," Lucille said, trying to force herself to be in control. "Robby, call the police. Eric, you get Mrs. Wander a glass of water."

The twins ran for the kitchen.

Down the block, a scruffy-looking man watched the Wander house from the darkness of his van. He'd waited for the mother to come home, waited to see how she'd react. It was so much like that other time, thirty years earlier. Same story, different day. He laughed, but quickly stopped himself from making more noise. He didn't want to wake up the children, bound and gagged in the back of the van.

But that wasn't likely to happen. Both kids had been as

silent as the dead from the moment he had covered their mouths with chloroform.

He turned on his engine and drove off.

By the time the night air was filled with the sound of police sirens, the man and his captives were many, many blocks away.

FOUR

▼

LIEUTENANT EDA CRISPIN, one arm firmly on the shoulder
of another woman, pushed her way through the nighttime
crowd of a Queens, New York, police station. Her "collar"
moved reluctantly, staggering, a pout on her heavily
made-up face. They came to an abrupt halt at the sergeant's desk.

"Take care of her, Neal," Eda said. "It's started to rain
and she needs a place to spend the night."

"I didn't do nothin'!" the hooker snapped.

Leaving her in Neal's care, Eda went to the locker
room, in passing greeting a fellow officer and ignoring the
leers of two pushers who had been brought in a short
while earlier.

She dressed quickly, trading her uniform for black den-
ims and a red T-shirt studded with rhinestone stars. She
pushed her fingers through her tight cap of curls to fluff

them up. In a million years, no one would know the woman she saw in her locker mirror was a cop. Eda hoped to put that to an advantage someday, when she earned the gold shield of a detective.

She was exiting the locker room, pulling on a raincoat, when her partner called her from across the floor.

"Hey, Cowgirl!" Tim Becker said. "There's a fax coming in for you!"

Eda had learned long ago not to react to the nickname she'd been given in the academy. When her friends had learned she'd come all the way from Montana, they'd started calling her that; her protests that her father was a newspaperman, not a rancher, were met by deaf ears. Tim had graduated with her, and so the name had been carried clear through to her assignment here in this Bayside precinct.

"It's from Montana," Tim said as he pulled the paper out of the machine.

In the time it took Eda to cross the room, a few words seemed to jump off the page at him: *Murder . . . Missing . . . Chris.* Tim realized it was bad news, and handed the paper to Eda with a worried expression. As she read it, he watched the color drain from her face. Eda's teeth clenched together and she began swearing under her breath.

"Eda? What's wrong?"

Eda found herself unable to speak. She crumbled up the fax and threw it on the floor with all her might. She just couldn't believe what it said.

Tim picked up the wad of paper, opened it, and read for himself.

"Damn," he said.

He took Eda by the arm and steered her into an empty office.

"Chris is in a lot of trouble, it seems. But Lucille doesn't explain everything. Only that Chris was taken into custody for her husband's murder . . ."

"And that their two children are missing," Eda said. "But it's the way Brian was murdered, Tim! His head cut off! The same thing happened about thirty years ago, when we were kids. Two young boys were kidnapped when that crime occurred. As far as I know, they were never found."

She shut her eyes tightly and grabbed two fistfuls of wavy blond hair.

"They were never found!" she repeated emphatically.

Tim was thoughtful for a few minutes, playing with the heavy silver-and-onyx ring he wore. Eda had spoken of her friends so often that he felt they were his friends, too. He'd met Lucille once when she came to New York to visit her literary agent. Finally, he said:

"You won't do your friend much good here. I think you should go to her."

Eda rubbed her face, then looked up at him.

"I want to go," she said. "But I'm not due any time off."

"Call it a family emergency," Tim said.

"They know I don't have a family here," Eda said. "My parents are overseas."

"From what you've told me about them over the years, Lucille and Chris are as close to family as anyone can get!"

"You'll cover for me?"

"You know I will," Tim said. "And I'll make arrangements for you to get the quickest flight out."

"I can do that," Eda said.

"The hell you can," Tim replied.

Eda stood up, seeming taller than five-foot-six by the way she squared her shoulders. She glowered at him.

"You know my background better than anyone here, Tim," she said. "You know I had servants to take care of my every need while growing up. It didn't make me helpless. It made me want to prove to my mother and father that I could do things for myself."

"So you applied for, and got, one of the toughest jobs of all," Tim said. "Being a New York cop. A decorated one, at that. Eda, I'm not pulling any macho shit and doubting your abilities. I'm just trying to help you through a distressing time. Besides, if you let me handle the airline tickets, it'll give you more time to pack what you need to take. I have a feeling you're going to be there for a long time."

Eda relaxed, even smiled a tiny bit.

"Sorry," she said. "I should know that you, of all people, wouldn't try to take command of my life. Ask for the next flight to Regina. It's a few hours' drive from Aberdeen, but the closest you'll get."

"I'll handle it right away," he said. "And don't worry, I'll talk to the chief about your sudden absence. If he doesn't understand, well . . ."

"The hell with him," Eda grumbled.

Tim was as good as his word, and Eda was on a flight to Regina, Montana, by way of Chicago, within a few hours. She hadn't slept much the night before, and gazed drowsily out the window. The plane had been in the air about an hour and was passing over Ohio now. The clouds had parted to reveal squares of farmland in various shades of green.

The flight attendant came by with soda and peanuts. Eda undid her flight bag and stuck the little silver packet inside. Maybe Josh would like to have them.

But Josh wouldn't be there to get them, would he?

No, she had to remain hopeful. It was certainly possible the children had been found by now.

"Yeah, like they found Teddy and Adrian Gammel," Eda mumbled to herself.

When she finished her soda, she closed her eyes and tried to sleep. Images of Chris and her family, laughing and happy and alive, kept coming to her mind. Things like this weren't supposed to happen to nice people like the Wanders.

Why had it happened? Eda wondered. What did a crime committed thirty years ago have to do with her friends now?

She fell asleep pondering these thoughts. When the plane touched down in Chicago, she was jolted momentarily awake. But exhaustion after a sleepless night, combined with the hum of the big engines, lulled her back to sleep once more. When she woke again, she opened her flight bag and pulled out a hardcover copy of Lucille's newest mystery novel, *The Clock Struck One*. Lucille's vivid imagination had helped her turn out four mystery novels. The picture on the back cover made Eda smile. It was a glamorous shot, very flattering.

When Lucille met her at the gate, Eda's first thought was that the publicity shot didn't do her justice. Lucille, with her long legs, high cheekbones and jet-black hair, had always been the exotic beauty of the group. She certainly stood out in the small crowd now, dressed in a blue linen pantsuit. Eda had always felt like a munchkin next to her. She was surprised to see the feeling hadn't changed. But she let these thoughts go and turned her concerns to Chris.

"How is she?" Eda asked.

"Heavily sedated," Lucille said. "She was completely hysterical last night, and the hours in the police station wore her out completely. I'm glad you're here. Chris is going to be so grateful that you came."

"I couldn't leave her alone," Eda said.

She retrieved her suitcase from the revolving carousel at the front of the terminal. The moment she exited to head to Lucille's car, she was struck by the clean, thin quality of the air. She stopped and sighed deeply.

"Oh, I didn't know how much I missed being able to breathe," she said.

"Chris and I were wondering just the other day how you handle big city life."

She unlocked Eda's door, then went around to her own side.

"I handle it just fine," Eda said, fastening her seat belt. "I love the city. I'm not sure I could get back into country life again. Too quiet."

Lucille humphed.

"Not these days," she said. "There are reporters and nosy people all around Chris's house."

"The goons come out of the woodwork at times like this, don't they?" Eda commented.

"It's the most exciting thing to happen in Aberdeen in . . ."

"Thirty years," Eda completed. "Lucille, I keep thinking about the similarity between this and the Gammel case. Maybe this person has come back to cause trouble again?"

"I wonder what the police are doing about it?"

"I understand Mike Hewlett is chief of police now," Eda said. "You remember how nice he was to us kids when he was just a rookie cop? He was my father's good friend, too. I bet he'll talk to me."

They drove in silence for a while, until finally Eda slammed a hand down on the seat beside her.

"Damn!" she cried. "I'm so worried about those kids! If anything happened to them, it would destroy Chris."

"She's pretty near destroyed already," Lucille said. "Brian was her life. You know how things turned around for her when he married her. He actually rescued her from a horrible existence."

Eda nodded. "Her knight in shining armor. Who would want to hurt such a great guy?"

"I'm afraid the killer might still be nearby," Lucille said. "I sent my own kids to stay with their grandparents in Rose Park. The twins weren't too happy about it, but I don't care as long as they're safe."

Eda turned back to the subject of the old murder.

"I'm going to do some sleuthing on my own while I'm here," she said. "There must be some connection between those long-ago crimes and what's happened now. I'm sure the police are pursuing that route, but I want to see what I can learn on my own."

"I have a feeling you won't be the only one," Lucille said. "Stories like this attract amateur detectives like cotton candy attracts yellow jackets."

"But none of those people care as much as I do," Eda insisted. "I won't rest until they find those children."

But they're never gonna find them.

Eda tilted her head, a confused expression coming across her face. Where had that thought come from?

The voice was not her own, but it sounded very familiar. Where had she heard it?

But they're never gonna find them.

She looked at her friend and knew at once where she had heard the voice. It was Lucille's, but not the Lucille she knew today. It belonged to a nine-year-old, and the words had been spoken three decades earlier.

"You knew that they wouldn't find the Gammel kids," she said.

Now it was Lucille's turn to look confused.

"I did?"

"You said, 'They're never gonna find them,' " Eda replied. "Of course, you were always making up wild stories. Probably how you got to be such a good mystery author. But it's funny how it came true."

Lucille pointed to a big green sign. White letters spelled out ABERDEEN, 1 MI. She turned off at the exit.

"Here we are," she said. "Don't worry about what I said when I was a kid. I exaggerated a lot."

"But you were uncannily correct," Eda said. "I remember so clearly you saying that. It just popped into my head now."

"Well, it won't be true this time," Lucille asserted.

They finally pulled up to Lucille's house. Eda wasn't sure why the crowd outside the Wanders' modest home surprised her. There were reporters from all media, gawkers and thrill-seekers. A yellow police banner was tied across the front lawn.

"What a bunch of ghouls," Eda said. She started to pull her suitcase from the backseat, but Lucille stopped her.

"Don't," she said. "If they see the suitcase, they'll wonder if you're somehow connected with all this. Some of those people remember you, Eda. We'll bring your luggage in after dark."

"That's a bit cloak and dagger, don't you think?"

"You'd understand," Lucille said, "if you'd been confronted by reporter after reporter in the last twenty-four hours. They learned somehow that I was the one who called the police, and they keep trying to interview me. They won't take a hint that I don't know anything."

"Disgusting," Eda said. "And they say New York is bad." She paused, then asked, "Has a date been set for the funeral?"

"Not yet," Lucille answered, "because of the ongoing murder investigation." Eda nodded—police procedure was the same in New York. Lucille continued, "But I've spoken to the minister at St. Elizabeth's, and he'll help Chris when it's time."

In the kitchen, they were surprised to see Chris seated at the table. She looked up at them with bloodshot eyes.

"Chris!" Lucille cried. "What are you doing up?"

"Did they find my babies?"

Eda and Lucille looked at each other.

"I haven't heard anything, honey," Lucille said gently.

Eda had to blink back tears of shock at the sight of her friend. While Lucille had been the exotic beauty of the trio, Chris always had a gentle, almost Victorian quality about her. But this was no innocent sitting here in this little yellow-and-orange kitchen. This was someone who had once lived in hell, and had just been brought back there again.

Someone who had seen her husband's headless body.

Someone who might never see her children again.

"Hi, Chris," Eda said. "I came as soon as I heard what happened."

"Do you hear that?" Lucille spoke as if to a child. "Your two best friends are here to help you. We're going to get through this, Chris!"

Chris stared at her, but the sedative she'd been given kept her from reacting to Eda's presence.

"They're never going to find them," she whispered.

Eda looked at Lucille, and saw the surprise in the other woman's face. Those were almost the exact words that had come into Eda's mind during the car drive. Quickly, both women took chairs to either side of the smaller woman. Lucille grabbed her hand.

"Don't you worry," she said. "They *will* find them! You have to keep hoping!"

"Chris," Eda said. "I know it must be hard for you to talk about what happened, but—"

"They made me tell the story over and over at the police station," Chris said wearily. "If my watercolor students hadn't verified where I'd been when it . . . when it happened . . ."

She covered her face, but didn't cry.

"I thought the three of us could brainstorm," Eda went on. She knew there was little time to waste being overly gentle with her friend. "Somehow, there's a connection between this and the Gammel crime."

Chris's head snapped up.

"They kept asking me about that!" she cried. "I couldn't tell them a thing! What could I possibly know? I was only seven!"

"But if there was anything that happened to us back then," Eda said, "anything at all to help us make sense of this, we have to try to remember it."

Lucille frowned at her. "You're upsetting her, Eda. That isn't what you came here to do, I'm sure."

"Of course not," Eda said. "But I just can't sit back and let the police go off on their own. If there is a link, I want to do my part to find it."

Chris pulled her hand gently from Lucille's. She nodded, rubbing at her eyes.

"I don't remember much," she said. "But maybe, if we start talking, something will come to me."

She turned to stare out the window. For a moment, the blank look on her face made Lucille believe the sedative was taking effect again.

But Chris wasn't going into a fugue state. She was remembering, her mind racing back to a long-ago day on a school playground.

"We wanted to read the article in Eda's father's newspaper," she said. "Lucille had money to buy one after school. . . ."

Lucille nodded eagerly. "That's right! You were only in second grade and couldn't handle the bigger words yet. So you wanted me to read."

With that, the three women brought themselves back in time, trying desperately to remember anything at all that might save the Wander children.

FIVE

▼

THE DAY AFTER Christy went home with bloodstains on her blouse, Eda met her at the swings in the school yard. Christy was kneeling on the seat, not sitting. And she was wearing long sleeves even though it was very warm out. Eda's chubby hands tightened into fists. She knew what that meant. She hated Christy's parents for being so mean.

But Christy was smiling. She beckoned Eda over and indicated an empty swing. Eda climbed aboard and began to ride.

"Eda, I made a new friend yesterday," Christy said. "Her name is Lucille and she's in the fourth grade."

"Wow!" Eda cried from up high. She came down and let the heels of her MaryJanes brake into the sand. The swing wobbled back and forth as she hugged the chains. "You made friends with a big kid?"

Eda jumped off and ran for the empty seesaw. When she reached it before another child, she stuck out her tongue in triumph. Christy came up after her and climbed on. Eda saw her wince as her thighs rubbed the wood, but Christy didn't complain. Eda was certain if her daddy walloped her like that she'd complain a whole *lot*.

"Lucille's great," Christy said as they teeter-tottered. She explained how the bigger girl had come to her rescue the day before.

"Didn't keep your daddy from hitting you," Eda grumbled.

Christy lowered her eyes and didn't respond.

"Well, I'm glad that lady didn't get you," Eda went on. "It must have been real scary."

"It was," Christy said with an emphatic nod.

"Gee, my parents were talking about that crazy woman this morning," Eda said. "Her neighbors called the police because she was running around screaming. It's on the front page of Daddy's newspaper."

Eda's father was publisher of the *Aberdeen Chronicle*. About a month earlier, he had decided life in Chicago was too hectic. He'd spent his childhood in Montana, and when the opportunity came to buy a network of small-town papers there, he took it. It was a big change for Eda, especially having to say good-bye to her friends. Meeting Christy had been the best thing about the move.

"Did your father tell you about the story, Eda?"

Eda shrugged. "Well, not really. Mom says it's grown-up stuff. I wish I could read better. Then I'd look for myself."

Christy pouted.

"I really want to find out about that Irene Gammel," she said. "That's the lady who ran after me. I got in trouble because of that dummy!"

"But the paper has too many big words to read," Eda said.

They seesawed for a few moments. Then Christy's eyes got big.

"Lucille!" she cried. "We can ask Lucille to read the paper to us!"

"Yeah!" Eda cried. "I bet a fourth-grader knows lots of big words."

She was so excited about the idea that she jumped off the low end of the seesaw, making Christy smash to the ground.

Christy gasped in pain, the shock of hitting the sand exacerbated by her already sore muscles. Eda ran around to her.

"I'm sorry, Christy!" she cried. "Oh, gee, I'm so sorry! Here, here, you can pinch my arm really hard."

Christy frowned at her.

"I mean it, go ahead," Eda said, holding out her bare arm. There was no need for this rich man's daughter to wear long sleeves on a warm day. "Pinch it, and we'll be even-steven."

A boy in their class, Willy Keel, looked up from a hole he was digging and shouted.

"You belong on the ground, Creepy Christy! Good place for slime!"

"Shut up, Keel!" Eda cried, her freckled face scrunching up.

"Make me, Brillo head!"

Eda started for him, fists doubled. Christy got up and grabbed her friend.

"No!" she cried. "You'll get in trouble! You don't want to stand in the corner again, do you?"

Eda pouted. She recalled how David Marzallo, the boy in the desk behind hers, had whispered "Brillo head" over and over. She'd gotten so mad she turned around and yelled at him to "Shut up!" The teacher had punished her, and nothing at all happened to stupid, moon-faced David.

Eda *hated* the corner and didn't want to go there again. Although it had happened a week ago, memory of that humiliation was enough to save Willy.

"Let's go find Lucille," Christy said as Eda made a gooney face at the boy.

There were two recess areas at Chandler—one for first through fourth grades, the second for the older kids. Long before any of these children had started school, invisible barriers had been set up between the divisions. As Christy and Eda crossed into fourth grade territory, a few kids turned to stare at them. One girl even started walking towards them. Eda saw she had a mean look on her face, but she wasn't afraid. She glared at the big girl, thinking she looked like an ugly moose. To her surprise, the girl turned away.

"Do you see her?" Eda asked now.

Christy looked around. Lucille was taller than the other girls in her group, and easy to spot. She smiled to see her younger friend.

"Hi, Christy!" she said. "How'd it go yesterday?"

"Okay," Christy lied. "This is my friend, Eda."

Lucille said hi. Eda mumbled a reply as she gazed at the tall girl. She couldn't take her eyes off Lucille's long, straight black hair.

It's all the way down to her tush! Eda thought.

"Lucille, can you do us a favor?" Christy asked. "Can you buy one of Eda's daddy's newspapers? There's stuff about Irene Gammel in there, but no one will tell us the story."

Lucille's eyes rounded with glee.

"I don't have to buy the paper," she said. "I know the story. I wasn't supposed to hear it, either, but my big brother Tom is a teenager, and he's really cool, and he told me everything."

"What did he say?" Eda asked, excited.

"It was a murrrderrrr," Lucille drawled in a voice that made her sound like the announcer on "Chiller Theater."

Both little girls gasped.

"Tom says she went upstairs to her bedroom and found her husband there," Lucille said. "Only it wasn't his whole body. Just his head! There was blood all over the place."

Eda turned to Christy and saw her make a sick face. It was murder blood that woman had rubbed on her friend yesterday!

But Lucille was talking again.

"That's not the worst part," she said. "The worst part is that they had two kids and no one knows where they are!"

A fifth grader playing marbles nearby, added his two cents' worth:

"She cut the body in little pieces and made the kids eat 'em!" he cried.

"Stop talking like that!" Christy protested. It was no joke to her.

Lucille made a bored face.

"Flake off, Tommy," she said.

"Squares," Tommy growled, gathering up his marbles to put them in a leather sack.

Eda looked up at Lucille. Boy, she sure was big! Eda thought she must be seven feet tall.

"What's the rest of the story?" she asked.

"Well, the police are looking everywhere for Teddy and Adrian Gammel, of course," Lucille went on. "And they've got that woman in jail. But Tom says she'll probably get out because she probably didn't do it."

"What do you think, Lucille?"

"I think," she said, "that the kids are either dead or far, far away. They'll look and look, but they'll never find them. Well, maybe not for years and years. It's like the little princes in England."

"Who?"

"A long, long time ago," Lucille explained, "there were these two little princes in England. One of them was supposed to grow up to be king. Anyway, they disappeared one night. Nobody found them until years later, when they were doing some work in the palace. They tore down a brick wall and found two little skeletons behind it."

"Yuck," Eda said, making a face.

"I don't want to talk about this anymore," Christy said. "It scares me."

The bell rang, and the children lined up to return to their classrooms. It seemed to Eda that the day dragged on *forever*, but at last the final bell rang.

"Can we go to your house today?" Eda asked as they walked out of the school yard. Eda rolled her bike between them.

"I don't know," Christy said. "I have to see if Mommy's okay."

Eda wasn't exactly sure why Christy had to see if Mrs. Burnett was okay every time she wanted to play.

"All right," Eda said. "If she isn't okay, you can come to my house again."

Christy smiled. "I like your house better. You have so many toys."

Christy had very few playthings, but Eda didn't care. Christy lived over a pizzeria, and that was *neat*.

They crossed the street and walked into the door on the side of the corner building. Eda *had* noticed some bad things about the Burnetts' apartment, but she was too nice to say so. It was always so dark in there. And it smelled funny. One time when she was living in Chicago, her father had brought her down to the police station with him. He went there a lot to do his newspaper stories, so when he offered to bring Eda it was a big treat. She loved watching the policemen at work. The captain even let her sit on his desk and got ice cream for her. But a scary thing had happened.

An ugly man in filthy clothes came up to her. He smiled a smile with no teeth, and tried to touch her. Eda wasn't usually afraid, but she was glad when her daddy pulled her into his arms and a policeman took the weird guy away. He had smelled *terrible*. That was the smell she'd sometimes noticed in Christy's apartment.

But when Christy opened the door and led Eda inside, she was completely surprised. Today, the apartment was immaculately clean and smelled like Christmas trees. All the windows were opened, letting in fresh air.

"Gee," Christy breathed. She was as surprised as Eda.

Sarah Burnett was busy dusting the coffee table. She was wearing a crisp white apron over a lavender dress, and her hair was combed into a flip. She looked up and smiled.

"Hello, sweet angel," she said to Christy. "Hello, Eda."

"Hi, Mrs. Burnett," Eda said. She couldn't say more. It was the first time Christy's mother had actually greeted her.

"It smells good in here, Mommy," Christy said as she took off her coat.

Sarah put her hands on her hips and looked around the room with a satisfied expression.

"Yep, been pretty busy," she said. "Place sure needed cleanin'."

She turned and went back to work. Christy led Eda into her room, where she changed out of her school clothes, carefully hanging up her blouse and jumper. Then she sat on her bed and pulled off her stockings. Eda gasped to see the purple bruises that marked her friend's thin legs.

"Oh, Christy," she said. "Does it hurt a lot?"

"Only if I touch them," Christy said, blushing. She quickly pulled on a pair of jeans. She was usually embarrassed to wear castoffs purchased at Goodwill in front of her friend. Today, however, Christy was grateful they were loose enough not to bind her sore legs. As she fastened a safety pin at the waist, she asked:

"What do you want to do?"

"I dunno," Eda said. "Want to play dolls?"

"I only have one doll," Christy replied. "I have lots of paper and crayons. Want to draw?"

Eda didn't like drawing very much, because she wasn't good at it. But she knew it would make Christy happy, so she agreed. They stretched out on the floor and began to sketch with crayons.

"You know what?" Christy asked after a while. "I don't think Lucille knew the whole story."

"Why?"

"Well," Christy said, "I think something more happened."

Eda sat up, Indian-style. She leaned forward and reached for a green crayon to scribble leaves on a tree.

"How come?"

"I'm not sure. I had a real bad dream last night. A man tried to hurt me with a knife."

She shivered. The dream came back vaguely, nothing more than a pair of ugly green eyes and a flash of metal.

"Maybe you were just scared," Eda suggested. "Like when you watch 'Chiller Theater' or 'Twilight Zone.' Those shows give me nightmares."

"I don't watch them," Christy said.

She colored for a few moments, filling in a rainbow.

"Well," Eda said, "I sure hope you don't dream it again!"

"Me, too," Christy said.

Eda picked up a red crayon and colored apple blobs on her tree. Christy found a black crayon and started to draw clouds over her pretty rainbow. She made them really dark, really big, and really scary-looking. Soon, they blocked out the rainbow completely.

A tear ran down her face. Eda stared at her for a minute, but she didn't say anything. Christy looked like she was really scared because of that dream, and Eda didn't know what she could do to help her.

SIX

▼

On Saturday morning, Christy moved very quietly through the apartment. It was her father's day to sleep in after a long week at the Cable and Wire Factory. Waking him up, even by accident, was a great way to invite a whipping. At least her brother had already gone out. The jerk would risk punishment himself just to get her into trouble, too.

Her mother was at the kitchen sink, washing a dish. Christy fixed a bowl of Frosty-Os and watched her. Sarah seemed to be gazing beyond the cactuses that lined the window in little green plastic pots. Her eyes seemed to look farther than the empty lot behind the building. Christy wished she could ask just what it was her mother saw, but knew even at her young age that she wouldn't get an answer.

The vacant lot down below reached to the next corner. In warmer weather, when the storm window was replaced by a screen, Christy would be able to hear kids shouting as they played kickball or ring-a-levio. She'd wish she was down there with them, instead of all by herself in this dark little apartment. Mostly, she wished it when the paddle was being applied to her thin legs. In the summer, she'd grit her teeth and not scream because letting those kids below know she was getting a beating made her feel like a big, fat jerk. But this was the fall, and the window was shut tight. She could yell all she wanted. No one would hear.

But more important, she didn't have to wish for playmates like last year. She had two of them now—Eda and Lucille. A smile spread across her face as she thought of them. Eda was so much fun, and so nervy. Sometimes she acted just like a boy! Christy wished she could be as brave and strong. And Lucille was so smart and so nice. She liked Christy even though she was nine and Christy was only seven and a half. Christy couldn't figure out *why* Lucille liked her, or Eda. Nobody had ever liked her before. They sneered at her and said mean things about her clothes. Tiffany Simmons once said she probably had lice. Christy had wanted to protest, to say she had learned how to wash her own hair when she was only four and she was very clean so she couldn't have lice, no way! Too bad Eda hadn't been living here when Tiffany said that. Christy wondered what Eda would have done.

When she finished the cereal, she realized her mother was still washing the same dish. The wild cleaning spree was over now, and the way her mother's lips were moving told Christy she was talking to nobody again. Gently, she took the clean dish away and replaced it with her used one. Her mother didn't acknowledge her. Christy dried the clean dish and put it away, then left the apartment.

She walked carefully on the creaky staircase. First step, second step, skip the third. It made a loud noise, and once her father had knocked her down the whole flight because she'd awakened him. As soon as she got out the door, however, a grin spread across her face and she broke into a run. Eda and Lucille were waiting in the school yard, taking turns on the slide.

"Hi!" Christy cried as she approached them. She looked at the clothes Eda was wearing. "Wow, Eda, that's a pretty sweater."

Eda looked down at the cableknit pullover she wore.

"Thanks," she said. "Mommy ordered it from Ireland."

Lucille jumped off the end of the slide, her blue Keds kicking up sand.

"Well, are you ready?" she asked, adjusting the pink gingham headband that held back her hair.

"For what?" Christy asked.

"Eda and I were talking," Lucille said. "We want to go take a look at the murder house."

Christy backed away, shaking her head.

"Oh, no!" she cried. "I'm not going near that terrible place again!"

"Don't be such a baby," Eda said. "We just want to look at it."

"It's empty, anyhow," Lucille said. "That lady is in jail. What could happen?"

"Besides, you're the only one of us who knows where it is," Eda said.

Christy shifted from one foot to the other.

"I don't remember," she lied. "Besides, the pizzeria is still closed. I can't get my bike."

"We walked this morning," Eda said. "Now come on, Christy. We're just going to walk past it, okay?"

"Please?" Lucille implored.

Christy looked from one friend to the other. How could she disappoint the only people who really cared about her? She'd only met Lucille two days ago. Maybe if Lucille thought she was a baby, she wouldn't want to be Christy's friend.

And the house *was* empty now.

An image flashed in her mind: eyes, hateful and staring. They were the eyes she'd seen in her dream, and the memory of them chilled her. She'd tried to tell Eda about them, but she wasn't sure if her friend understood.

"Christy?" Lucille pushed.

Christy rubbed her arms and forced the image away.

"Oh, okay!" she cried. "But I'm staying across the street."

She did exactly that when they reached the house, but Lucille and Eda ran ahead, stopping at the end of the walkway.

"I'm going to take a closer look!" Lucille announced. "I'll bet there's blood!"

"Oh, don't!" Christy yelled, but Lucille was already walking up the path to the house, Eda close behind her.

"Please, come back!" Christy cried, terrified someone would grab her friends.

But that's silly, she told herself. *There's no one there!*

Suddenly, she felt a hand clamp around her arm. She was turned around, and faced an old man with faded blue eyes. His breath had a spicy smell, like the beef sticks her father chewed on when he watched "The Red Skelton Show" on their little black-and-white television.

"You and your little friends oughta stay away from that devil house," he said. "Weird place, weird family. Always had the shades drawn, never acted friendly. And those noises at night, out in that big field in back. Big bulldozer digging. Probably buryin' something. . . ."

Christy finally found enough voice to let out a small scream. The man let her go as Eda and Lucille came running across the street.

"Get away from my friend!" Eda cried, her fist raised.

"You get away!" the old man retorted. "Get away from that devil house!"

Christy broke into a run, racing down the street. Her thoughts were wild, and she didn't hear Eda and Lucille begging her to wait up. Maybe the man with the ugly green eyes was watching her, maybe he would grab her as easily as the old man had, maybe there really was blood all over the house. . . .

"Chris-teee!"

Eda's shout cut through the little girl's panic, but she didn't stop until she reached the park near Lake Aberdeen. She plunked down onto a swing and pouted. Tears spilled from her eyes.

"I told you I didn't want to go there!"

"Well, we didn't know an old guy was gonna grab you!" Eda said defensively.

"Are you okay, Christy?" Lucille asked. "He didn't hurt you, did he?"

Christy thought a moment, then shook her head.

"I guess not," she said. "He just talked about that family. He said they were weird and did funny things at night."

"Like what?" Eda asked.

"I don't know," Christy said. She gazed down the hill to the water. It was speckled with fallen leaves of red, orange and yellow and looked pretty. "You want to take a walk along the lake?"

But Lucille wasn't going to let her off that easily.

"Maybe they were witches," she said, a gleam coming into her eyes. "Maybe they had a coven and they danced naked in the moonlight and made blood sacrifices—"

"Stop it, Lucille!" Christy begged.

"What's a coven?" Eda wanted to know.

Another voice cut into their conversation.

"Aww, there ain't no such thing as witches."

The girls turned, and gave a collective moan to see Willy Keel riding up to the park on his bike.

"Oh, yecch," Eda said, sticking out her tongue.

"Wait, I was wrong," Willy said. "There are witches. I'm lookin' at three of 'em right now."

Lucille squinted and clicked her tongue.

"Oh, get lost," she sneered.

"Make me!" Willy said, jumping from his bike.

Lucille simply turned away, but Eda couldn't resist a challenge. There were no teachers to stop her now. She pounced on Willy, and the two started rolling around in the sand. Eda punched Willy anywhere her fists could connect; Willy pulled Eda's curly hair and bit her ear.

"*Stop it!*" Christy begged.

"Eda, you'll get hurt!" Lucille cried.

But the two were oblivious. Eda had seen what a bully Willy was, and now she wanted to make him pay for all the mean things he said. She grabbed his ear and started to twist it, hard.

"Okay, kids, break it up!"

This wasn't a kid's voice. This was a man's voice, full of such authority that Eda and Willy were both shocked into obeying. Willy stood up, touching his bloody nose, while Eda rolled onto her back and stared up at the young police officer who'd suddenly appeared. He shook his head at her. He tried to look stern, but his face was too young and his eyes too bright blue to succeed.

"Hi, Officer Mike!" Eda cried.

Mike Hewlett offered a hand and pulled her up from the ground.

"Your mother isn't going to be too happy to see you all messed up," he said.

"She started it!" Willy cried.

"That's not true," Lucille said.

Mike turned to the little boy, who stood wiping blood from his nose with the back of his hand.

"And what'll your mom think," he asked, "if she hears you were fighting with a girl?"

Willy's sneer turned into a frown, and he hung his head.

"Let me see that nose," Mike said gently, taking out a handkerchief. "Here, you can keep this."

He carefully checked Willy's nose.

"It's not broken," he said.

He looked around.

"I'm surprised your parents let you out alone," he said.

Eda giggled. "I always go out by myself! I'm nearly eight, you know."

"I know you're a big girl, Eda," Mike said. "But it's dangerous to wander around without an adult these days."

" 'Cause of the murder?" Willy asked.

"And the kidnapping," Mike said.

The children looked at each other.

"Do you think they'll find those boys?" Christy asked. She wanted to ask if they'd caught a man with mean eyes, but she was afraid of sounding silly. It had just been a dream, hadn't it?

"I hope so," Mike said. "We're certainly doing all we can."

As if to prove the point, the sound of a dog barking came from the nearby woods. The children looked across the lake to see half a dozen hounds exiting the trees, closely followed by their trainers.

"Those men are looking for the missing kids, aren't they?" Lucille asked.

"That's right," Mike said. "Teddy and Adrian Gammel. Teddy is in the fifth grade in your school. Do you know him?"

The girls shook their heads, but there was a hint of pride in Willy's voice when he said:

"My sister does, and she says he's a geek."

"That's not very nice," Lucille said.

"Adrian is just a baby, barely four years old," Mike went on. "You kids would do well to say a little prayer in church for their safety."

"You know I can't go to church," Eda said. "I'm Jewish."

"Then go to temple," Mike said. "But listen, no matter where you go, stay in a group."

He looked directly at Willy.

"We don't know what happened to the Gammel boys," he said. "The kidnapper could be far away, or still right here in Aberdeen."

Four little pairs of eyes went completely round.

"But . . . but we thought their mother . . ." Eda said.

"Irene Gammel was let out of jail this morning," Mike told them. "There was another . . . a similar killing last night. She's innocent."

"Where was the killing?" Eda asked.

"Did any other kids disappear?" Lucille wanted to know.

"Never mind where it was," Mike said. "And no, no kids disappeared this time. Let's keep it that way. You walk back to town together, you hear?"

"I don't want to walk with girls!"

Mike smiled at him. "I could drive you home."

Willy thought about what his mother would think if a cop brought him back home all dirty, with a bloody nose.

"Okay, I'll walk," he moaned. "But they better not tell anyone."

"Fine," Mike said. "I have to get back to work now. Remember what I said."

He walked toward the squad car that was parked in the nearby lot.

Willy mounted his bike and started off.

"You have to wait!" Eda cried.

"You have to hurry up," Willy called back.

The three girls ran after him. As soon as the police car was out of sight, Willy picked up speed and took off. Eda stopped abruptly, and Lucille and Christy nearly crashed into her.

"Oh, let him go," she said. "I don't want to walk with that jerk, either."

"But the policeman said . . ."

"Mike's okay," Eda answered Christy. "He treats me like a grown-up, not a baby. Besides, it's not our fault that dumb Willy took off."

"How come you call him Mike?" Christy asked. "He's a grown-up!"

"He's my father's friend," Eda replied. "When we moved to Aberdeen, and Daddy wanted to do a newspaper story on some houses that were robbed, Mike is the guy who helped him."

"He's real cute," Lucille said.

Eda shrugged. She hadn't really noticed. Now she looked around.

"Well, what do you want to do now?"

"Let's get our bikes," Lucille suggested. "We can ride around town."

"It's safe there," Christy agreed, "with so many people."

"My house is nearest," Lucille said. "We'll get mine first."

The children enjoyed riding through town, stopping to look at the new display in the toy store window, oohing over little French lop rabbits in the pet store window. They circled around the town square several times and rode in and out of alleys. Eda was always way ahead of the others. They called to her to wait up, but no sooner did they reach her than she was off again. Finally, Lucille got tired of the chase and sped up herself. Christy didn't dare force her rickety old bike to do more work, and so she was forced to wait until her friends circled around and met her again. She stopped in front of a bakery and wished she could eat everything in the window.

As she was admiring an apple strudel, someone came up behind her. It was a man, and he stood very close to her. Christy's eyes were brought up to his head, his flattop making it look square. But it was his eyes she noticed. Even in their reflection they were ugly eyes, like in her dream. She was about to move away when he raised his hand—and something flashed in the sunlight.

Christy was sure it was a knife. Her dream was coming true! Too frightened to scream, she could only push her bike away awkwardly. She stumbled up onto it, not daring to look back, racing until she reached her friends. She was so upset that she nearly crashed into the back of Eda's bike.

"What's the big idea?" Eda demanded.

"There was a man . . . a man with a knife . . . and . . ."

"Catch your breath, Christy," Lucille suggested.

Christy gulped in big bubbles of air, then finally calmed down enough to say what had happened.

"We better find Officer Mike," Eda said.

"We'll ride back down to the lake," Lucille agreed. "But first, Christy, let's take a look."

Christy led them back into the main part of town, keeping a safe distance from the bakery in the town square. She looked up and down the road, trying to spot the man who had tried to kill her. Finally, to her terror, she saw him walking slowly past the medical building.

"There he is!" she cried, pointing.

Lucille and Eda looked carefully in that direction. Then Lucille began to laugh.

"It isn't funny, Lucille!" Eda said.

"Oh, yes it is," Lucille said. "Christy, you're a nut. That's old man Pierpont. Mother says he's a drunk, but Daddy says he wouldn't hurt a fly."

The old man raised his hand, as he had done near Christy, and metal flashed in the sunlight. With a cry, she covered her eyes. Lucille put a hand on her arm.

"Christy, that isn't a knife," she said. "That's the thing he drinks out of. It's okay."

Christy didn't uncover her face. Was this what she was going to feel like until they caught the murderer? Was every man who came close to her, every flash of metal, suspect?

SEVEN

▼

"THEY'RE PLANNING TO drag the lake this afternoon."

A week had passed since the Gammel boys' disappearance. Christy was spending Saturday afternoon at Eda's house. They sat in the middle of a bedroom that seemed as big as the Burnetts' apartment, surrounded by Barbie and all her accessories. But the dolls lay forgotten on the floor as the girls knelt down close to an air vent and eavesdropped. Eda's parents were talking in the parlor, directly connected by the heating system to her bedroom.

The children leaned closer to the vent.

"Oh, Dean," Eda's mother said. Her voice sounded echoey. "Do you really think those poor little things are . . . dead?"

"If you ask me, Rita," Dean Crispin told his wife, "I think they're alive someplace."

"Well!" Rita said. "I refuse to fall into a false sense of security just because there was no kidnapping with the second murder. What's Sheriff Barnard doing to protect our children?"

Eda had to clasp a hand over her mouth to keep from giggling. Through the vent, the sheriff's name sounded like "Barnyard."

"We'll find out at the rally tonight," Dean said. "Now, Rita, I've got the Sunday *Gazette* to print. I'll be back by dinner."

When it seemed obvious the conversation was over, the girls crawled away from the vent.

"What does 'drag the lake' mean?" Christy asked. "It sounds scary."

"They're looking for bodies under the water," Eda replied, making a disgusted face. "But I think Daddy's right. I think Teddy and Adrian are alive."

Christy felt icy across the back of her neck. She didn't like talking about dead kids, even kids who, maybe, weren't dead at all.

"I saw posters for that rally," she said. "Your daddy put them up all over town."

"Are your parents going?"

Christy shrugged, then slowly shook her head. What would her parents care about protecting children? They did a pretty good job hurting their own right at home.

"Well, mine are, of course," Eda said. "And you know what? I'm going, too."

"What do you mean you're going?" Christy asked in disbelief. "It's at night. You can't go out at night."

"I'm gonna sneak out," Eda said. "My parents won't be here, and the servants will all be busy."

Christy's eyes were full of worry.

"But if you get caught," she said, "you'll be whipped for sure!"

"I won't get caught," Eda insisted.

The terrified look on Christy's face told Eda she'd need

more reassurance. It wasn't enough to say that her parents never laid a hand on her.

"I'll hide in the bushes," she said, "and I'll come home long before anyone knows I'm gone."

"But why do you want to go?"

"Because no one will tell us a thing," Eda said. "And I bet the grown-ups do plenty of talking tonight."

She jumped up.

"Come on, let's check the kitchen," she said. "I'm hungry."

Christy followed her friend out into the hall and down a huge staircase, hoping there would be something delicious to eat. Christy planned to take all that was offered. It might be the best she had to eat all day.

That night, Eda gave her parents fifteen minutes' head start, then snuck out of the house. It was slightly less than a mile's walk into town, but the crisscross of shadows and light from the street lamps made the roads seem to stretch forever. Eda wasn't afraid of the dark, but out here in the night, out where a killer might be hiding, she felt strange.

She turned a corner and saw a pair of glowing eyes peering out from behind some bushes. Yellow eyes, like the devil might have. Eda stopped short, staring at the pinpoints of light. Were they staring back? she wondered. Was something going to pounce?

Then one light disappeared, quickly followed by the other. The devil was gone. Eda started to walk faster, wanting to get to town right *now*. In minutes, she reached the relative safety of the bushes surrounding Town Hall.

It seemed to her, as she gazed through the branches, that every single mom and dad in town was in front of those wide steps. Eda's father stood high above the others, a hand resting on the head of a stone lion. People were carrying signs. Just beginning second grade, there were many that Eda couldn't read, but she could make out words like SAVE OUR CHILDREN.

Her father waved both hands over his head to silence the crowd, then began to speak. Eda thought he looked very handsome, and very important, in his best gray suit.

"We have come here tonight," Dean Crispin began, "to demand action! We demand to know what is being done to protect our loved ones, especially our children, from the madman who stalks our town! Two murders have been committed. Will there be more?"

Shouts from the crowd; Eda wished she could understand what they were yelling.

"Two innocent boys have vanished! Will there be more?"

More shouts.

"We must protect our homes and families!"

Signs bounced up and down and fists waved in fury. Eda watched her father in fascination.

"Where are those children, Sheriff Barnard?"

A hand rested lightly on the back of Eda's neck. She froze, her shoulders pulling up, her eyes widening.

"I know where those boys are," a voice whispered. "Do you want to see them? I think I'd like you to see them."

Eda was too frightened to answer.

"But I don't want you, little girl," the voice said. "I want your friend. They call her 'Creepy Christy,' don't they? Cruel children! Such a beauty! So perfect . . ."

Eda found her strength at last and ducked down quickly. Free of the stranger's grasp, she stumbled away and started to run as fast as she could. In her fear, it didn't even occur to her that her parents were only a few feet away, near a police station. Eda ran blindly, certain the killer was right behind her. She'd never reach home in time! He'd catch her, and maybe cut off her head, or make her disappear like Teddy and Adrian Gammel, or . . .

She suddenly remembered that Christy lived nearby. The safety of her apartment was much closer than Eda's own home, so she headed in that direction. She was relieved to see a light on in Christy's room.

Eda tucked herself into the doorway of the pizzeria. She looked down the street, only to find it completely deserted. With a sigh of relief, she stepped onto the sidewalk again and went up to the Burnetts' apartment door. But she stopped, thinking: what if Christy's parents were home? Did she dare knock on the door? How would she explain what she was doing there?

She danced from one sneaker to the other—it was getting cold out here. Then a smile spread across her face. She could climb up to Christy's window! It would be easy—first she'd use the stones in the wall as footholds, then she'd catch the fire escape and go up that way. It would be as easy as climbing monkey bars.

In minutes, Eda was tapping at Christy's window.

Inside the house, Christy looked up from the picture she was drawing. Someone was tapping at her window! She turned to look at the curtains, drawn tightly now. If she opened them, would a pair of ugly green eyes be looking at her?

Then, faintly, she heard:

"Christy! Open up! It's Eda!"

Eda? Christy jumped up and hurried to the window. Carefully, she pulled a tiny bit of the curtain back. When she saw her friend, she opened the window.

"What are you doing out there?"

"Christy, the killer almost got me!" Eda said breathlessly, climbing through the window.

"Oh, no!"

Eda took a deep breath. "Where are your parents?" she asked, sitting on the edge of the bed. "I didn't see them at the rally."

"Mom's inside, watching 'Bewitched,' " Christy said. "Daddy's . . . out."

Eda nodded, and told her friend what had happened. When she finished, Christy said:

"Maybe you should tell that policeman."

"Officer Mike?" Eda asked. "Are you kidding? My parents would *kill* me if they knew I snuck out."

Christy lowered her eyes.

"Oh, well, they wouldn't really kill me," Eda amended quickly. "But I'd be grounded forever. Besides which, well, I didn't really get a good look at him. They wouldn't know who to look for. But Christy, he asked about *you.* Why would he do that? Is he the guy you dreamed about?"

"I . . . I don't know," Christy said.

Green eyes, flashes of metal . . .

She looked at her friend with fear in her eyes.

"Maybe he knows I saw that woman," she said. "What am I going to do, Eda? No one would believe me now."

Eda bounced on the edge of the bed.

"Gee, I wish I could have heard more at the rally!" Eda said.

Christy went to the window and looked out, half expecting to see someone lurking under the street lamp.

Eda leaned down and picked up the picture Christy had been drawing.

"This is good," she said. "Those look just like real leaves."

"It's the tree across the street," Christy said.

"I wish I could draw like you," Eda said. "Hey, Christy, I gotta go home now."

"All by yourself?"

"You sure can't walk me," Eda said. "Don't worry, I'll be okay. I'll run as fast as I can."

Christy was worried for her friend, but could see there was no other choice.

"Wait a second," she said.

She left the room, then came back with a pocketknife. "Harvey keeps it in his dresser," she said.

She didn't tell her friend that Harvey's dresser was actually the bottom drawer of his parents' bureau.

"Won't he be mad?"

"He won't even know it's gone," Christy said. "Grandpa gave it to him for Christmas a few years ago. He never even uses it. Says pocketknives are for wimps."

She leaned closer to her friend and whispered, even though no one could hear them.

"He's got a switchblade."

"Wow!"

Eda put the pocketknife inside her jacket. Then she turned and opened the window. As she climbed out on the fire escape, she said, "I'll call you tomorrow morning."

"Let's call Lucille, too," Christy said. "Maybe she'll want to play with us again."

Eda nodded, then disappeared down the fire escape. Christy held her breath as Eda jumped from the bottom, but she landed squarely on her feet. She waved her hands over her head, then ran off.

Across the street, a stranger waited until Christy's curtain was drawn before stepping out of the darkened doorway of the hardware store. He smiled with satisfaction. He now knew exactly where Christy lived.

EIGHT

▼

T HE BRIGHAMS' STATION wagon was pulling out of the driveway just as Christy and Eda rode up on their bikes the next morning. Lucille poked her head out the window and waved.

"We're going to get fabric for costumes!" she said. "Wanna come? Can they come, Mom?"

"If they want to squeeze in," Mrs. Brigham said.

The girls parked their bikes behind the house, then wiggled in next to Lucille. Her brother, five-year-old Stannie, groaned and pushed himself as close to the window as possible to avoid touching his sister. Eda leaned over and stuck out her tongue at him. Stannie crossed his eyes in response.

"Halloween's coming up pretty fast," Mrs. Brigham said. "Have you girls decided what you're going to be?"

"I saw a cowgirl costume in the Sears catalog," Eda said. "It's got fringe and little silver buttons."

"Mom's making all our costumes," Lucille said. "I'm going to be a witch this year."

"I'm gonna be a cat!" said three-year-old Greta.

Mrs. Brigham tilted her head back a little as she drove.

"How about you, dear?" she asked Christy. "Have you decided on your costume?"

Christy hadn't even thought about Halloween. How could she tell them she didn't have a costume, that she probably never would?

"Not really," she said softly.

There was silence in the car for a few minutes, except for the baby's babbling. Then, as she turned in to downtown Aberdeen, Mrs. Brigham said:

"Maybe Lucille could lend you a costume. What about that pink outfit you wore to your recital a few years back?"

"Oh, Mommy, that's perfect," Lucille said. She held up both hands. "It is *so* beautiful, Christy. You can be a fairy princess."

A shy smile spread across Christy's face. Maybe she could have fun on Halloween, after all.

They parked in front of Wittig's Five-and-Ten and got out. Entering the store, Mrs. Brigham wheeled the baby to the pattern books, her children following like little ducks. The store was the biggest in town, with rows and rows of shelves cluttered with merchandise. While her mother went off to look at fabric, Lucille led her friends to the candy and toy counter. Glass apothecary jars lined the wall near the cash register, each one brimming with treats. Christy stared up at them, wishing she had a penny or two. Those malt balls looked delicious, or maybe the licorice, or the MaryJanes . . .

A whirring noise made her turn. Stannie had found a friction gun. A blue-and-red wheel shot sparks as he pulled the trigger.

"Get lost, Stannie," Lucille said.

"Mom said I could look at the toys!"

He put the gun down and started fishing through the water pistols.

"How come boys like guns so much?" Lucille asked.

"I think it'd be neat to have a gun," Eda said. "My father's friend Mike has a gun."

"But he's a cop," Lucille said. "So it doesn't really count. Does it, Christy? Christy?"

Christy was admiring a bag of pop beads, thinking how much fun it would be to make jewelry. Eda laughed and tapped her on the shoulder.

"Wake up!" she said.

"Huh?" Christy started. "Oh! I was just . . . looking."

Lucille seemed to understand how Christy was feeling, looking at so many things she couldn't have. She reached into the pocket of her corduroy slacks and found a nickel.

"Let's pick out some candy," she said. "We can each have one thing. Then I'll have two pennies left for Greta and Stannie."

They were looking over the candy when two women brushed by them. Laden with purchases, they headed to the register and began to talk as if the children weren't there at all.

"Did you hear that Gammel woman left town?" one woman asked. "As if her boys don't matter none!"

"I still say she's guilty," the second replied. "She had blood all over her. You mark my words, they'll . . ."

Eda poked Christy in the ribs.

"They're talking about the murder," she whispered.

They pretended to be busy choosing candy while they eavesdropped.

"Well, my sister's beautician lives down the block from them," the first woman was saying, "and she told my sister they were the most unfriendly family. Her son is in Teddy

Gammel's class. Said the boy was always dirty. He was sent home with head lice! I wouldn't be surprised if Irene Gammel beat those poor children."

"Who knows what her husband was like?"

"Well, anyway, it's just disgraceful," the first said, "her leaving town like that. If my children had vanished, I'd stay right here until they were found. It just proves, in my mind, that she's guilty."

"But what about the other murder?"

Lucille's younger sister came running into the aisle.

"Mommy's ready to go," Greta said.

"Now?" Lucille whined, disappointed.

"Yes, now," Mrs. Brigham called from across the store.

Lucille looked at her friends with surprise. How could her mother have such good hearing? Disappointed they couldn't hear more about Irene Gammel, the children made their candy choices, and Lucille paid for them all. After Mrs. Brigham had purchased her fabric, they went out to the car, enjoying their treats. Christy had picked a jawbreaker because she thought it would last the longest. Besides, it was fun to take it out of her mouth every few minutes to see the color change.

In the car, Lucille told her mother what they'd overheard.

"Why would Teddy and Adrian's mother leave them?" Lucille asked.

"I think that poor Mrs. Gammel was trying to get away from gossips like those women," Mrs. Brigham said with sympathy in her voice.

"Where do you think she went?" Eda asked. She blew a big, pink gum bubble.

"I heard it was to Washington," Mrs. Brigham said. "People were talking about it after church. She has family there. It surprises me that the police let her go, but I'm sure they know where to find her."

"What about—"

Mrs. Brigham waved a hand. "Let's not talk about this, children. Does anyone want an ice cream cone?"

The vote was unanimous, and for a short time the Gammels were forgotten.

On Halloween night, Christy pulled on the pink leotard and sparkling silver-pink tutu Lucille had given her. It was a little big, but Mrs. Brigham had taken it in in a few places, and Christy couldn't help feeling pretty.

She wanted to have fun tonight. She hadn't had a dream about the ugly green eyes or flashes of metal in several weeks, and thoughts of the murders and kidnappings were all but gone from her mind.

Christy walked into the living room, where her father slouched in his chair. He was drinking beer and watching a football game. She tried to sneak past him, but he turned and said:

"Where'd you find that getup?"

Christy swallowed, her heart beginning to race. Was her night going to be ruined?

"Lucille Brigham gave it to me," she said softly.

Harvey Sr. grunted: "No loss to her."

Wanting to get away before he could say more, Christy hurried from the apartment. Eda and Lucille were waiting in front of the pizzeria. Blond braids peeked out from under Eda's pale blue cowgirl hat, the silver fringe of her jacket ruffled in the wind. Lucille wore a funny nose and made appropriate witch noises.

"You look great, Christy!" Lucille said.

"Thanks," Christy replied.

Her brother seemed to appear out of nowhere. He had a pillowcase in his hand. Christy could only guess what nasty tricks were hidden there.

"This Halloween business is all bull, y'know," Harvey

Jr. said. "It said on the news that the Russians are building missile bases all over Cuba. I bet they're gonna bomb Florida any day now."

Christy's eyes widened. She'd heard about the trouble in that little country. She didn't understand a word of it, but the thought of being killed by a bomb scared her.

Almost as much as mean eyes and flashing knives scared her.

"Oh, they won't either!" Eda insisted, but her eyes were big, too.

"My father says nobody can beat the U.S.A.," Lucille said. "Besides, this is Montana. We're far, far away from Florida."

Harvey chuckled mirthlessly.

"Huh!" he snorted. "First they get Florida, then New York, then maybe California. Then the radiation cloud covers the whole country. And then you puke all the time and your hair falls out and—"

"Stop it, Harvey!" Christy begged. He was ruining her fun!

Just then, an older boy came running across the street. "Mrs. Garone just made fresh popcorn!"

"Oh, boy!" Lucille cried. "Let's get some!"

The children raced across the street, trick-or-treat bags flying, the trouble in far-off Cuba momentarily forgotten.

As the night progressed, their bags grew heavier and heavier. They moved from the main part of town to the nearby streets, knocking on door after door. When they came to the block where the Gammels had lived, some of the older kids began to tease.

"Darren's gonna getcha! Darren's gonna getcha!"

"Look at the woods! I see someone without a head!"

Somehow, this street seemed darker than all the others.

"Can we get away from here?" Christy asked. "I don't like it here. It gives me the creeps."

"Yeah, there aren't any houses lit up here anyway," Lucille said.

The girls turned the corner, unaware that they were being watched.

Inside the Gammel garage, a stranger hid in the shadows and watched the children parading by. He'd been waiting all night for one particular child, Christy Burnett. There would be no chance to get her tonight, not with all these people around, but he hoped that following her would give him a clue that would help him snatch her one day soon.

He had used a pair of garden shears to poke holes in a tarp he'd found piled in a corner. When he saw Christy and her friends, he pulled the makeshift ghost costume over his head and snuck out of the garage. He looked just like any other adult accompanying the kids on their rounds. No one paid any attention to him. He moved quickly, searching for the little girl he had made his prey. A boy in a skeleton costume and mask jumped in front of him. He roared in anger, but the kid only laughed. Scary noises were part of the night's fun.

Christy and a group of other children were walking away from a house, laughing.

"I got another Tootsie Roll Pop!" Lucille cried.

"Nestlé bars are my favorite," Eda said.

Harvey, just coming up the walk, said:

"Christy! What've you got in that bag?"

Christy's fist tightened protectively around the handle.

"Nothing," she said, her eyes wary.

Eda stepped forward, looking defiant. She pulled herself up as tall as she could, barely reaching Harvey's shoulders, and said:

"Don't you even think about stealing Christy's loot!"

"Huh, big talker!" Harvey sneered. "What're you gonna do, Brillo head? Shoot me with a water pistol?"

"Someday I'll have a real gun," Eda said. "Then you'll get it!"

"Oh, forget him," Lucille said. "Come on, it's getting late. Let's go home. We'll walk Christy back first."

The children headed back into town, unaware that their exchange had told the stranger exactly how he was going to get Christy Burnett.

NINE

▼

HALLOWEEN CANDY WAS quickly gobbled up, and soon talk of spooky things gave way to Thanksgiving plans. Eda and Christy came to school one day to see the whole classroom decorated with cutouts of Pilgrims and Indians. But Mrs. Mincini didn't seem happy about the upcoming holidays. Her face was very serious as she called the class to order.

"Today, children," she began, "we have something very important to discuss. I'm sure you've all heard your parents talking about the trouble President Kennedy is having with Cuba. Can anyone tell me who the leader of Cuba is?"

Tiffany Simmons's hand shot up.

"Fido Castro!" she said.

"Don't speak out of turn, Tiffany," Mrs. Mincini scolded. "And his name is Fi-*del*. Say that with me. Fi-*del* Cas-tro."

"Fi-*del Cas*-tro," the children singsonged.

"Now, Mr. Castro wants us to take away our naval base in Guantanamo Bay," she said. "Guantanamo is a big word, isn't it? Here, I'll write it on the board."

As the chalk squeaked over the slate, Christy felt a tap on her shoulder. She turned to see Eda pointing at the window.

"Look across the street!" Eda whispered. "I think it's the guy I saw at the rally!"

Christy's heart began to flutter. She stretched a little and gazed outside. A man was standing there, his back against a big oak tree. He seemed to be staring right at Christy. He picked up his hand, and something metal flashed in the sunlight.

It was just like the flash of metal she saw in her dreams. With a gasp, Christy turned her eyes away.

"Do you think it's him?" Eda whispered.

"Miss Crispin!" their teacher snapped. "Do you want to stand in the corner again?"

"N-no, ma'am," Eda replied.

"Then stop whispering."

Christy gave Eda a worried glance, then looked to the front of the room. She wished she could watch the man again, to see if he was really the one she had seen in her dream. But Mrs. Mincini was going on about Cuba, and missiles, and President Kennedy.

Harvey had scared her when he talked about this on Halloween, but hearing her teacher confirm everything was even more frightening to the little girl. It seemed it was just a matter of who would get her first—that bad man or the Commies.

"We're going to watch a little film," Mrs. Mincini said, rolling the projector down the aisle between the two center rows. "It will teach us what to do if there is an attack."

When the lights went down, Christy was able to look

out the window for a moment before the shades were pulled down. The man was still standing there, waiting, holding up that knife.

It had to be a very *big* knife if she could see it from so far away.

It had to be big enough to cut off somebody's head.

The loud sound track of the filmstrip jolted her attention back to the screen in front of the room. She watched a show about the bomb, listened to a tune called "Duck and Cover" and saw schoolchildren rolled up in balls along the walls of their school corridor. But she turned to the window every once in a while, as if she could see through the fawn-colored shades.

When the lights went up, her eyes were huge. No one noticed, because they were all wide-eyed with terror.

"Now," Mrs. Mincini said, "some time today, we're going to have a drill. Did you see how nicely those children in the film exited their classroom? Did you see the way they covered their heads and crouched down in the hall? They had an air raid drill. We're going to have one here. I don't know exactly when that will be, but I'm sure that you will all do well. Better than the third-graders, right?"

The children nodded eagerly, but fear was still stamped on their little faces. Only two children felt differently. Christy was more afraid of the man outside, and Eda revealed her own thoughts at lunch two hours later.

"That was a stupid movie," she said, pulling meat from a tiny chicken leg. "Like a tablecloth is gonna protect you from a bomb!"

"Those people were practicing 'duck and cover,' " Christy reminded her friend. "There was no place else to hide."

She looked down at her own meal. Her mother had been in a good mood that morning, and had given her enough money to buy a hot lunch. She dug her spoon into the lumpy mashed potatoes.

"Do you think that guy is still outside?" she asked.

"I hope not," Eda said. "What a creep! I'll bet he's watching the school to find new kids to take!"

Christy shuddered so violently that her mashed potatoes plopped into her lap. She heard giggles from across the room and thought Tiffany's crowd was laughing at her. Quickly, she cleaned her dress with her napkin.

"Gee!" Eda said, "I didn't mean to scare you. You want my ice cream?"

"It's okay," Christy said, forcing a smile.

"Well, you don't have to worry," Eda insisted. "That man wouldn't dare touch you with all the teachers around."

"Uh-huh," Christy agreed.

"Share my pretzels," Eda insisted. "I got too much."

"You always eat a lot," Christy said. She didn't mean it as an insult, but as a statement of fascination.

"Mommy says I'm going to get fat," Eda said, "but I don't care. I like food."

After lunch, they found an empty bench in the school yard and started to play a clapping game, Miss Mary Mack. When the chant came to an end, they dropped their hands into their laps and giggled.

"Christy!"

The voice was deep, and faraway.

"Did you hear that?" Christy asked.

"Christy, come here!"

"It sounds like the man at the rally," Eda said.

Tears welled up in Christy's eyes. Eda wriggled around on the bench and glanced at the trees across the street. No one was there.

"Maybe . . . maybe it was just another kid calling another Christy," she offered.

"No, it was him," Christy said. "He wants to get me, just because that lady put blood all over me! But I didn't see his face! I can't tell the police what the murderer looks like! So why does he want me? Why?"

"I dunno," Eda said. "How come you don't tell a grown-up about him?"

"My father told me not to," Christy said, remembering his dire threats.

"Your father is scary, too," Eda replied.

Both girls were glad when the bell rang to beckon them inside. Christy hardly heard the story Mrs. Mincini read about the Pilgrims. She could only think about the man outside. Maybe he'd get her on the way home from school. . . .

As promised, the surprise air raid drill came, right in the middle of arithmetic. As their teacher snapped out orders, the children filed quickly from the room. Christy turned to face the wall, studying a tiny crack for a moment before she was told to tuck herself into a ball. She didn't understand why she had to do this, but she threw her arms over her head and squeezed her eyes shut.

She heard a siren wailing and teachers shouting, but in her private darkness she saw only ugly green eyes staring at her.

I won't let him get you, Christy. I'll protect you. I'm strong, because I'm the head . . .

And he popped his head right off his neck.

. . . of the family!

Christy didn't realize she was screaming until Mrs. Mincini jerked her to her feet and shook her.

"Christine Burnett! Stop this at once!"

Christy burst into tears. As the other children watched in awe, she stood sobbing.

"He's gonna get me! He's gonna get me!"

"Who, dear?" Mrs. Mincini asked, her voice a mix of concern and annoyance.

"The . . . the man who took Teddy and Adrian!" Christy blubbered. "The man who cuts off heads! He's after me!"

As her teacher stood holding her by the shoulders, she hung her head and sobbed uncontrollably.

TEN

▼

CHRISTY SPENT THE afternoon in the nurse's office, lying on an uncomfortable little cot, staring up at a water mark on the ceiling. The door to Mrs. Babcock's office was ajar, and the nurse was talking quietly with the principal. Not quietly enough, though, because Christy could hear everything they were saying.

"It's the father that puts fear in that poor child," Mrs. Babcock commented. "That man ought to be in jail. All this talk of bombs and Communists only exacerbates the problem."

"I must agree," Mr. Milton said. Christy imagined his bald head bobbing up and down like the little statue she'd seen in the back of Mrs. Mincini's car. "The child is too nervous. Perhaps we should consider giving her some time off from school."

Oh, no! Christy thought. *My father will kill me!*

Almost as if she'd read the girl's mind, Mrs. Babcock said:

"And what do you suppose her father would have to say to that?"

There was no reply, but in Christy's mind the principal's head was bobbing again.

It was a funny image, but she didn't smile. And she didn't close her eyes and go to sleep the way Mrs. Babcock had told her. She was afraid she'd see that man again, darkly shadowed and evil. Christy never saw his whole face, but those horrible eyes were enough to bring terror.

When she heard the door open, she closed her eyes and pretended to be asleep.

"What a darling," Mrs. Babcock was saying. Christy thought the school nurse was *so* nice. "How could such a beautiful child be so unhappy?"

The door to the office closed again, and Mr. Milton's reply was lost.

At last it was time to go home. Christy was grateful that Eda met her. She didn't want to face the other kids alone. With Eda at her side, no one would dare tease her.

"Gee, what happened?" Eda asked.

"That man I saw scared me," Christy explained as they walked down the hall.

Just outside the door, Christy came to a halt on the steps.

"Oh, Eda," she said. "I wish I knew why that man was so scary! When we were having the air raid drill, I had a dream about him!"

"Dreams in the middle of the day are weird," Eda said.

A loud noise made them turn towards a cluster of holly bushes that grew next to the stoop. Tiffany and a few other kids were huddled together, staring at Christy.

"Creepy Christy!" Tiffany cried. "Creepy Christy!"

"No, Crazy Christy!" said another girl. "She's really wacko!"

"Stop it!" Eda shouted, fists doubling.

She started down the steps, but Tiffany's group ran away in a chorus of squeals.

"I hate her so much," Eda said.

Christy watched them go, too ashamed to say anything. She came down the steps and walked with Eda to the gate.

"How come you don't have a bike today?" she asked.

"I got a flat tire," Eda said. "I was doing wheelies in the driveway. Mom's really mad and she says she isn't going to fix it. But Dad will when he gets a chance."

They were halfway across the yard when a loud honking made them both look towards the street. A long blue Cadillac had pulled up to the curb. Christy recognized Eda's mother behind the wheel. Rita Crispin pulled herself out of the car, waving to her daughter. She was wearing a light brown coat with dark fur trim, and a little brown fur hat. Her sunglasses had sparkles on them.

"Your mommy looks just like a movie star," Christy said.

"I wonder what she's doing here," Eda said, frowning. She was disappointed she couldn't walk home.

Mrs. Crispin came across the pavement, high heels clicking.

"Hello, darling," she said. She smiled just a little at Christy. "I've come to drive you home."

"Why?"

"You know perfectly well why," Rita said. "It isn't safe to be alone these days."

"Oh, Mom . . ."

"Don't argue," Rita said. "Come along. Say good-bye to your friend."

Defeated, Eda said good-bye to Christy and followed her mother to the big car.

Left alone in the school yard, Christy wrapped her arms tightly around her books and started for the gate with her head lowered. Maybe if she didn't look up, no one would see her. She didn't want to face any mean kids without Eda to help.

But then, a big boy she'd never seen before jumped directly in her path. He waved his hands at her like a mesmerist.

"Hoooo . . . hoooo," he sang. "The killer's gonna getcha!"

Christy tried to get around the boy, but another one cut in front of her.

"He's waiting for you!" this second boy said.

"He's going to get you and bury you with the other kids!" the first boy cried.

Christy swung around. Maybe Lucille was nearby! But Christy was all alone in a throng of cruel faces.

"Hooo! Hooo!"

"Hey, is that the crazy kid?" someone shouted from far away.

"Crazy Christy! Crazy Christy!"

"Hooo! Hoooo!"

Christy's eyes squeezed shut.

"Go away!"

"Crazy Christy!"

Suddenly, a familiar voice cut in.

"She said 'Go away,' " Harvey echoed.

Christy looked up to see her brother standing nearby. His hands were curled into tight fists, and there was an angry look on his face. The other boys knew his reputation, and they backed away with fear in their eyes.

"Come on," the first boy said. "I ain't messin' with him!"

The group disbanded, running in different directions.

"Come on," Harvey said, still glaring at them. "I'll walk you home."

Christy fell into step with her brother.

"Thanks," she said softly. "What're you doing here?"

The junior high was two blocks away, and until today Harvey wouldn't have been caught dead near the grade school.

Harvey snorted. "I just was walkin' by and I heard those morons picking on you. But just 'cause I'm being nice don't you go getting any funny ideas."

"I won't."

They didn't speak again during the walk home. Upstairs, they changed into everyday clothes. Harvey left the apartment as soon as he was dressed. Christy headed to the kitchen, hoping there might be a snack. Just then, the apartment door opened and her mother walked in with a bag of groceries.

"Hi, Mommy," Christy said.

"I can't hear you," her mother replied. She put a hand to her ear. "The voices are too loud."

She looked around the dark little room with worry in her eyes.

"I wonder why Dr. Markel doesn't make the voices stop?"

Christy didn't know what to say.

Sarah went into the kitchen, ignoring her daughter. Christy followed, setting up her papers on the table. As memories of her nightmarish day began to fade ever so slightly, she tried to busy herself with a Thanksgiving drawing. Her mother flitted about the kitchen, pulling food from the refrigerator to prepare dinner. After a few minutes, she stopped and leaned over Christy's shoulder.

"What a pretty Indian maiden," she said. "Thanksgiving is coming, isn't it? I have to make plans. Oh, yes, I have to make a lot of plans! I have to buy a goose. No, a turkey.

It's turkey for Turkey Day! Turkey with stuffing. Might use the stuffing from the couch. Daddy won't yell, oh, no, he won't, because stuffing from the couch is so cheap."

Sarah ranted on like that for twenty minutes, then lapsed into silence again. Most of what she said made little sense and frightened Christy. By the time her mother was quiet, big tears had spilled down the little girl's cheeks and splattered over her drawing.

The Burnett family celebrated Thanksgiving two days late, on Saturday. *Celebrate* wasn't the word in Christy's mind as her family ate roast chicken, potatoes and canned corn in silence. Her mother had awakened in one of her "moods" that morning, and had sent Harvey Jr. to the butcher for a turkey. By now there were none available, but he'd chosen the biggest chicken he could find.

"Chicken," Harvey Sr. grumbled, washing the meat down with beer. "Supposed to be turkey on Thanksgiving. Supposed to be Thanksgiving on Thursday."

Harvey Jr. and Christy exchanged glances, but knew better than to speak. Sarah, however, smiled brightly. Christy took a bite of stuffing and gazed at her mother. She looked pretty today. Her light brown hair was pulled into a neat bun, and she was wearing a little makeup. Christy wished her mother could always look this way.

"Well, isn't this nice?" Sarah said, as if Harvey Sr. hadn't spoken at all. "All of us together. And just the family—none of those . . . others."

Christy thought she said the word *others* the way some people said *Communist*.

Somehow, Christy had managed to survive the weekend with neither Eda nor Lucille. Eda had gone to Chicago. Lucille was at an aunt's house. Christy imagined both of them were laughing and having a grand time. By the time dinner was over, her father was snoring on the couch with a half-empty beer can dangling from his hand, her mother had announced that she was tired, and Christy knew Sarah's good mood was over. Harvey Jr. helped her wash dishes, then disappeared from the apartment. Christy thought about leaving herself, but wondered where she would go. Besides, what if that man was still out there?

She hadn't seen him since that day in the school yard. But she didn't believe he wasn't around, just waiting for her. So she stayed in the safety of her bedroom, drawing pictures.

When she saw Eda in school on Monday, she was so happy she hugged her friend.

"I missed you!"

"I missed you, too!" Eda said. "We had such a good time. We went to a zoo and a puppet show, and Grandma made the best turkey ever!"

They walked to the swings together.

"What did you do?"

Christy shrugged. "Not much. Sure sounds like it was fun for you."

"It was," Eda said. "I can't wait until Hanukkah. Everybody's gonna come to our house."

Eda's freckled face seemed to light up as she swung around.

"I have a super idea!" she said. "You want to come have dinner with us one night during Hanukkah?"

"Oh, Eda, could I?" Christy asked. She wasn't exactly sure what Hanukkah was, but imagined the dinner in the Crispin mansion would be wonderful.

"I'll ask my parents," Eda promised. "Maybe Lucille can come, too. It'll be so much fun."

After school, the two girls rode bikes to Eda's house. They found Mrs. Crispin in Eda's bedroom, going through piles of old clothes with the housekeeper. Eda bounced up onto the bed, scattering dresses.

"Eda Crispin!" Rita cried in exasperation. "Get off the bed! Can't you see Mrs. Slocombe and I are busy?"

"Did you have a nice day at school, dear?" the house-keeper asked.

"It was okay," Eda said, jumping off the bed again. "Whatcha doing?"

"Gathering up some of your outgrown clothes," Rita said. "We're boxing them up for Rabbi Horn to distribute among the poor children in town."

She turned around with a pile of blouses that Mrs. Slocombe had just neatly folded. For just a moment, she stared at Christy, taking in the child's too-long corduroy pants and raggy-looking sweater. Having one of those "poor children" right here made her feel uncomfortable.

She turned quickly and put the blouses down in a box. Then she picked up a coat and started to fold it. She gazed up at a poster from the Montana Ballet Troupe that decorated Eda's pink-and-white floral wallpaper, thoughtful. Finally, she turned to Christy.

"You know, Eda outgrew this coat so quickly," she said. "I wonder if it might fit you? Would you like to have it?"

Rita watched Christy's expression, fearing the child would feel insulted. Instead, the little girl nodded eagerly.

"Oh!" she gasped.

She took the coat, royal blue with silver buttons, and ran her fingers over the rabbit fur collar.

"Oh, thank you!"

"Try it on, Christy," Eda said.

Christy did so eagerly. The coat fit perfectly, and unlike the coats she'd received other winters from charities, this one didn't have holes in the pockets. She twirled around in it.

"Thanks!"

"You're quite welcome, dear," Rita said.

"How pretty it makes you look," Mrs. Slocombe said.

"That was my Hanukkah coat last year," Eda said. "Oh! Mommy? Can Christy come for Hanukkah dinner? And can my friend Lucille come, too?"

"Certainly," Rita said. "You just tell Cook, all right? And be sure to let Daddy and me know what night they'll be coming."

Christy frowned. They'd be coming on Hanukkah, wouldn't they? She asked Eda about this as they headed to the kitchen.

"Hanukkah's eight days long," Eda said. "I get a present every night, but on the first and last nights I get extra stuff."

"Eight nights!" Christy cried in wonderment.

She couldn't imagine anyone being that lucky. Like Thanksgiving, Christmas was something she didn't dare get her hopes up about.

They entered the kitchen, where Eda told the cook about her plans. Christy breathed deeply, taking in the aroma of pumpkin pie. She hoped someone would offer her a piece, but instead, Eda said:

"Let's go outside. I saw a nest in a tree the other day and I want to try to get it."

Eda's backyard was so big that Christy could hardly see the trees at the other end. Her friend raced ahead of her, blond hair bouncing crazily in the wind. The sky was gray with the promise of rain. The air was crisp, but in her "new" coat, Christy didn't notice. She ran after her friend, laughing.

"Look up there," Eda said. "Do you see it?"

Christy tilted her head back and gazed through the bare branches of a huge oak tree. She spotted a dark clump.

"That's really high, Eda," she said.

"Oh, it is not," Eda insisted. She braced a sneaker on the side of the tree and hoisted herself up. "I'll throw it down! You catch it!"

Christy held her breath as she watched Eda shinny up the tree, certain Eda was going to fall and get killed. It was all Christy could do not to cover her eyes. She was so intent on her friend's progress that she nearly jumped out of her skin when she felt a tap on her shoulder. With a cry, she turned around.

"Lucille!"

"Gosh, I'm glad I found you!" Lucille cried. "Wait 'til you hear what happened!"

She looked up into the tree. Eda was almost to the bird's nest. For a moment, Lucille stood mesmerized, astounded that anyone could climb that high. She watched as Eda grabbed the nest, working it loose from the tangle of branches.

"Christy! Catch!"

Eda let the nest drop, but it was Lucille who caught it.

"Come down!" Lucille shouted. *"I want to tell you something!"*

By the time Eda jumped onto the ground, Lucille was almost breathless with excitement.

"Listen to this," she said. "One of my mother's friends called to tell her—they found Teddy Gammel's jacket!"

"Where?" Christy asked.

"Behind a gas station just outside of town," Lucille said. "The guy there keeps lots of old hubcaps and tires and things in a pile. He went to get something and he found it."

"How do they know it's Teddy's jacket?" Eda asked.

Lucille rolled her eyes as if the answer was obvious.

"He had his name written on the tag, of course," she said. "But listen! There were stains on it. Funny brown stains. My mother's friend said it might have been old blood."

"Ewww!" Eda cried, making a face.

Christy wrapped her arms around herself and looked

away. Somehow, the blue wool coat no longer made her feel warm. She thought of her school blouse, and the blood Irene Gammel had left on it. She thought of her dreams of flashing metal and mean eyes. Had Teddy and Adrian seen those same things?

"I—I think I better go home," she said, feeling sick.

"Don't go by yourself," Lucille said. "Wait for me."

"But you just got here," Eda protested.

Lucille held up her hands. "Mommy doesn't know I came out. She doesn't even know I heard what Mrs. Gaudiello told her. I have to hurry back."

Eda accompanied her friends to the front gate. She told Lucille about her Hanukkah plans, and Lucille gladly accepted.

"I'll see if it's okay with my parents," she said. "I hope so! It'll be fun."

Christy felt as if another blow had been dealt to her. Her parents! She hadn't thought about how they'd react. She was so unhappy about the prospect of asking them that she hardly said a word to Lucille as they biked home together. Lucille said good-bye at her house, and Christy went on alone.

The streets seemed strangely deserted. Christy felt uneasy, and pedaled her old bike as fast as she could. She was certain that the man knew all about the bloody jacket that had been found. He was back in town, here to make certain no other clues were discovered. He'd come looking for her, too.

She thought about Teddy Gammel. She didn't know what he looked like, but she pictured a big boy screaming as an ax came swinging towards him. She saw him crawling away, as she'd crawled in her nightmares, but unlike her nightmares he didn't escape the weapon's swing.

As clear as the day it had happened, she heard Irene Gammel screaming: *"He took off his head!"*

And as she raced down Central Street, the image of a boy's head floated in her mind. Then two boys, one big and one little. She imagined little Adrian still sucking on a pacifier.

Christy crashed up onto the sidewalk and hurried into the pizzeria. Mr. Venetto was working today, and when he saw the tears in Christy's eyes he came hurrying from behind the counter.

"What is it, Christy? What has happened?"

"I—I . . ."

Christy didn't know what to say.

"They found Teddy Gammel's jacket!" she blurted. "It had blood on it!"

Mr. Venetto said something in Italian, shaking his head.

"This frightened you," he said. "Do you want to sit down? Do you want a cola to relax you?"

Christy shook her head. "N-no. You just have to lock up my bike."

"I'll have Jimmy do it," the older man said, referring to his teenage delivery boy.

He watched Christy hurry outside to the apartment entrance, bothered that such a young child heard such terrible news.

Upstairs, Christy hurried into her room and climbed under her covers. She was so frightened that she didn't ever want to leave her room. Only the threat of a whipping coaxed her out to the dinner table. As usual, dinner was eaten in silence. But afterward, as they did the dishes together, Harvey confided in her.

"Did you hear about the jacket?"

Christy's eyes widened with surprise as she looked up at her brother.

"Everyone in town's talking about it," Harvey said. "They're tearing that gas station apart, looking for more clues. But you know what?"

"What?" Christy choked as she washed a dish. She wasn't sure she wanted to hear this.

"I don't think they're going to find those kids, ever."

"That's . . . that's what my friend Lucille said," Christy recalled. "Harvey, I'm scared."

"Me, too, kid," Harvey admitted. "Me, too."

Christy bit her lip to keep from bursting into tears. If a big, strong boy like Harvey was afraid, there was no hope for her at all.

ELEVEN

THE DISCOVERY OF Teddy Gammel's bloodied jacket had the parents of Aberdeen in an uproar again. A curfew was set for all children, and no child was allowed to leave school unaccompanied. Under the threat of dire punishment, Harvey begrudgingly met his sister to walk her home.

"What a crock," Harvey said. "They don't think that guy's still around, do they?"

"You think he might be gone?" Christy asked hopefully.

"He'd be pretty stupid to hang around here," Harvey said. "Geez! First those dumb air raid drills, then this! These grown-ups just want to make my life difficult. I can't wait until Christmas vacation. Then we can forget about school and Commies and all these rules for a while."

Christmas! Christy realized then that she hadn't asked her parents about Hanukkah. She made a vow to do so at dinner that night.

But her father was drunk, and there was no getting past her mother's voices. The same thing happened the next night, and the next. A week went by, and still Christy couldn't get up the nerve to ask. One Sunday afternoon about two weeks later, Eda asked what had happened.

"So, did you ask yet?"

"I—I haven't had a chance," Christy said.

They were sitting around the dining room table in the Brighams' house, making paper snowflakes. Christy traced a circle with a paper plate, then folded the paper several times.

"Well, hurry up," Eda said. "Hanukkah's just a week away."

"Next week?" Christy cried, nearly dropping the scissors she was using to cut little triangles in her folded circle. "But it's two weeks to Christmas!"

"Hanukkah comes earlier this year," Eda said. "Gosh, Christy. I sure hope you can come. Cook's gonna make a *great* dinner. And it's the first night so Daddy's gonna read the Hanukkah story. It'll be so much fun."

"I can't wait," Lucille said. She opened up her piece of paper, revealing a lacework of hearts and diamonds.

"Let's go hang some on the tree," she said.

She led the girls into the den, where a huge Christmas tree glowed warmly with blue, red, yellow and orange lights. It was so laden with ornaments that it was hard to see the boughs. At the top, a lighted star flashed and sparkled.

"I can't wait until Christmas," Lucille said. "I asked Santa for a horse. My brother Tom got one when he was ten, so I think Santa ought to bring me one, too. I mean, I'll be ten in January, anyway!"

Christy frowned. She'd stopped believing in Santa years ago. If he was so good, he'd come to everyone's house, but he didn't always make it to the Burnett apartment. So he just had to be fake.

But she didn't say anything about this to her friends. Instead, she helped hang the paper cutouts on the tree. The facets of a crystal ornament caught her reflection and broke it into pieces. The ornament was so beautiful that she couldn't help reaching out for it. She only wanted to touch it, to feel the smooth, cool crystal in her fingers. Somehow, the ornament slipped off its bough, and before Christy knew what was happening it fell to the floor and shattered.

"Oh, no!" Lucille cried.

Christy dropped the paper snowflakes she'd made. They fell slowly to the rug, like real snow, but unlike the crystal bauble they didn't break. The little girl brought both hands up to her opened mouth. She looked at Lucille with big eyes, and burst into tears.

"I'm sorry!" she cried. "I didn't mean it!"

"Christy, you gotta be careful!" Eda said.

"I'm sorry! I'm sorry!"

Christy started bawling. She could only think that Lucille would tell her mother, and her mother would tell Christy's father, and he'd get out that Ping-Pong paddle he kept in a drawer and . . .

"Christy, stop crying!" Lucille said. "It's just a dumb ornament!"

A door slammed nearby, and Mrs. Brigham entered the room, wearing riding clothes. She had the baby in her arms, all bundled up in a snowsuit. The cold air had nipped bright pink into their cheeks, and their eyes sparkled as if snow crystals had formed in them. Mrs. Brigham was smiling, but her smile faded when she saw the wet streaks down Christy's reddened face.

"What happened?" she asked, setting the baby down.

"Christy accidentally broke an ornament," Lucille said. "We were hanging paper snowflakes."

"I'm sorry," Christy said again. "Please, please don't tell my father!"

Mrs. Brigham looked at her strangely, as if she didn't understand. She turned to the baby and started to free him from his snowsuit. Christy couldn't tell how angry she was, and this frightened her all the more. She stopped crying, but great hiccups racked her small frame as she stared at the woman and the baby.

"Which ornament, Lucille?" Mrs. Brigham asked, pulling off the baby's knit cap.

"The crystal one with the silver flower on top," Lucille said.

"It was an accident, Mrs. Brigham," Eda put in.

Mrs. Brigham stood up, and when she turned around she was smiling gently.

"I'm sure it was," she said. "Christy, that was just a little thing I bought for half price at the end of the Christmas season last year. I'm sorry it broke, but it really isn't that important."

Christy sniffled.

"It isn't?"

"Not enough to cry about," Mrs. Brigham said.

"You—you aren't gonna tell my father?"

Mrs. Brigham shook her head.

"Of course not," she said. She came to Christy and gave her a big hug. Christy, unused to kindness, stiffened in her arms.

Mrs. Brigham pulled away and frowned for a moment. She'd never met such a strange child before. She wondered why Christy was so nervous all the time.

But the children were staring at her, and she quickly regained her composure.

"Lucille, can you finish undressing Matthew?" she said. "I'll get something to clean up the glass."

She started to leave the room, but turned and said:

"Have you looked outside?"

The girls raced to the window.

"Snow!" Lucille cried.

"It's snowing!" Eda said.

"First snowfall of the season," Mrs. Brigham said. "I should have known it was coming, since Major grew a thicker coat. I'm just surprised it's so late this year."

The three girls stood in the window, admiring the flakes as they fell to the ground. Already, everything in sight was covered with a dusting of white. It was so beautiful and peaceful that Christy started to forget what had happened. Mrs. Brigham left them alone.

Eda breathed on the windowpane, then drew a smiling face in the frost.

"Christy, why were you crying so much?" she asked.

"I—I was scared," Christy said softly. She stared down at the window ledge. "I thought Lucille's mom would call my father."

"About that?" Lucille asked. "My mom wouldn't make a big deal about anything. She's real sweet."

Christy nodded, thinking this was true. If only her mother was as nice as Mrs. Brigham. If only her father . . .

"You two kids better let me drive you home," Mrs. Brigham said as she came back into the room. "The weatherman predicts a bad storm, and your parents will worry."

"Can I come?" Lucille asked.

"Daddy will be coming back in from the barns with Stannie," Mrs. Brigham said. "And Greta is due to wake up from her nap. I need you to watch the kids."

She found her keys and purse and waited until the girls had their coats on. Lucille said good-bye, and her friends walked out to the station wagon. They dropped Eda off first. As they headed on into town, Christy had the feeling Mrs. Brigham was glancing over at her every once in a while. She looked up, and Mrs. Brigham's head snapped quickly forward.

"Are you okay now, Christy?" she asked.

"Yes."

The woman fidgeted a little with the fur collar on her coat.

"How's your mother doing these days?"

"Fine," Christy said. She didn't realize Lucille's mom knew hers.

"And your daddy?"

Christy shifted uncomfortably. Why was Mrs. Brigham asking about him? Nobody asked about him. Nobody liked him very much.

"Fine," she said in a smaller voice.

She felt Mrs. Brigham's gloved hand on top of her own.

"If you ever need to talk to someone," she said, "someone grown up, you can come to me, okay?"

Christy didn't say anything. She didn't understand why Mrs. Brigham was being so kind. It would be nice if she could tell her about the strange man who had been following her. But everyone thought she was crazy. Why should Mrs. Brigham be any different?

At last, they reached the apartment. By now the snow had covered the streets, and the wind was blowing crazily. Christy pushed open the door, letting in a blast of cold.

"Looks like a blizzard!" Mrs. Brigham cried over the wind. "Guess you won't have school tomorrow!"

"Hope not!" Christy said.

"You remember what I told you, now, honey!" said Mrs. Brigham.

Christy didn't reply, but hurried into the apartment. She was about to race up the stairs to the warmth of her home when she remembered the snow on her shoes. She took them off and set them carefully on the floor near the bottom of the stairs. Then she went upstairs to her room. There, she took her snowflakes from her pocket and taped them to her windows. For a long time, she stared outside, gazing past the bars of the fire escape at the white school yard across the street. Everything seemed so quiet, so clean. And safe—bad people would be locked inside just like good people. That meant that, if the killer was still in town, he couldn't come looking for her. The idea made her feel completely at ease for the first time in months. It made her so comfortable that, by dinnertime, she finally got up the nerve to ask her father about the Hanukkah celebration.

"I don't care," Harvey Sr. said with a grunt. "Let someone else feed you."

"But it's a Jewish celebration," Harvey Jr. said. "Isn't it a sin for a Christian to attend?"

Christy glared across the dinner table at her brother.

"Oh, it's not like church."

The two children and their father turned with surprise at the sound of Sarah's voice. She looked from one to the other, guileless.

"Well, it's just a dinner," she said.

She seemed completely unaware that she had just come awake. Most nights, she sat at the dinner table eating slowly, rubbing at her ear to make the "voices" stop. Christy felt relief, seeing she'd found an unexpected ally in her mother.

"Well, okay," her father said. "When is it?"

"Next Saturday night," Christy said.

Sarah turned around and looked at the calendar that hung on the kitchen wall.

"Oh, that's just a week away!" she cried. "We have so much to do, Christy! We have to get you some new clothes and new shoes! And of course, you'll have to bring a gift. And—"

"Hold it!" Harvey Sr. yelled. "You ain't spendin' all my money for one night!"

Sarah gave her husband an exasperated look.

"You don't want her to look like poor white trash, do you?" she demanded. "The Crispins are one of the richest families in town. You know the father owns some newspapers. And Rita Crispin always looks so pretty when she comes to town. I see her sometimes, all dolled up in her fancy Paris fashions. Why, she had a suit on the other day just like the kind Jackie Kennedy wears. It must have cost—"

Harvey Sr. snorted.

"Probably thinks she's better'n us," he said.

But he didn't change his mind about the celebration. Christy walked on eggshells for the next week, careful not to incur his wrath. She wouldn't do *anything* to ruin her special plans. She even tried her best to be tolerant of her brother. He still walked her to and from school every day, but most of the time he had nothing to say to her. They plodded across the snow in silence, their breath coming in gasps that condensed into puffs of vapor.

"Tell Mom I'll be down by the lake," Harvey said one afternoon.

"You're going alone?"

Harvey sneered at her.

"What're you, the police?" he asked. "I'm meeting my friends there, okay? That dumb rule about staying in groups isn't gonna keep me from having fun. Besides, I told you—that guy is long gone."

He turned away and headed down the block. Christy entered the apartment, pulled off her boots, and went upstairs. She almost hated entering the apartment after spending so many hours in Mrs. Mincini's cheerfully decorated classroom. Her mother had been too sick lately to do any decorating. They didn't even have a tree.

The first thing Christy noticed when she opened the door was a warm, cinnamony smell. Her mouth dropped open as she looked around. Instead of a dark and drab living room, she found one as beautifully decorated as Lucille's house. Wreaths hung in the windows, red candles lined a bureau, and there was even a manger scene on the radiator. Christy took it all in with astonishment. She hung up her coat and came farther into the room. It was then she noticed the opened boxes and bags scattered all around. Her mother had decorated, but she'd left a mess behind.

Christy followed the spicy aroma into the kitchen. Sarah was pulling gingerbread men from the oven. She turned to Christy with a grin. Flour grayed her hair, and a splotch of batter clung to one cheek. Her eyes were big.

"Just in time," she said. "There's one on the table I made to look like you, and one for Harvey."

"Harvey went to the lake," Christy said, staring at the kitchen table. She couldn't guess how many cookies and other baked goods were there, but the kitchen looked like a bakery. There were piles and piles of cookies, all different kinds. She saw two pies, and several loaves of shiny bread, braided and decorated with poppy seeds.

But there were also mixing bowls stacked cockeyed into each other, icing and batter dripping over their sides. The sugar and flour sat open on the counter, and an unwrapped stick of butter had made a yellow pool on the stove. A container of milk had fallen, and most of the contents had dripped all over the floor. Christy felt her heart sink. She would have to clean all this up before her father got home.

"You . . . you sure did a lot of cooking," she said.

Sarah smiled broadly. "Just getting into the spirit. I have so many mouths to feed, you know. They kept asking me when I was going to do my holiday baking, so I thought today was as good a time as any."

Christy put the lids back on the sugar and flour canisters. Then she picked up the milk carton and threw it into the trash. She didn't understand who "they" were, but she knew not to ask.

"Don't you want your cookie?"

When she turned, Sarah was holding the gingerbread out to her. Christy took it and was amazed to see it really did look like her.

"Wow," was all she could say.

"I started baking as soon as I came home from the store," Sarah said. "I'll freeze some for Christmas, but we can enjoy some now. Your father likes butter cookies—I made some especially for him."

Christy found a place to sit down and began to eat her gingerbread girl. Her mother, singing "Jingle Bells" at the top of her lungs, placed a steaming cup of hot cocoa in front of her. This was completely unexpected, since cocoa was very expensive. Christy knew this because her father had once said so while backhanding Harvey for knocking over a can.

"I've been so busy," Sarah said. "It was hard carrying all those packages home. I'm glad we live close to town. I bought so many nice things. Oh, wait!"

She hurried from the room. Christy stood up with her cookie and started to clean again. She was just wiping up the spilled milk when Sarah returned a few minutes later. Her mother didn't acknowledge that Christy was helping, but said:

"Look!"

Christy turned around. Her eyes widened at the sight of the red dress her mother was holding. It had long, puffy sleeves and a big white satin sash. The yoke was smocked, and there was lace around the neckline.

"Isn't it lovely?" Sarah asked. "You can wear it to the Crispins' house."

Christy stood up and ran to give her mother a hug. Maybe she acted strange sometimes, and maybe she didn't stop Christy's father from being mean, but sometimes she was just the best mother in the world.

"I love you, Mommy," she said.

"My angel from heaven," Sarah replied. Then she gave her hands a clap. "Now! To pack up all these goodies!"

She set to work, singing loudly and off-key. As she wrapped the baked goods, she suddenly seemed unaware that Christy was even in the room. The little girl cleaned diligently, stopping once in a while for a sip of cocoa.

She noticed some poppy seeds on the counter and went to wipe them up. A few of them started to move. Christy screamed and backed away. Ants had come into the kitchen, drawn by the sweet smells! With a disgusted face, she turned to ask her mother for help. But Sarah was staring down at the kitchen table, laden with baked goods. Her mouth was moving rapidly.

She was talking to nobody again.

Christy knew her mother wouldn't be any help. She took a deep breath and grabbed a dish towel. Quickly, just allowing herself a glance to see where she had to work, she knocked the ants into the trash can. Then she double-checked every nook and cranny for crumbs. If her father came home and found ants in the kitchen, he'd beat up her mother. Then he'd beat Christy for not helping to clean properly.

By the time she finished, she was exhausted. But when she looked up at the clock and saw her father would be home in twenty minutes, she knew she had to clean up the living room, too. She raced about, gathering up packages and bags. She crumbled them up small and stuffed them into the kitchen wastebasket. Then, with a yawn, she went into her room to lie down.

She only meant to close her eyes for a minute. But she was so worn out she fell deeply asleep, and began to dream.

She was riding her bike in front of the Gammels' house. She looked up at the towers and saw a little boy in the window. He waved to her, his hand moving slowly. She waved back.

"Want to go upstairs and play?"

Christy turned around and saw a man on a bicycle. In the mist of the dream she could just make out his eyes. They were green, crinkled around the edges in a mean look.

"Want to go upstairs and play?"

"I have to go home."

"Don't get your blouse dirty."

"I have to go home."

"Don't get blood on it!"

The man's hand came at her, a gleaming knife sparkling in the dream sunshine. Christy screamed.

But somebody else was screaming. Christy sat up in her bed, clutching her pillow. Her room had grown dark as the sun went down. As her heart pounded, she listened to her father yelling and her mother screaming.

"You really are crazy!" Harvey Sr. shouted. "What the hell possessed you to buy all this junk?"

"Christmas is coming!" Sarah yelled back. "Why shouldn't I buy gifts for the kids?"

"But all this?" Harvey shot back. "Christ, there's four dolls here! What's Christy gonna do with four dolls? And that stereo for Harvey! How much did that set us back?"

Christy heard crashing noises, as if something was being thrown across her parents' room. So her mother had bought Christmas presents and not just food. Her father must have just discovered her purchases. She wondered if he'd seen the bags in the kitchen trash. If he thought Christy had hidden them there . . .

"I'll teach you to waste my money!"

"Harvey, no!"

There was a slapping noise, and a scream, and more things falling. Christy covered her ears and wiggled under her covers. Even then, she could hear her mother's cries of pain.

Some time later, her door opened. Harvey Jr. came in and poked hard at the mound she made under her blankets.

"Supper's ready," he said, his voice dull.

Slowly, Christy made her way into the kitchen. Sarah had made meat loaf with gravy for dinner. Christy sat quietly at her place. No one spoke through the entire meal. No one said a word about Sarah's black eye, or even about the nice meal she'd prepared.

Christy knew there would be no more baking that holiday season.

TWELVE

▼

By COINCIDENCE, THE annual holiday party at the Cable and Wire Factory fell on the same night as the Crispins' Hanukkah celebration. Harvey Sr. dressed in his one-and-only good suit, and saw to it that his wife put on her best dress. Sarah moved like a robot, never smiling, simply staring into the mirror as her husband zipped up the dress.

"The party's over at eleven," Harvey Sr. told his kids.

They were sitting together on the living room couch, as ordered. Christy was wearing the red dress. Harvey, by contrast, had on his jeans and a sweatshirt. He was shoeless, and a toe poked through the end of one white sock.

"That means I expect you home at ten," their father said as he opened a bottle of cologne. "And don't think you can pull a fast one on me. I might come home for a bit just to check on you."

"It'll be dark then," Sarah said in a quiet voice. "How

will they walk home in the dark, with all the snow? Things hide in the dark, bad things . . ."

"I'm goin' to a party right near Christy's," Harvey volunteered. "I'll pick her up on the way home and we'll walk together."

"Fine," his father said. "Come on, Sarah, we'll be late."

He helped his wife into her coat, then steered her towards the door. Before leaving, he turned and pointed an intimidating finger at his kids.

"Ten o'clock," he said. The threat was clear; he didn't need to say more.

When they heard the downstairs door shut, the two kids leaped from the couch.

"Are you really gonna walk me home, Harvey?" Christy asked.

"Why not?" Harvey replied. "Is it a crime?"

"Well, no," Christy said, uncertain. "But . . ."

"Forget it," Harvey said. "Let's go. The guys are waiting for me."

They put on their coats and left the apartment. As they sat on the bottom steps and pulled on their boots, Christy asked:

"What kind of party are you going to? Is it for Hanukkah?"

Harvey snorted. "No, it isn't for Hanukkah. It's just for the holidays. Don't ask so many questions."

Christy pulled on her gloves. Then the children walked out into the night. For a second, the sight of downtown Aberdeen, decorated for the upcoming holidays, made Christy stop and stare.

"Oh, Harvey, look!" she cried. "Isn't it beautiful?"

"I guess so," Harvey said, his breath making a cloud of mist.

Arches of colored lights had been strung over Central Street, beginning and ending at lampposts that had been wrapped to look like candy canes. The storefronts were decorated with their own lights, all blinking merrily. In the distance, someone was playing a recording of Bing Crosby's "White Christmas."

Christy sighed. "I love Christmas. I think it's going to be great this year. I think we're going to get presents."

"Yeah, sure," Harvey said sarcastically. "After Dad makes Mom take all those things she bought back again, we won't get shit."

"Harvey!" Christy cried. "Don't talk like that! She won't take them back! She just won't!"

"I don't want to talk about it," Harvey said. "Come on, will you?"

Christy followed him, climbing over an embankment of snow. The going was easier in the streets, and they walked right down the middle. Once in a while a car would come, crunching on the freshly plowed snow, and they'd separate to let it pass. The snow made made it difficult to hurry—it was a full twenty minutes before they reached the gates of the Crispin house. Not a word was spoken in that time, although Christy couldn't help softly singing Christmas carols.

"Here it is," she said. "Thanks for walking with me, Harvey."

She realized then that she hadn't thought of the stranger even once during their walk. It *was* going to be a good night!

"I'll pick you up at nine-thirty," Harvey said. "Be ready. I don't want a whipping just 'cause of you."

"I'll be ready," Christy promised.

She pushed open the gate and started towards the house. About halfway up, she turned to wave to her brother. But the road in front of the house was empty. Shaking her head in wonder at her brother's speed, she turned and hurried up to the front door.

There were no wreaths or colored lights on the Crispins' front door, but every window held a candle that flickered warmly in the darkness. Christy rang the bell. A man with black skin pulled open the door. He smiled at Christy and welcomed her into the house. He was wearing a suit with a short coat and white gloves.

"The guests are in the parlor," he said. His words sounded strange to Christy, unlike any voice she'd ever heard. They were beautiful words, warm and rounded.

"What's a parlor?" she asked.

The man laughed, a baritone laugh.

"Like a living room, *ma cherie*," he said. "You come with Jean-Robert. He will show you the party."

She followed him, and in a few moments heard music. It wasn't Christmas music, of course, and for a second that didn't seem right. Christy had to remind herself that Jewish people didn't celebrate Christmas. She couldn't wait to see how they *did* celebrate.

Jean-Robert, a butler hired for the night, pushed open a pair of doors and showed her into the parlor. Eda came running up to her, all smiles. She was wearing the most beautiful blue dress Christy had ever seen. The top part was satin, and the skirt hung in tier after tier of lace.

"Here you are!" Eda cried.

Rita Crispin came up behind her daughter. She reminded Christy of pictures she'd seen of Elizabeth Taylor as Cleopatra. Rita wore a long, flowing dress clasped with a gold sunburst at one shoulder. Thick bangs came down to her darkly lined eyes, and her hair was perfectly straight and cut just where her chin was. A smile lit up her face.

"Did your parents drive you, dear?"

"My brother walked me," Christy said, a hint of pride in her voice. Having Harvey as an escort was still something amazing to her.

For a second, Rita's frown faltered. But her smile quickly reappeared.

"What a nice brother," she said. "And it must be so cold out!"

"It's okay," Christy said.

"You look pretty," Eda said.

"So do you," Christy answered.

Eda made a face that showed she'd rather be in play clothes. Then she took hold of Christy's hand and pulled her towards a table full of presents. They were wrapped in blue, gold and silver. Eda pointed to a few of them.

"That one's mine, and that one, and that one," she said. "I don't know which one I get to open tonight, but I hope it's the big one."

Christy's eyes widened. Eda was so lucky to get all these presents!

Her friend pulled out a small box.

"Guess who this one is for?" she asked.

"I dunno," Christy said with a shrug.

"You!"

"Really?"

She looked at the box, no bigger than the palm of Eda's hand, and wondered what it could possibly be. She was about to ask when the big double doors opened again and Lucille came into the room. Eda put the box down, and the two girls ran to greet their friend.

Lucille's long back hair had been pulled back into a French braid, a stark contrast to the white dress she wore. The three little girls giggled with each other.

"You kids look more like Independence Day than Hanukkah," Dean Crispin said.

They turned around. Christy's father was standing behind them. Christy thought he looked like a handsome prince in his black tuxedo, his dark hair slicked back with something that smelled really good. Through his glasses, she could see a sparkle in his eyes—or maybe that was from the tiny white lights that had been strung across the ceiling. He had a drink in one hand, and something golden in the other. Christy tried to see what it was, but Eda jumped at her father and took his hand.

"Gold coins! Gold coins!" she cried.

"Eda! Be a little lady!" Rita cried, a huge diamond ring glimmering as she held up her hand.

Dean Crispin laughed heartily, then passed bags of gold-foil-wrapped chocolate coins to the children.

"Let them have their fun, Rita," he said. He winked at Eda. "Thought you might like a snack while I read the story."

"Now?" Eda asked, hope in her voice.

"Sure," Dean said. "Our guests are all here, aren't they?"

An announcement was made, and the people in the room found seats. Small children cuddled into mothers' laps, men sat on the edges of chairs, and older kids sat on the floor.

"My dad used to be an actor," Eda whispered. "He's *great*."

She was right. Christy sat mesmerized as he told the Hanukkah story. She thought the Syrians were really mean to keep the Jewish people from practicing their religion.

"But for three years," Dean Crispin said in a booming voice, "an army of rebels struggled to free their home once again. At last, they succeeded. Now it was time to make the temple holy once more. Eda, what was one of the most important things they had to do?"

Eda wriggled in her seat, but Christy saw that she was grinning when she answered.

"They had to light a lamp for eight days."

"That's right," Dean said with a nod. "But did they have enough oil for eight days?"

This was directed at everyone in the room. In a chorus, the children drawled, *"No!"*

"But they didn't want to wait for more oil to arrive," Eda's father continued. "So they lit the lamp that very night. And what happened? The lamp stayed lit one day, then two ..."

With each number, he held up a finger. The children in the room joined him. Christy found herself counting in amazement. Eight days! How could a little bit of oil light a lamp for eight days! It was just like magic!

"Now, we will light the menorah," he said. "If you'll follow me ..."

Christy caught up with Eda and Lucille and whispered: "What's a menorah?"

"A special candlestick with eight candles," Eda replied. "You light one each night with a *shammash*."

"That's a funny word," Lucille said.

"I think it means 'servant,' " Eda replied. "I don't get to light the candle tonight. Daddy always lets the youngest family member do that. It's my cousin Martha. She's just three years old."

The family and their guests watched as the little dark-haired girl was lifted up to light the first candle. A prayer was said, and then everyone was called in to dinner. There were many kinds of foods that Christy had never seen before. Her eyes widened at the sight of bow-shaped noodles being spooned into her dish.

"This is kasha varnishkes," Jean-Robert told her.

Christy smiled up at him. Then she started to eat—pot roast with fruit sauce, honey cakes, challah, noodle pudding.

Her fourth helping of potato pancakes did not go unnoticed. Rita saw Jean-Robert stop at the child's plate and serve her more of the treats. Her heart went out to the little girl. She ate as if she'd been starved! Rita thought perhaps she might have been. The type of family Christy came from was common knowledge in town. Everyone at the beauty parlor had something to say about that crazy Sarah Burnett. And her husband! Well, if ever there was a man who belonged in jail—

"Who's for presents?" Dean announced, interrupting her thoughts.

"Me! Me!" Eda cried.

Rita, embarrassed by her daughter's lack of decorum, tried to say something, but Eda was already bounding out of the dining room.

"Christy! Lucille! Come on!"

The children gathered in the parlor, laughing and talking excitedly as the first night's gifts were brought out. Christy hadn't been expecting a gift, and she thought she'd just burst wide open if someone didn't give her the small package Eda had showed her. At last, it was handed over the sea of raised hands. Christy thanked the woman who had passed it and hurried to find a seat. The silver paper was torn off in a matter of seconds.

Christy gasped when she pulled a charm bracelet from the box. There was a little dog on it, and a key, and a small object she didn't recognize.

"Oh! Oh, it's so pretty!"

"Look what I got," Lucille said, showing her own gift. "It's a necklace. I think it's real gold. Look at the colors in the stone!"

"That's an opal," someone said.

Lucille and Christy turned to see that Mike Hewlett was standing behind the couch. The police officer, still in uniform, smiled at them.

"Hi, Officer Mike!" Eda cried. She held up a gold locket. "Look what I got!"

"That's great," Mike said.

"How come you didn't come to dinner?"'

"Sorry, I was on duty," Mike said. He looked across the room. "You have a nice time, kids. I've got to talk to your father."

When he left, the three girls gathered on the couch and compared gifts. Christy asked about the unusual charm.

"That's a dreidel," Eda said. "It's a game you play. My uncle Max has a big one made of wood. You want to ask him if we can play with it?"

"Okay," Christy said. "Wait, can you put the bracelet on for me?"

"I'll do it," Lucille said. "Then you can latch my necklace. And I'll latch Eda's."

Once properly adorned, the children ran off to find Eda's uncle Max. Christy enjoyed the Hanukkah games. To her, the night was like a fairy tale. She wished she could stay with the Crispins forever—Eda's father was so *nice*, and her mother was the prettiest woman she'd ever seen. Christy was disappointed when Jean-Robert came in to announce:

"A young man is waiting for Miss Burnett."

"That's my brother, Harvey," Christy explained. "He's going to walk me home."

Rita frowned at her husband.

"Should they be walking, Dean?" she asked. "It's late, and so dark. And I'm not sure it's safe. . . ."

"Harvey's strong," Christy insisted. "We have to be home by ten—we promised our father. And it's just a short walk."

She knew Harvey would never accept a ride home, and was afraid they might both get in trouble if she didn't join him.

"I'll walk you to the front door," Eda said, pushing back her chair.

"Me, too!" Lucille added.

Christy wasn't much surprised that Harvey wasn't waiting for her. She knew he'd be too shy to come in. After the butler helped her into her coat and boots, Christy hugged her two friends. She carefully pulled the cuff of her glove over her new bracelet to keep it safe.

"I had a super time," she said. "Hanukkah's a great holiday, Eda! You're so lucky it's eight days long."

"Maybe we can do something at my house for Christmas," Lucille suggested. "Maybe we can have hot chocolate and bake sugar cookies."

"Yeah!" Eda cried, clapping her hands.

Jean-Robert leaned down.

"Pardon me, miss," he said, "but it's getting late."

Eda made a face, gave Christy another hung, and watched her friend hurry down the snow-covered sidewalk to meet her brother. Harvey was jumping back and forth to keep himself warm. His cheeks were bright red under the lamplight, and there was frost on his eyebrows.

"Hi, Harvey!" Christy greeted. "Did you have a good time at your party?"

"It was okay," Harvey grunted.

"My party was like a story," Christy said dreamily. She gazed up at the stars. "I wish this night could last forever and ever!"

They walked for a block before Harvey answered.

"I know a way we can make it last longer," he said. "I heard they're giving away toys and things to the poor kids at the Salvation Army. You know, that brick building behind the high school?"

"Gee, it's kinda late," Christy said. "Do you think they'd be open? And do you think we'd get home in time?"

"Aww, those places stay open all night long," Harvey said. "And we've got plenty of time, if we hurry. I know a shortcut that'll save us ten minutes."

Christy made an indecisive little moaning noise.

"Well, do you want a present or don'tcha?" Harvey demanded.

His sister thought about the beautiful silver charm bracelet she'd received. It didn't seem fair that she got something and Harvey didn't, so she nodded eagerly.

"Then let's go!" Harvey cried, breaking into a run.

Christy raced after him, slip-sliding on the snow, yelling for him to wait. He took a turn down the road that led to the industrial part of town. Aberdeen's biggest employers were its cable-and-wire and furniture factories. Right now, the huge stone building that housed Glemby's Furniture was dark. Harvey pointed to the lights shining in the top floor windows of the Cable and Wire Factory.

"That's where our parents are," he said. "You really think they'd even know if we were home by ten on the dot? Dad's probably stinkin' drunk by now."

Christy could hear muffled laughter and music. She wondered if the people inside that big brick building were having as much fun as she'd had tonight. Still, it was dark and creepy down here on the street.

"Can we hurry?" she said. "I don't like it here."

"This is the quickest way," Harvey said, leading her. "Come on, just around this corner."

He disappeared into the shadows.

"Harvey, don't go away!" Christy cried, starting to run again.

She followed him around the side of the building.

Suddenly, a man jumped out from behind a big dumpster. Christy screamed.

"Haaarveeeeeee!"

The man grabbed her, leaning close to push something that smelled bad against her face. Her last vision before passing out was a pair of mean, hateful eyes.

THIRTEEN

▼

SOMEONE WAS TYING her up. She couldn't see in the dark, but she could feel the rough texture of rope against her small wrists, cutting into her, tighter, tighter . . .

"My bracelet . . ." Christy whispered. Another voice spoke, but she didn't understand it. Then she heard:

"Shut your mouth, Harvey." That wasn't Harvey's voice. A man's voice. A man was tying her up.

"Harvey?" She tried to say her brother's name, but her mouth felt funny.

Laughter.

"Shhh!" said the man.

"What're you gonna do?" *That* was Harvey's voice.

"Take her to the boys. Take her to stay with Teddy and Adrian, forever. She saw. She knows. They have to stay together."

Something was being pressed against her face.

Something cold and wet.

"Christy? Christy, oh, shit, please wake up!"

Christy obeyed the voice with a terrified yelp. She back-crawled across the snow, making a wide track over some-one's front lawn. Her eyes gazed up in fright at the figure towering over her, the golden lamplight behind it making it look like a ghost.

"Go away!" she yelped.

"Christy, it's me," Harvey yelled. "Can you get up? I thought that guy killed you!"

Christy lay in the snow for a few moments, her wits slowly returning. The sensation of being tied up, the pres-sure against her face, the voices—were they all a dream?

"What—what . . .?"

"Some creep jumped us in the alley," Harvey said. He came closer and held out his hand. "I found an old hubcap in the trash and clocked him over the head. I had to hit him three times, but finally I knocked him out! Then I dragged you away as fast as I could. But you got heavy, Christy. I had to rub snow in your face to make you wake up."

Christy accepted her brother's hand and let him help her to her feet.

"I . . . I heard him talking to you," she said. "He called you Harvey. Who was it, Harvey?"

"Nobody!" Harvey snapped. "You were delirious."

"Deler . . .?"

"You were zonked," Harvey said. "Look, I rescued you, okay? That guy didn't know my name! You were just hearing things! It was a stranger. You oughta be glad I was here!"

"But, Harvey . . ." Things didn't seem right.

"I saved your life," Harvey insisted.

Christy brought her hands up to her face. As she did so, she saw the charm bracelet was still safely locked around her wrist—but her gloves were gone. She buried her face in her hands and began to cry.

"Don't do that," Harvey said. "It's okay. We hafta hurry, though. It's getting late and I'm afraid we won't get home in time."

Christy went on crying. She hurt all over. What would happen now? Would her parents believe her? Or would she get another beating?

Harvey hooked his hand around her elbow.

"Come *on*," he urged. "We may just make it in time."

"I—I thought they weren't gonna be home until eleven?" Christy asked as she stumbled along.

"It's almost that now," Harvey said. "I told you, it was hard fighting that guy and then pulling you through the snow. I think he drugged you. I couldn't wake you up!"

Christy sobbed as she hurried along the street, her arm still caught by her brother's tight grasp. It wasn't fair! This was the best night in her life and now it was ruined!

"Harvey? Harvey, slow down!"

"We can't!"

"Do you . . . do you think it was the kidnapper?"

"I dunno. Look, there's the pizzeria," Harvey said. "Oh, *damn!*"

"What?" Christy yelped, unable to stand more trouble.

"They're already home!" Harvey whispered. He pointed up to the lighted window. "Shit! I thought we'd beat them."

He pulled her towards the door. Before he opened it, Christy looked into his eyes and saw they were full of fear.

"Harvey, I'm so scared," she said. "I don't want to be hurt!"

Harvey breathed deeply.

"I'll tell Dad everything that happened," he said. "He won't hurt you."

"You can't stop him!"

"Oh, I can—"

Harvey stopped talking. Suddenly, he seemed to become more like his nasty old self.

"Just get inside!"

They sat together on the bottom steps and removed their wet boots. Then, in stocking feet, they dragged themselves up the stairs to face the uncertain.

The living room was empty. Harvey leaned close to his sister.

"Make a dash for your room," he whispered. "I'll do what I can."

"Harvey . . ."

"Go!"

Without another word, Christy obeyed him. She closed her door, then sank down on the floor in the dark and listened. Moments later, she heard her father's footsteps thumping over the wooden floor.

"You're late."

"We . . . we had some trouble, Daddy."

Harvey never called his father Daddy.

"You were told to be home by ten. It's almost eleven. Where the hell have you been?"

"We woulda been home by ten," Harvey said. "Even earlier. We were walking and all of a sudden this man jumped out from behind a building! He tried to hurt Christy! I tried to stop him, Daddy! But he was bigger than me! I think maybe it was the kidnapper, the guy who took those little boys—"

"Shut the hell up!"

Christy jumped.

"You expect me to believe that cock-and-bull story? You *liar*! Tell me the truth, Harvey! Tell me what you've really been up to! You're fifteen now, huh? I know what fifteen is like! More brains between your legs than in your head! Did you get any tonight, Harvey? Did you? Was she worth it? Was she worth . . . *this?*"

The sound of a face being slapped.

"I'm telling the truth!"

"*Liar! Li*-ar!"

A blow with each syllable. Screaming, yelling. Christy flinched with each loud slapping noise as if she was being beaten. Something thundered across the floor—a piece of furniture.

Why wouldn't her father believe Harvey? Harvey had saved her life! He was a hero!

"*Stinkin'* Liar!"

"*Lemme* go!"

Crashes, more screams . . .

And, finally, a door slamming. Christy froze, listening as footsteps raced down the stairs. She jumped away from the door, hurrying to the window, pulling away the snowflakes she had hung there. In a few moments, her brother's silhouette stumbled into the street. He turned and raised a fist, shaking it. With the street lamp shining down on him, making his face as bright as the moon, he shouted:

"I ain't your son no more! *No more!*"

"Harvey!" Christy shouted through the frosty glass, but her brother couldn't hear her. By the time she worked the lock and opened it, he had disappeared down the street.

"Shut that damned window," her father's gruff voice said from behind her. "You want to heat the neighborhood?"

Christy obeyed at once. Then she turned slowly, grabbing a pillow to clutch against herself, as if that might offer her some protection.

Her father looked like a giant, standing in the doorway with his fists clenched. A shadow fell across his face, almost hiding his angered expression.

"Had to come home early tonight," he said. "Your crazy

mother started in with her voices. Said they were singin' Christmas carols. So someone kids around and asks what they're singing. Your mother tells 'em "Oh, Little Town of Bethlehem." And she starts singin' herself, only she puts in dirty words. My boss had invited his minister to the party. I'm probably gonna lose my job because of your mother."

Christy didn't say a word. Sometimes silence was her only defense. She'd heard what had happened when Harvey tried to tell the truth.

"Bad enough my wife is crazy," Harvey Sr. went on. "But now I got a looney for a daughter. And you're makin' your brother lie for you. Well, the hell with him. If he can't take his medicine like a man, good riddance."

He isn't a man! He isn't big like you!

Harvey Sr. took another step into the room.

"But then, maybe you talk like that because it's what you want," he said. "Maybe you want some guy to take you away because anyone, even a killer, is better than your stinkin' drunk of a father! *Right?*"

Christy shook her head vigorously, her eyes widening with terror.

"Maybe you *want* him to get you," Harvey Sr. said, moving closer and closer. "You think it'd be fun to be in all the newspapers, huh? Just like Teddy and Adrian Gammel? Bet their heads are propping up their father's. All nice and cozy."

With that, he reached out and grabbed Christy by her ears. She yelped in pain, but didn't dare struggle. Her father was strong enough, and drunk enough, to rip them right off her head.

"What would he do with *your* head, Christy?" her father asked, his alcohol breath like poisonous gas. He began to shake her back and forth. "It's such a pretty head. Bet he's got heads in all his rooms. Maybe he'd put yours in the kitchen, right in the middle of the table. With flowers all around. Real pretty, huh? *Huh?*"

The bed creaked noisily beneath them. Christy squeezed her eyes shut, silently begging her father to stop.

"Or maybe he'll put you on the back of the toilet seat," Harvey Sr. ranted. "Right there with the *crap* where you belong!"

He gave her a hard shove that bounced the back of her head against the windowsill. Christy lay there, frozen. Her bed rose up as her father got off it. For a few moments, there was such silence in the room that Christy dared to believe he'd gone. Slowly, she opened her eyes.

He was standing in the middle of her room, his eyes darting about. He looked just like a wolf in search of something, ready to pounce as soon as he found it.

The room was quiet. Christy cried in silence, the only noise an occasional hiccup that escaped her. Finally, her father grabbed a little plastic doll her mother had bought her from the drugstore.

"If you don't stop this talk about a man chasing you," her father said, "I'm gonna see to it that he does get you. I'm gonna take you out one night and leave you for him, right by that gas station where they found that kid's bloody jacket. Then you'll get what you really want, Christy. The killer will have you, and he'll make you look just like *this*!"

He gave the doll's head a quick turn, pulling the head from the socket. Then he threw the pieces at Christy. The body hit the wall, but the head connected with her cheek, leaving a stinging pain.

"Not another word, Christy," her father warned.

He turned and left the room.

Christy stared at her closed door, too frightened to move, too miserable to cry.

FOURTEEN

▼

I GOT FOUR dolls for Christmas that year," Chris Wander said in a quiet voice. She shifted in the chair where she was sitting, tucking one thin leg beneath her. "My father never made my mother bring the gifts back."

The women had been talking for hours. The table in front of them was laden with empty mugs, cups of coffee finished an hour earlier. Lucille had a pad of paper on her lap. She'd filled nearly ten pages with notes.

"I remember that Christmas," she said. "It was the year I got my first horse. I was so excited about him. I named him Wenceslaus, after the king in that Christmas carol. Only I couldn't spell it, so I called him Wency."

She looked at Chris, who sat with her head resting against the side of a wing-backed chair. Her friend's eyes were red, the skin beneath them darkly circled. Telling the story of that night had drained her, as much as if her father had been alive and beating her right here and now.

"There's something else I remember," Lucille went on. "I rode Wency to your apartment to see if you wanted a ride. I was amazed at all the presents you got, because I thought you were poor. But you didn't seem happy at all. You were surrounded by boxes and boxes, but you didn't seem pleased."

Eda leaned forward.

"You didn't tell us about that night, Chris," she said. "Not until now. Lucille's right—you did seem more miserable than usual that Christmas. And every holiday season after that, you were like a changed person. I tried to invite you to another Hanukkah dinner, but you always refused."

Chris closed her eyes. Someone was staring back at her in her mind. She opened them quickly.

"I couldn't stop thinking about my father's promise to give me to the killer," she said. "I was just seven then, so I believed him."

She said it in a way that suggested a plea for understanding.

"You thought you couldn't even tell your friends about it," Lucille said, her voice full of sympathy.

"I thought . . ." Chris took a breath. "I thought he had spies everywhere. People watching me, listening. My mother kept telling me there were bad people everywhere. I started believing they were working for my father. I became more afraid of them than the man who had been following me."

"What a rotten thing to do to a little kid," Eda said. "Your father has a special place in hell, I'm sure."

Lucille stood up, collecting empty coffee cups and a crumb-filled cookie plate.

"Harvey really did run away, didn't he?" she asked. "I think I remember that."

"Who could forget when he came back?" Eda said.

Chris turned to look out the window, thoughtful. She

could remember Harvey's homecoming very clearly. She could see him at the apartment door, seventeen years old. He hadn't been alone.

"Let's talk about that later," Lucille said, interrupting Chris's thoughts. "I think we all need a break. Are you hungry? I could start an early dinner. Nothing fancy, but . . ."

"I'm not hungry," Chris insisted.

"You have to keep up your strength, Chris," Lucille replied.

"Maybe in a little while . . ."

Chris picked up her own coffee cup and followed Lucille into the kitchen. As she went to place the mug in the sink, it slipped from her hand and crashed to the floor. That was all the catalyst needed to send the distraught woman into hysterics. Quickly, both Eda and Lucille put their arms around her. They let her cry for a few moments, then helped her to sit down.

"What if he's back again?" Chris asked. "What if, somehow, he's kept track of me all these years? He's got my kids now. He's got my kids and I'll never see them again the way no one ever saw the Gammel children!"

She put her head down into the crook of her elbow and began to pound the tabletop with her fist.

"I'll never see my babies again! *Never!*"

"Oh, Chris, of course you will!" Lucille insisted.

"Damn him to hell! Damn him!" Chris slammed her fist on the tabletop.

Eda stood back and watched the scene. Chris continued to bang on the tabletop, her brown hair falling over her like a shroud. Lucille tried desperately to comfort her. Lucille was worn, her French braid coming out in wisps, the outfit that had been so trim and pressed now wrinkled and tired-looking. They'd been talking for hours, and it showed. Through all of it, Chris had shown all ranges of emotion—even short-lived humor. But she'd never shown anger the way she was now.

Eda was about to say something when the phone rang. Still keeping an eye on Chris, Lucille answered. She spoke quietly, but Eda could hear the concern in her voice. When she hung up, she took a deep breath and said:

"That was Mike Hewlett. They're searching the woods around Lake Aberdeen."

"That's good, Chris," Eda said by way of encouragement. "They're not wasting any time."

Chris rubbed away the last of her tears. She stood up and ran her fingers through her hair.

"I have to be there," she said. "Can you drive me, Lucille? I have to help look for my children."

"Oh, Chris!" Lucille cried. "I don't think you should!"

But Chris wasn't listening. As if she was being moved by some unseen force, she was already heading out the back door. Eda moved quickly to stop her.

"Please let me go," Chris implored.

From the time she'd come home from the police station very early that morning, Chris had felt completely helpless. Talking about the past, trying to find the connection to her missing children, had helped a little. But she needed to do more. She needed to do something more physical than sit around doped up on sedatives.

"I know you need to help," Eda said. "But if you walk out that door now, you'll be bombarded by reporters."

"What do you think will happen down at the lake?" Lucille protested.

"Mike Hewlett will be there to protect her," Eda said. "Come on, Lucille. Find a pair of dark glasses. Do you still have one of those big hats you used to wear?"

Lucille sighed, but reluctantly gave in and worked on helping Chris go incognito. When they pulled out of the driveway a few minutes later, a few of the reporters looked their way. But no one seemed to realize the woman they wanted to question was just a few yards away.

"We went to Lake Aberdeen just yesterday," Chris said, staring out the window. Through the dark glasses, everything had a gloomy cast of gray. "The kids had a great time."

"You'll be back there again with them," Eda maintained.

Still upset that Chris was going to take part in the search, Lucille kept silent. It was only a few minutes' ride to the lake, and when they arrived Lucille circled the parking lot until she found a pair of squad cars.

"There's Sheriff Hewlett," she said. "Your father was good friends with him, Eda. Maybe you ought to talk to him."

Eda got out of the car and walked over to the group of twenty volunteers. Although daylight savings time provided a good deal of remaining daylight, some were already equipped with flashlights. A half dozen dogs sat obediently to the sides of their trainers, waiting the signal to begin.

Mike had been giving out instructions, and when he was finished the group dispersed. Eda went over to him, her blue eyes wide with inquiry. She hadn't seen him in years. Would he recognize her? He'd certainly changed himself. His face was a little more wrinkled than she had remembered. But when he saw her his eyes became full of the kindness that had endeared the children of Aberdeen to him. Without a word, he opened up his arms. Years of hard work had hardened his muscles, and he seemed as strong as an oak as he hugged Eda tightly.

"Welcome home, Eda," he said. "Chris must have been pleased to see you."

"I'm not sure if *pleased* is the word, Officer Mike," Eda

said. She'd been calling him that when she left Montana years earlier, and it still came naturally.

She looked back towards Lucille's car.

"She's here," Eda said. "She wanted to be part of the search. Lucille didn't think that was such a good idea, though."

Mike took off his cap and wiped sweat from his forehead with a light blue handkerchief.

"I don't know if it is, either," he said. "But if Chris wants to help, let her. Psychology be damned. I don't see how it could hurt any more than finding her husband like that."

Eda felt a shiver rush down her arms despite the July heat.

"I'll get her, then," she said.

She went to the car and told her friends Mike had given his approval. Chris looked all around as she approached the sheriff, as if she might see Josh and Vicki at any moment. He greeted her, but she didn't acknowledge him.

"I don't see any media," Lucille said.

"We kept this as quiet as possible," Mike told her. "I'm sure someone will show up, but hopefully we'll be done by then."

Chris looked at him.

"What should I do?" she asked quietly.

At first, Mike thought it was a plea. Chris had moaned almost the same words when she'd been questioned at the police station. Before he could answer, Eda said:

"Maybe Lucille and Chris can have an area to reconnoiter. I'd like to walk with you, if I can, Officer Mike."

Mike smiled. "Just Mike, okay? Or Sheriff, if you want. And I'd be glad to have a fellow cop at my side, Eda."

He pointed towards a narrow path on the other side of the lake.

"Walk around to there," he said. "It cuts through to a

field about a mile back. Look in every branch, near every leaf on the ground. Anything at all can be a clue. A cigarette butt, a piece of fabric . . ."

"We understand," Lucille said. She was impatient, wanting to get this over with and have Chris safely home again.

After they left, Eda walked along with Mike. He watched the other two women for a few moments, his expression troubled.

"I wish I knew what to say to her," he said.

"She knows you're doing your best," Eda said. "But she's fluctuating between shock and hysterics. We spent the last few hours talking about the Gammel murder and kidnappings. I'm sure you haven't missed the bizarre similarities. We can't help recalling that Teddy and Adrian Gammel were never found."

"Not for lack of trying," Mike said, taking off his cap again and running his fingers through hair that had gone from black to almost steel-gray. "That case is still open, and we've gone through those files again and again. The forensics team spent hours going over the Wander house— you know the routines. We've sent samples to the lab in Marylborne, and we hope to get results back quickly."

As he walked along the lakeside, his eyes scrutinized every inch of ground. A bottle cap caught his eye, and he bent for a closer look. Eda saw that it was rusted, a piece of litter that had probably been stamped into the dirt years earlier.

"It's a good thing your friend had an alibi," he said. "I'm sorry to say it, but she was a prime suspect. Having those six people from her art class verify her whereabouts at the approximate time of death certainly helped."

"I don't see how anyone could accuse Chris Wander of such a horrible crime," Eda said, almost indignant. "She's the most gentle soul I've ever known. And she loved Brian and the kids almost to the point of obsession."

"I was just thinking of the parallel between the two crimes," Mike said. "To this day, there are a lot of us who believe Irene Gammel is somehow implicated. Of course, evidence proved she didn't actually commit the crimes. Remember the second murder, that took place while she was in jail? That helped clear her of any suspicion. Still, the whole thing seemed strange."

"Mike, do you think those boys might have survived?"

Mike shrugged. "I don't know. It was wishful thinking in the town for years. But, since this is a parallel crime, knowing the fate of those kids would certainly help us. We're trying to locate Irene Gammel."

"She left town not too long after the kids vanished," Eda recalled. "My mother's friends used to gossip about it. They thought she was a horrible mother, that she was deserting her kids. Where was it she went? Oregon?"

"Washington," Mike corrected. "We knew where she was thirty years ago, but today? You can't keep tabs on a person forever. Irene Gammel was not accused of any crime. Following her for the rest of her life would be tantamount to harassment."

Mike put a hand on her arm and steered her into the section of woods he'd chosen for his own search.

"You don't even know that she's still alive," Eda said.

"It's a chance we have to take," Mike said. "We're hoping she might be able to fill us in on a few more details."

"Well, that's partly why I wanted to walk with you," Eda said. "I might have some details myself."

Although he was still carefully scrutinizing his surroundings, Mike listened attentively as Eda told him an abridged version of the story the three women had pieced together that evening. He interrupted once in a while, asking for clarification or more detail, but for the most part he was a captive audience. When she was finished, he mumbled words of amazement.

"I don't understand why Christy didn't tell anyone she was being followed," he said, running his fingers through his hair again. After hearing of the woman as a child, he couldn't help using her nickname.

"How could she?" Eda asked. "She was a lonely little girl being terrorized by both her father and brother. Her mother was certifiable—probably schizophrenic now that I think of it. If she couldn't trust her own family, whom could she trust?"

"She had you and Lucille, at least," Mike said.

"That's probably what kept her from going insane herself," Eda said. "That, and meeting a great guy like Brian Wander. He was her savior."

"Well, someone wanted that savior dead," Mike reminded her. "And we're doing all we can to find out who. In the meantime, what you've told me is certainly going to help. I appreciate it, Eda. You've got quite a mind for detail and memory. No wonder your father was always very proud of you."

Eda laughed. "Dad would have been prouder if I'd taken over the newspaper when he decided to retire. He never was too happy about me being a cop."

"Oh, yes he was," Mike said. "He subscribed to every New York City paper, just to see if there was anything about you in them. If he could have taken them on his world tour, he would have."

He sighed. "I wish Dean was still here. He was my mentor, Eda. We were good friends, even though he was ten years my senior. I never met such a man for bouncing ideas off of. If he was here now, things might go more smoothly."

He smiled at Eda, and she recalled how handsome she'd

thought he was when she was little. He was still just as attractive, in a more mature way.

"But I'm glad I've got his daughter," Mike said. "Eda, if there's anything you can do for us, we'd appreciate it."

"I'll do whatever I can," Eda said.

Something bright blue caught both their eyes. Mike moved towards it and crouched down. He held up a jay's feather. When he got up again, his weary sigh spoke of the hard work he was doing.

"I hope," he said, "that we can prevent another thirty-year mystery from haunting Aberdeen."

The search team moved ahead slowly, carefully scrutinizing everything in sight. Forty minutes later, Chris was stopping to rest when a dog's bark made her look through the trees. A few yards away, a woman held fast to a German shepherd's leash. Something bright yellow was sticking out of her pocket. Chris gazed at it for a few moments.

"Lucille?" she called.

Lucille was a few yards ahead. She turned and came back to Chris.

"Look at the woman with that dog," Chris said. "Do you see her pocket? She's got Vicki's unicorn!"

"Well, I think . . ."

But Chris was already plowing through the trees, her steps made awkward by roots and branches. Lucille called to her to wait, but her friend didn't seem to hear.

"What are you doing with Vicki's unicorn?" Chris demanded. "That's Vicki's favorite stuffed animal! Why do you have it?"

The woman backed up, taking the leash halfway down with her free hand to steady her dog. The shepherd stared up at Chris, it's expression seemingly full of curiosity.

"I was given it for my dog," the woman said. "It helps him pick up the scent."

Lucille came up to them.

"Chris, it's okay," she said, putting an arm around the smaller woman's shoulders.

Exhaustion and frustration combined with residual effects of the sedative she'd been given, and Chris began to cry again.

"It's Vicki's favorite toy! She loved that! She must miss it so much right now!"

The woman with the dog gave Lucille an inquiring look.

"She's the mother," Lucille said.

She didn't wait for the woman's reaction, but turned Chris around and led her firmly down the path.

"You've had enough," Lucille insisted. "We're going home."

"I didn't find anything," Chris protested weakly.

"There must be thirty people combing these woods," Lucille said. "If anything's here, *they'll* find it."

When they reached Lucille's car, she helped Chris inside. Then she leaned into the opened door and said:

"I'm just going to tell Eda we're going home."

Eda and Mike were on their way back when Lucille caught up with them. They both looked very tired and dejected.

"Not a thing," Eda said.

"I'm sure the kids aren't here," Mike put in. "But a second team will come in later to see if we missed anything."

Lucille pointed back at her car.

"Eda, Chris is hysterical," she said. "She saw a dog trainer with one of Vicki's toys, and it set her off. I'm taking her home."

Eda looked at Mike.

"I think I'd like to discuss things further," she said.

"You can come back to the station with me," Mike said. "And I'll drive you home later."

"Just don't be too long, okay?" Lucille asked. She felt

a little annoyed that Eda had let Chris come here to-day. "Chris needs both of us now."

Eda nodded and watched Lucille stride back to her car. Had it been wrong to bring Chris here?

"It's my fault she's upset," she said.

"Of course it isn't," Mike insisted. "You're just doing what you think is right. You're just being a friend."

Eda linked her arm through his and walked with him to the car. She hoped that being a friend was enough to make things right.

FIFTEEN

▼

J OSH WAS THE first of the children to awaken, into a fog that was more like a dream than reality. His entire body hurt, he was shivering with cold, and it was dark. Shaky, he moved slowly until he was in a sitting position. He was on some kind of cot, he guessed through the mush of his thoughts. He could feel the cold metal of its frame through his cotton pajamas.

"What's this place?" he demanded, although he sensed no one could hear him.

He tried to get up. Bad idea—his legs buckled out from under him. Josh thought he might get sick, but he closed his eyes and chewed on his lip until the nausea passed. Then he tucked his head between his knees and tried to remember what had happened.

They'd been watching TV, he knew. Mom had gone out teaching, and they were playing video games. Dad had just made popcorn for everyone when the doorbell rang. He'd gone to answer it. Josh had seen a scruffy-looking man at the door.

Then, for some reason, Vicki had screamed.

Then . . .

Then . . .

Josh sat up slowly. That was all he could remember. He knew something bad had happened, but not what it had been.

Josh thought, for now, he didn't want to remember.

He just wanted to get the heck out of here.

"The bad man, Daddy! *The bad man!*"

Somewhere in the darkness, Vicki was screaming.

"Vicki!" Josh cried.

He groped around until he found her. The little girl was thrashing about on the bed, her arms waving wildly.

"The bad man!"

"Vicki, wake up!" Josh commanded.

As if his words were magic, she snapped awake, then sobbed loudly in the darkness. Josh felt awkward, wishing his mother were here to help. Mom always hugged Vicki when she had a bad dream, until the kid calmed down. But the idea of hugging his little sister was, well . . . gross.

"Are you gonna cry forever?" he asked.

"It was the bad man, Josh," Vicki blubbered. "The bad man I saw at the fireworks."

Josh had no idea what she was talking about. She saw him at the fireworks? The guy who'd rung the doorbell?

"Where did Daddy go?" Vicki asked. "Did the bad man hurt him? Why is it so dark, Josh? Where's my unicorn? Where's Mommy? I want *Mommy!*"

Josh got up. He couldn't answer most of her questions, but there was one thing he could do right now, no matter how crummy he felt.

He could find light.

"I don't know where we are," he said, although Vicki

was crying too hard to hear him. "But there's gotta be a light switch somewhere."

Josh reached out, walking slowly until his hands hit a wall. He slid along it, feeling the rough, cold cement. When he bumped into what seemed to be metal shelves, the resulting rattle made Vicki scream again.

"Be quiet!"

Josh found a switch just beyond the shelves, and flipped it up. His eyes squinted shut in protest to the bright overhead light. After a few moments he opened them again, to find himself looking up at three big racks of food.

"Look at all this stuff," he said, reaching for a bag of potato chips. "Wow!"

"I don't want food," Vicki grumbled. "I want to go *home*!"

Josh returned the chips. He didn't want any food, either.

"Let's look for a door," he said, turning around.

They seemed to be in a cellar of some kind, Spartanly furnished with two cots, and table and chairs, and the pantry. An open door revealed a bathroom. The floor in both rooms was made of cement. But Josh felt something was wrong.

It took him only an instant to realize what it was. There were no windows.

"Where are we, Josh?" Vicki asked, more calm for now.

"Looks like a basement," Josh said. "Except there isn't much down here. I mean, people store things in cellars, don't they? How come there isn't anything down here but all that food?"

Vicki stood up and shuffled over to him.

"My feets are cold," she said. "I want my slippers."

Josh ignored her. He had spotted a door all the way at the back of the big room, a black door with a round, rusted metal knob.

"Come on!" he cried.

He hurried to the door, expecting to push it open and make a run for it.

"Hurry, Vicki!" he urged. "That guy might be coming back! Maybe this is our only chance!"

Vicki raced to his side. Josh took hold of the knob and tried to turn it.

It stuck.

"Oh, no!"

"Josh, open it!"

He tried again. And again. And even when he knew the door was locked tight, he went on trying.

"We're stuck," he moaned. "There's no way out."

"Yes, there is!" Vicki insisted. "I want out of here! I want *out*! Lemme *out*!"

Vicki threw herself on the floor and began to kick the door, screaming and crying. Josh watched her for a moment, amazed, despite their terrible predicament, at how loudly his sister could scream. Then he picked up his fists and joined her, pounding hard against the metal, hoping that someone was out there to hear them.

SIXTEEN

CHRIS WAS SO tired when she came home that she collapsed into bed without needing another sedative. And in her dreams, her mind played tricks on her. Everything was just fine. Brian was with her, and the children slept soundly in their beds. As she lay sleeping, a smile spread over her careworn face as her dreams carried her to one of the happiest times of her life.

"Come see your new baby sister, Joshua," she told her then five-year-old son as Lucille brought him into the house. He'd been staying with Lucille while Chris was at the hospital.

Victoria Rose Wander lay in a beautifully decorated bassinette, one tiny fist curled up towards her chubby little face. Chris watched with a smile as Josh leaned into the crib.

"Can I touch her?" he asked.

"Of course," Chris said. "Vicki's your baby, too."

"Wow . . ." Josh said in awe.

He reached into the bassinette, then looked up at his mother, beaming.

"I like her," he said.

Chris looked at Lucille, who gave a knowing wink.

"And you thought he'd be jealous," Lucille whispered.

"Hey, Josh!"

It was Brian, calling from outside. Josh ran out the front door. Chris looked out the window to see Brian holding a shiny red bicycle. She went outside herself, shaking her head.

"Brian, that's much too big!" she protested. "Josh is only five!"

"Chris, Josh is seven," Brian said.

And when she looked at her son, he'd grown older. Chris's dream self accepted this segue.

"Come on, Josh," Brian said. "Hop on. I'm going to teach you to ride."

"Yay!" Josh cried. "No more training wheels!"

Brian held the bike steady as Josh climbed on the seat. He looked over his son's head and said to Chris:

"His other bike was getting too small."

It was his way of explaining the expensive purchase.

"It's fine, Brian," Chris said. "He really needed a new bike, now that summer's here."

But it wasn't summer any longer. It was early spring, and they were all watching through the living room window as snow fell.

"I wish winter would go away," Vicki said. She was nearly five years old now.

"Well, long winters are part of life in Montana," Brian told her as he picked her up. "But it'll be spring before you know it."

"I'm glad Easter is late this year," Chris said. "We should be seeing some flowers by then."

"How come Easter changes all the time, but Christmas is the same day every year?" Josh asked.

Brian put Vicki down and took Josh into the kitchen, where a calender hung near the telephone. He turned the page to April and pointed.

"See that white circle?"

"Yeah?"

"That's a full moon," Brian said. "It's the first full moon after the first day of spring. Now, you go to the next Sunday. See?"

"Easter!" Josh cried.

"Right," Brian said. "Easter falls on the first Sunday after the first full moon after the first day of spring."

"Oh, brother," Josh said. "I'm glad Christmas and Halloween and my birthday aren't so crazy to remember."

Chris had entered the kitchen.

"It is crazy, isn't it?" She laughed. "But that's just the way the Church decided to do it."

"Crazy like Christy," an unfamiliar voice said.

Chris swung around. Her house was gone, her family was gone. She was in the old apartment, facing her brother. He was a young man now, and there was a woman at his side.

"You don't want to think about it," Harvey Jr. said cryptically.

And in that instant, Chris woke up to reality. Her heart beat rapidly as she lay in bed, Harvey Jr.'s image fading slowly from her mind. But the other images, the memories of things that had really happened, stayed with her. Things had been so wonderful all these years, but now it almost seemed that idyllic life had all been a dream itself.

Chris climbed slowly from the bed, rubbing the back of her neck. She didn't cry for those lost memories. She was beyond tears. The sun was already bright outside the window, and the clock told her it was nearly nine in the morning.

Eda was reading the morning paper when Chris entered the kitchen.

"Where's Lucille?" Chris asked, heading to the coffee maker.

"She went to run an errand," Eda said, "and to check up on the kids. She made corn muffins before she left."

Eda pushed the basket towards Chris as she sat down with her coffee. Chris was surprised to find she was very hungry. The muffins were delicious.

"How'd you sleep?" Eda asked.

"Okay, I guess," Chris replied. "I dreamed about nice things, like Brian teaching Josh to ride a bike. It was only when Harvey showed up in the end that things turned bad."

"Harvey would do that, wouldn't he?" Eda said. "How did he figure into a nice dream?"

Chris sipped her coffee.

"I don't know," she said. "He was just *there*. He said something strange to me. He said: 'You don't want to think about it.' I wonder what it meant."

"Could be your subconscious sending you a message," Eda said.

Chris laughed a little.

"That sounds like something Lucille would say."

"It makes sense," Eda said. "You have a lot on your mind. My God, do you ever! But there must be some missing pieces, some things that haven't come to you yet. We left off our talk yesterday when Harvey ran away from home. Today I think we ought to talk about the time when Harvey returned. The fact that he appeared so suddenly in your dream must mean something."

The back door opened, and Lucille came in, bearing a bundle of papers. She set them on the table. Chris took one and studied the side-by-side pictures of her children. Underneath, three-inch-high letters declared: "MISSING."

"Eda and I are going to paste them up all over town," she said. "And some of the people who work on the school newsletter for me have volunteered to help saturate the county. If there could possibly be anyone who doesn't know what happened, after all the media attention, they'll certainly know now!"

"I never did like that picture of Josh," Chris said softly. She put the paper back on the pile and stood up to give her friend a hug. "Thank you so much."

"It's the least we can do," Eda said. "Lucille told me she's already contacted ChildFind and the Center for Missing and Exploited Children. It's possible they're still in the area, Chris. Kidnappers usually stick around for about forty-eight hours."

"Not all kidnappers are murderers," Chris pointed out.

Lucille picked up half the pile of papers and handed them to Eda.

"Don't think about that now, Chris," she said. "We're all doing our best to find Josh and Vicki."

"And we will!" Eda insisted.

Chris held out her hand. "Let me have some of those."

"No," Lucille said simply. "Chris, I didn't like the idea of you going on that search last night. I don't think you should be driving around town, either."

"For heaven's sake, Lucille," Eda said, "she's a grown woman!"

Lucille gazed at Eda for a moment, then at Chris.

"Am I being a mother hen again?" she asked.

Chris managed a smile. "It's okay. I guess I don't really feel up to it, either."

"You can stay by the phone, in case someone calls," Eda offered. She knew Chris hated feeling helpless.

"Good idea," Lucille said. "But listen to the answering machine first. That way you can screen out any weirdos."

Chris frowned. "Why would weirdos call here? No one knows I'm here!"

"But my number is on these posters," Lucille pointed out. "And tragedy brings out the worst people. Still, we could also get a hopeful call!"

So Chris stayed home, staring at the telephone. It never rang, and soon the silence became so frustrating that she switched on the television. Tiffany Simmons was on Cable 75, and two pictures of Josh and Vicki seemed to float in space behind her. Chris stared at her children's faces, not hearing Tiffany at all.

She could hear only the sound of her own coarse breathing, as tears fell once more.

SEVENTEEN

▼

Eda SPENT AN hour at the police station looking over files from the original Gammel case. Mike was more than happy to have her input, not only as a fellow police officer but as a close friend of Chris Wander's. When she finally decided to quit for the day, he drove her back to Lucille's house. The sight of a police car attracted reporters like ants to honey, but Eda waved them all away impatiently.

"Sheriff Hewlett just gave me a lift," she explained. "I don't have any information on the case."

"But aren't you Christine Wander's old friend?" someone asked.

"Of course," Eda said. "And I'm here to offer emotional support. That's all."

"Where is she staying?" another reporter demanded.

Mike was out of the squad car, holding up both arms.

"All right, all right," he said. "Leave her alone. Mrs. Wander is in protective custody."

Everyone turned to Mike with more questions. Eda shot him a grateful look, then hurried up Lucille's driveway. She was halfway to the kitchen door at the back when she heard someone calling her name. A woman, smartly dressed in a suit with a bow tie at her neck, hurried up the driveway. Her heels clicked softly on the cement.

"Eda? Eda Crispin, is that you?"

The voice was overly friendly. Eda braced herself.

"Yes."

Eda turned slowly—and stifled an urge to make a face. Acting like the kid she'd once been wouldn't do for a decorated officer of the N.Y.P.D. But it was difficult to maintain her composure when she saw Tiffany Simmons.

"Hello, Tiffany," she said.

Tiffany's hair was as fussily coifed as ever, each strand exactly in place. It irked Eda. She wished she *was* seven again, just so she could reach out and mess it up.

"What do you want?"

Tiffany's pretty face was full of concern.

"Oh, I'm so sorry about Christy's husband," she said. "Poor Christy! And those children! Have you talked to Christy? Is that why you're here?"

Eda nodded. "I flew in to be with her."

"What a great friend you are," Tiffany said. "Christy must appreciate you."

A great enough friend to know we haven't called her "Christy" in years.

"She does," Eda said. "Look, I'm tired. Good-bye, Tiffany."

"Wait!" Tiffany cried. "I haven't had a chance to explain what I'm doing here. You might have heard I'm working at the TV station over in Garvey. You know, Cable 75? I'm with the news department. Would you mind if I asked a few questions? You know, old friend to old friend?"

Eda's growing exhaustion was exacerbated by a slight case of jet lag. She breathed in deeply, like a bull readying itself for the fight.

"You are not my old friend," she said evenly. "You hated Chris thirty years ago, and you probably hate her just as much today. You're as bad as those other ghouls across the street!"

She left Tiffany standing openmouthed, and walked up the steps to the back door. Finally, just before she entered the house, she heard Tiffany gasp.

"Having money didn't keep you from being trash!" she cried. "All I wanted was to ask where Christy is staying!"

"I wouldn't tell you," Eda said, closing the door behind her.

Lucille was still in the kitchen. She looked at Eda with inquiring eyes.

"I heard shouting," she said.

"Oh, Tiffany Simmons was outside," Eda said.

Lucille smiled a little. "I've seen her on television. She's as obnoxious as ever."

"Little Miss Perfect," Eda recalled. "Where's Chris? Resting, I hope."

"It took some effort," Lucille said. "Did you learn anything?"

Eda told Lucille about her conversation with Mike. Together, they decided it wasn't worth waking Chris up.

Outside, Tiffany stared at the house for a long time. She thought Christy Wander would be crazy to hide so near to the scene of the crime. But then, where better to hide than right under everyone's noses?

Tiffany slid on a pair of sunglasses, then walked down the street to her car. She knew she wouldn't get a story today. But she was patient. She could wait until the others had given up. Then she'd confront Eda (that bitch) and Lucille. And she'd find Christy, and have her story.

The cameraman, suddenly aware she had left the crowd, hurried to catch up with her.

"What's up, Ms. Simmons?"

"There's no story here, Frank," Tiffany said. "Let's call it a day."

"But what about . . .?"

"Never mind," Tiffany said. She waved a hand, like a queen dismissing a servant. "Go on home. I'll call you when I need you."

She got into her car before he could say a word.

Vicki looked down at her bowl of soup and made a face. "It tastes funny," she said.

"You're just saying that 'cause I cooked it," Josh retorted. "Sorry if I can't do it the way Mom does."

But when he lifted a spoonful into his own mouth, he spit it back into the bowl.

"Gross!"

They'd found a portable stove in the room, and a can opener. After dumping noodle soup concentrate into a pot, Josh had realized there was no sink in the room. Investigation found a large water tank in one corner, with a tap at the bottom. He'd filled the soup can with that.

"It tastes rusty," he said. "I guess I shoulda let it drain a little. Forget it—there's some potato chips over there. They've got to be okay."

He took a bag down from the shelf and popped it open, spilling crumbs all over the floor. Then he and Vicki sat on the edge of the cot, sharing them.

"Does your tummy still hurt?" the little girl asked.

"Not so much," Josh said.

Vicki took another potato chip and stuffed it whole into her mouth.

"What're we gonna do, Josh?"

"Gee, I don't know," Josh admitted. "If it's really late at

night, there's nothing we can do. It's stupid to yell for help
if no one can hear you. We can't get out as long as the
door is locked.

Vicki yawned noisily. "I'm tired. I wanna go to sleep
again."

"Maybe one of us should stay awake," Josh suggested.
"I mean, if anyone comes."

He didn't admit his fear that "anyone" might be the kidnapper. Having had to time to think, he was convinced that
was what had happened. He had vague memories of his father fighting with someone, but he was afraid to push the
recollection any further. The underlying sense of something horrible was too much for him to take. Vicki had
stopped talking about the bad man, and he was glad. She
scared him when she screamed like that.

"I don't wanna," Vicki said, yawning again.

"Then lie down and go to sleep," Josh said. "I'll wake
you up if help comes."

Vicki stretched out on the cot, pulling a green army-
issue blanket over herself.

"Wish I had my unicorn," she mumbled drowsily.

Josh got up and cleaned the soup bowls. The soup was
gross enough as it was, he thought, without letting it sit
around. There was a bent and rusted trash can on the other
side of the room, where he dumped the inedible noodles.
He rinsed the bowls and spoons under the tap of the water
tank and stacked them on the table again.

Once finished, he started another trip around the room.
He hoped he'd find something he'd missed before, some
way out of this strange place. He was convinced they were
in a basement, since there were no windows. There *were*
vents, and he wondered if he might be able to unscrew the
cover of one to crawl through. Then he shook his head.
The vents were too small.

The lights flickered suddenly. Vicki, not quite asleep yet, bolted upright.

"Josh?"

"It's okay," Josh said, though he wasn't so sure himself. What would happen if the lights went out. What would he do then? He hadn't been afraid of the dark for a couple of years now, but . . .

"Are you awake?"

The voice sounded far away, like a radio just off a station. Josh didn't answer.

"I asked: Are you awake?"

"Yeah!" Josh yelled back, looking all around. "Let us out of here, will you?"

"In time," the voice said. *"Did you eat?"*

"The water is gross," Josh said.

"What did you eat?"

"Soup," Josh answered. "And potato chips."

"What kind of soup?"

Josh gave his sister a look that asked: what kind of question was that? Who cared?

"Just let us out of here!" he shouted. "You better let us out, or our father—"

"What kind of soup?"

It was almost a scream.

"Chicken noodle," Josh said, raising his eyebrows at Vicki.

She twisted her mouth. This guy was *weird*.

"You open that door!" she yelled. "You open that door and let us out, you *criminal*!"

There was a long silence.

Finally:

"What door?"

"The door that's locked, stupid!" Josh snapped. "The way out of here!"

The unseen figure burst into laughter. The sound of it

bounced around the stone room, growing more maniacal by the minute. Josh lost his bravado, and suddenly hugging his sister didn't seem so repulsive. They looked around themselves. Where was the voice coming from? It seemed to be everywhere!

At last the hideous laughter stopped.

"I'll be back in the morning," the voice said. *"I'll bring the key."*

"We want out now!" Vicki shouted.

They waited for a few minutes, but there was no answer. Vicki cuddled more tightly against her brother.

"Josh, why won't he let us out?" she asked.

"I don't know," Josh said. He pulled away. "What makes you think I know everything?"

He hurried away from her, feeling bad that he couldn't save them. He was the big brother, the smart one, the brave one. If this were a video game, he'd know what to do. He'd know where to find weapons, a secret door to another level, a special code to make him invincible. But this wasn't a video game. It was real, and it was scarier than anything he'd ever experienced.

As Vicki watched, Josh went into the small bathroom and shut the door. He didn't want her looking at him when he felt so little and helpless. He plunked himself down on the floor and gazed for a moment at the cracked toilet bowl. There was no water in it, and it didn't flush at all. The back had no lid, and a spider had long abandoned a web inside the tank.

Josh stared a little longer, as an idea began to form in his head. Slowly, he rose. He could stand on the tank and reach the ceiling, couldn't he? He'd watched a house being built once, and he knew there was space between a ceiling and the floor above it. Not much space, but probably the right size for a kid. If he could get up in there, if he could find a weak spot in the floor above . . .

No, it was a crazy idea.

He looked up at the ceiling. It was covered with dingy tile, spotted brown and black with water stains and mildew.

"What the heck," he said out loud, standing up.

It was worth a try. He climbed onto the tank. Then he reached up and started pulling the tiles away. One by one they crumbled to the floor. He had to avert his eyes, and he sneezed a few times, but after the dust settled he looked up at his handiwork.

He expected to see a network of pipes and wires, or perhaps just some wood beams.

Instead, there was solid cement, just like the walls around him.

Defeated, Josh jumped down to the floor. Then, in the privacy of that dingy, waterless bathroom, he buried his face between his knees and began to cry.

EIGHTEEN

THE THINGS THE children used had to be replaced. Everything down there had to be kept precise or terrible things would happen. There had to be fifteen cans of soup, fifteen bags of chips, fifteen of everything. Fifteen was a very important number.

He knew he couldn't buy anything in town. The people of Aberdeen were certainly on the lookout for strangers, and in a town this small he'd be spotted. So he drove to the next town, Longacre, and bought what he needed there. He parked his car at the bus station on the edge of Aberdeen and walked the rest of the way. He kept away from the main roads, kept his head ducked down so no one would see his face.

When he reached the corner nearest his lair, he waited for nearly half an hour to be sure he was alone. Then he raced across the street, cutting through nearly two acres of tall grass, until he reached his destination. Even then, he waited at the door another ten minutes, breathing hard from the run. Then, very, very slowly, he opened the door.

He peered at the children, who cuddled together on the cot, sound asleep. Moving carefully (like a stalking tiger, he thought), he entered the room and replaced the soup and chips. He was about to leave when he remembered the boy had asked about a key. A laugh tried to escape, and he covered his mouth with a dirty hand. Then he reached into his pocket and pulled out a rusty old key. He put it on the table and left.

The sound of a door slamming pulled Josh out of his sleep so abruptly that he fell from the cot. He sat holding his head for a few moments, dazed, unable to comprehend his surroundings. Finally, he realized where he was and that what he'd hoped had been a nightmare was all too real.

He stood up and looked around. Had he heard a door slam? He looked back at his sister, who slept curled like a baby. He wondered how long they'd been asleep and if it was morning yet. A terrible ache turned his attentions to the bathroom, and with great reluctance he used the old toilet.

"Gross," he mumbled.

When he came out again, he noticed something on the table. A key! He hurried to pick it up. It didn't look like any key he'd ever seen. It was all rusty and very heavy. Josh didn't care, though. He just wanted to try it.

"Vicki!" he called. "Wake up! He left the key, just like he said he would!"

Maybe it was all a joke, and maybe now it was over.

"Vicki!"

The little girl sat up and began to whine.

"I want Mommy!"

"Can it," Josh said, holding up the key. "Look what I've got!"

Vicki's eyes widened. "Yay! Are we goin' home?"

"Soon as I get the door open," Josh said.

Vicki walked across the room to stand at his side as he pushed the key into the lock. At first, it wouldn't turn. Josh bit his lip, and tried harder.

"Are we stuck?" Vicki asked. "Are we stuck?"

"No!" Josh snapped. They couldn't be stuck! He was sick of this game and he wanted to go home!

He wrapped both hands around the key and put his weight into the effort. At last, with a pop, it turned the lock. Vicki's look of apprehension turned into a wide grin. Josh pushed the door open . . .

. . . and walked into a closet.

"What the . . .?"

"Josh," Vicki said softly, "this isn't the way out."

"I can see that!" Josh said, trying hard to fight tears. What kind of cruel trick was this?

The closet measured about four-by-four feet. The walls were cement, without windows or vents. The room was completely empty.

Vicki turned and ran to the middle of the room. She turned in circles and shouted:

"I want out! I want out! I want ouuuuuut!"

"Vicki, shut up!" Josh snapped. Her voice was bouncing off the walls. "Nobody can hear you!"

"Hey you stupid people out there! You make a door for us!"

Josh sat on the edge of the cot and covered his ears. As Vicki went on shouting, he thought about her words: "make a door." There *had* to be a door! There had to be a way out of here! Maybe it was just blocked off.

"Hey, Vicki!" he called.

By now his little sister was jumping up and down, her fists waving angrily.

"Vicki, let's find a door!"

Somehow, that cut through her tantrum. She stopped, took a few deep breaths, and stared at him.

"Let's find a door," he said again. "We got in, we'll get out."

"Okay," Vicki said almost calmly. It was as if she hadn't had a fit of temper at all.

"Let's look very carefully," Josh said. "Like detectives. You know, like Encyclopedia Brown would look. The door has to be hidden."

"Yeah, hidden," Vicki agreed.

"We'll start over there," Josh said, pointing to a wall.

They walked along, feeling carefully for any sign of an exit.

"It's cold," Vicki said.

Josh didn't answer. He was concentrating too deeply, peering at every little crack, checking the places between the cement blocks. There was a way out of this place, and if it took him a million hours, he'd find it.

Vicki walked over to the shelves. She felt hungry suddenly, and took down a bag of pretzels. As she ate them, she peered carefully behind the shelves of food. It was silly for a door to be behind shelves, she thought. But she kept looking, and kept seeing nothing but solid wall. Finally, she came to the end of the shelves. She was about to turn back to her brother when the light flickered.

"Not again!" Josh moaned.

Vicki looked up at the flickering bulb. And as she did so, she noticed something they hadn't seen before.

"Josh, look!" she cried. "What's a ladder doing up there?"

Josh turned to see at the same time she ran across the room. There really was a ladder, and it was bolted to the wall. Vicki reached up, but couldn't grab the end of it.

"How come it's on the wall like that, Josh?" she asked. "How come it's so high?"

At once, Josh knew the answer. They hadn't been able to find the door because it was overhead! The ladder led to a trapdoor!

"Help me push the table over!" Josh cried.

The two children pushed the table to the wall. When he stood on it, Josh could see that it was an extension ladder and that it had been pulled up and hooked in place. All he had to do was unhook it and climb right up to the trapdoor above.

He took hold of a rung and tried to lift the ladder. But it was much too heavy. Josh studied it, scratching his head in thought.

Well, why did he need to unhook it? He could reach the bottom rung right from the table! He climbed onto it, then looked over his shoulder.

"We'll be outta here in a minute," he told Vicki. "Then we'll go home and tell Mom and Dad what happened."

"Yeah," Vicki said. "Daddy'll beat up the bad man who put us in here!"

Josh paused suddenly. Something about the words *beat up* brought back that vague, frightening memory that had had been trying to surface since he woke up down here. But he pushed it away. Whatever it was, it didn't matter so long as they got out of here.

He started up.

"I'll climb out," he called down. "And then I'll unhook the ladder and you can climb up."

"Okay!"

The ladder shook slightly with each step, but Josh held tightly and kept ascending. He had no idea that his weight was working the latch free until it was too late.

Suddenly, the lower half of the ladder came loose. It shot towards the floor with lightninglike speed. The clanking blended with the sound of the children's screams. When the ladder hit the floor a few seconds later, the impact threw Josh off. He fell backwards, smashed his head on the table edge, and passed out.

Vicki stood staring at him for just a moment. Then she started to shake him.

"Josh, wake up!" she cried. "Please!"

But Josh wouldn't wake up. Vicki stared at the ladder that had hurt him. How could they get out if the ladder hurt them?

She went to the ladder and grabbed it. Shaking it with all her might, she gazed up at the ceiling. She could see the door now, a funny round door.

"Open up!" she shouted. *"Open up! Open up! Open up!"*

But no one heard her.

NINETEEN

▼

THE FOLLOWING MORNING, as soon as the coffee maker had brewed a pot, Lucille went up to Chris's room to wake her friend. Christ was curled in a fetal position, her arms wrapped tightly around a pillow. Lucille wondered who she was hugging in her dreams. She put her hand on her friend's shoulder and shook gently.

Chris didn't respond.

"Chris?" Lucille called. "Wake up. Do you want break-fast?"

There was a knock behind her, and Lucille looked over her shoulder as Eda entered the room.

"I heard her get up in the middle of the night," Eda said. "She's probably exhausted. Maybe you should let her sleep."

Agreeing, Lucille followed Eda from the room and softly closed the door. While Lucille prepared breakfast, Eda went outside for the newspaper. She felt a twinge of

nostalgia to see the paper's banner: *"Aberdeen Chronicle."*
It hadn't been in the family for nearly a decade, but she recalled vividly the days when her father had first bought it.
That had been at the time of the original murders. Strange
how things came around again.

Dean Crispin had sold the *Chronicle* after Rita died, and
was spending his retirement years traveling the world. The
last Eda had heard, he was in Singapore. She wondered
what he'd have to say about this latest turn of events.

"Good morning!"

Eda winced at the familiar-sounding voice.

"Don't you ever go home?" she asked.

"Not until I get my story," Tiffany said. She was
dressed in a sky-blue linen suit. "Eda, please talk to me.
I'm not stupid. I know that you're here because of Christy,
and I also know where she's staying."

Eda looked the other woman in the eye, her expression
even.

"You do, do you?" she asked. "That's a pretty good
trick."

"Oh, come off it," Tiffany said, beginning to sound annoyed. "You three were like peas in a pod when we were
growing up. I can't imagine that you'd dump Christy in a
strange place at a time like this. She's in there with you,
isn't she?"

Eda shook her head and turned away.

"Don't you walk away from me!" Tiffany snapped.
"Who do you think you are?"

Eda still didn't answer. She thought that if she opened
her mouth, she'd explode and Tiffany might end up all
over the sidewalk.

"You listen to me, Eda Crispin!" Tiffany cried. "I
thought I'd do a sympathetic piece on this crime! But everyone in town knows what kind of background Christy
comes from! Everyone knows what kind of man her father

was! An abused child grows up to be an abusing parent. People are talking, Eda! They're getting suspicious!"

That was too much for Eda to take. With a cry, she turned and ran down the driveway, hands outstretched. In training to be a police officer, she'd studied combat techniques and the martial arts. But all these skills were forgotten as the little girl she'd been came to the surface, the little girl who had hated Tiffany and all snobs like her.

"You *bitch*!"

"Eda, no!" Tiffany cried, turning to run.

Eda came up behind the other woman, one hand reaching out to grab her. She almost had her by the collar when someone grabbed her from behind. It was Lucille.

"Eda, stop!" she cried. "She isn't worth it!"

"She's a lying, cruel-mouthed bitch!"

"I'll have my story, Eda Crispin!" Tiffany cried as she backed across the street. "I'll see Christy if I have to haunt you day and night!"

Eda was about to yell out a choice epithet when Lucille gave her a yank and pulled her back to the house.

"Calm down," Lucille said in a gentle voice. "You aren't helping Chris this way."

"You should have heard what she said," Eda replied as they entered the house. "She knows that Chris is here, and she won't let us alone until she talks to her."

"Well, we certainly can't allow that," Lucille said.

Eda went to the coffee maker and poured herself a cup she didn't really want. She just needed something to do.

"I'll talk to Mike again," she said. "I'll have him talk to her, threaten her with harassment charges."

"I don't think you can do that," Lucille said. "I think the First Amendment protects witches like Tiffany."

Eda sat down, setting her cup hard on the table.

"Then I'll find another way to stop her."

Lucille shook her head, sitting herself.

"You're amazing," she said. "You haven't changed a bit. I never met anyone who could fly off the handle one minute, then be sweet the next, like you!"

"It's gotten me into some trouble at the precinct," Eda said. "But I guess they're getting used to me by now. Oh, that reminds me. Do you mind if I make a long-distance call? I want to check with my partner."

"Go right ahead," Lucille said. "I've got some writing to catch up on."

"A new mystery?" Eda asked. "I really loved *The Clock Struck One.*"

"Thanks," Lucille said. "Yes, I've been working on my newest book for a few months now. But I tell you, nothing in fiction compares to real life, does it?"

"I guess not," Eda said.

Lucille went to her office while Eda dialed the phone. She knew Tim Becker had off today, and hoped to catch him at home.

"Hi, Tim," she said.

"Eda!" Tim cried. "How are you, Cowgirl? How's your friend?"

"I'm okay," Eda said. "It's a horrible situation, Tim. I don't think I'm going to be back any time soon."

She gave him an update. When she was finished, Tim had some ideas.

"It seems like too much of a coincidence," he said, "especially considering that creep that was following Chris so long ago. But what about her husband? Could there be a connection there?"

"The police are working on it," Eda said.

"And you're just going to leave it at that?"

"You know me better than that, Tim," Eda said. "Of course I plan to check up on Brian Wander."

"Talking about the past seems to have been a good

idea," Tim said. "You should go on doing it. You might come up with some other clues."

"Well, Chris is asleep now," Eda said. "I think she took a sedative in the middle of the night. But when she wakes up, we plan to continue our discussion."

Lucille came into the room.

"Hey, Tim, I have to go," Eda said, although Lucille shook her head to indicate it was fine to keep talking. "I'll keep you posted. Tell the captain I'm using my vacation time."

"Good-bye, Eda," Tim said.

Eda hung up the phone.

"I'm heading to town," Lucille said. "I need printer paper, and I thought I'd pick up a few groceries. Are you going to call Mike about Tiffany?"

"You bet I am," Eda said. "If she has ideas about harassing Chris, you can bet there'll be others."

A worried looked crossed Lucille's face.

"I just hope we don't have to leave," she said.

Her father had been right.

There was a whole collection of heads in the old Gammel house. Heads on the tables, heads decorating the bedposts, heads in pots on the stove.

Chris walked slowly, staring at every head, searching for the familiar ones.

Josh and Vicki were here somewhere.

She head a footstep behind herself.

"I'm so glad you've come, Christy. Now I can add you to my collection."

Chris woke with a gasp. It was dark in the room, and silent except for a low hum from the clock. She turned to look at the time, and frowned to see it was ten-thirty. In that short space of time, the dream was forgotten.

But not the real nightmare that had caused it.

Groggily, Chris tried to make sense of the time. It had been early midnight when she went to bed. Had she slept through a whole day? Bewildered, she threw her covers aside and jumped from the bed. Without putting on the robe Lucille had left for her, she hurried down to the kitchen to find her friends drinking coffee at the table.

"Why didn't you wake me up?" she demanded. "Why did you let me sleep?"

"Chris, there was no waking you up," Lucille said. "We tried a few times during the day, but I guess the sedative you took was stronger than we imagined. Besides, you needed your sleep."

"But a whole day!" Chris exclaimed.

"There wasn't any news," Eda told her. "We would have tried harder to get you up if there had been. I spoke to Mike Hewlett again, and he promises they're working round-the-clock. But right now, I'm afraid there isn't anything to tell you."

Lucille regarded her friend with concern.

"Are you up to eating?" she asked. "I made a nice shepherd's pie for dinner. I could heat some in the microwave. . . ."

Chris shook her head.

"I don't think I could eat," she said. "But I could use a cup of coffee."

Instantly Lucille was on her feet, filling the request. Chris accepted the cup gratefully. She drank nearly half before speaking again.

"I can't understand why there hasn't been a phone call," she went on. "I mean, the children were kidnapped, weren't they? Why hasn't anyone made a ransom call?"

"I don't know, Chris," Lucille said. "Maybe . . . well, maybe the kidnapper is biding his time. Anyone cruel enough to do what he did . . ."

"I don't want to think about that," Chris said suddenly. "I just want to get my children back! Eda, did Mike say anything at all that I should know?"

Eda thought a moment.

"He was interested in that man who had been following you," she reported. "He'll probably want to ask questions about him, Chris."

Chris ran a hand through her hair, looking worried.

"I don't know," she said. "A lot of people believed that was only my imagination."

"A lot of people?" Eda echoed. "Just some mean kids and your father, Chris. And who the hell cares what he thought? He was a vicious child abuser."

Chris moved uncomfortably in her chair. Lucille watched as an expression of fear crossed over her friend's features, one she'd seen many times in their childhood. She shot Eda a warning glance. Then she stood up and took Chris's cup.

"Refill?" she asked in a cheerful tone that was only slightly forced.

"Please," Chris said.

"I think," Lucille said, "that we should keep talking about the past. What we remembered from so long ago may provide important clues for the police to follow."

Eda nodded in agreement.

"Chris, if you try to remember the times you saw that man, maybe we can establish a pattern."

"Let's sit in the living room," Lucille said. "It's much more comfortable there. Chris, are you sure you won't have any dinner?"

"Not right now."

The three women left the kitchen. Chris had always felt instantly comfortable when she entered Lucille's living room, where the floral-print couch and ruffled curtains beckoned visitors to relax. But today, when she sank in among overstuffed cushions and put her coffee cup on the oak table, she only felt tense. Resting an arm across the back of the couch, she turned to look out the window.

"They're still there," she said.

"Don't look, Chris," Lucille said. "There isn't anything to see. And if anyone looks this way and sees you, you'll never have any peace."

She was thinking of Tiffany. Did the woman really know Chris was here? She was tempted to peek herself, to see if Tiffany had come back. The woman had rung her doorbell earlier that day, but Lucille had refused to answer.

"So, let's get started," Eda said.

Chris reached for her coffee cup.

"I just wish we could do more than talk," she said.

"It's the best place to start," Lucille said.

"Chris, the last thing we talked about was that blackout you had, and then your father . . ."

"Your brother was with you that night," Lucille said.

Chris stared at a reproduction Remington on the table, focusing her eyes on the fierce look of the horse's face.

"Harvey kept saying he saved my life," she said. "But I never felt right about that. He ran away, remember, so I couldn't question him further."

Eda jotted down some notes to herself. Something about this whole story was suspicious, and she planned to do a little research of her own regarding Harvey Burnett, Jr.

"But he came back three years later," Lucille said. "Did you talk to him then?"

"There was no time," Chris said. "My father treated him like the Prodigal Son. They spent most of Harvey's time in Aberdeen together. It was as if nothing bad had ever happened between them. Then Harvey left, and I never saw him again. But, somehow, I think he knows the truth. I think he knew it when he came home."

Lucille gave Chris's hand a squeeze.

"Then we have to go back again," she said. "We have to talk about what happened."

With those words, the three women's minds were transported back in time once more.

TWENTY

▼

CHRISTY BURNETT TURNED ten three days after the end of fifth grade. She didn't expect much of a birthday celebration. Her mother had been getting worse, and seemed completely unaware of her daughter. Christy's father, unable to keep up with medical bills, took the brunt of his frustrations out on Christy. Most of the time, his anger wasn't even directed at her. She was just unlucky enough to be in the line of fire.

She hardly ever thought about that strange day when Irene Gammel ran from her house all covered with blood. The nightmares about the man with strange green eyes came back every once in a while, as if to remind her that he was still out there, somewhere. But it was enough to deal with her family. The added burden of worrying about someone who'd frightened her three years earlier was something she couldn't accept.

Recently it seemed to Christy that her father was even

meaner than usual. She didn't even dare look at him without getting yelled at. Christy wondered if his mood had
something to do with a telegram her father had received a
week earlier. Curled up in a corner of the sofa, she'd
watched him carefully as he read it. His face had gone
very pale, then very red. His lips were set hard. Christy
snuck into her room for safety. A short while later, she
heard her parents having an argument. Harvey's name
came up a few times.

Christy hugged her pillow and wondered how her
brother was getting along. He surely had to be doing better
than she was, now that he was far away from their father!
She wondered if the telegram had something to do with
him.

But when her birthday came, Harvey Jr. was the furthest
thing from her mind. Christy ate breakfast quickly that
morning. She just wanted to get away from the apartment
and meet her friends. To her surprise, her father handed
her a five-dollar-bill just as she was leaving.

"I don't want you home until six," he said. "I've got . . .
business I don't need a little kid running around."

No "Happy Birthday." Christy wondered if he remembered.

Her parents might have forgotten she was ten now, but
her friends hadn't. They had asked her to meet them in the
town square. Christy was first to arrive. She went to a
bench and sat down to wait, her back partially hiding graf-
fiti: STOP THE DRAFT. Vandalism was uncommon in Aberdeen, and the townspeople had been infuriated to see this.
Nobody would admit to it, but Christy had heard that
Willy Keel was responsible. Christy could hardly blame
him, though. Maybe he was a jerk, but even a jerk didn't
deserve getting his brother killed in Vietnam.

Christy didn't understand much about the conflict in
Southeast Asia. She just knew it had something to do with

Commies, the same group that had frightened everyone so much when she was smaller. And she also knew that boys could be drafted when they were seventeen. Harvey was eighteen now. She wondered if he had been sent to Vietnam without anyone in the family knowing it.

"Happy Birthday to Yoooouu!" sang two happy voices from behind her.

Christy turned around, grinning. Eda handed her a balloon, and Lucille pinned a ribbon corsage to her shirt.

"It has ten Tootsie Rolls on it," she said. "Plus one piece of bubble gum to grow on."

"Thanks," Christy said. "It's great."

"I made it myself," Lucille said.

They sat down on either side of her, and Eda put a small package in her lap. It was wrapped in pink-and-white paper, secured with a big pink bow. Christy opened a card no bigger than the palm of her hand and read:

"A friend is someone who shares happy times. Hope your birthday is the happiest time of all!"

She smiled at Eda, and then at Lucille.

"Now it is," she said.

"Open your present, already!" Eda coaxed.

She squirmed with anticipation as she watched Christy unwrap the paper. Christy gasped when she pulled out a transistor radio.

"We put batteries in it, too," Lucille said. "Here, try it out. . . ."

She showed Christy the different knobs. Christy played with it until she found a music station. The sound was a little crackly, since the nearest station was over a hundred miles away, but Christy thought it was great.

"Who's singing?" she asked, listening to a rock-and-roll song.

Both Eda and Lucille leaned forward to look at each other. Then they laughed.

"Those are the Beatles!" Lucille cried. "Don't you know anything?"

Christy looked down at her lap.

"I heard of them," she said, sounding insulted. "I just never really heard their music. My father hates rock and roll."

"My cousin Martha, who lives in New York, got to see them on the Ed Sullivan show last year," Lucille said with some pride. "She even got Ringo's autograph."

"What kind of name is Ringo?" Eda asked.

"It's a great radio," Christy said, ignoring Eda. "It's the best present I ever got."

The song came to an end, and the announcer made some comments about "The British Invasion." A commercial for Q-T Tanning Lotion followed, and then a song by the Dave Clark Five. A group of teenaged girls walked by, long hair flowing from center parts, eyes bright with blue makeup. Christy's mouth dropped open when she saw the short skirts two of them were wearing.

"Eda!" she gasped, tugging at her friend's sleeve. "You can almost see their underwear!"

Lucille watched the group as they crossed to the five-and-ten.

"I like miniskirts," she said. "There's a really pretty one in the Sears catalog that looks like it's made from a serape. But my father says 'No daughter of mine is going to look like that!' "

She tucked her neck into her chest and lowered her voice to imitate her father.

"I think they're stupid," said Eda, who lived in slacks whenever possible. "You always have to worry about your fanny sticking out."

Christy giggled as the radio played a new song. Then Lucille stood up and said:

"Party isn't over yet. Let's go to the Ice Cream Cottage!"

"My father gave me five dollars," Christy said in awe. "I guess that was my birthday present."

Eda wanted to comment that it was a pretty lousy birthday present, but caught herself. It would be mean to say such a thing to her friend, who was probably grateful her father remembered at all.

"Put it away," Lucille said. "This is on me and Eda."

Inside the Ice Cream Cottage, they found three empty seats at the counter.

"You can have anything you want," Lucille said. "Even a banana split."

"Oh, get one!" Eda cried. "Then you can break a balloon and get a prize."

There was a line of balloons taped to a beam above the counter. When a customer purchased a banana split, he or she could puncture a balloon. Christy agreed it would be fun, especially since she'd never done it before.

"Here you go, honey," the counterman said with a smile. He handed her a dart.

"Try the pink one!" Lucille said.

"No, that blue one there!" Eda suggested.

Christy looked carefully at the long stretch of balloons. Then she found a lonely white one. She reached up for it.

"Oh, white's so boring," Eda said.

Christy poked at it. A loud *pop* filled the shop, and a piece of paper floated down. As her friends watched, Christy read it.

"A free bag of candy!" she cried. "I get free candy!"

Her grin was a mile wide.

The counterman bent down and stood back up again holding a small white paper bag. He handed it to Christy and said:

"Happy Birthday, honey."

Then he went off to fill their ice cream order.

Christy opened the bag and spilled out the contents. She divided the candy evenly among her friends, then put her own share back into the bag. It might come in handy if there wasn't much for dinner tonight. Eda immediately opened a Jolly Rancher and started to suck noisily.

In the mirror, Christy saw Tiffany Simmons turn around. She was sitting at a nearby table, and there was a look of disgust on her face.

"You sound like a pig!" she said.

"You look like one," Eda retorted. Then she sucked all the louder, just to annoy Tiffany.

Lucille and Christy snickered.

Tiffany rolled her eyes and turned her attention back to her own treat.

"Figures," Tiffany mumbled. "Some people are such trash!"

"Takes one to know one," Christy shot back.

Christy ducked her head a little, surprised she'd said it. But the look of approval from her friends made her smile. This was turning out to be a pretty good day, after all.

When she finished her banana split, she decided to use the rest room. She excused herself and went to the hall at the back of the store. There was only one bathroom, with one inner stall and a sink. Christy took care of her needs. She was fastening her belt again when she heard the door open. She unlocked the booth and started to open the door, only to find it wouldn't budge.

"Hey!" she cried. "Let go!"

She looked under the door to see a pair of boots and the bottoms of denim jeans. As she fought to open the door, Christy tried to peek through the crack. It was closed too tightly for her to see a thing. She wondered if Tiffany had been wearing jeans.

Of course not, she thought. Tiffany wouldn't be caught dead in blue jeans!

"Christy . . ."

It was a man's voice, deep and evil.

And deadly familiar.

"Let me out!" Christy shouted.

"I've come back for you. . . ."

She knew that voice. But how could it be? How could the man who had frightened her so terribly be back again?

Christy shoved the lock closed again, backed into a corner of the booth, wedged between the wall and toilet, and began to scream.

Moments later, someone came into the bathroom and demanded:

"What's going on in here?"

It was a man's voice, but not the same one that had whispered to her. Christy stopped screaming. Still, she cowered back and stared at the locked door to the stall. The man knocked at the door.

"Answer me, kid," he said.

Christy finally recognized the counterman. She moved forward. Her hand was trembling as she unlatched the door. She stared down at her sneakers, not knowing what to say. Nobody ever believed her before. Why would they believe someone was after her now?

"What gives?" the counterman asked, staring hard at her.

Christy edged past him, shaking her head.

"Christy, are you okay?" Lucille asked.

Christy was embarrassed to realize her screams had attracted a small crowd, people pushing each other to get a look into the bathroom. She had to think quickly, and blurted out the first thing that came to her mind.

"I . . . I saw a roach," she whispered.

"Ewww!" screeched Tiffany.

The counterman looked into the stall, then shook his head.

"No roaches here," he said. "You must have imagined things."

Lucille put an arm around Christy's shoulder.

"Back off, you guys," Eda commanded as they left the bathroom.

"There are no roaches in my store," the man insisted to no one in particular.

Eda helped clear a path for Christy and Lucille. She heard some nasty remarks, and fixed a killer gaze on Tiffany. "Take a picture, it'll last longer!"

They were halfway out of the store when Tiffany thought of an answer.

"Wouldn't want to break my camera!"

Once they were away from the Ice Cream Cottage, the girls all started talking at once.

"Christy, what . . .?"

"Everyone heard you . . .?"

"I was so scared! I thought . . ."

Lucille held up a hand. "Wait, wait. Let's take a walk to the lake. We can talk in private there."

She had noticed some people watching them from the shop window. Christy was still in tears, and Lucille didn't want anyone to stare at them.

They walked to the park in silence. Both Eda and Lucille would glance at Christy, then at each other. Silent wonder passed between them. They hadn't seen their friend hysterical in a long time, not even when she knew she was in for a thrashing from her father.

"So what happened?" Eda finally asked as they entered the park.

"I . . . I think that man is back again," Christy said softly.

"What man?" Lucille asked.

She pointed to a shady spot under a huge elm tree. Lucille and Christy leaned against the tree trunk. Eda plunked down on her stomach and crossed her ankles up behind her. With her chin in her hands, she watched Christy with interest.

"You know!" Christy said. "The man who was following me when I was seven. He's back again!"

"Oh, Christy, he can't be!" Lucille cried. "That was three years ago! Why would he come back now?"

Christy turned to her friend, her eyes growing large.

"It was him!" she said.

She proceeded to tell them what had happened in the bathroom. Eda turned around and sat up straight.

"Maybe we should tell my father," she said. "He could tell Officer Mike—"

"No!" Christy said. "Then he'd tell *my* father. And I don't ... I don't want him to ... to know!"

She started to cry again. Lucille patted her arm.

"I don't blame you," she said. "But you can't let him terrorize you again."

"Who?" Eda said with dead seriousness. "Her father or that stranger?"

Lucille shot her a look. "Both of them! Christy, you've got to let someone help you!"

Christy stared down at her lap and shook her head.

"I can't," she said. "He's back again, and maybe this time he'll get me!"

Eda thought for a while.

"Well, I can't figure it out," she said finally. "Three years go by without a word from this creep. Why would he come back now?"

"And how come we didn't see him at the Ice Cream Cottage?" Lucille asked.

Eda had a quick answer for that one.

"There's a back door," she said. "He could have run down the hall and left before anyone saw him."

"He said he came back for me," Christy recalled. "He wants to take me away! He tried to do it when I was little, but Harvey stopped him!"

She gazed past the trees to the lake.

"I wish Harvey was here now," she said. "I bet he's big and strong."

"I bet he's a bigger geek than ever," Eda grumbled. "Why do you want that jerk back again?"

Lucille nodded. "He was just another bad thing in your life. Be glad Harvey is gone. At least he can't pick on you the way he always did!"

"But if he was here—"

"He'd probably be just as mean as ever," Eda said.

"But I don't want to be alone!" Christy cried. "My parents can't help me!"

Eda and Lucille moved closer to her.

"We can," they said in unison.

"We'll make sure you're *never* alone," Lucille said.

"Yeah, by the time summer is over," Eda put in, "you'll be sick of us."

Christy was thoughtful.

"You . . . you know they never found Teddy and Adrian," she said. "What if he's come back to take me away, too? What if he's going to kill me?"

Tears were starting to well up in her brown eyes again. Eda squeezed her hand hard.

"He won't!" she said. "Just let him try! I'll punch him in the nose!"

"I'll hit him over the head," Lucille put in.

"I'll kick him where it counts," added Eda.

"Eda Crispin!" Lucille gasped. "The mouth on you!"

Eda wriggled. "Well, it'd work, wouldn't it? What do you say, Christy? Will you let us help you?"

Christy nodded, and braved a smile for her friends. But she couldn't help looking beyond them to the road leading into town. Where was the man now? Was he hiding somewhere, waiting for a new opportunity to kidnap her?

Maybe to murder her?

TWENTY-ONE

▼

CAREFUL TO OBEY her father's orders, Christy didn't return that night until six-fifteen. Even though it was still light out, she was grateful that Lucille and Eda had kept their promise to be with her at all times. Still, she kept looking back over her shoulder as they walked down Central Street.

"It's okay, Christy," Lucille said, understanding. "Even if that guy was here, he wouldn't show up right in the middle of town."

"He came to the Ice Cream Cottage," Christy pointed out worriedly.

"And ran out the back door to the alley," Eda said.

Lucille stopped a moment, looking thoughtful.

"You know what?" she said. "I'll bet it wasn't that man at all! I'll bet it was one of that mean Tiffany's friends."

"That could be right!" Eda agreed, her eyes looking

hopeful. "Tiffany would do something like that, wouldn't she?"

"But this was a man," Christy said. "He had a man kind of voice. Just like that guy when I was seven."

They started walking again. The early summer evening was pleasantly cool, and shopowners had their doors wide open to welcome customers. The sidewalks along Central Street were shaded with pear trees. Eda reached up, picked a piece of fruit, and tasted it. She made a face.

"Ugh!" she said, throwing it into the gutter. "That tastes horrible!"

Lucille giggled. "I bet Tiffany would like it."

"Nahh," Eda replied. "She's already sour enough."

"Rotten to the core," Lucille agreed.

"Green and moldy," Christy put in.

"Good for you, Christy," Lucille said, glad Christy was joining in their teasing. The three girls started laughing. But when they reached the Burnett's apartment building, Christy's smile fell. She opened the door and looked up the dark staircase. Eda and Lucille turned to each other, recognizing Christy's worried expression. What would be waiting up there? They knew the fact that this was Christy's birthday wouldn't make a difference if her father was in a bad mood.

"Well, I'll see you tomorrow," Christy said.

She went up the stairs. Christy tried to think about the nice day she'd had so far. She tried to concentrate on her new radio, safe in her hands. But with each step, the familiar feeling of dread grew stronger. It had been a long time since her father had hit her, but that didn't mean he wouldn't start again tonight. Only after she opened the door would she know.

She wondered about the meeting her father had said he was going to have. He'd seemed worried about it this morning, and she prayed it hadn't put him in a bad mood.

It was funny that he had to see someone in the apartment. He *never* brought anyone home. Christy knew he was ashamed of her mother, who sat around all day in a bathrobe, staring at the television. Her mother didn't even bathe unless her father turned on the shower and shoved her underneath it. Then Christy would hide in her room, covering her ears to mask her mother's screams.

She took a deep breath and opened the door.

To her surprise, her father was sitting at the table with a cup of coffee, reading the evening paper. Her mother sat there, too, with her own cup. Her hair was combed, and she was wearing a fresh housecoat.

Christy was even more surprised when her father smiled at her.

"There's the birthday girl," he said.

Christy stopped short. Her father had remembered her birthday after all!

"Hi," she said uncertainly.

"Sit down," Harvey Sr. said. "What did you do today?"

Christy told about the celebration at the Ice Cream Cottage and showed off her new radio. She spoke carefully, glancing at her mother once in a while. Her father's good moods were rare, and the littlest thing could turn him around. Sarah didn't look at her daughter.

"Do . . . do you want me to get dinner?" she asked uncertainly.

"I have a surprise," Harvey Sr. said. He got up and fetched a large bag from the counter.

Christy's eyes widened as he pulled out a quart of won ton soup and a container of lo mein. Chinese food was expensive!

"Wow," she said. "Thanks, Dad."

"Thought we could celebrate," Harvey Sr. replied. "Good things are happening today, Christy."

Christy got up and started to serve the food. What good

things? she wondered. Her father had never made a fuss over her birthday before. What was going on now? Why was he in such a rare good mood?

She thought again of the meeting and wondered who had come to the house. Her father seemed so pleasant she thought she might ask, but bit her tongue instead. Being nosy might be the thing that made him mean again.

"There's going to be a surprise later, Christy," her father said.

Christy looked up from her soup.

"For my birthday?"

Could that be possible?

"Sort of," her father answered. "Finish your dinner."

Nothing else was said. After dinner, Christy cleaned up the table, put away the leftover food, and helped her mother to the couch. Then she went downstairs to Venetto's. She thought Mr. or Mrs. Venetto might say something about whoever it was who had visited her father.

The pizzeria was busy, so Christy went behind the counter to the soda machine. Mr. Venetto had shown her how to use it last summer, and said she could have a soda any time she wanted. At first, she'd felt shy. But the kindly Italian couple had made her feel so welcome that she didn't hesitate.

"*Bella* Christina!" Mr. Venetto called as he opened the large steel oven and checked his pies. "How are you today?"

"I'm fine," said Christy, taking a sip of orange soda. "It's my birthday."

"Is it?" the old man said. "Then that must be why—"

"Joey!" Mrs. Venetto cried. Then she said something in Italian. Christy didn't understand her, but she guessed the woman was telling her husband to be quiet. He shrugged.

"Happy Birthday," Mrs. Venetto said. "Here, you take some zeppoles. Did you have cake and candles?"

Christy hated to lie, but the old couple seemed to worry so much about her that she didn't want to tell them her father had almost forgotten her birthday. She nodded, then quickly added:

"We had Chinese food, too."

"That's nice," Mrs. Venetto said.

"Next birthday," said Mr. Venetto, "you come and have special Italian dinner, okay?"

Christy grinned. "Okay!"

When the couple turned back to their waiting customers, Christy slipped from behind the counter and went outside. Now that it was summer, she could sit on the bench outside Venetto's and daydream. But just as she reached the bench, she remembered the stranger at the ice cream parlor. What if he really was back again, and it wasn't Tiffany at all? Maybe he was hiding somewhere, right now, watching her!

The thought was so disturbing that Christy went back to the apartment. Her father had settled on the couch next to her mother, and they were watching the news. On the small set, Christy could barely make out a rocket heading to outer space.

She went into her room with the soda and pulled her drawing box out from under the bed. For a few moments, she wondered what to draw. Then her hand seemed to take on a life of its own, and crayons sketched over the blank page until a picture of a little girl in a fancy birthday dress appeared. She was surrounded by balloons, and two friends sat to either side of her. Of course, one had long black braids and one had curly blond hair. Christy wrote HAPPY BIRTHDAY TO ME in big letters across the top.

"Wish it was really like this," she said.

She crawled over to her dresser and reached up for her

new radio. Turning it on low, she tuned in some nice music. Humming along, she started to draw another picture.

The sound of the doorbell made her look up in surprise. Nobody ever came to the apartment, and now two people had been her in one day! Wondering who it could be, she turned off the radio and left her room.

"Get the door, Christy," her father said.

Christy turned on the light at the top of the dark stairwell, then went down to see who had come to visit at this late hour. When she opened the door, she looked out on Skye Street, but no one was there. Some teenagers were playing basketball in the school yard across the street. Christy wondered if they'd rung her bell before running over there, just to be mean.

She was about to close the door when a small noise made her look down. There was a box just to the side of the door, with holes punched in the top. Christy bent down to pick it up, her heart beating faster. Holes in boxes meant pets. What could it be?

When she pulled off the lid, the tiniest kitten she'd ever seen looked up at the light and mewled. Christy took the little thing and cuddled it up to her neck. The kitten nuzzled her, crying.

"Oh, you are so adorable!" she said. "You're so sweet!"

Someone jumped from behind the corner of the building and shouted:

"Surprise!"

For a split second, Christy thought of the man who had frightened her in the ice cream parlor. He had found her again, and . . .

But it was Harvey Jr.!

Christy gasped, stepping back as she held fast to the kitten.

"Where . . . where did you come from?" she demanded. "You scared me!"

Harvey grinned, hopping from one foot to the other. He had grown six inches since he'd left home, and he was more than a head taller than his sister. He wore his hair long, like the pictures Christy had seen of the Beatles. Before she could protest, he leaned forward to hug and kiss her. He'd started growing a beard, and the stubble hurt her cheek.

"Owww!" she said.

"Is this the way you welcome me home?" Harvey asked. "Even Dad was glad to see me."

Now Christy understood. "You were the person Dad was meeting today?"

"Yeah," Harvey said. "I would have stayed home to meet you, too. But when I heard it was your birthday, I had to go out and find you something. Felicity got the idea for the kitten."

"Who's Felicity?"

It was only now that Christy noticed the girl who was standing a few feet away. She smiled at Christy, then with a toss of her long blond hair came forward. Christy couldn't help noticing how fat she was around the middle. She'd seen Lucille's mother pregnant so she knew what condition Felicity was in.

"Hi," she said uncertainly.

"Hi, Christy," said Felicity. "You sure are a pretty kid. Harvey told me all about you."

Old habits die hard, and Christy shot Harvey a suspicious look. What could he have said, except bad stuff? He hated her!

"Oh, come on," Harvey said. "I'm not the brat I used to be. I'm eighteen now, Christy. All grown up. I even got myself a wife. Felicity and I are married!"

Felicity rubbed her stomach, her eyes taking on a dreamy quality.

"Peace brought us together," she said. "It was Karma."

Christy made a face.

"Peace? Karma?"

"I'm going to name our baby Peace," Felicity said, looking down at her tummy. "And Karma is ... well, Karma is the magic way things just seem to happen. The wonderful way."

Her eyes were so full of admiration when she looked at Harvey that Christy had to bite her lip to keep from making a snide remark. Yuk! What mush!

"Do you like the kitten?" Harvey asked.

"She's great," Christy said. "I ... I hope Dad will let me keep her."

"Sure he will," Harvey said. "I already told him about it. Dad's in a great mood since I came home."

Christy was about to ask why, but thought better of it. She couldn't imagine how Harvey's homecoming could make her father anything but meaner. But *something* must have happened to straighten out things between them.

"Let's go inside," she said finally.

Harvey and Felicity followed her up the stairs. Even at the young age of ten, Christy noticed that Harvey walked ahead of his wife and didn't even help her.

That figures, she thought.

"What are you going to name your kitty?" Felicity asked.

"She's sweet," Christy said. "So I'm going to call her Sweetie."

She gave the kitten a kiss and opened the apartment door.

Her father was standing there, beaming. He completely ignored Christy and her kitten as he came to put his arms around Harvey. The whole thing seemed so phony that Christy slipped away unnoticed and went to her room.

"Something's up, Sweetie," she said, lying on her bed and holding the kitten close.

The cat found purchase in her T-shirt with its tiny, sharp claws. Christy stoked it and stared up at the ceiling. She wished she could call Eda and tell her what had happened. Because in spite of all the smiles and good words, in spite of the nice gift she'd received, Christy still didn't trust Harvey Jr.

TWENTY-TWO

CHRISTY SAT ON her bed with the cat, dangling a piece of string over its head. It tried to bat at it, but was too clumsy and ended up falling head-over-paws.

"I guess you're too little right now, Sweetie," Christy said. "But you'll be big enough to have fun before you know it. We'll have lots of fun together. You can be my friend when Eda and Lucille aren't with me."

She picked up the kitten and nuzzled it.

"You can be my friend even when they are!"

A knock on the door turned her attentions from the kitten. Felicity poked her head in and asked if she could come in.

"Okay," Christy said, sitting on the edge of the bed.

Felicity looked around the room.

"This is nice," she said. "It must be nice to have a room of your own. Do you ever get lonely? I had to sleep with three sisters when I was a kid. On the commune, Harvey and I have a curtained-off area to sleep in. But no place of our own."

She seemed different from the shy girl who had smiled at Christy out on the street. Christy didn't know which question to answer first. What was a commune, anyway?

"It's okay, I guess," was all she could say.

"Are these all your own drawings?"

"Yeah."

"Groovy," said Felicity. "This one with the rainbow is so . . . deep."

Christy didn't reply, not really understanding what the other girl meant. She studied her new sister-in-law for a few moments. Felicity looked a lot like the teenagers who had walked across the town square that day wearing miniskirts. Only there was something different about Felicity, something strange in her eyes. She was looking at pictures, and sometimes at Christy, but it was as if she wasn't really *seeing* anything.

Christy watched her in fascination. She wore a loose-fitting floral dress with buttons down the front, and a pair of sandals. Necklaces of tiny flowers made from seed beads were strung from her neck, and when she tossed back her long blond hair Christy saw a pair of feather earrings.

Felicity finally at on the bed, grimacing for just a second as she settled. She rubbed her back and said:

"I hope we can be good friends, Christy. I want Peace to know his aunt Christy real good."

Christy couldn't help looking down at the girl's roundness.

"When are your gonna have the baby?"

"Two more months," Felicity reported, sounding proud. "That's why Harvey decided to come back to Aberdeen now. See, kid, we're real scared Uncle Sam is gonna call my husband to 'Nam. I don't want to raise Peace without a daddy around."

Christy couldn't imagine what kind of daddy Harvey would make. If he was anything like their own father, Peace would be better off without him.

What kind of name was Peace anyway?

"Maybe he won't go," Christy said. Much as she didn't like Harvey, she didn't want him killed thousands of miles away. Not like Willy Keel's brother.

"Well, we can't take a chance, you know?" Felicity said. "So we're here to ask your old . . . your daddy for some money. Then we're heading for Canada until this all blows over."

Christy frowned, bringing the kitten up to nuzzle her. This explained why Harvey had come home after two years. But it didn't tell her why her father was in such a good mood. If Harvey had asked him for money, why wasn't her father angry? Why hadn't he thrown Harvey out?

What was really going on?

She looked at her new sister-in-law. Felicity's bright eyes told her that she'd get nowhere asking questions now. She just had to wait and see.

"Hey, Feliss!"

Felicity jumped off the bed so quickly that Christy gasped. The pregnant young woman made a face, and Christy could tell she was hurting.

"Harvey's calling," she said, smiling. "We'll talk later."

"You don't hafta jump when he calls," Christy pointed out.

"It's just his way," Felicity said.

Another call, this time more urgent, sent Felicity out into the living room. That was the Harvey Jr. Christy remembered. Mean-spirited and impatient. Poor Felicity!

Poor baby! Christy wished they could stay here. Having a little niece or nephew would be great.

She went to her dresser to retrieve a book she'd borrowed from the library. She tried to concentrate on the story, but once in a while a word spoken too loudly would turn her attention to the people in the living room. She wondered what they were talking about in there. There was no point in joining them. She was certain she wouldn't be welcome. But as the night grew long and she became tired, it was finally necessary to cross the living room to use the bathroom.

All conversation stopped the moment her door opened. She glanced at them quickly, noting that her mother wasn't in the room. Felicity had her head on Harvey Jr.'s shoulder, and her father was sunk down into his favorite chair with a can of beer in his hand.

"I'm going to bed now," she said softly.

"Good night, Christy," Felicity said. "Sleep well. Hope the kitty doesn't keep you up."

Christy managed a tired smile for her new sister-in-law. Felicity was nice, she decided. Too nice to be married to Harvey.

"Don't take her into bed with you," Harvey said. "You might squash her."

Not wanting to set her father off, Christy resisted the urge to stick out her tongue. Only Harvey would say something so mean!

But when she went to bed, the thought of hurting Sweetie was so terrifying that she laid the kitten down on a bunched-up old sweater. It cried for her warmth, but Christy was so tired after her exciting day that she was soon unaware of the kitten, and sound asleep.

When she woke up the next morning, her father had already gone to work, and Felicity was scrambling eggs. Christy was so used to fixing breakfast herself that she stood awkwardly in the kitchen doorway for a few moments. There was a funny smell in the kitchen, and Christy wondered if it was drugs. She'd heard marijuana had a funny smell.

"Sit down, Christy," Felicity said. "I made herbal tea, if you want some."

Christy took a seat and reached for the container of milk. As she poured, she decided to find out if Harvey had drugs in the apartment.

"What's that yucky smell?" she asked in the blunt way of ten-year-olds.

"Rose hips, cloves, other stuff," Harvey said. "Felicity always likes organic shit."

"Harvey don't say words like that," Christy said.

Felicity put a plate of eggs in front of Harvey, who immediately smothered them in ketchup. Christy wrinkled her nose. She thought ketchup on eggs was gross.

"So what are you gonna do today?" Felicity asked as she handed the little girl her own eggs.

Christy reached for the salt.

"I dunno," she said. "Play with my friends."

"I'd like to meet them," Felicity said.

"You still hanging out with the Brillo head?" Harvey asked, his mouth full of eggs.

Christy thought the eggs looked bloody with all that ketchup.

"You know her name is Eda, Harvey."

She finished her eggs without looking up, then carried her plate to the sink and washed it.

"Thanks for breakfast, Felicity," she said. "I'll see you guys later."

She had Mr. Venetto retrieve her old bike from the garage. She'd grown into it, but it was so rickety the ride was very uncomfortable. Still, it was a quick way to get to Lucille's house. When she arrived, Lucille was helping her mother dress the younger children. With the newest baby girl, there were six kids now in the Brigham house. Christy wondered what it would be like to have a baby in the apartment. She couldn't wait to tell Lucille she was going to be an aunt!

"Why are you smiling like you've got a secret?" Lucille asked.

"Because I do," Christy said.

"Tell me!"

Christy shook her head. "Not until we get to Eda's house."

Lucille looked over at her mother, who was changing the baby on the other side of the nursery.

"Can I go out now, Mom?"

"Are your chores done?"

"Yes," Lucille said. "And I already went out to the field and got Dad's thermos for a refill. It's Greta's turn to take it back."

"All right, then," Mrs. Brigham said, lifting the baby. "Have fun."

Lucille lifted her three-year-old brother from her lap and set him on the floor. Then she stood up.

"We're going to ride bikes, Mom," she said.

"Fine," her mother said. "Why don't you bring your friends here for lunch later?"

Christy and Lucille gave each other big smiles, nodding. Then they ran off, giggling, to get Lucille's bike. In no time, they were at Eda's house.

"Christy has a secret!" Lucille said.

"Tell us!" Eda demanded.

They all sat down on Eda's front steps.

"I'm gonna be an aunt pretty soon," Christy blurted out, all excited.

In unison, the excited looks on her friends' faces dropped away. Now they appeared confused.

"How can you be an aunt?" Lucille asked.

"Harvey came back last night," Christy said.

"Oh, no!" Eda moaned.

"He came back with a girl," Christy went on. "Her name is Felicity. She's really nice, and she's gonna have a baby. She and Harvey got married, and they came back to visit us."

Eda pulled a flower from one of the bushes next to them and played with it for a few moments, thoughtful. Then she looked up at Christy and said:

"He's just a teenager. How can he be married?"

"I don't know," Christy said. "But he is. Felicity said they lived on a place called a commune in San Francisco. Do you know what that is?"

"It's a place where a whole lot of people live together," Eda explained.

"A commune!" Lucille echoed. "Did Harvey turn into a hippie? Does he have really long hair?"

"It's kinda long," Christy said.

Lucille came down a step so she was sitting right next to Christy.

"Does Felicity look like a hippie?" she asked. "Is she a flower child? Does she have flowers painted on her?"

Christy laughed. "No! She doesn't have flowers painted on her."

She paused.

"But she is strange," she went on. "She talks kind of funny. And you know what she's going to name her baby?"

"What?" Eda and Lucille asked together.

"Peace!" Christy revealed with a laugh. "Can you believe it?"

"Oh, that poor kid!" Eda cried.

"She's gotta be kidding," Lucille said.

The three girls couldn't imagine going through life with a name like that.

"What's Harvey like?" Eda asked finally. "I bet he's still a creep."

Now Christy didn't know what to say. Harvey had been pretty nice to her, but she hadn't felt right about that. How could she explain it?

"He ... he bought me a kitten for my birthday," she said.

"A kitten! Lucky!" Eda cried. "I wish I had a kitten, but my mother hates cats."

"I can't believe Harvey remembered your birthday," Lucille said suspiciously.

"Well, it was really Felicity's idea," Christy said uncertainly. "You can come back to my apartment later and see her."

"Felicity?" Eda asked.

"No, Sweetie!" Christy said. "My kitten. I named her Sweetie. She's the cutest, tiniest little thing."

"Oh, let's go see her now," Lucille said.

Eda got up and opened her front door. "I'll just tell my mom where I'm going."

The trio biked back to Christy's apartment, parking in the Venettos' garage. Christy wondered if Felicity and Harvey were there. She knew her friends wouldn't much want to see Harvey again, but she did want to introduce them to Felicity. When they went upstairs, however, they found Mrs. Burnett in front of the television, but no one else.

"Sweetie's in my room," Christy said, leading the way.

Eda and Lucille had been up here many times before, and so paid no attention to the dull-eyed woman sitting on the couch in her bathrobe.

They fussed and cooed over the kitten, taking turns holding her.

"Oh, can I give her some milk?" Lucille asked.

"Sure," Christy said. "There's a saucer on the floor over there. You can pour some in it."

Lucille went off and got the milk.

"Can we take her outside?" Eda asked. She wanted to say that it was too dark up here, but didn't. She never wanted to hurt Christy's feelings. At least the place didn't smell funny, like it did when Mrs. Burnett had been talking all the time. Eda knew it was because Christy worked hard to keep everything clean.

Lucille returned with the milk and poured some for Sweetie. Eda set the kitten down and the three girls watched it lap up the milk.

"That's so cute," Lucille said.

Eda repeated, "Can we take her out?"

"I don't see why not," Christy said. "I bet she'd like the fresh air."

"I know!" Lucille said. "We'll put her in a basket and go down to the lake. Maybe my mother can pack a picnic lunch for us."

Everyone thought this was a great idea, and soon they were on their way back to Lucille's house, Sweetie safely tucked away in the basket on Eda's bike. Christy had packed a little bag of food for the kitten. When Lucille told her mother their plans, Mrs. Brigham gave a weary sigh and said:

"A picnic is fine, but you can make your own lunches. I've got too much to do!"

In the kitchen, Lucille found cream cheese and home-made strawberry jam. She made sandwiches while Eda washed some apples and Christy located a half-full bag of potato chips. Then Lucille filled a thermos with lemonade.

"This is going to be fun," Eda said. "Do you have a ball and mitt?"

"We can borrow one of Stannie's," Lucille said.

Christy handed Lucille the chips to pack in a big paper bag.

"We better see what time the movie starts before we go," she suggested. "We don't want to miss it."

"The paper's on the table," Lucille said.

"I looked it up in Daddy's paper this morning," Eda said. "The show's at twelve-thirty."

"Good thing we're eating an early lunch," Lucille said. "We'll have plenty of time to get Sweetie back to Christy's."

Lucille tied the lunch bag to her bike, and Eda hung Stannie's mitt from her handlebars. Christy put the ball in her own little basket. The banks of the lake were crowded with people enjoying the summer day, and it took a few minutes to find a place to lay their blanket down. Eda fished the borrowed softball from the bag and tossed it up and down.

"Who wants to play catch?" she asked.

"You and Lucille," Christy said. "You know I can't catch a ball."

"That's 'cause you never try," Eda said. "Come on, Lucille can hold Sweetie for a while."

"Oh, okay," Christy said, rolling her eyes. "But you know I'll miss."

They moved a few yards away from each other. Eda wound up and threw the ball. Christy ducked.

"Christy, you don't have to be afraid of it!"

Lucille watched Christy's clumsy attempts at the game, then finally decided her friend needed help. She put Sweetie back in her basket and closed the latch. Then she got up and went to Christy's side.

"Here, watch," she instructed.

They became so involved that none of them saw Sweetie wiggle out of the basket and run towards the nearby woods. The kitten was so small that no one at all noticed her.

"That's enough," Christy said finally, never having actually caught the ball. "Catch is for boys, anyway."

"It is not!" Eda cried.

"Girls can do anything boys can do," Lucille insisted. "Except, I bet we do it better."

They went back to the blanket. Christy went for the basket at once, eager to hold her kitten. She let out a little scream when she opened it.

"She's gone!"

"What?" Lucille cried.

Lucille and Eda leaned forward to look into the empty basket.

"Sweetie's gone!" Christy cried.

Eda jumped to her feet and looked around.

"She's just a baby," she said. "She couldn't have gone too far. Let's look right away."

"I'll ask people about her," Lucille volunteered.

"You go look in the woods, Christy," Eda suggested. "She might be just behind one of those bushes. I'll look around here."

"Oh, what if someone stepped on her?" Christy wailed, hurrying off to the woods.

She'd never forgive herself if anything happened to Sweetie. Frantically, she looked all around herself as she ran, but there was no sign of the animal. In the woods, she moved leaves aside with her feet and pulled away roots. Sweetie didn't seem to be anywhere!

Christy tried to stop herself from crying. She'd feel stupid, in front of all these people. But a tear streamed down her cheek as she moved deeper into the woods. Could Sweetie have moved so quickly, so fast?

She looked back at the open field. She could see Lucille talking to some older girls, waving her arms. The girls started looking around themselves. Christy was glad they had help. She studied her own surroundings, making little noises she hoped would attract the animal.

"Sweetie! Ssss! Sssss!"

A cry made her look up. Suddenly, something dropped on her head from above. Christy screamed, batting at her head in fear. Then she saw Sweetie lying on the ground. With a cry of joy, she bent down to pick up the kitten.

It was then she saw the drop of blood on the corner of Sweetie's tiny mouth.

"Oh, no!" she cried. "Oh, no!"

She began to scream.

Something else dropped from the branches above, with a loud thump. Before Christy could turn, she was struck across the back of the head. She fell into darkness, still clutching the lifeless kitten.

TWENTY-THREE

▼

LUCILLE HAD FOUND ten more people to join in the search, and word kept spreading. When Willy Keel heard it was Christy Burnett whose kitten was missing, he sneered:

"Only Crazy Christy would be dumb enough to bring a cat to a park!"

"Shut up, Willy," Eda warned. "Unless you want me to flatten your nose."

Willy made an obscene gesture at her, but turned away. He knew Eda could carry out her threat. Who cared about a dumb cat anyway? All cats did was make him sneeze. He'd come to the park to look for pieces of bark in the woods. He was going to cover a can with them and make a neat present for his father's birthday.

He ran to the trees, hoping his father would like the present. Ever since Greg died, his father didn't smile. There was only Willy and his Dad now. Mom had died soon after Willy was born. So Willy had to do things to make his father happy again.

Willy spotted an old tree and went to investigate. As he got down on his knees to retrieve bits of bark, he began to sneeze profusely. Wiping his eyes, he looked around to find out what was bothering him.

He saw Christy's kitten lying in a pile of leaves. It looked kind of funny to him. Wiping his nose, he stood up and went closer.

"Hey!" he cried when he saw the blood.

A movement deeper in the woods made him look up, and he saw someone duck behind a tree.

"Who's that?" he demanded.

No one answered. Willy went to the edge of the woods and called out:

"Hey, Brillo head!"

Eda ignored him.

"Eee-*daaa!*"

He gestured broadly, beckoning her to the woods. Eda ran after him. Lucille followed quickly.

"I found the cat," Willy said, sneezing again. "It's ... well, I think it's dead."

"No!" Lucille cried, pushing by him. "Where's Christy?"

"Willy Keel, if you're lying to us ...." Eda began to threaten.

"Eda, I don't see Christy!"

Willy pointed into the woods.

"The cat's by that first fallen tree," he said. "And I saw someone running away up ahead. Maybe it was Christy."

The girls ran into the woods, calling to their friend. Neither one wanted to see the dead kitten.

"Christy! *Christy!*"

Through the fog in her mind, Christy heard her friends' voices. She tried to get up, but her head hurt so badly she thought she might get sick instead. She crawled out from behind a tree.

"There she is!" Eda cried, running.

Lucille caught up with her, and the two girls knelt on either side of their friend. Christy's head was bleeding.

"Gee, you're hurt!" Lucille cried. "You're bleeding."

Christy touched her head gingerly.

"Something fell out of the tree," Christy said. "It hit me on the head."

She looked around with sudden panic.

"Sweetie! Something bad happened to Sweetie!"

Lucille moved away a bit, looking worriedly at Eda. What would they tell Christy?

"I think the cat's dead," Willy announced bluntly.

Eda got up and walked slowly towards him, her fists doubled.

"That isn't true," she said. "You just go away."

"I will!" Willy said. "Who cares about a dumb cat getting killed anyway? It isn't like a person!"

Eda thought she saw tears in Willy's eyes as he turned to run away. But her concerns at the moment were with Christy. She joined Lucille in helping her friend up.

"Willy's right," Christy said dully. "Sweetie's dead. She must have climbed a tree and fallen."

"Maybe she'll be okay," Eda said. "Maybe we can take her to a vet!"

"Yeah, we don't know if she's really dead," Lucille offered hopefully. "Let's go see, Christy. We'll take her to Dr. Simson!"

Christy walked slowly, holding her head. It throbbed terribly. What could have hit her? A branch?

"I held her," she said. "I know she's dead. And I think I know who did it, too! That man really *is* back again! He killed my new kitty!"

Reluctantly, Eda and Lucille followed their friend to the

site where Sweetie lay. Eda let out a cry of anger and disgust to see the innocent little animal lying like that. Lucille
began to cry. It was so horrible she had to turn away.

Then she saw the paper stuck on the branch of another
tree.

"Eda, Christy, look!"

She retrieved the paper, and all three read it together.
THIS TIME, I'LL GET YOU.

Christy covered her face and began to wail.

"He really is back! He is!"

"Christy, we're gonna tell my father," Eda said. "He'll
tell Officer Mike, and they'll catch that guy for sure!"

"No!" Christy cried. "*No!* No one will believe me, and
my father will say I'm making up stories and he'll beat me
up!"

"Christy, we have this note!" Lucille cried. "We have
Sweetie!"

"*No!*" Christy screamed.

She ran off, weaving through people who turned to gaze
in wonder at her. Ignoring Eda's and Lucille's yells, she
raced off on her bike. She wasn't headed in any particular
direction, only moving blindly away.

Away from the terror that had come back again.

Eda and Lucille returned to the Crispin house, where
they found Eda's father working in his study. Dean smiled
to see his daughter, but the smile quickly faded when he
saw the red blotches on Lucille's face.

"You've been crying," he said. "What's wrong, honey?"

"Mr. Crispin, something terrible happened!" Lucille
said.

Eda told her father about the kitten and the note. But
she held back on Christy's belief the man who had killed
Darren Gammel was back in town again. That would be
telling secrets, and she'd promised.

Immediately, Dean Crispin was on the phone to his friend Mike Hewlett. He explained the situation, and Mike soon showed up at the house. The handsome young cop did his best to ease the girls' fears.

"Are you sure the cat didn't just fall from the tree?" he asked. "She was only a baby. It might have been easy to get up, but not down."

"We found the note," Eda pointed out. "And someone hit Christy on the head!"

"She thought it was a branch," Lucille offered, "but Willy Keel saw someone running away."

Dean Crispin's eyebrows went up.

"Willy Keel?" he asked. He looked at the police officer. "Isn't that kid a troublemaker?"

"Well, he's had problems," Mike Hewlett said, never wanting to bad-mouth a child. "But I doubt he'd ever kill a cat or hit Christy."

"But could he have written the note after he found the cat?" Dean asked. "Just to be mean?"

Eda's eyes thinned. "He'd do a thing like that."

Lucille nodded in agreement.

The cop stood up.

"I think we'd better talk to Christy. Do you girls want to come along? It might make her feel more relaxed."

"Sure," Eda said. "Except I don't think she'll talk to you."

"Christy's afraid," Lucille said.

"Don't worry," the policeman said. "I won't scare her."

The two girls followed him out the office door. Dean Crispin stood in the doorway and said:

"Good luck. If there's anything really going on, I want to know. We can have it in tonight's edition, and warn the townspeople there may be trouble brewing."

Outside, Eda realized to her excitement that they were going to ride in a police car. She and Lucille climbed into the front seat, and immediately Eda started asking questions.

"Is that the mike?" she asked. "Can you call people on that? How do you turn on the siren?"

Officer Mike laughed and told her all about the car as they drove into town. He parked on Central Street, near the corner. The policeman had heard what Harvey Burnett was like, but had never actually dealt with him. He wished there were laws to deal with jerks like that, but unless someone actually made an accusation against him, nothing could be done to help Christy. He knew from talking with Dean and Rita Crispin that no one had ever *seen* the man hit his daughter. Only her bruises stood as evidence.

Now Mike knew he had to talk to Burnett. But he also hoped the man wasn't at home. In his short career as a cop, Mike hadn't yet faced someone with a hair-trigger temper. He didn't want to now, not with three little girls nearby.

He rang the apartment doorbell.

"Maybe Christy isn't home," Eda suggested.

But, to her surprise, a big-eyed Christy opened the door. She stared up at the officer for a moment, then looked questioningly at her friends.

"Hi, Christy," the policeman said gently. "May we come in?"

"I guess so," Christy said, backing up.

They followed her up the stairs.

"Is your father home?"

"He's at work," Christy said. "No one is here."

When he entered the apartment, Mike Hewlett looked around. The place was simply finished, and neat. But it was too dark, and the air of gloom in the place was instantly noticeable. He saw Mrs. Burnett on the couch, staring at a soap opera.

"Hello, Mrs. Burnett," he said politely.

Christy didn't look at her mother.

"She doesn't talk," she said. "She's sick."

Officer Mike nodded. "Well, we need to talk. Your friends tell me you had a terrifying experience this afternoon."

Christy turned abruptly to face Eda and Lucille.

"Nothing happened!" she cried.

"Christy, someone killed Sweetie," Eda said. "That isn't nothing!"

"And someone wrote a mean note to you," Lucille said.

Officer Mike looked back at the kitchen.

"Can we sit down, honey?" he asked. "Maybe in there?"

Christy thought about it a moment, then nodded slowly. In the kitchen, the patrolman tried to get her side of the story. She spoke in a near monotone, as if in shock. Poor kid, the man thought. There was no one here to help her. He wished he could take her away.

"Do you think you know who wrote that note?" he asked finally.

Christy nodded vigorously. Lucille sat up straight, looking hopefully at Eda. Maybe Christy was finally going to tell someone about the man who had been following her!

"Harvey did it!" Christy blurted.

"What?" Eda asked in surprise.

"He told me he did it to be mean," Christy said. "He . . . he got mad because he thinks Felicity likes me better!"

"Who's Felicity?" Officer Mike asked.

"Harvey's wife," Lucille said. "He got married."

"They're gonna have a baby," Eda put in.

Mike Hewlett whistled. "How old is he? Eighteen?"

Eda ignored the question. "Christy," she said. "Why would Harvey kill the cat he bought for you?"

"He did!" Christy screamed, tears springing into her

eyes. "He told me he did! *Why won't you leave me alone?*"

She ran to her room, slamming the door. Officer Mike sighed and got up.

"I'm going to have a talk with Harvey," he said. "That j.d. has caused enough trouble."

"What's a j.d.?" Lucille asked as they left the apartment. The girls knew there was no point in trying to talk to Christy. They would question their friend later, when she'd calmed down.

"A juvenile delinquent," Mike said, his expression grim. "Come on, kids. I'll drive you back to Eda's house."

The girls remained silent during the drive, each deep in thought. Lucille hoped Christy would be okay. Eda was thinking it wasn't a j.d. that had frightened Christy.

It was something far, far worse than that.

TWENTY-FOUR

▼

CHRIS WANDER SAT ON Lucille's couch with her head in her hands, very much like the young girl she'd once been. Their conversation had taken them through two pots of coffee, and Eda had nearly filled a writing pad. She leaned back with a deep sigh.

"What time is it?" she asked.

Lucille looked up at the mantel clock.

"Twelve-fifteen," she said. "I think we've done enough talking for one night."

Chris gave her a weary smile.

"Thanks," she said. "I'm really not up to explaining why I acted like that. At least not now. It's just ꞏ uch to think about."

"We need to talk to Harvey Jr.," Eda said. "Do you know where he lives now, Chris?"

Chris shook her head.

"I remember something else," she said. "When Officer

Mike came back to the apartment to talk to Harvey, Felicity suddenly collapsed, screaming. I think she'd gone into early labor. They rushed her off to the hospital. That's the last I ever saw of either of them. I don't think Mike ever did talk to Harvey."

"So we aren't sure it really *was* Harvey," Eda said thoughtfully.

Chris didn't answer, but tried to busy herself by standing up and gathering coffee cups.

"Forget those," Lucille said. "Let's just go to bed."

They walked upstairs together.

"I don't think I can sleep," Chris said.

"You want to take one of your pills?"

Chris stopped in the hallway. She thought a moment, then shook her head.

"No," she said. "I have to clear my head. My kids are out there somewhere, and I'm not going to find them if I'm drugged out."

Eda agreed with her, and said good-night when she reached her bedroom. They'd spent a long time talking, reminiscing, but tomorrow morning she wanted to take action. She planned to tell Mike her suspicions about Harvey, perhaps see if he could find out where Christy's brother was now living. Harvey knew something, she was sure, and she was determined to find out.

The smell of coffee and home-baked muffins lured Eda out of bed early the next morning. She found her two friends already at the table.

"I wish I could eat like this in New York," Eda said, buttering a huge, fluffy muffin. "The local bakery just doesn't make 'em like this."

Chris managed a weary smile.

"You told us once that Tim Becker's quite a cook."

"He never made me breakfast," Eda said. "But his cheesecake's incredible."

Lucille freshened everyone's coffee cups. She wanted to ask Eda if she missed Tim, but it didn't seem right. How could she bring up Eda's partner when Chris would never see her husband again? She decided the question was best left for private conversation. As if to stress the point, tears welled in Chris's eyes as she unrolled the morning paper. Photographs of Josh and Vicki were prominent under the headline: LITTLE VICTIMS: THE SEARCH FOR THE WANDER CHILDREN.

"I never liked that school picture of Josh," she said softly. "He's so much cuter."

Lucille took the paper from her.

"I'm glad to see them on the front page," Eda said. "The more people who are aware of them, the better chance of finding them."

"Like they found Teddy and Adrian Gammel?" Chris asked, bitterness in her tone.

"Don't forget that was thirty years ago," Eda said. "Forensics has come a long way. We have computers now, fax machines, and more. I'm sure Mike will send pictures of the kids all over the country. There's a much better chance of finding Josh and Vicki than there was for the Gammel boys."

Lucille squeezed her friend's hand.

"They *will* find them," she insisted.

Chris's shoulders heaved greatly in a sign of frustration.

"It's been days," she said. "I feel so helpless! I hate sitting around doing nothing while my babies could be in terrible danger. What if they're hurt or sick?"

She recalled hearing Josh cough the other night.

"I think Josh was coming down with a cold," she said. "And I'm not there to help him!"

Lucille stood up and left the room. A moment later, she

returned with a pad of paper and some drawing pencils she'd found in Jerry's room. She lay them on the table.

"There is one thing you can do right now," she said. "Do you think you can draw a picture of the man who was following you years ago?"

Chris stared at her friend, momentarily shocked by the request.

"Why?" she demanded. "I don't want to remember that horrible man!"

But Eda understood at once.

"I think it's a great idea," she said. "Chris, it will give the police something to work with. Right now, they have no real suspects."

Chris gave it a moment's thought, then nodded. It would be difficult to conjure up an image of that hideous face, but she would do anything to help get her children back.

Eda excused herself and went upstairs to get dressed. She planned to drive to the police station for a talk with Mike. As she was pulling her belt through the loops of her slacks, Lucille entered the room.

"I wish there was something *I* could do," she said.

"Giving Chris a safe haven is a lot," Eda told her.

Lucille shook her head.

"I was thinking about my mystery books last night, and trying to recall the different ways my detectives worked. But this is real life, and I don't know where to begin."

"Maybe there is something you can do," Eda said. "When we were talking last night, we recalled wondering why the Gammel house was still there after seven years. Now it's been thirty years, and the place is *still* there. Someone must be paying property tax on it, or it would have gone into foreclosure. That's a nice piece of land someone could have developed years ago. Can you find out who owns the house?"

"That sounds easy enough," Lucille said. "I bet it's Irene Gammel."

"Then we'll have another clue," Eda said. "We'll find out where she's living. And when we find her, you can bet I've got a lot of questions to ask her."

TWENTY-FIVE

▼

JOSH CAME TO in the middle of the night, but without windows he had no way of knowing the time. Vicki was curled up in a ball next to him on the floor, her back pressed tight against his side. She had her thumb in her mouth. She'd taken a blanket from one of the cots to cover them both.

Slowly, Josh sat up. His head hurt badly, and when he touched it his fingertips came back dotted with blood. It took him a few moments to remember he had fallen from the ladder.

The ladder—their only hope of getting out of this place.

He shook his sister.

"Vicki, wake up," he said.

Vicki stirred, then sat up.

"You're not dead," she mumbled, her eyes still closed.

"Of course not," Josh said. "But my head hurts enough to kill me."

Vicki opened her eyes and brought up a chubby hand to scratch her head. Her red hair was a mess of tangles.

"You banged your head real bad," she said. Her voice was tiny, distant. "I tried and tried to wake you up, but you wouldn't. I thought it killed you."

"Well, I'm alive, all right," Josh said.

He tried to stand up, but the room started spinning. It was a lot like the Tilt-and-Flip ride he'd gone on the previous summer. He put his head in his hands. For a few moments, he did and said nothing, just letting his brain steady itself. As soon as he could speak again, he said:

"Vicki, check those shelves. Mom always gives me medicine when I get hurt. See if there's a bottle of Tylenol or something."

Still half asleep, the little girl stood up and padded over to the shelves of food. The cans and boxes seemed to swim in front of her. Although she couldn't read she'd recognize the box right away. But there was none to be found.

"Sorry, Josh," she said. "Does your head hurt real bad?"

"Is the Pope Catholic?" Josh asked irritably.

"I dunno," Vicki drawled. Why was Josh talking about the Pope anyway?

She reached up and pulled down a box of cereal.

"I'm hungry," she said. "Is it time for breakfast yet?"

Josh shrugged. He wished he had the watch his mom's friend Lucille had given him on his last birthday. But it was lying on his father's tool bench at home, waiting for Dad to have a chance to fix it.

He closed his eyes again. An image of someone running through the house filled his mind, so frightening that he opened his eyes to stop it.

"I'll fix that," he said, walking to the table where Vicki stood with the cereal box. "We'll need milk. See that can over there? It's powdered milk. You have to mix it with water."

Vicki got the can down while Josh filled a metal pitcher from the water tank. He prepared the milk and filled the two bowls with cereal. Vicki took a bite, then turned and spat it on the floor.

"Ugh!" she cried. "It's disgusting."

"I did the best I could," Josh insisted.

Vicki pushed the cereal bowl away.

"I don't want any disgusting milk in my cereal," she whined. "I want the nice cereal Mommy makes. When are we going home, Josh?"

"In two minutes," Josh said sarcastically. "Like I'm supposed to know."

Vicki stood up and ran to stand under the ladder. She looked up towards the dim light of the ceiling, at the trap-door.

"Hey, you! Open the door! I want outta here!"

Josh rubbed his head.

"Oww, Vicki," he complained. "Your big mouth is giving me a worse headache."

Vicki swung around, tears streaming down her cheeks.

"But I wanna go home," she cried. "I want my mommy and daddy. How come they don't come to get us?"

Josh opened his mouth to make another smart-aleck remark. But he stopped, realizing he was just as scared and bewildered as his little sister. He wouldn't cry in front of her. No way, José! It wasn't her fault they were stuck down here. He guessed he didn't have to be such a creep.

"Vicki, they must be looking for us real hard," he said softly. "I'll bet the whole police department in Aberdeen is looking for us. Maybe the whole police department in Montana. Maybe the FBI!"

Vicki stopped crying and stared at her brother in wonder.

"Really?"

"Yeah," Josh said, pushing away his own cereal bowl. It did taste disgusting.

"I'll bet our pictures are in the newspaper," he said. "Maybe even on television. Don't worry, Vicki. Someone is looking for us, for sure."

Vicki thought about this for a few minutes, staring down at the floor. Finally, she looked up and said:

"Josh, how can they find us? How can they see us?"

"What do you mean?"

"They can't see us," Vicki insisted. "There's no windows in this place."

Not far away, the stranger slept fitfully on a cold wooden floor. He tossed and turned as his dream self thrashed about on a bed.

A man was looking down at him.

"You'll get over it, kid. We'll be a big, happy family."

"Where's my daddy?"

"I found just the playmate for you. She's a girl, but there's something special about her. I'm going to get her for you."

"Where's Mommy?"

"She's with Adrian. You want a toy, kid? A ball? I've got a nice, round one. A special one with eyes, and a nose, and teeth . . ."

The man snapped himself awake, but an image of a severed head floated in the darkness for a millisecond before it vanished. He looked up at the small window over his head and saw that it was still night. His nightmare was instantly forgotten as he wondered what his little prisoners were doing.

He found his shoes tumbled against a box, pulled them on, and went downstairs. He was standing over the trapdoor within a few moments. When he unlocked it and pulled it open, he was surprised to see bright light below. A little face turned up to him. It was the girl. This time was better than thirty years ago. This time, there was a boy *and* a girl. Pretty kid, too. Not like Christy, but pretty in her own way. He was proud of his achievement.

"Hey!" Vicki shouted.

"Hey, yourself," the man shouted back. He knew the surrounding darkness would keep him invisible. "Why are you awake?"

Now the boy came into view. The man noticed blood on his head, but it didn't faze him. There had been plenty of blood, that other time, and everyone had come out okay.

"Who can sleep in this dump?" Josh demanded. "When are you gonna let us out of here?"

The stranger didn't answer. He stared into the unnatural light of the room below, studying the two kids. He wondered how he'd be able to get them out of Aberdeen, get them to their new home where life would begin again. Christy would surely come with him if he had the two kids. That's what had happened before, too.

He could see part of the table from up here, and noticed cereal floating in a bowl of bluish-white milk.

"Did you eat?" he asked.

"I wouldn't eat this crap if you paid me," Josh snapped.

"Did you open anything?" the man shouted. He had to know that. He had to know exactly what they'd taken, so he could replace it.

"Some powdered milk and some cereal," Josh told him, begrudgingly. "What's the big deal?"

"That's all you opened?"

"I guess so."

"Be certain!" the man yelled, his anger rising. Didn't they understand how important it was to keep things just right? He'd replaced the food they'd eaten earlier, while they slept soundly. Now he'd have to replace new food, and it wasn't even four in the morning.

"I'm certain, for cryin' out loud!" Josh said.

Vicki started to cry. The man stared down at her, and his heart began to race. Something hot moved through his blood, pooling in his joints. He remembered someone crying and afraid, so long ago ...

No! He didn't want to think about that! He slammed the door shut and locked it, ignoring the protests of the children.

He had to find an all-night store. He had to replace that food. Having things out of order for too long would ruin all his plans.

There had to be fifteen of everything. Fifteen. It was a very important number.

TWENTY-SIX

▼

When Eda went to the police station to tell Mike her misgivings about Harvey Burnett, the sheriff gave her his full attention. He listened with interest as she related the memories that had come back to Chris, Lucille and herself.

"I have to agree that Harvey looks suspect," Mike said, "although tormenting his sister would hardly make him a murderer."

"Living with that mother and father might," Eda said. "But I'm not suggesting that Harvey came back and killed his brother-in-law. I'm just saying he seemed to show up at strange times. He always was a troublemaker. I'd be curious to know where he is nowadays."

Mike jotted a note.

"That shouldn't be too hard," he said. "I'll have someone get on it. If he's connected in any way at all to this, I want to know."

There was a knock at the door, and a young policeman came in. He handed a file folder to the sheriff.

"Another sighting was reported this morning, sir," he said.

Eda glanced from the young cop to the sheriff.

"Sighting?"

"A few people claim to have seen the Wander children," Mike said. "But you understand that we take these reports with caution. Some are from people who are genuinely concerned, but even in Aberdeen we have our share of mean-spirited bastards."

"That's right, sir," the young cop agreed. "Until we see those kids for ourselves, there's no proof."

Mike signed a form and handed the folder back to the younger man. He left the office, and the sheriff resumed his conversation with Eda.

"This kind of thing happens when the story is all over the news," he said. "In a way, publicity helps our cause. Having people aware of the Wander children may help find them. On the other hand, too many interested parties muck up the investigation."

"It's hard to sort between the useful and useless information," Eda agreed. She stood up. "Speaking of information, you said I could have access to the old files."

Mike got up, too, and led her out of the office.

"We've perused them carefully," he said. "But it never hurts to have someone fresh take a look. Just the way you women are trying to make a connection between the events of your childhoods and what happened now, I've been trying to connect the few facts we have in this case with the old information. So far, I've come up with nothing helpful."

Eda followed him through a small reception area filled with four desks, each occupied by a very busy person. When she was a child, there had been only one desk with a secretary who manned a little black rotary dial telephone. Now there were computers, fax machines and the like. She hoped every one of them was dedicated to helping Chris find her children.

They entered a large room. Tall windows striped the back wall, letting sunlight pour over a long conference table. There were several large bulletin boards hung on the walls, covered with scraps of paper, newspaper clippings, and announcements. Two file cabinets flanked the door. Mike went to one and pulled it open.

"Here's the old file," he said. "You can sit here and have a look."

The fact that only two file cabinets were needed to keep track of crime in Aberdeen reminded Eda just what a quiet little town it was. Or at least, seemed to be. She wondered if Harvey Burnett Jr. was in there somewhere. And what about Chris's father? Was there any file on him, on the way he had abused his family? She doubted it. People just hadn't discussed those things back then.

And one thing leads to another. Maybe if they had talked, Chris's family would be alive.

"Eda?"

She blinked, realizing her mind was wandering.

"Can you get me some coffee?" she asked.

"I'll have someone bring it in," Mike said.

He left her alone. Eda sat down with her back to the window and opened the thick folder. Her first sight was a grainy black-and-white photograph of Darren Gammel's remains. Although his back was to the camera, and his arm thrown up over the empty space that should have been his head, the picture was gory enough to send a shiver down Eda's spine.

She wondered what it had been like for Chris, finding Brian.

With a sigh, she put the old photographs aside and started to read.

Before Eda and Lucille had left that morning, Lucille had repeatedly asked if Chris minded being alone for a few hours. Chris had insisted she was okay, but now she wasn't so sure. She had been sitting at one of the desks in the twins' bedroom, a blank pad of paper before her. As if she were a child again, she felt terribly afraid of being alone. How long had her friends been gone?

It was difficult to draw the man's face. Every oval she sketched for his head, every shadow she rubbed for his beard, sent such chills through her that she crumpled up each effort. She buried her head in her hands and sighed deeply. Except for a faint hum from the refrigerator, the house was still. She could hear an occasional car pass on the road below, and once a dog started barking.

It was the kind of stagnant silence that filled a movie a split second before the murderer jumped out.

Chris tried to hum a Randy Travis tune, just to hear something. She was getting nowhere. She had to stop being so afraid!

You're not seven now, Chris. You aren't a helpless little girl.

But her kids *were* helpless, and she had to do what she could to save them.

Hoping to clear her head, she went to the window and looked outside. A yellow police banner had been stretched between the trees that flanked her front yard. There were still a few people there. A policewoman sat guard in her squad car. Two television trucks were parked along the curb. One was marked CABLE 75, Tiffany's station. Chris tried to find the woman in the crowd, but surprisingly she wasn't there.

Even more surprising was the second TV van, which

had come from North Dakota. Had her story spread that far so quickly? Good. The more people who knew about Josh and Vicki, the better.

She turned abruptly and headed back to the desk. With determination, she picked up a pencil and started to sketch again. People had seen her children's pictures. Now they would see a likeness of the man who probably kidnapped them, of the murderer who had taken Brian away from her.

Her hand flew over the page, the picture forming in a matter of seconds. When she finished, she recognized the devil eyes she'd been so afraid of as a child. Was this really him? Was he back again?

She stared at the hateful portrait for a long time, her teeth set. She wanted to tear it up, stomp on it, set it on fire.

No, she wanted to do those things to the man she had drawn.

How could he have done that to her, to her family? Why was he so full of hatred? Her only involvement in that long-ago crime was the blood Irene Gammel had smeared on her blouse. So why had he stalked her?

Who *was* he?

Suddenly she pushed the paper away as if it had become searingly hot. There was something familiar about the face she'd drawn. It wasn't just that she'd seen him years before. It was more than that.

"It's impossible," she told herself with a wide back-and-forth sweep of her head. "It can't be! Just coincidence!"

But in her heart, she was disgusted to realize it might not be coincidence at all.

She had seen eyes like that in another face. Softer, kinder eyes, but with the same shape. And probably the same color. Chris *knew* where she'd seen those eyes, but she didn't want to believe it.

While Chris drew, and remembered, and Eda studied the old criminal files, Lucille visited the town hall. Many years ago, it had been part of the building that also housed the library. But Aberdeen's growing population of school-children had prompted the town fathers to separate the two. Now the library was a huge glass-and-stone building situated on the opposite side of town. The town hall remained in the old brick building, although it had expanded to fill the space left behind when all the books were moved out. The records room was now in the place where the children's library had been. Instead of Dr. Seuss and Nancy Drew, the room held birth certificates, death certificates, blank marriage licenses waiting to be filled in, and tax records.

Lucille hadn't been here since her divorce was finalized, and she was both surprised and pleased to see her old schoolmate, Stephanie, working behind the counter. Stephanie had gained a good fifty pounds since graduation, and there was a lot of gray in her hair. But she still had the same nice smile and friendly manner that had lured Lucille into her brief stint as a sorority girl.

"Lucille Danton!" Stephanie cried. She frowned. "Oh, I'm sorry. It's back to Brigham again, isn't it? I was so sorry to hear about you and Sydney."

"Thanks," Lucille said.

Stephanie looked straight into her eyes.

"How are you doing now?"

"I'm fine," Lucille insisted. She didn't want to talk about her divorce. "I need a favor, Stephanie. I need to find someone's tax records."

"Income tax?"

"Property tax," Lucille corrected. "I was wondering if you could tell me who's been paying the property tax on the old Gammel place."

Suddenly, Stephanie's eyes widened with understanding.

"Oh, this has something to do with the Wander family, doesn't it?" she asked. "I couldn't believe it when I heard Tiffany Simmons on the news. It sends chills through me."

"We're all concerned," Lucille said. "Can you get me that information?"

"Well, property tax is usually paid along with a mortgage," Stephanie said. "You might do better at Western National Bank."

"I'd be surprised if there was still a mortgage on that house," Lucille said a little shortly. Maybe it wasn't such a good idea to have an old friend here after all. She wanted work done, not conversation. "Will you please look it up?"

"All right," Stephanie said, a slight hint of hurt in her voice. "Wait here. Taxes paid by individuals rather than banks come in twice a year. The last pay period was May thirty-first. It shouldn't take too long to find it."

Lucille sat down on one of five ladder-back wooden chairs that lined the wall. She picked up a pamphlet titled "How to Apply for a Passport" and flipped through it without really seeing the words. Then she simply watched the clock for the next five minutes.

Stephanie came back with a thick book. She was shaking her head as she plunked the volume down onto the counter.

"You didn't have to come here to find out who's paying the tax on that property," she said sharply.

Lucille stood opposite her, perplexed. "What do you mean?"

"You could just ask Chris," Stephanie said.

Lucille looked at her with bewilderment. Stephanie turned the book in her direction and pointed halfway down the page. Lucille read the words. Then she read them again, because she was certain she'd made a mistake.

But it was there, all right, in black ink. The name of the person who had paid the tax.

Brian Wander.

TWENTY-SEVEN

▼

A SHORT TIME after their captor left, Josh and Vicki heard
the overhead door squealing open again. They ran to stand
beneath it, shouting as loudly as they could. The door
clanked back on its hinge, and Vicki pointed.

"Josh, the sky!" she cried. "Look at the sky!"

Josh could see a circle of gray dotted with dark spots.
There were storm clouds up there. But why was there sky?
Weren't they in a basement?

"Hey!" he shouted.

This time, their captor didn't answer. Josh moved
around to get a glimpse of him, but only his hand and
forearm came into sudden view. A paper sack, attached to
a string, came slowly down into the room.

"Untie it!" the man yelled.

"Come do it yourself!" Josh snapped.

"Yeah!" Vicki agreed with false bravado. She didn't
want that man down here for even one second.

"Untie it or I'll chop off your stupid little head!"

Josh froze. The now-familiar, if vague, image of his father running through the house filled his mind again. And something more. Something bright and metallic flashing through the air . . .

"Are you doing it?"

Vicki gave Josh a shove, and the boy snapped out of his stupor. He quickly untied the knot.

"Y-yes," he croaked.

"What?"

Josh's voice, congested with fear, hadn't carried.

"Yes!"

The rope snapped up, and while the children yelled the door slammed shut. They heard a lock being thrown across it.

"You *creep*!" Vicki yelled. Then she began to cough. "Josh, I don't think I can yell anymore. My throat hurts a whole lot."

Josh put the bag on the table and started to open it.

"Don't!" Vicki begged. "It's something scary, I know it!"

"No, it isn't," Josh said. He pulled out a can of powdered milk and box of cereal. "How come he's giving us more food? We didn't even finish what we opened."

How come he said he'd cut off my head?

Josh shook the thought away. He took the food to the shelves, and for the first time noticed how neat the rows were. He counted the cans of powdered milk. Fifteen. There were fifteen juice cans next to them. Fifteen chicken noodle soups, fifteen tomato soups, fifteen cans of ham.

"Fifteen," Josh said out loud. "There's exactly fifteen of everything."

Vicki reached around him for the bag of chips they'd opened the day before. She started munching on them. Josh counted the bags of chips. Not counting the opened one, there were fifteen of those, too. For some crazy reason, this guy wanted fifteen unopened cans or boxes or bags of everything down here.

An unexpected pain flashed through his head. He touched the bruise over his eye, the one he'd gotten when his skull met the floor last night. For a second, he thought he'd throw up. He held fast to the metal rack.

"Josh, are you okay?" Vicki's voice was full of worry.

"I think I'm gonna puke," Josh groaned.

Vicki made a face and backed away. She didn't want any yucky stuff on her.

Josh drew in a long breath and straightened his head. The pain was gone. Something new replaced it, an idea that spread a smug grin across his face.

"You know what, Vicki?" he asked. "I think I know a real good way to get back at this scuzz."

Eda and Lucille had planned to meet each other in two hours. Eda didn't have enough time to read all the reports from the Gammel investigation, but she was beginning to agree with Mike's idea that there was no way to make a direct connection to the Wander murder and kidnappings. She'd read through all the autopsy reports, and now she was reading Darren's a second time. She had a feeling she had missed something, but she just couldn't be sure what it was.

Although she tried to read the faded, blurry pica type with a clinical eye, Eda could only see Brian's name, instead of Darren's. The coroner had stated the lines of the cut through Darren's throat were clean enough to suggest a quick blow. There were numerous other blows, but the autopsy concluded he'd probably died quickly. Had Brian's death been quick?

Again, she had the feeling she had missed something. She went back to the second report. This man's name was

Basil Horton, a bachelor who seemed to have no family. Eda thought it was sad that no one talked much about that crime. She guessed the Gammel murder was stressed because it involved the disappearance of children. But maybe, within Basil Horton's report, she would find the thing that was eluding her.

The young deputy who had been in Mike's office earlier knocked gently and opened the door.

"Are you expecting a Lucille Brigham?" he asked.

"Sure," Eda said with surprise. Had two hours passed already?

Lucille came into the room, her face ashen. The dark hair she usually kept so neat had come loose from her braid in tendrils, as if she'd run all the way here and the wind had had its way with her. She took a deep breath and dropped into the chair next to Eda's.

"What happened to you?" Eda said. "You're all flushed!"

"Got here as fast as I could," Lucille said. "Eda, this is worse than we imagined."

"How could it be worse?" Eda asked.

"You'll never believe who's been paying the tax on the Gammel land," Lucille said. She didn't wait for her friend to prompt her. "Brian Wander!"

Eda opened her mouth to reply, but nothing came out.

"You heard me right," Lucille said. "*Brian* was paying the property tax. He's been doing so for about eleven years."

"About as long as he was married to Chris," Eda said. "Somehow, Brian Wander is connected to all this, and not just as a victim."

Lucille's eyes thinned suspiciously.

"You know, he was always going on business trips," she said. "I wonder about that."

Eda closed the file. She wanted to check the other autopsy report again, but decided this was more important.

"Maybe you should go to the department store," Eda suggested. "Find out just what he did there and where he went on those trips. Somehow, I wouldn't be surprised if Washington came up."

"Washington?"

"That's where Irene Gammel moved to after it all happened," Eda reminded her.

Eda stood and picked up the file she'd been studying. She returned it to its place in the cabinet, then the women left the room together. Eda knocked at Mike's door, but there was no answer, so she left a message with the desk sergeant that she'd be back. Outside the blue sky had gone overcast with the promise of rain. The day was thick, muggy.

She wondered how Josh and Vicki were doing. Were they cool enough, and dry?

"I could drop you off at the store," Lucille suggested, "then head home. Someone needs to be with Chris."

Lucille unlocked the doors of her car. She'd never felt it necessary to lock them before, but in the last two days it had become automatic. Once inside, Eda answered her.

"We don't have time," she said. "I want to visit the Gammel house. If Brian was in charge of it, maybe he left a clue there. It shouldn't take too much time. When I'm finished, I'll swing around and pick you up. *Then* we'll go home."

The women drove in silence until they reached the shopping mall where Brian had worked until a few days before. Lucille got out and Eda moved into the driver's seat. As she pushed open one of eight glass doors leading into the mall, Lucille confronted a large poster bearing photographs of Joshua and Victoria Wander. The word MISSING was printed in block letters over their heads.

Brenley's Department Store was at the end of a long corridor of shops. Inside, Lucille passed cosmetic counters, ignoring a beautiful young woman who wanted to spritz her with a new perfume. She cut through an accessories department, where the cutesy name FUN-TO-SEE FANTASY arced over the entrance in gaudy neon letters. Her long legs gave her a stride that was purposeful, businesslike. Just beyond the jewelry island, she stepped onto the escalator. It took her to the third-floor offices.

A few inquiries led her to the store manager. A young man, perhaps in his twenties, he introduced himself as Jamie McEntire and shook Lucille's hand. She pulled up the chair he indicated.

"Brian Wander?" he said curiously. "But I've already spoken to the police."

"I just need some questions answered," Lucille said. "I'm a friend of his wife, and there are things she needs to know."

McEntire closed the ledger he had been studying.

"I can't tell you much," he said. "I don't remember him very well. I've only been on this job six months and haven't gotten to know everyone who works here."

He made himself taller in his seat, as if daring Lucille to challenge him. Lucille had the feeling he was holding back, perhaps because he was resentful of this interference in his workday.

"If you don't mind my saying this," she commented, "you seem young to be in such a high position. That tells me you have brains. Someone as smart as that should be able to remember a man who made that kind of money."

"I wouldn't call twenty-five thousand dollars a year a lot of money," Jamie said.

Lucille stared at him for a few seconds.

"There must be some mistake," she insisted. Chris had told her Brian made a lot more than that.

"No, that's what he earned. After all, he only worked part-time," the young man said.

"Part-time?" Lucille echoed. This was getting harder to understand by the moment. "Brian worked a forty-hour week. More, when you consider the business trips he took so often."

"I think someone's been lying to you, Ms. Brigham," McEntire said. "No *part-time* employee of Brenley's makes business trips. I don't know where he went, but it had nothing to do with us."

Lucille sank back in her chair, staring into space as she tried to sort things out. Brian had lied to Chris, but why? Where had those bogus trips taken him, if not on business?

She wondered if he had been having an affair.

She turned her eyes back to McEntire, who was watching her patiently as he drank from a big cup that said: WORLD'S BEST DADDY. Brian had been one of those, too, Lucille thought.

"Could I see Brian's résumé?" she asked.

"Sure," the manager said. "I happen to have it right here, since I haven't had the chance to refile it."

He pushed aside some papers until he unearthed the paper.

"Good report on the guy," he said, handing the sheet across the desk. "A model employee, always on time. His résumé doesn't say much."

Lucille took the paper and read it carefully. She was hoping it would list his place of birth, but that information wasn't here. She did, however, find the name of the first company that had employed him when he came to Aberdeen.

"Thanks for your time, Mr. McEntire," she said as she stood up.

"Hope I was of help," he replied.

Too much help, Lucille thought as she walked from the store. *I'm not sure I want to know all this.*

She glanced at her watch and realized Eda wouldn't be picking her up for a while. Though she wished she could talk to Brian's first employer in person, she didn't want to wait that long. She opened her purse, collected as much change from the bottom as she could, and headed for the nearest pay phone. Information gave her the number of Mooney's Fine Furniture.

The line rang twenty times before someone finally answered, in a voice that was out of breath. Lucille introduced herself and explained what she needed.

"Brian Wander?" the man on the other end said. "What a shame about that guy, huh? Nice fella. He worked here for about two years."

"Could you possibly tell me where he came from?" Lucille asked.

"I think he used to drive a UPS truck," the man said.

"No, I mean where did he live before he came to Aberdeen," Lucille explained.

There was a hum on the wire.

"I don't recall exactly," the man said. "Wait here."

Lucille heard the buzzing sounds of saws and the pounding of hammers in the background. A recording cut in and asked for "twenty-five more cents, please." Lucille dropped a quarter into the slot. Finally, the man came back.

"Got his papers right here," he said. "It took a few minutes to look it up. Been a few years, you know. Yep, yep, here it is."

"It says where he used to live?"

"Sure does," came the reply. "Brian Wander came all the way from Washington."

Lucille nearly dropped the phone.

"What?" she gasped.

"Washington," the man repeated. "Don't know what brought him all the way to Montana just to make furniture. Guess he must—"

Lucille cut him off, thanked him, and hung up the phone. Her stomach was starting to feel sour. Her surroundings became a blur of lights and colors as she walked slowly to the mall entrance.

She'd thought they'd gotten wiser over the years. She'd thought Chris had earned her happy place in life after the nightmarish childhood she'd lived. No one had been happier than Lucille the day Chris announced she was getting married. Brian was such a nice guy. Eda had even called him Chris's "knight in shining armor."

It made Lucille sick to think that knight had more than a few chinks in his armor, chinks cut there by the swing of an ax.

TWENTY-EIGHT

▼

"WHAT'RE WE GONNA do, Josh?" Vicki asked, watching her brother build a pyramid of cans.

"We're gonna fight back," Josh said. "This is our arsenal."

"Our what?"

"Never mind," Josh said. "Just pretend we're going to have a snowball fight. Only instead of snowballs, we're gonna use cans. See the way I'm putting them here? You make a pile like that across the room."

Vicki began working eagerly on her own pile. Josh picked up a can of corn, hefted it a few times, and pretended to throw it.

"We can get him coming down the ladder," Josh said.

"But he *never* comes down," Vicki protested. "And I can't throw all the way up that high."

"He'll come down, all right," Josh said, his plan almost

completely worked out. "He'll come down, and we'll get him. Then we'll get out of here."

"Really?" Vicki asked hopefully.

Josh didn't answer. There was nothing he could say to reassure his sister. His plan seemed to be a good one, but he was praying it would work.

It had been years since he was last here, but the man felt he knew every sound of the house. The wood had a certain creak when it swelled and contracted, the glass window-panes rattled a particular way in the wind. He knew every scratch of a tree branch, every skittle of a rat's feet. Hidden in the shadows of the attic, he slept peacefully through the day, until the sound of something *wrong*, a noise that didn't belong, jerked him into instant wakefulness. He sat up and cocked his head to one side to hear a car's engine being shut off. He ran down to the hall and looked out the front window. Someone was parked out there!

Terrified someone would discover his secret, he raced into the bathroom. There he found the small bottle of chloroform he'd used to knock out the children a few nights ago. He hadn't planned to use it again until it was time to leave, but he couldn't take a chance of the children's being discovered. He soaked a rag and hurried out the back door of the house.

The yard had been neglected for years, and the grass had grown as tall as his shoulders. He pushed through it like an old-time hunter. But he wasn't the hunter now. He was the tiger, every muscle tense, every nerve tuned to the world around him. He heard squirrels chipping, rabbits bounding through the thick growth. Above these, from far away, the sound of a car door slamming. The enemy was approaching the house. . . .

It was beastly hot out here, stagnant with the pledge of a storm. Mosquitoes nipped at him, drinking blood undis-

turbed. He didn't notice them. Every few seconds, he
glanced back over his shoulder, terrified the unwelcome
one would come around the side of the house. But the yard
remained empty.

The round metal door that led to the children had ab-
sorbed enough heat to make it difficult to touch. Burning
pain seared through his hand as he grabbed the latch, but
he didn't care. Pain was something he'd overcome years
ago. Nothing could hurt him physically. But they could
hurt his mind. That person in front of the house could send
him back to the hospital again.

He had to keep that from happening. He had to make
sure things happened exactly as they had before. Only this
time around, they'd all get it right.

The door fell back with a clang. The man called down
into the hole.

"Sit on the floor and cover your eyes!"

"Hey, you up there!" the boy called. "We ate ten cans
of soup!"

"Sit on the floor and cover your eyes!"

"Yeah, we were real hungry!" said the girl.

"Sit on the floor and cover your eyes!"

"Come down and make us!" the boy cried. "Or we'll
eat even more food. And we won't tell you how much!"

The man stopped to consider this. He hadn't thought
two small children could consume that much food. It
hadn't been that way long ago. *Those* children had been
polite, had taken only what they really needed.

Ten cans! A sense of panic began to rise in him. Things
were not in perfect order now. Did he dare shop in the
daytime? That would mean leaving the kids alone . . .

No!

"You're trying to trick me!" he called.

"Come down and see!" Josh yelled back.

The man tucked the rag into his pocket and unlatched

the top of the ladder. The other piece sped to the floor below, landing with a crash that rattled the metal shelves. He started to climb down. Vicki gasped, recognizing him at once.

"Oh, Josh!" Vicki cried. "It's the bad man from the fireworks!"

"Let him have it, Vicki!" Josh commanded.

In seconds, cans were sailing at the man from every direction. He roared at the children to stop, crunching up his shoulders and throwing his arm over his head. The barrage impeded his descent, and one can hit him so squarely on the head that it nearly knocked him from the ladder.

"Let us out, scuzz!" Josh cried.

"Yeah, let us out, scuzz!" Vicki echoed. She turned around to get another can, but her eyes rounded in dismay. "Oh, I'm all out of snowballs!"

The man stopped midway down the ladder and glared at her. Vicki was standing clear across the floor from her brother. Josh seemed to understand what was in the insane green eyes that studied his sister, for he flashed across the room. But the man was quicker, and with a jump and two strides he had Vicki up in his arms. The little girl screamed and kicked. The man shoved the cloth on her face, thinking how much easier it had been the other night, when she was already asleep.

"Leave her alone!" Josh shouted.

The man let Vicki's limp form drop to the ground. He lunged for the boy, but Josh dodged him as easily as he'd pull away from another kid playing football. Josh raced for the ladder and was actually halfway up it, yelling, when the stranger grabbed his ankles.

"You're all boy, aren't you?" he asked. "The way boys are supposed to be. That's what my mother would say. She never said it to me, though. She said I was a wimp. She . . . Quit kicking!"

"Lemme go! *Help!* Help me!"

Josh thought his voice might carry clear up to the darkening clouds.

He felt a sharp pull, and then was falling back. His headache came back in a flash as gravity seemed to tug at his brain before the rest of him. He screamed, but never hit the cement floor. The man kept his arms wrapped firmly around the boy and took the fall for him.

But not before shoving the poisonous cloth over his mouth and nose.

Eda stood on the front porch of the Gammel house; much the way she had when she was a teenager. Things were different now, though. There were no longer boards on the windows, and the porch had been swept clean. The building was a sharp contrast to the dilapidated condition of the surrounding acreage. Grass and weeds grew shoulder high as far as she could see. Numerous animals had made their homes here. There were wasps' nests clumped in the old trees; gopher holes dotted the ground. A few squirrels raced boldly across the porch.

Eda wondered who had maintained the place. Brian? That would explain the terrible shape of the yard. He could hide his work near the house, but yardwork was too much to go unnoticed.

She wished she knew what Lucille had learned.

Though some work had obviously been done on the house, Eda was tempted to walk off the porch and look for a broken window. But she took a chance on the front door. To her surprise, the knob turned easily and the door swung open. It didn't creak, though. Eda thought a door on such a creepy old house ought to scream in protest when it opened. She glanced at the hinges, suspecting someone had oiled them recently.

She stood in the foyer and looked from the living room

to the dining room. The place was swept and dusted. It was downtrodden, to be sure, but clean. She moved down the hall to the kitchen.

The window over the sink had been left open, perhaps by a careless investigator. Eda could hear thunder, promising a downpour.

And something more.

She moved closer to the sink and curled both hands around its rusty ledge. Turning her ear towards the open window, she listened again.

Someone was shouting!

"Josh?" she said out loud. Her voice resounded through the empty room.

God, it had sounded just like him.

She hurried to the kitchen door and tried to open it, but unlike the front door, it was locked. She rushed back to the main entrance, nearly crashing through it in her desperation. She had to get to those kids!

Outside, she raced to the backyard, shouting their names.

"Josh! Vicki!"

Only thunder answered her, a loud clap that immediately preceded the rain. Eda stood, shouting, oblivious to the fact that she was getting soaked. No voices answered her.

She pushed through the tall grass, squinting as rain pelted her face, until she reached the barn. The weeds were so tall here that it was difficult to open the door. She grabbed the broken handle with both hands and braced her feet in the mud. With a jerk, the door fought the thick weeds and won.

The barn was big, airy, and empty. There was no hay here, no equipment to hide two children. With a sigh, Eda put her hands over her face. It had only been wishful thinking that she'd heard Josh's voice. Of course the children weren't here. Mike would have found them days ago. . . .

She turned to walk back to the house. As she did so, she spotted something small and white on the ground. Eda bent to pick it up. It was a card from one of Aberdeen's two real estate companies. Eda tucked it in her pocket. Now there was someone else she could talk to. But first she had to have a look around the old house.

Although it was July, the house was so cold that her wet clothes made her shiver. Her hair was plastered against her head like a yellow swim cap, water dripping over her face. She wiped it away with her hand and proceeded to check the basement. Finding it completely empty, she went to the second floor.

Like the main floor, it had been recently cleaned. There were no cobwebs, no dust. She wondered how Brian had managed to remove all the furniture without being spotted. To her modern cop's eyes, it seemed strange that the house hadn't been sealed, kept the way it had been found when Darren Gammel was murdered. Eda reminded herself that that had been thirty years ago, and the forensic technology used today hadn't been available. If the crime had happened today, there would have been much more to do than dust for fingerprints and take photographs. The investigators would have taken minute samples of dust, hair and blood. The house would have been sealed off against the chance a jury might want to come take a look at the crime scene.

She wondered how long Chris's house would remain sealed.

Eda came to the master bedroom, and here she finally found evidence of that long-ago crime. Though it had faded, there was no mistaking the spray of bloodstains on the wallpaper. In places the wallpaper was coming loose, drooping nearly to the floor. Obviously, Brian hadn't worked on this after moving the furniture out.

Finally, she headed for the attic. Slowly, she ascended the wooden staircase. Halfway up, she could see the entire attic. There were a few boxes that merited investigation, but nothing else. Eda opened each one, finding old clothes and a few toys. It was much warmer up here than in the rest of the house, and the combination of rain and heat made the air unpleasantly musty. She was about to leave when she spotted a pad of paper in the corner. She pounced on it, careful to touch only one corner. Bringing it over to the window, she held it up to the light and read:

> *Houghton Psychiatric Hospital*
> *Spokane, Washington*
> *Dr. Marion Niles*

Eda couldn't help a triumphal cry. Tucking the evidence into her purse, she hurried downstairs. How had Mike's people missed this? Perhaps it hadn't been here a few days ago. She'd bring it right to him, as soon as she picked up Lucille.

As she got into her car, she was momentarily discouraged as she remembered the voice she'd heard earlier. Wishing she could have found the children, she drove away from the old house.

She never noticed the blue BMW parked across the street. If she'd looked in her rearview mirror, she would have seen Tiffany Simmons climbing out. The reporter had been trailing Lucille's car ever since it left that morning. Unable to follow Eda into the police station, she had continued on to the town hall, where she had followed Lucille to the records office.

Tiffany kept reminding herself that she had tried to ask for information in a professional, civilized way. But Eda turned out to be the same little bitch she'd been years earlier. Tiffany couldn't imagine why a grown woman would try to start a fight. She knew Eda hated her, but she didn't care. She was after a story, and if it took clandestine efforts to get it, the end justified the means. She could hardly believe her luck when she walked into the records office and spoke with her old sorority sister. Stephanie was full of gossip, pondering what Brian Wander had to do with the old Gammel house. Tiffany meant to find out for herself, so she'd driven to the site of that ancient crime. She'd almost run into Eda, slowing up at just the last minute when she saw the woman getting out of her car. While Eda poked around inside the dark house, Tiffany waited impatiently, tapping her perfectly manicured nails on the leather seat beside her. She wore sunglasses despite the rainy weather, but she knew it wasn't much of a disguise. Eda would know at once who she was. But Eda never looked her way. She came out of the house some time later, a serious expression darkening her face. From the unkempt look of her, Tiffany guessed Eda had been caught in the sudden downpour.

As soon as Eda left, Tiffany hurried to do some investigating of her own. She was as surprised as Eda had been to see how clean the place was.

"It's still horrible," she said out loud. Her voice bounced around the empty living room. "What would Christy's husband want with a place like this?"

Like Eda, she was disappointed to see the house was not only clean but completely devoid of clues. Even so, the second floor was still exciting. Tiffany caught her breath when she entered what seemed to be the master bedroom—the site of the first murder. The bloodstains had faded years ago, but there was no mistaking them.

"Have to figure out a way to get a camera crew up

here," she whispered. "Too bad there's a rule about trespass—"

She was turning around as she spoke, but her last words changed into a scream that bounced crazily around the big, empty room.

A man was standing in the doorway. A man with an unshaven face, wild green eyes, and a snarl.

"You don't belong here! This is Christy's room!"

Christy? What the h—

Tiffany's thoughts were sliced off as the man lunged at her with a rag soaked in chloroform. She collapsed to the floor.

For a few moments, he stared down at her. There was something familiar about this woman, and it didn't make him feel good. He wished he could think what it was.

He'd used up all his sleeping drug. Filing away a mental note to buy some more when he had the chance, he bent down and gathered Tiffany into his arms.

Throwing the unconscious woman over his shoulder in a fireman's hold, he lumbered down two flights of stairs to the basement. Outside, the sky had grown even darker. The earlier downpour had been a mere herald of the storm to come, and now the only light came from flashes of lightning. He dumped Tiffany on the floor, then looked around for something to use to tie her up. He saw some moldy old books wrapped in twine, and used his pocket-knife to free them. He took the twine and bound it tightly around Tiffany's small wrists. Then he wrapped a piece of the cloth he'd used to knock her out around her eyes. He kept her mouth free, though. He wanted to talk to her.

There had been only a small amount of the drug on the cloth, and he guessed she would be waking up shortly, unlike the children, whom he knew were still sound asleep. Sure enough, Tiffany soon began to struggle. The blindfold was unnecessary in the near-total darkness, but when she let out a scream he wished he'd gagged her. At least until he could trust her.

He clamped a big hand over her mouth and nose.

"Shut up!" he said. "I could hurt you, right now. So just shut up!"

Tiffany whimpered beneath his hand.

"I want to talk to you," he said. "I just want to talk. I wanted to talk to Brian, too, but he gave me a fight. That's why I had to kill him. You don't want me to kill you, do you?"

With a small cry, Tiffany shook her head.

"Can I pull my hand away?"

She nodded.

Pull it away, you bastard. The first chance I get, I'm going to kill you. Because, God help me, I know you're going to kill me if you get the chance.

Tiffany thought about the gun she had in her purse, the purse that was probably on the bedroom floor upstairs. If she could only loosen the ties around her wrists . . .

Slowly, he moved his hand away. Tiffany had to bite her tongue to keep from yelling. She had a strong feeling no one would hear her anyway. Not just because of the noisy storm outside but because this seemed to be the most deserted street in all of Montana. For a split second, she wished she hadn't followed Eda here. But she pushed that thought away with annoyance. Investigating was her job!

"Now, let me talk," the man said. "What's your name?"

"Tiffany Simmons," she said, her voice strong.

"Tiffany Simmons, Tiffany Simmons . . ."

He seemed to know it.

"I'm an anchor on the news," she offered.

"Don't watch TV," the man said. "But I know you. Oh, yes! I remember now! You're the little girl who thought she was so much better than everyone else. So much better than Christy. But you can't be better than Christy, because she's an angel. And angels are perfect."

That little sleaze was no angel, believe me.

Somehow, she knew it was dangerous to say that out loud.

"You were mean to Christy, weren't you?"

"I don't recall—"

"Of course you recall," the man said. "You were the one who spread rumors about her being crazy."

"No!" Tiffany insisted.

"I have to do something to make all that right," the shadow said. His voice was strangely, dangerously calm. "You'll have to pay for hurting an angel."

"I never did!" Tiffany cried. Suddenly, her false bravado fell away from her like a flimsy outer shell. Her stomach twisted into knots, and she tried to back-crawl into the darker shadows. But he reached out and grabbed her.

"I've seen men get their heads chopped off," he said. "But I've never seen it happen to a woman. What do you suppose that's like?"

Tiffany said nothing.

"Do you suppose they bleed differently? Hmmm, why don't we find out?"

He spoke in strange, lilting tones now. Tiffany was crazily reminded of a schoolteacher giving a lesson.

"Please, don't—"

"Be quiet!" the man snapped. She heard him moving around in the darkness. "I have an ax hidden outside. You be patient, okay? It'll take me a few minutes to get it."

Tiffany listened as he thunked up the stairs. When the back door slammed shut, she began to scream, and scream, and scream.

Even though she knew there was nobody to hear her.

TWENTY-NINE

▼

Aᴄᴛᴇʀ sʜᴇ ᴘɪᴄᴋᴇᴅ up Lucille at the mall, Eda headed back to the police station. She wanted to give the pad she'd found to Mike, and to hear if he'd learned anything new in the past few hours.

The rain was pouring down in sheets now, slowing driving considerably. It gave the women time to fill each other in. Eda was fascinated to hear how Brian had lied about his job, but she couldn't figure out why he'd do such a thing.

At the police station, the women dashed through the rain to get inside, where they found Mike talking on the phone. He waved at Eda and Lucille, who pulled up chairs to wait for him. Finally, he hung up.

"I was on the phone with the sheriff in Belfield, Washington," he said. "That's the last known address for Irene Gammel. I had a theory that the killer might have made contact with her again, the way he's come after Chris Wander."

"Is the sheriff going to find her?" Lucille asked.

Mike shook his head, his expression weary. Eda knew at once what that look meant—she'd seen it enough when working on cases in New York. He'd hit a wall.

"Irene Gammel is dead," he said. "She's been dead since last August."

Lucille was thoughtful for a moment. Then her head snapped up, her eyes wide.

"That's about the time Brian started going on those business trips!" she said, excited.

Mike looked from one woman to the other, curious. Now Eda handed him the pad of paper she'd found.

"I found this in the attic," she said. "You did check the old Gammel house, didn't you?"

"Hell yes," Mike said. "We didn't find a thing, which tells me someone's been there since. We noticed the place had been fixed up a bit."

"Brian Wander," Eda said. "I think he must have cleaned up."

Mike leaned back in his chair and folded his arms across his chest. He looked like a man settling in to hear a good story.

"Fill me in," he said. "It sounds like you two have come up with some interesting information about our victim."

Eda and Lucille took turns telling what they knew about Brian. This information, they all agreed, only led to more questions. But it established a connection between the victim and the perpetrator.

"You know, Eda," Mike said when they'd finished, "I wish I could lure you back from New York. We could use someone like you around here."

"I love Aberdeen," Eda said, "but my home is in Queens now."

She thought about Tim Becker and felt a slight twinge. How much quicker would things go if she had her partner's professional input along with her own? She was reminded of the autopsies she'd read. Once again, the feeling she'd missed something important washed over her. Tim had a good eye for detail. Would he have seen what she had missed?

"I think you should check the autopsies again," she said. "I don't know why, but I feel there's something there we've overlooked."

Mike nodded. "I'll have someone do that."

Lucille tapped Eda gently on the arm.

"I think we'd better be going home," she said. "We've left poor Chris alone long enough."

After a quick good-bye, the women headed back to Lucille's. When they walked into the house, they found Chris sitting on the living room couch, the drawing she had made held tightly in white-knuckled fists. Behind her, the picture window offered a view of the rain, slowing down now but still virtually obliterating the yellow-roped scene across the street.

Chris's red eyes were an ugly contrast to the sick gray of her skin. The last few hours had obviously been a terrible ordeal for her, and Lucille felt a twinge of guilt about leaving her alone for so long. She hurried to sit by her friend. Eda settled into the armchair, leaning forward with her hands clasped together. A look of concern crossed her face as she said:

"Chris, what's wrong?"

Chris stared at the picture and said in a dull voice:

"I know these eyes. Do you know who this is?"

Both women studied the picture for a few moments before shaking their heads. Lucille shuddered, and Eda said:

"Whoever he is, he's evil-looking. Is that the guy who was following you?"

"Yes."

"But it was so long ago," Lucille protested. "And you never saw him up close."

"Oh, yes I did," Chris said. "He was right outside my bedroom window once. But look at his eyes. Don't you know his eyes? He has Brian's eyes."

"Oh, Chris, that's impossible!" Lucille cried. Even with all the evidence she'd uncovered, she still wanted to believe Brian was an innocent victim. Hearing Chris's words shattered her last hopes.

And Chris was right. The eyes *did* look like Brian's. In fact, they also looked like Vicki's eyes, only bigger and with an added dimension of meanness.

"Is it?" Eda wondered aloud. "It would explain a lot of things. Brian could be related to the killer."

Chris turned to her, blinking a few times.

"What?" Her voice was a soft choke.

"Chris, we have a lot to tell you," Eda said. "The very start is that Brian came from Washington. Did he ever tell you that?"

"So?" Chris asked, feigning unconcern. She knew the significance of Eda's statement. "Lots of people come from Washington."

"Do you remember?" Lucille said gently. She felt as if pushing Chris too far would be dangerous. "Irene Gammel moved there after the—"

"Brian was an orphan," Chris cut in. She was trying to break any connection between her late husband and that crazy woman. "He was brought up in a foster home, and he was very happy. It's just coincidence."

Like the eyes in that portrait are coincidence?

As if in reply to her unspoken question, a soft chiming

filled the room from an anniversary clock that sat on an end table.

"It's time for dinner," Lucille said.

"I'm not hungry," Chris insisted.

Lucille stood up. "Maybe not, but you should eat. If you're not careful, you'll get sick. I'll just put together soup and a salad."

She left Eda and Chris in the living room. Chris reached for her sketch and turned it over so she wouldn't have to look at it.

"What else did you find out about Brian?" she asked. There was a slight hint of annoyance in her voice, as if she resented her friends checking up on her husband.

Eda sighed. "Chris, maybe we should all have dinner first—"

"Tell me," Chris said abruptly. "I want to know what else you learned! Those business trips—something was happening then, wasn't it? Brian was in some kind of trouble, and I have a right to know what it was."

"We didn't find out that much," Eda said apologetically. She wished she hadn't found out anything at all.

"Then tell me what you do know," Chris said. She saw Eda hesitate and leaned forward. "Eda, my husband is *dead*. My children are missing. I don't want them to be missing for thirty years! Please!"

"All right," Eda said with a quick nod. She'd wanted to protect Chris, but she saw now that keeping the truth from her was only hurting her. "But we'll talk over dinner. Let's go into the kitchen."

There, over a simple meal of tossed salad and vegetable soup, Eda and Lucille told their friend all they'd learned that day.

THIRTY

THE GAG THAT blocked Tiffany Simmons's mouth was wet with tears of fear and outrage. Her captor had removed the blindfold, using the cloth to stop her from screaming. It hadn't really been necessary. She'd figured out quickly enough that no one could hear her.

The man had propped Tiffany up against a cold metal pole, then taken a seat across the floor from her, with his back to the ancient oil burner. He sat cross-legged with the ax resting across his lap. Tiffany wasn't certain if he was staring at her, but imagined that his eyes could bore right through the dark shadows. She glared back, for what it was worth, all the while using the cover of darkness to try to undo the binds around her wrists.

About twenty minutes after leaving, he'd come back, carrying the ax, and after propping her up he'd moved to his current position. He'd been sitting there, without moving, long enough for the sun to begin setting, bringing even more darkness into the damp, cold cellar. Somehow, his silence unnerved Tiffany more than the ax he held.

When he spoke, it was so sudden that she gave a small cry of surprise, muffled by the gag.

"I was thinking," he said. "You said you were a news reporter, huh? I don't watch TV, I said. But you want to hear a good story? You want to know what Brian did to me?"

Tiffany's answer was a quiet whimper.

"See, it's all his fault he got killed," the man said. "If he'd left my things to me, I wouldn'ta hurt him. Like I'd never hurt Adrian. He got away from *her*, when I had to stay. She put him out for adoption, you know. That's 'cause *he* said he couldn't take care of two of us. I was worth something 'cause I was big 'nuf to work, but Adrian, he was just four and too little. *He* told my mother that Adrian had to go or he'd go to the police and tell everyone what they'd done. You know what they did, don't you?"

Tiffany didn't move or make a sound. The reporter in her was absorbing every word, fascination overcoming fright. What the hell was this crazy man talking about?

"They killed my father, they did," the man said.

Tiffany straightened up.

"Chopped off his head," the man went on, "cut him up in fifteen different places. Fifteen is my favorite number, you know. I gave it to Brian fifteen times. Maybe it was number five or six that did his head in. I dunno. I wasn't so good at it as she was."

She?

"They never knew I was hiding in the closet," the man went on. His voice was distant, as cold as the surrounding darkness. "Mother went screaming out of the room, and the man ran after her. Then he was carrying my little brother under one arm. I said: "How come Adrian ain't moving?" But then he hit me hard and shoved something up against my face. Same thing I did to you, I guess. Same stuff. Knocked me right out."

Tiffany struggled against her bonds. Her head was spinning, full of disbelief. Was this who she thought it might be? He'd mentioned an Adrian. Hadn't one of the missing Gammel boys been named Adrian? And what did Brian Wander have to do with them?

"I woke up in a dark room," the man went on. "Adrian was screaming and crying, but I just looked around and made sure of where we were. I knew the place right away. It was a fallout shelter my father had built when the Cubans was causin' so much trouble. I wasn't afraid, then. There was plenty of food and water, and even a place to go to the bathroom. So I told Adrian to just shut up and let me think. But Adrian wouldn't, so I hit him and knocked him right out. Stupid little kid."

Is this Teddy Gammel? Tiffany wished she wasn't gagged. She was full of questions.

"I had a plan," the man said. "I thought everything would be okay now that Daddy was gone. They took care of him okay. He wouldn't be beatin' up on me and Mother and Adrian anymore, no sir. So things were gonna be okay. I figured Mother and *him* was just hiding us until it was safe to escape. That man said he had a farm in Washington. He was a truck driver. He helped Mother with a flat tire once, she said, and that was how they met. Mother said he was going to rescue us from Daddy. Daddy said he was a Commie, and he was gonna kill us all if Daddy didn't stop him. He built that fallout shelter to protect us, he said. He made us practice 'duck and cover' to protect us, he said. Only the trouble was Daddy said I couldn't get it right, he said I was lazy and he would *show me how* it was done."

The more he rambled, the closer he moved to Tiffany,

and she could barely make out his face. His eyes seemed
to glow with malevolence. She shrank against the pole,
working harder at the twine, wishing to God she had her
gun.

His hands came up. Tiffany saw now that he no longer
held the ax.

"Daddy said he'd show me how to cover myself," the
man went on. There was a choke in his voice, which had
risen half an octave. "He threw the blanket over me . . ."

His hands lurched forward. Tiffany started, but realized
he wasn't aiming for her. He was throwing an imaginary
blanket, she guessed.

"And he held it there and held it and held it and I
couldn't breathe and I wanted him dead and then *he* came
and they had a fight and Daddy called him a Commie and
he said 'I got a Purple Heart fighting in Korea what did
you ever do for America?' And then Daddy came with the
ax and there was a big fight and Mother, and Mother, and
Mother . . ."

He stopped then, his words choked off by big, racking
sobs. As if Tiffany wasn't there at all, he threw himself
around the cellar like a caged animal, crying with the
memory of a horrible, long-ago day.

And Tiffany realized her hands were free.

When the shuffle of her captor's footsteps seemed far-
thest from the stairs, Tiffany bolted for the steps and raced
up to the door. He was after her in a flash.

"No!"

She felt him grab at her legs, but she was fast. She
didn't hesitate or look back. She crashed through the cellar
door and raced upstairs to find her purse, the purse with
the gun in it.

She heard him lumbering after her, and screamed as he
touched her arm. There was fire where he touched her, and

she realized to her horror that he hadn't *grabbed* her after all. He'd hit her with the ax!

"Stop it!" she screamed, stumbling up the next staircase.

"You weren't supposed to be here," the man said. "You're Christy's enemy! I have to stop you!"

Tiffany reached the top of the stairs. She turned back just in time to see the ax swing forward again. It connected with her foot, skinning her shoe but hardly injuring her.

"You *bastard*!"

There were too many doors in this hall. Which one led to the master bedroom?

The ax swung into the wall, fragmenting old sheetrock.

Tiffany pushed open the first door—the bathroom. She rolled against the wall, looking back as Teddy gained on her, stumbling towards the next door.

With a scream, she finally fell into the master bedroom. Her purse was in the middle of the floor.

She'd slammed shut the door to give herself a moment's extra time, and hurried to find her gun. But Teddy—if it was Teddy Gammel—was just a few seconds behind her, and the door crashed open just as she was pulling the weapon out.

With a war-cry-like yelp, Teddy flew at her. The ax came down as Tiffany rolled onto her back, the blade connecting with her shin. She screamed, pulled the trigger, and nothing happened.

The safety! The friggin' safety!

"*Get away from me!*"

She fumbled until the gun was operable, then fired again. She missed, but Teddy's aim was better. He swung the ax at Tiffany's hand, cutting through three of her fingers, knocking the gun across the room.

Tiffany screamed in horror and pain, staring at the mess

of her hand. She scrambled to her feet and tried to get to the gun. But Teddy blocked her path.

He stood with the ax gripped in both hands, his green eyes wild, his shoulders heaving. The gun was a few feet behind him.

"You bastard . . ." Tiffany whimpered. Fire seemed to engulf her arm, her shin, her hand.

Teddy stared at her, a look of dismay coming over his face.

"Nobody ever got away before," he said. "You threw me off count. How many was that? How many? It has to be fifteen total. How many times did I hit you?"

"Fuck you," Tiffany growled.

"How many times did I hit you?" he said, louder, harshly.

He took a step at her, the ax held high. Tiffany screamed. She closed her eyes, waiting for the next blow to fall.

But nothing happened. Slowly, Tiffany opened her eyes and saw that Teddy had moved to the window and was looking out.

"There's a car coming up the block," he said quietly. "I have to finish now. Hold still."

Tiffany glared at him.

He glared back.

Then the ax went up again. Tiffany screamed as the weapon came flying towards her head.

Everything went black.

THIRTY-ONE

▼

CHRIS WAS SURPRISED when she looked down and saw both her soup bowl and salad plate were empty. She'd been listening so carefully to Eda and Lucille that she hadn't been aware of eating at all. Now she regretted even this small meal. The unexpected news about Brian was enough to turn her stomach.

"Are you going to be all right?" Lucille asked, concern vivid on her face.

"I don't know," Chris said softly. "This is so much to take in at once."

Lucille looked across the table at Eda.

"We shouldn't have told her," she said. "We should have held back a little."

"No!" Chris said. "I want to know everything. Somehow, the fact that Brian was taking care of that house is a clue to finding my children. I only wish . . ."

She felt heat behind her eyes and blinked a few times. She didn't want to start crying again.

"I only wish Brian was here to explain things," she said. "I can't believe he was deceiving me on purpose. I know he had a logical reason for all this!"

"Of course," Lucille said.

"Brian really did love you," Eda insisted. "That was no lie."

Chris thought for a few minutes.

"Before he—" she began, then had to stop to collect herself. "The other day he told me he had his eyes on a house with five bedrooms. We talked about needing room for another baby."

"Oh, Chris!"

Lucille's voice was full of sympathy.

"I told him I thought we had a perfect family," Chris said. She wiped the tears away. "But maybe we would have had a third. I don't know. Brian really loved kids."

The phone rang, and Eda volunteered to answer it. Lucille said she'd take care of the supper dishes, pushing Chris gently back into her chair when she tried to help. When they heard Eda greet the sheriff, they both turned full attention to her.

"Really?" Eda was saying. "Blueriver Jail? That's just two hours from here, isn't it?"

Chris and Lucille exchanged glances. Who was in jail?

"Did he kill his wife?"

"Who?" Lucille whispered.

Eda sighed. "I'm glad. From what Chris said, the woman was a flake, but sweet. So what are you going to do now?"

A few minutes later, Eda hung up, shaking her head.

"Well, this doesn't surprise me," he said. "They found your brother, Chris. He's in the jail up in Blueriver, doing time for manslaughter."

Chris brought her fingers to her lips. An image of Felicity, dreamy-eyed as she toyed with her love beads, came to mind.

"You . . . you asked if he killed his wife?"

"Felicity left him twenty years ago," Eda said. "Nobody knows where she went, and she took their daughter with her."

Chris sighed, feeling a loss for the niece she would never meet. Still, she was glad Felicity had had the sense to get away from Harvey. She could only imagine what kind of life he'd provided for her.

"Good for Felicity," Lucille said.

"The creep probably beat on her," Eda said. "Anyway, Mike wants to ask some questions. He thinks Harvey may know something about the man who was following you years ago."

Chris shook her head.

"Harvey didn't believe in him," she said. "He thought I was crazy, just like everyone else." She stood up, and wasn't surprised to find that her knees felt weak. She yawned and rubbed her eyes.

"I'm overwhelmed," she said. "I'm going to lie down for a while."

"That's a good idea," Lucille said. "A rest might clear your head and help you sort things out."

"Do you want one of your sleeping pills?" Eda asked.

Chris waved a hand at her.

"No," she said. "I don't need it. I just want a nap, a couple of hours' rest. Any more and I'll never sleep tonight." Her legs were so heavy she could hardly face the stairs. Still, somehow, she got to her room. Her mind was a cauldron of thoughts and questions, all jumbled together and boiling, with answers rising like elusive steam. Brian would have told her everything in due time, she thought as she lay down on the bed and closed her eyes. Brian loved her. . . .

She was asleep within moments.

Brian was standing on the banks of Lake Aberdeen, the wind tousling his red hair.

"I'm not like them, Chris. I'm one of them, but I'm not like them. I got away soon enough."

"I don't understand, Brian!"

"I love you, Chris. That wasn't a lie. I love you."

Chris moved towards him. Although the wind was softly blowing his hair, her nightgown hung straight and still. The wind was Brian's alone.

"Why didn't you tell me about the house?"

"I love you. That wasn't a lie. I love you."

Chris came closer to him and reached out to touch him. He backed away.

"Don't touch me! I'll break if you touch me. Here, you forgot this."

He held out his hand. Something glimmered in the sunshine. It was a chain, and it turned slowly as it dropped to the grass. Chris bent to pick it up, and found the charm bracelet the Crispins had given her one long-ago Hanukkah.

"Oh, Brian, how . . . ?"

But Brian wasn't there. Harvey was there, and beside him stood an older man with red hair and green eyes. Red hair and green eyes like Brian's—but there was malevolence in those eyes.

"No!"

"What're you gonna do?" Harvey asked.

"Take her to the boy. Take her to stay with Teddy, forever. She saw. She knows. They have to stay together."

"Leave me alone!"

"Christy, it's just a joke. . . ."

The man started laughing. He came closer to her, a rope

stretched between his two big hands. Chris screamed and fell to the grass.

But it wasn't grass at all. It was snow, deep and cold. The sunshine had vanished instantly, replaced by a darkness so complete its only purpose could be to hide evil.

The man picked her up as if she was just a little girl. No one heard her scream. Harvey just laughed at her.

The man opened a door, and she could see a pit of darkness. She didn't want to go in there. She knew it was going to . . .

. . . hurt.

Chris opened her eyes and rolled over onto her side. She hurt everywhere. She rubbed her face and felt tears on her cheeks. The dream should have faded, as dreams do, but this one stayed with her in complete clarity. And she knew it had to be a sign. The bracelet, the evil man, Harvey—Brian had been trying to tell her something.

"Harvey," she whispered. "He was trying to tell me about Harvey. But what?"

Though she lay awake for a long time, nothing came to her. She thought about talking to Lucille and Eda, but finally decided they'd given her enough of their time. She would just lay here and think, and when the answer came to her, *then* she would talk to them.

Sleep came before she found the answer, and next thing she knew she was gazing out the window at the morning sun. Her hand went to her wrist in search of a charm bracelet she hadn't worn in decades. And instantly, she knew what Brian had been trying to tell her.

Something had happened that Hanukkah night, and Harvey knew exactly what it was. She had to talk to him.

When she got out of bed, she saw it was only eight o'clock in the morning. It was a two-hour drive up to the prison in Blueriver, and she wasn't even sure about visiting hours. Would they let her see Harvey?

She didn't give herself another moment to think. Quietly, not wanting to wake her friends, she washed and dressed. Part of her said she should wake Lucille and Eda, but she ignored the suggestion. She moved like a robot, still a little disoriented from her nightmare, but successfully found Lucille's keys and slipped quietly out of the house.

This was something she had to do on her own. She doubted either Eda or Lucille would be permitted to see Harvey. They weren't family. And Harvey would certainly refuse to talk to them. But she'd make him talk to *her*. She'd make him tell her what happened when they were kids.

There was nobody near her house as she pulled out of the driveway. Only the yellow police banners, flapping in the wind, gave witness to the horror that had occurred there. Harvey might know something about that.

"I've been terrified of that Hannukah night all my life," Chris said out loud. "But now I'm going to face it. Damn it, if it means finding my babies, I'm going to find out what Harvey did to me!"

THIRTY-TWO

▼

ABERDEEN, MONTANA, PROPER was a small town, but its surrounding farmland stretched for miles. It took Chris nearly half an hour to drive beyond its zip code. She was thinking about Harvey, and about all the things that had come back to her during her discussions with Eda and Lucille. Harvey figured in a lot of her memories, didn't he? He seemed to show up at strange times. When she got to Blueriver, she planned to confront him once and for all.

The endless stretch of sky and land that gave Montana the nickname Big Sky Country seemed to envelop her. In a state with barely a million in population, it wasn't unusual that Chris was alone on the highway for long stretches of time. It was a lonely road, without even the sight of mountains to break the view. Funny this state had been named Montana. Chris had seen the mountains only once in her life, on a camping trip years ago with Brian.

Josh had been a rambunctious three-year-old back then,

and it seemed she spent every moment making certain he didn't run off the edge of a cliff. The whole trip had exhausted Chris, and she vowed she'd never go camping again. But seeing the beautiful Rockies had been worth it.

Chris realized she was crying. She suddenly felt more alone than she had in years. Brian had teased her for months about the trip, but he'd never do that again, would he? Damn, she didn't even have her best friends at her side right now. She hadn't felt this alone since . . .

Maybe since before Eda Crispin had moved to Aberdeen from Chicago and had become her best friend. She'd been alone at other times, too. Her twenties had also been virtually friendless. Of course, Eda and Lucille had still been close to her. But Eda had surprised everyone after high school graduation by announcing that she was planning to become a cop—in New York. Lucille had already left Aberdeen, after her own graduation two years earlier. She and her boyfriend, Sydney, were sharing an apartment in Bozeman while they attended Montana State. Years passed with the women corresponding mostly by phone and letter. Chris had missed her friends terribly, but there was one good thing about that time. The man who had been stalking her hadn't shown up.

A few years later, Lucille announced that Sydney had finally asked her to marry him. Eda came back from New York to be a bridesmaid, and for the first time since they were teenagers the women were together again. Lucille's wedding had been huge, as befitted the oldest daughter of Aberdeen's "most important sugar beet farmer." Chris couldn't help smiling as she remembered how proudly Lucille had spoken those words. There had been eight bridesmaids. Lucille wasn't a show-off, but she had six sisters in addition to her two best friends. Lucille's younger brother Stannie, who had grown dark-eyed and handsome, had been Chris's escort.

She looked up at the sky and thought the peach-colored layer of sun shining beneath the clouds was very much like her bridesmaid's dress.

"I think I look ridiculous," Eda had whispered as she tugged at the off-the-shoulder neckline of the soft batiste gown. "My mother is so happy I'm wearing a formal. She keeps inviting me to her parties, but I'm never comfortable."

"You look adorable," Chris had replied.

"No, I don't," Eda insisted. She pointed to the flower girl, eleven-year-old Marcia Danton. "Marcia looks adorable. *You* look adorable. Maybe you'll get lucky and meet someone today."

Chris snorted. "Maybe I'll get lucky and leave Aberdeen. That's when I'll meet someone, Eda, not before."

Eda turned and busied herself with her blond curls. She'd pulled them up into the circlet of orange blossoms Lucille had provided for all the attendants, but already her wild locks were coming loose in the misty spring weather.

Chris waited for Eda to lecture her, telling her to put Harvey Sr. in a nursing home. A few years earlier, he had had her mother committed, and soon after that he'd had a stroke. Although she had a nurse come in every day to take care of the old man while she went to work, she had a lot to do herself. And Harvey Sr.'s last days had not been brief.

Ten years into the future, Chris found a tissue in the glove compartment and blew her nose. How had thoughts of her father's long dying crept into her mind? Biting her lip, staring hard at the stretch of road ahead, she steered her memories to the moments just after the wedding.

They were standing on the steps of St. Gregory's Church, throwing birdseed at Lucille and Sydney. Lucille was a stunning bride, her black hair a dramatic contrast to the white silk and Chantilly lace gown. Chris's heart had been full of empathetic joy as she watched her beautiful friend race down the steps. Everyone was clapping and cheering the newlyweds.

Everyone but one man, who stood in the crowd on the other side of the church steps. As Chris scanned the group of well-wishers, her eyes met his—or, rather, they met the black emptiness of his sunglasses. He smiled, and lifted a hand as if in salute. Something bright gleamed in the early afternoon sunlight. . . .

He had come back, Chris thought as her hands tightened around the steering wheel. It was the man of her nightmares, the evil man who had chased her up a fire escape, who had followed her. He had come back again.

Twenty-three-year-old Chris, charming in her peach batiste gown, froze. Was he was going to plunge his knife into the neck of the old woman who stood in front of him, oblivious? Chris let out a cry and pointed. The man ducked away and disappeared through the crowd.

Eda took hold of her arm on one side. Stannie Brigham tapped her shoulder.

"What's going on?" he demanded.

"Chris, what is it?" Eda asked.

Chris was about to tell them what she just saw, but stopped herself. The man was gone. This was Lucille's day, and talk of evil would only spoil things. He couldn't hurt her with all these people around. She would try her best to put him out of her mind. It was only fair to Lucille.

"Nothing," she had said. "I thought that old lady was going to slip on the birdseed."

Stannie laughed. "Her? That's my aunt Susannah. She may be old, but she's feisty as hell. I'm surprised she's not wearing roller skates!"

Eda laughed, and Chris forced herself to join them. The next thing she knew, she was being herded towards a trio of waiting limos. Eda was nowhere near her, so there was no chance to discuss what had happened. And, to Chris's surprise, the day was so much fun that she was able to put the man completely out of her mind.

Eda had had to return to New York the very next day, so they'd had little time to talk. Dean Crispin's Mercedes pulled up outside her apartment in the early morning, and Eda had come up to say good-bye. She was running late, she said, but promised she'd call soon.

Then, once more, Chris was alone in Aberdeen. Eda was back in New York, while Lucille and her new husband were honeymooning in Florida.

Chris was working at The Geode, a small shop that specialized in rocks and minerals. Dr. Scott, her boss, was a retired professor from Montana College of Mineral Science and Technology. He often left her on her own at the shop while he set out on geologic expeditions. Today, Chris was planning to set some Easter baskets in the window to reflect the upcoming holiday. She'd placed different colored stones on the grass to represent Easter eggs. As she was gathering her equipment, her eyes fell on a small, oval geode. It sparkled beautifully under the track lights. Chris decided it would look cute with a baby chick coming out of it, as if it had just been hatched.

She was pulling out the previous window display when she saw him. He was standing directly across the street, just the way he had a few days earlier, at Lucille's wedding. Chris stared at him, frozen. His hand came up in a mock salute, silver glistening off the gleaming blade.

Chris dropped a slab of agate to the floor. The crash shocked her enough to tear her eyes from the man, and she looked down at the stone. Carefully, she picked it up and carried it to the counter, where she checked it over for damage. To her relief, the six-inch-long agate slice was intact.

She set it on the counter and went to look out the window again. The man was gone, having disappeared as he had so many other times. Heart pounding, Chris tried to concentrate on her work. When the bell tinkled to announce the first customer of the day, she nearly dropped an entire basket of stones. She swung around, her eyes wide, half expecting to see that her tormentor had walked into the little, dark wood-filled shop.

"Sorry!" a cheerful man's voice said. "Did I startle you?"

When Chris saw him, her heart stopped once more— only this time, it wasn't out of fear. Her first customer of the day was one of the most attractive men she'd ever seen in her life. She found herself making instant analogies to the minerals around her. His hair reminded her of burnished copper, and his eyes were like . . .

. . . well, like emeralds, Chris Wander thought as she sped towards Blueriver.

"No-no," Chris had faltered, back then, setting the Easter basket in the window.

The man gazed at her for a few minutes, and she realized he was studying *her*. Feeling a warm blush wash over her, she turned away and pretended to be busy.

"I was just setting up a new display," she said. "I guess I was concentrating too deeply."

"You look like a woman who has many thoughts to think," the man said.

He moved farther into the store and started to look at its wares, displayed on rough-hewn shelves.

"Are you looking for a gift?" Chris asked, trying to

bring the conversation into familiar territory. He was probably married, anyway. "Or a souvenir?"

"Just looking," the man said idly. "I just moved to Aberdeen, and want to see what's here."

Chris laughed. "Not much. There are fewer than ten thousand people in this town."

"It's gorgeous," said the man, "the kind of homey, quiet place I like."

He came to her and held out a hand. Chris felt a surprising giddiness as she took it, and was embarrassed to think she'd developed an immediate crush on a complete stranger. She hadn't dated much in the last five years, but she recognized the feeling of powerful attraction.

"My name is Brian Wander," he said, his smile gleaming.

"I'm Christine Burnett," Chris said. "Call me Chris."

"Hello, Chris," said Brian.

It was in that way she met her future husband. Brian came back to the store a few times that first week, and actually bought something when the proprietor himself was in. As Chris was wrapping the block of amethyst crystals, Brian leaned over the counter and whispered:

"Would you like to have dinner with me tonight?"

Chris didn't know what to say. New relationships had never been easy for her. The thought of this man meeting her father, all glassy-eyed and drooly in his bed, made her stomach turn.

She shook her head.

"I can't," she said.

Brian didn't pursue the matter then, and that impressed Chris. He seemed both outgoing and gentle. But he wasn't the type to give up. He asked her out two more times, but both times she found excuses.

"Don't tell me you locals don't cotton to strangers," he said one day, pulling the last three words into a drawl.

"No," Chris said softly. "It's just that . . ." She couldn't explain.

"Never mind," Brian said patiently. "I'll try again."

After he left, a number of people flooded the store. It was the largest group of shoppers The Geode had ever seen at one time, and the woman who seemed to be their leader said they were on a bus trip from Helena to Granite Park.

"We have another two hours to drive," she said, "and your little town seemed a nice diversion."

By the time they left, the sun was coming down, and Dr. Scott announced it was time to close up shop. Seeing him yawn and rub his neck wearily, Chris volunteered to do it herself.

"Why, thanks," the old man said. He looked down at his big, rough hands. They weren't a professor's hands at all. His dirty fingernails seemed proof of his hard work. "It was a rough day at the dig yesterday, and I've got another one tomorrow. I'd appreciate a good night's sleep."

The professor spent four days a week away from the store, digging for minerals and preparing new stock. It was the main reason he had hired Chris. She, in turn, had enjoyed the solitude of the job. The Geode was around the corner from downtown, and they had only a few regular customers. The shop obviously was more of a venture of love than a money-maker, but he paid Chris well enough.

He said good-bye and left. A few minutes later, the phone rang. Chris answered it, but there was no one on the other end. The darkness outside the shop window seemed suddenly full of potential danger. Perhaps the stranger was checking up on her. Perhaps he was out there, waiting in the dark.

It was ridiculous, she told herself. She was a grown woman, not a frightened little girl.

She flitted nervously around the store, finding work that

would delay her, ringing out the cash register and cleaning up. She reminded herself it was just a short walk home, and at this hour there would be numerous people on the street. She would be quite safe, of course.

As she was leaving the shop, locking the door behind her, she felt a tap on her shoulder.

"So grown up and pretty," the voice whispered.

Chris screamed, breaking into a run, but the man was quicker. He grabbed her arm and pulled her close to him, covering her mouth with his hand. Chris thought frantically how very alone she was, how isolated the little shop was.

"Please, please," the voice said. Somehow, it seemed different than she remembered, younger. "He told me you were beautiful, but he didn't say how beautiful. I won't hurt you, Chris. I've dreamed of you all my life! I only want to talk to you!"

Chris's teeth found purchase on a small pad of skin, and she bit down as hard as she could. The man cried out in dismay, and she broke into a run. She raced towards the corner, passing a small parklike area. Trees shadowed her path, trees that could easily hide a murder. . . .

"Please wait!" The pleading tone seemed incongruous with the rough voice. "Wait! I want to talk to you!"

"Leave me alone!" Chris screamed.

Chris ran towards her apartment, her heels clicking on the sidewalk. There were a few people in the street, and they turned to gape at her. But no one helped her. Why had she thought they would? They were probably whispering that "Crazy Christy" was at it again, the way they'd done all her life.

Her fear mixing with a surge of hatred for all of them, she looked back over her shoulder. The man was about a block back, and gaining on her.

Suddenly Chris crashed into someone.

To her chagrin, it was Brian Wander. He took her by the shoulders.

"Hey, slow down!"

Chris tried to pull away.

"Let me go," she begged. "Can't you see he's after me?"

Brian looked behind her.

"Who?"

Chris turned around slowly. The man had disappeared once more.

"He was there," she said, a defiant tone in her voice.

"Of course," Brian said. "But he's gone now."

Chris's expression softened as she realized Brian wouldn't know about her crazy past. She blinked the last of her tears away.

"You're shaking like a leaf," Brian said. "Please, come into the coffee shop and talk to me. I'd like to hear what happened."

Grateful to have a sympathetic ear, Chris followed him down the street to Mayer's Luncheonette.

Her voice was soft as she ordered a coffee, light and sweet. Brian took his black, but let it sit as he listened to her story. He interrupted a few times to ask pertinent questions, but mostly left the floor to her. With a sigh, she finally brought the strange story to an end.

She looked him straight in the eyes, challenging him to ridicule her. If he did, if he even suggested she was as crazy as people said, she'd walk out and . . .

"My God, you must have been terrified," Brian said.

His sympathetic response was so unexpected that Chris simply sat there with her mouth open.

"Wasn't there anyone at all you could tell?" Brian asked. "I mean, a little girl living a nightmare like that, all alone . . ."

"I wasn't really alone," Chris said. "I had my best

friends to help me—Eda and Lucille. But I couldn't tell my parents. I was afraid of my father, and my mother was in her own world. There was a nice cop named Mike Hewlett—he's still on the force, actually—but I'd grown to distrust all adults."

Brian nodded, finally taking a sip of his coffee. He made a face, since it had grown tepid, and pushed it away.

"I can't say I blame you," he said. Then his expression grew even more serious. "What do you suppose brought him back after all these years?"

"I don't know," Chris said, shaking her head. "It's been more than fifteen years since I saw him. I can't think where he's been, or what he wants. All I know is that for some reason he can't put me out of his mind."

She felt an urge to start crying again, and pinched the bridge of her nose between her thumb and forefinger. She tried to keep her voice steady, but there was a choke in it when she said:

"He's had plenty of opportunity to grab me, if that's what he's after. Maybe he thought taking a child would be too conspicuous all those years ago."

"That didn't stop him from taking the Gammel boys," Brian pointed out.

Chris blinked, her eyes wet as she looked up. "They never found them, you know. Most people think they're dead. It's only some twist of events that kept me from that same fate, whatever happened to those poor little boys."

The waitress came by to refill their cups at that moment. When she left, Brian spoke.

"Maybe you should report this incident," he suggested. "The police ought to know you've been followed."

Chris shook her head vehemently. "No! I don't want to involve the police. And besides, there's no proof. No one else has ever seen him."

Chris shifted uncomfortably in her seat. Brian reached

across the table, took her hand, and held it tightly. His grasp was warm and strong, supportive.

"No one should have to put up with harassment the way you have," he said.

"You don't know about me," Chris said. "You don't know what people have been saying about me all my life. I have a . . . well, people think I'm disturbed. You see, my mother and father . . . uh . . . my mother . . ."

She lowered her head and began to cry, unable to say more. How could she tell this kind, handsome stranger about her family's problems? About her mother, diagnosed schizophrenic and living in a home? About her father, who couldn't even feed himself?

"Hey," Brian said, softly, "hey."

He came around to her side of the booth and took her in his arms. It felt good to have someone to hold her close.

"Come on," Brian said. "Let me walk you home."

Chris wiped her eyes with a paper napkin.

"I'd appreciate that," she said. "I don't know if that man is waiting for me."

Brian paid for the coffee, and they left the shop. Keeping his arm around her, he led her down the street. It was dark out, and there were few people. No one looked in their direction.

"This is my place," Chris said when they reached the pizzeria. "I live upstairs."

"Should I walk you up?"

"No," Chris said. "No, thank you."

The last thing I want is for you to meet my father.

Brian studied her for a few minutes.

"Will you let me take you to dinner Friday night?"

"I don't . . ."

"Please?"

Chris managed a smile. Why not? Why shouldn't she be happy, if only for a little while?

"Okay," she said. "But it has to be an early evening." She was grateful that Brian didn't ask why.

On the lonely highway between Aberdeen and Blueriver, Chris looked up to see her destination was only ten miles away. She put thoughts of Brian aside for the time being, after allowing herself the quick memory of their pleasant first dinner together. But those memories were crowded out by a sense of foreboding. In a short while, if things went well, she would be facing her brother for the first time in years.

"Oh, Brian," she whispered, tears streaming down her face. "I wish you were here to help me!"

THIRTY-THREE

▼

TEDDY WAS PROUD he'd remembered to have a backup plan. The grown-ups had had one when they took him away so long ago. They thought he'd grown up slow, but he knew they were wrong. He had a backup plan.

Slow people couldn't remember things they did yesterday, but he remembered things that happened thirty years ago. He remembered how the man had hidden Adrian and him in that underground shelter. It was just for safekeeping, he had said, until the police went away. Because the police wanted to take them away from their mother. No one knew about the fallout shelter. Daddy had built it at night, using a bulldozer he rented. No one saw it in the daytime because it was so far back from the road. The top was flush with the ground, and Daddy had covered it with a patch of sod to make it completely invisible almost until you were on top of it. The police had probably looked out over that vast stretch of yard and had seen nothing at all.

They'd never known Teddy and Adrian were almost literally under their noses.

When he was a kid, Teddy remembered, the grass had been cut short and neat. Now the shelter's hatch was surrounded with tall weeds and thick tangles. Once he unlatched it, he could grab a fistful of grass and use it as a handle to pull the round lid back. But he understood it was just a matter of time before the police found the shelter. So, just as the man had moved the brothers after only a few days, Teddy knew he had to move these kids.

The man had paid a gas station owner to let him use an old metal shack with a lock. The owner had taken the money without asking questions, so he never knew what the plans were for that shack. Teddy hadn't liked the cold metal place very much, but he hadn't complained. He knew the man was protecting them, saving them from the police the way he'd saved from Daddy. Adrian, however, had screamed and cried so much that the man had given him medicine to make him sleep.

Teddy wondered if the little girl would scream and cry. He worried that he didn't have any more sleeping potion. Well, if he had to, he'd just stuff something in her mouth to shut her up. In the meantime, he had to go to that gas station to see if he could borrow the old shack, too.

He had decided he needed someone to keep an eye on the kids, in case they woke up before he got back. Of course, he had no friends in Aberdeen. But he did have someone who owed him, someone who had hurt his precious Christy, an angel. Tiffany still hadn't paid enough for that. She still had her head.

When he'd heard that car driving by outside, he'd been so startled his swing had missed. Then he'd been afraid to go further, not just because he thought the owner of the car might stop and come in but because he was even more afraid he'd go past the number fifteen. He'd decided he'd have time to count later, and if there weren't enough slashes he'd just use the ax a few more times.

A search of the woman's handbag found car keys. He went downstairs and waited for a long time inside the front door, watching the street outside. It was a quiet street; only two houses sat on the other side. One had a For Sale sign on it that was so faded there was no telling when it was hung. The other one was occupied, but Teddy knew the habits of its owners. They left for work early in the morning and wouldn't be back until six. Still, he watched for a long time to make certain no one was there.

At last, he went out to Tiffany's car, keeping his head ducked low. Somebody might see him, after all. People had binoculars and telescopes, didn't they? Nosy people who watched everything? Daddy had always said people watched you, waiting for you to make a mistake.

Quickly, Teddy opened the car door and climbed behind the wheel. He drove the car a few blocks, heading towards the outskirts of town, where he was less likely to be noticed. Then he went back home again, on foot. He didn't dare run, but he hurried as best as he could, wanting to be off the street.

The walk gave him time to think, and he smiled as a brilliant idea came to him. He would make Tiffany watch the children! She owed Christy that much, at least. He went upstairs and hoisted her limp form over his shoulder. Then he carried her downstairs and outside. In a few minutes, he was struggling down the ladder into the fallout shelter. Deeply drugged, the kids were sound asleep. Teddy was very quiet, and neither child stirred as he moved around the shelter. He sat Tiffany up in a chair. Her head lolled forward. That wasn't good at all. She couldn't see the kids wake up if she was looking at the floor.

He found a very large sack of flour, just big enough to fit on her lap, and wedged it under her chin. Her eyes were pointed directly at the children. Now they would be watched constantly, to make sure nothing went wrong.

Quietly, Teddy ascended the ladder and pulled it up after him. Then, afraid someone might come to the house the way Tiffany had, he crept off to the woods to fall asleep under a tree.

Eda came into the kitchen with a towel wrapped around her hair, wet from her morning shower. Lucille was draining bacon on paper towels, and three places at the table had already been set with sectioned grapefruits. Eda took a piece of bacon from the counter and sat down.

"Where's Chris?" Lucille asked. "Still sleeping?"

"She wasn't in her room when I looked," Eda said. "I thought she was down here already."

Lucille opened the refrigerator and took out a carton of eggs. As she cracked them into a bowl, she said:

"Well, she's probably taking a shower. She'll be down in a minute. I'll just keep some eggs aside for her."

Eda finished the bacon and said:

"No, she's not in the bathroom. I just got out myself, and I would have seen her."

A look of concern crossed Lucille's face.

"I'm sure she isn't down here," she said. "Wait . . ."

She parted the curtains behind the sink and looked out at the driveway. Letting them fall together again, she turned and said:

"The car's gone."

"Damn!" Eda cried. "Where could she have gone? We didn't even hear her leave!"

Lucille looked up at the clock.

"It's only eight-thirty," she said. "She must have gotten up very early. But where would she go at that hour?"

Eda played with her grapefruit spoon for a few moments, thoughtful.

"Blueriver," she said finally. "I'll bet she's gone up to see Harvey."

"Oh, no!" Lucille said. "I don't think that's such a good idea."

"I'm not sure it is, either," Eda said, standing. "Let me call Mike Hewlett. If she's on the highway headed up there, maybe he could have a state trooper find her."

When Mike heard Eda's suspicions, he promised to contact the state prison. However, he thought it might be good for Chris to talk to her brother, and finally convinced Eda of this. He had some interesting news for Eda, too, and when she hung up she reported it to Lucille.

"They called the doctor whose notepad I found," she said. "It seems she had a patient named Teddy Eastman who was supposed to show up for an appointment two days ago. She hasn't been able to locate him."

Lucille shook her head.

"You don't have to be a college graduate to figure out who Teddy Eastman really is," she said. "What now?"

"They're trying to locate Teddy's father," Eda went on. "His stepfather, I mean. I guess Irene Gammel made a new life for herself in Washington. She married a man named Douglas Eastman."

"It's amazing to find Teddy alive after all these years," Lucille said. "But it doesn't explain Brian's connection to him—unless Douglas Eastman can answer that."

"Unfortunately, the Washington police have been unable to locate him," Eda said. "In the meantime, our own force is on the lookout for Teddy. Mike put a guard on the Gammel house, but he says no one showed up last night. Unfortunately, it can't be a twenty-four-hour watch. The Aberdeen Police Department has a very small staff, and this case has given them more work than they can handle."

"Do you think Teddy has been hiding in his old house?"

Lucille asked. A shudder racked her tall frame. "To think you might have run into that maniac!"

"I'm okay," Eda reassured her. "It's Chris we have to worry about."

Lucille packaged the leftover breakfast food and put it in the refrigerator.

"I just hate waiting!" she cried. "What if she isn't going up to Blueriver at all? What if, after all these years, that creep has decided it's time to get her?"

For a few moments, neither woman said a word. Eda was trying to put together the facts she'd learned in the past few days. Lucille was thinking about Chris, possibly in great danger. And, as if they were psychically linked, the two women thought of the children at the same time. Their eyes met, and Lucille said:

"I'm scared. I'm so worried about those kids."

"So am I," Eda declared. "Dear God, so am I."

Chris had arrived before visiting hours, and sat impatiently in a small building just outside the prison gates. It was a sort of waiting area, where family members gathered until it was time for a little shuttle bus to take them inside the confines of the penitentiary. Chris hardly noticed the other visitors, except for a little boy with big brown eyes. He looked a lot like Josh had a few years back. Chris couldn't take her eyes from him, and when he caught her staring he moved closer to his mother and buried his face in her skirt.

Chris looked down at her lap. She imagined that Eda and Lucille had discovered her missing by now. And she was certain they could guess where she was. So when a young cop came in asking for her, she wasn't much surprised. She stood up and went to him. He led her out to a car, opened the door for her, and explained that the warden wanted to see her.

The warden was a tall man with thick glasses and slicked-back hair that would have been more stylish in the early sixties. But he had a kind smile and called Chris "ma'am" when he offered her a seat. His name tag said FITTERMAN.

"Seems some folks in Aberdeen are quite concerned about you," he said. "Sheriff Hewlett called to say you might be up here. Mike's an old friend of mine."

"I've come to see my brother," Chris said. "I think he has some important information."

Fitterman nodded.

"Mike seems to think so, too," he said. "Now, the problem is that Harvey's been in solitary for nearly a week. Broke a plate over another inmate's head. Harvey's a real troublemaker."

Chris shifted uncomfortably.

"I know," she said softly.

"He doesn't talk much," Fitterman said, "but Mike believes he'll talk to you. He says you haven't seen each other for a few years?"

"Nearly thirty," Chris admitted. "If he's in solitary, does that mean I can't see him?"

"Not at all," Fitterman replied. "I'm having him brought out right now. I thought you could talk better in private, so I'll have you go in a little earlier than the other families."

Chris tucked a lock of hair behind her ear.

"How much did Mike tell you?"

"Just about everything," Fitterman said. "It's been in the papers, too. Damn, you are one brave lady. If it had been my family, I'm not sure I could be as strong."

Chris, anxious to speak with her brother, didn't say anything. The phone rang, and Fitterman answered it. After he hung up, he stood and said:

"Harvey's waiting for you."

Chris followed him out of the office and down a long

hall. They stopped and waited for several gates to be unlocked and then relocked behind them. At last, they
reached a room with a metal door and a small window. A
police officer stood outside.

Suddenly, Chris froze. All she could think of was her father, a man who had hurt her time and again. Had Harvey
grown to be like him? Chris recalled he was in here on a
manslaughter charge. Had he become the animal their father had been?

When Fitterman put a hand on her shoulder, she jumped.

"Easy, ma'am," Fitterman said. "You're safe here. Officer Mascioli will be on guard the whole time."

Chris nodded mutely.

"Ready?"

"I guess."

Fitterman had the officer unlock the door, and he escorted Chris inside. Harvey was standing with his back to
the door, his hands clasped behind him. He wore a white
T-shirt with cut-off sleeves and a pair of khaki pants.

"Burnett, your visitor's here," Fitterman said.

"Yeah, yeah," Harvey sneered.

Chris felt a chill run through her. He sounded so much
like the boy she remembered!

"Who the hell would wanta visit—?" His voice broke as
he turned to see his sister. Chris, taken aback by his ap-
pearance, couldn't speak either. She'd expected Harvey to
be as big and mean-looking as their father. But this was a
scraggly, thin man, a wasted man. His eyes seemed huge
in his sunken face, his crew cut more gray than brown.

"Oh, shit," Harvey whispered.

"Hello, Harvey," was all Chris could think to say.

Fitterman left the room. Slowly, Chris made her way to
the table in the room's center. Harvey sat across from her,
staring into her eyes with haunted eyes of his own.

"Shit," he said again.

"Harvey, you know I never liked curse words," Chris said.

He said nothing for a few moments. Then a big grin spread across his face.

"God, you turned out pretty," he said. "You look like Mom did when I was little. Before stuff happened."

He pushed his fingers over the top of his head, as if to run them through a phantom head of hair.

"Before she got sick, you mean," Chris said.

They looked at each other for a few moments, then both started to talk at once.

"Harvey, I . . ."

"You're really . . ."

They both took a breath.

"How'd you find me?" Harvey asked.

"Mike Hewlett found you," Chris said. "Harvey, what happened to you? What happened to Felicity?"

Harvey shrugged. "She left. The baby changed her. She went to work, and I started stealing money from her for drugs. Guess it was too much."

"You had a little girl, I heard."

"Lolani," Harvey said, looking at the blank wall. A wistful look came across his face but quickly disappeared. "Pretty kid. Looked a lot like you."

"Really?"

Harvey nodded. "Felicity couldn't take any more of my shit. Not that I beat her or nothing. I'd never do that. Too much like Dad. But I was a dopehead."

Chris felt a momentary twinge of relief to think Felicity and the baby hadn't been abused. But she quickly turned the subject to her reason for being here. All this small talk was just keeping her from the truth.

"Harvey, do you remember the Gammel crimes?"

Harvey nodded. "Sure I do. Why?"

"A few days ago," Chris said, "my husband was murdered. Brian was . . ." She took a deep breath, concentrating on her brother's face to keep an image of Brian's body from coming into her thoughts. "Brian was decapitated. The same night, my two children disappeared."

"Holy shit," Harvey whispered. He ran his fingers over his head again. "We've had a lot of crappy things happen to us, haven't we?"

"I need your help, Harvey," Chris said. "We . . . my friends and I . . . think you might know something about all this."

"How the hell could I?" Harvey demanded. "I've been in this dump for nearly a year!"

Chris sighed deeply, trying to calm herself.

"Harvey, I have to ask you about that night when you walked me home from the Crispins' party," she said. "I keep thinking something more happened then, something you've kept secret for years. It might help me save my children. Please, Harvey, you've got to tell me what happened that night!"

Harvey stared at her for such a long time that Chris began to feel hot. Finally, he nodded.

"They told me someone working on a murder case wanted to talk to me," he said. "They said if I cooperated, I could cut my time here. You really want to know what happened that night?"

"Yes, I do," Chris said in a firm voice.

"Then you better brace yourself," Harvey said. " 'Cause you sure as hell ain't gonna like what I'm about to say."

"If it gets my kids back," Chris said, "that's all that matters."

"Boys or girls? Do I have nieces or nephews?"

"One of each," Chris said. "Joshua is ten, and Victoria is five. We call them Josh and Vicki."

"They know they have an uncle?"

Chris looked down at her lap. She had never mentioned

Harvey or her parents to her children. They were part of a past she had tried hard to forget. Strange how that past had caught up to her, overtaken her and destroyed her family. But if Harvey would help her, she might still save part of her life.

"They're very young, Harvey," she said softly.

"I get it," Harvey said.

Chris made no attempt to apologize for her actions. Harvey seemed to understand, and to her surprise he reached across the table and patted her hand.

"Okay, listen," he said. "You gotta realize something. I was a kid myself then. I wanted nothing more than to get outta that hellhole we called a home. But where was I gonna go? I was only fifteen, and I sure didn't have any money."

"You ran away that Christmas," Chris said. "You were gone for three years. How did you live?"

"I managed," Harvey said. "You'd be surprised what a kid can do. But that night, the one you're talking about, I didn't tell you the truth. That was no stranger who jumped us. At least, not to me. I'd seen him a few times, and I thought he was a worker from one of the ranches outside town. One day he came up to me and started talkin'. He was no ranch worker, Chris. He had a wad of bills you could gag on. Gave me five dollars just to mail a letter for him. He started talking to me more and more. That was a little after Halloween time, I think. He said he'd been watching our family, and he knew how badly we were being treated. He said he knew a nice couple that wanted a pretty little girl. I was supposed to get five hundred dollars if I turned you over to him."

Chris's eyes widened. "You tried to *sell* me?"

"Well, don't put it that way, Christy," Harvey said. "It ain't like it was white slavery. I really thought that guy had a family who wanted you. But I knew something was wrong when he put that stuff over your face to knock you out. He said it was to keep you quiet, since what we were doin' was really illegal. But then he started talkin' funny. He kept on about an ax, and how good it worked, and how much 'the boys' would enjoy you. I knew then and there that this was the man who murdered Darren Gammel and Basil Horton."

"Why didn't you ever go to the police?"

"Are you kidding?" Harvey asked. "With my reputation? And how could I explain that I knew this guy because I'd tried to sell him my kid sister. That night the bastard tried to cheat me—he only gave me two hundred dollars. That's when I got mad and hit him with a can."

"You said it was a hubcap," Chris recalled.

"A can, a hubcap, what does it matter? I saved you, didn't I?"

Chris buried her face in her hands and shook her head. The whole thing was unbelievable.

"Harvey, I can forgive you for what you did back then," she said into her fingers, her voice a steady drone. "Like you said, we were both kids. We were scared and desperate. But please don't insult me by pretending it was some noble act you performed. Because when you came back three years later, trouble started for me again. Did you see him a second time, Harvey? What brought you back to Aberdeen? You were trying to get money to escape the draft, weren't you?"

"That's right," Harvey said. "The first time I ran away, the same guy picked me up and drove me to Seattle. I worked for him for a while. He gave me the creeps, but I had no place else to go. Soon as I had enough money, I took off again. I finally ended up in San Francisco. But a coupla years later, both Uncle Sam and that guy found me."

"So you came back to Aberdeen," Chris said. "I could

never understand why Dad was so glad to see you, after all the trouble you'd caused. Why did you kill my new kitten, after you'd bought it yourself?"

"I didn't do that!"

"You said you did!"

"It wasn't me," Harvey said. "It was that guy. He followed me to Aberdeen. He had lots of money, and he said he'd give me some if I came back with him. Only I had to bring you along, too. I told Dad some people I knew were interested in adopting a little girl, and that they had lots of money to pay."

Somehow, that didn't surprise Chris. She felt no bitterness at her father's attempt at selling her. It was just one more flame in the fire. Like son, like father.

"You keep calling him 'that guy,' " Chris pointed out. "What was his name, Harvey?"

Harvey gave his head a rough shake. "No way. I ain't rattin' on him. The guy was a class-A weirdo, but he saved my ass back then. I couldn'ta survived without him."

"But Harvey—"

"No!"

Suddenly, Harvey's expression changed. His eyes seemed to go a shade darker, and he glared at something Chris couldn't see.

"He screwed it all up," Harvey grumbled. "It was his idea and he screwed it all up, following you like that and killing that kitten."

"The stranger killed Sweetie?" Chris prompted.

Harvey nodded. "Wanted to scare you silly so you'd be willing to leave town. But then you talked to that cop and he wanted to talk to me. If Felicity hadn't faked labor pains . . ."

Chris nodded, understanding. So Felicity *had* pulled a stunt that day.

"We ran away from the hospital," Harvey went on. "We headed up to Canada. But he found us and threatened to turn us in."

"You could have made the same threat towards him!"

Harvey shook his head. "This guy knew what he was doing. He was no drifter, Chris. He might have been crazy, but he was rich, too. He was crazy like a fox. So I had to do something about it. I had to stop him."

Chris stared at her brother for a moment before asking: "Did you kill him?"

"Didn't have to," Harvey said. "He died in a crash."

"Then he couldn't have hurt my family," Chris said distantly.

"It'd be a good trick," Harvey said.

It made sense, considering the man would be very old by now. But who, then? She needed to know the man's name. Maybe then she could make a connection.

"Please, Harvey," she said. "You can't hurt him now. He can't hurt you . . ."

"I said no!"

Harvey slammed his fist on the table, startling Chris so that her heart began to pound. The guard outside the door looked in on them, gave Harvey a warning stare, and closed the door.

"All right," Chris said gently. "But tell me what happened when you came back to Aberdeen."

"He found me," Harvey repeated, "and he said he would tell the authorities what I'd tried to do to you. He would do it anonymously, so he wouldn't be implicated. I was already in trouble with the police, being a druggie. It was a pretty scary thing. But the prospect of Vietnam was worse. When he offered to keep his mouth shut and pay me something to take off for Canada, I jumped at the chance. He still wanted you, Christy, he hadn't stopped thinking of you those two years. So I was supposed to try and get you again." He shook his head ruefully.

"What a mess it turned out to be! Mike Hewlett came to the hospital to talk to me. He said he'd seen me with a stranger and wanted to know who the guy was. I gave that cop a hard time, wouldn't tell him a thing! To this day, nobody's heard me mention his name."

He straightened his thin frame as if this was something to be proud of. Chris felt herself growing angry, and forced calm into her voice.

"What did you do after he died?" she asked.

I went back to San Francisco, and me and Felicity and the kid lived on a commune. They left me even before my number came up and I went to Canada. I stayed about twenty-years. That's all I can tell you, Christy."

Chris sighed, turning to stare up at the wired-glass window near the ceiling.

"Nobody calls me Christy now," she said in a quiet voice.

She had been right. Harvey *had* been connected to that horrible man from the past. But unless she knew his name, she might never find her children. Chris rolled her hands into tight fists and leaned forward.

"Listen to me, Harvey Burnett," she said. "I'm not the scared little twerp you remember as your sister. Something wonderful happened to me. A man named Brian Wander saved my life and gave me two beautiful children. Now someone's murdered him and taken my babies from me. And if I have to choke it out of you I'll find out that man's name!"

By the end of this tirade, she was shouting.

"Forget it!" Harvey yelled back. "I said I won't betray him! He didn't kill your friggin' old man! How could he? He'd be about seventy by now!" He got up and started to pace the room.

"You owe me," Chris insisted. "For God's sake, what difference does it make to you? The man's dead!"

Her brother stopped, and Chris felt the old fears returning as she watched a familiar snarl come over his face. He grabbed a chair and threw it.

"I don't owe you *nothing*!"

The chair crashed against the wall. A second later, the cop outside the door came in. He took Harvey by the arm and led him out.

"Sorry, lady," he said. "This interview's over."

He twisted Harvey's arm behind his back. "You must like solitary a whole lot, Burnett."

They left Chris alone in that barren room, with the miserable realization the whole thing had been a waste of time.

THIRTY-FOUR

JOSH WAS AWARE they weren't alone even before he opened his eyes. Although his stomach was churning and his head ached, he could sense the presence of someone new in the room. Slowly, he opened his eyes to find Vicki curled up on her own cot.

Groggily, he turned his aching head. Through a sea of dizziness, he saw the woman sitting on the chair. He blinked and tried to speak, but his tongue felt ten times too big. His mind was a jumble of half questions. Who are . . . ? Where . . . ? Why don't you . . . ?

It was too much to take, and the little boy passed out again.

Vicki's screaming woke him some time later, slicing painfully through the drugged stupor that surrounded him, jolting him completely awake and aware. First he looked at Vicki, beet-red and screaming. Then he looked at where her finger pointed.

And tried not to scream himself.

There was a woman sitting in a chair across the room, her head propped up by the blood-soaked flour sack in her lap. She was turned in such a way that she seemed to be staring at them, but Josh knew at once she couldn't see them. He turned to the other side of his bed and threw up.

"Josh, please!" Vicki whined. "Tell her to stop looking at me!"

Slowly, Josh got up. He took the blanket from his bed and walked towards the dead woman. Then he stopped cold, clutching the blanket tightly. What if she wasn't dead? What if she came to life? What if she grabbed him?

"That's stupid!" he told himself firmly.

Still, he looked at the woman only from the corner of his eye as he threw the blanket over her head. Now she was a shapeless form with legs, one ending in a heeled shoe, one cut and bloodied.

"Who—who is that, Josh?" Vicki asked.

"I don't know," Josh said. "I think I've seen her on television, though. Just don't look over there, Vicki, okay?"

Vicki obediently turned away.

"What happened?" she asked. "We were trying to stop that bad man."

Josh nodded, and the act made his head swim. He closed his eyes for a moment before answering.

"He jumped you," he said. "Then he got me. I think he poisoned us."

"I'm gonna get sick," Vicki said. She coughed a few times, then lost whatever food was in her stomach. The little girl began to cry softly. Without a thought, Josh went and put his arms around her.

"I wanna go home," Vicki said. "It's scary down here!"

"I know," Josh said, staring at the trapdoor overhead. "There's gotta be *some* way out of here!"

But there was only one way out—the locked trapdoor.

And in order to get to it, he'd have to move that lady in the chair. . . .

Shortly after hanging up with Eda, Mike Hewlett decided to take another look at the Gammel house. It had been dark when he'd sent a surveillance team to watch it. Deputy Katherine Jackson had reported the place was empty.

Katherine and her partner were still parked outside the house when he arrived, waiting to be relieved. He sent them home, sorry to hear there had been no activity, but thinking he might be able to come across another clue or two in the daylight.

He never expected that clue would be fresh blood.

There were spots of it on the stairs and trailing down the hall into a bedroom. Mike thought the search team should have seen it, but reminded himself that they had been looking for a human being, in the dark, and using only flashlights.

The sight of the reddish-brown stains made his heart stop for a moment. Slowly, he crouched down and touched a finger to it. It was sticky and cold. The sheriff got up and followed the blood spatters down to the cellar. For a second, he stopped halfway down the cellar stairs, afraid of what he might find, then swearing softly, he continued down, gun drawn. He swung his flashlight around, but saw nothing unusual. A more careful search confirmed there was no one present, but Mike spotted a high-heeled shoe. Certain it hadn't been there when the house was searched earlier, he left it for forensics to study.

Quickly, he bounded up the stairs and out to his car, where he radioed headquarters for extra help. Eda Crispin had gone to the station with more ideas, and she joined the team that came to the old Gammel house. When she saw the blood, a shiver ran down her spine.

"I don't think it's the kids'," Mike said, trying to sound more reassuring than he felt. "I found a high-heeled shoe in the cellar."

"Maybe it was one of Irene's?"

"No, it looked brand-new," the sheriff said.

The two officers were standing in the downstairs hallway, watching the flurry of activity as the forensics team went to work on the house. A man in a gray suit sidled past them, holding up a plastic bag containing the stylish shoe. Mike stopped him with a hand on his shoulder.

"Have a look, Eda," he said.

Eda recognized the shoe at once.

"That belongs to Tiffany Simmons," she said.

"The reporter?"

Eda nodded. "She was wearing this shoe—or its twin—just the other day. We had a confrontation in Lucille's driveway. Those are designer shoes—I don't think many people around here wear them."

Mike gave the bag back to the forensics technician.

"Have someone locate Tiffany Simmons," he ordered.

"Do you think something happened to her?" Eda asked, her gaze falling on the bloodstains.

"I don't know," Mike said. "But if there's been another victim, Chris and those kids are in more danger than ever. As soon as she gets back from Blueriver, I think you should make plans to get her out of Aberdeen."

Eda sighed, but nodded in agreement. It was just getting too dangerous.

"Mike, I had some thoughts," Eda said. "You probably figured this out on your own, but do you realize Teddy Gammel can't be the man who stalked Christy all those years ago?"

"Of course," Mike said. "He was only a child at the time. But he seems our prime suspect right now."

"If he is," Eda said, "then the person who murdered

Darren Gammel and Basil Horton is still free. Assuming he's alive, of course."

It was becoming crowded in the hallway, so the two walked out onto the porch.

"I was also wondering about Adrian," Eda continued. "Have you been able to locate his stepfather?"

"No," Mike replied. "But I've learned some interesting things about Douglas Eastman. He owns one of the biggest trucking companies in the West. Teddy's doctor, Marion Niles, was kind enough to provide some information. She also said Eastman is an extremely unpleasant individual. Dr. Miles says he's partly to blame for Teddy's problems."

"But not entirely," Eda said thoughtfully. "Not if he came into the picture after Irene left Aberdeen."

Eda grimaced, wrapping her arms around herself. She felt chilled despite the heat of the July morning. This house, with its tragic history, seemed to suck all warmth from the surrounding area.

"Maybe she had the kids with her later in life," she said, "but she sure didn't have them when she left here. What kind of mother dumps her kids that way?"

Mike didn't have an answer for her.

"Listen, I'd better get home," Eda said. "I want to be there when Chris arrives."

"Let me give you a lift," Mike said. "I've got things to take care of at headquarters."

Eda smiled at him. "Thanks. I walked to the station this morning. Chris took Lucille's car up to Blueriver."

Mike dropped Eda at Lucille's house. When she entered, she heard the soft clicking of a computer keyboard, and guessed Lucille was working on her new mystery novel. Eda decided to give Tim Becker a call, but as she was dialing the phone, she heard a car pull into the driveway. She hung up and hurried to look out the window. Then she called out:

"Lucille! Chris is back!"

The typing noises stopped at once, and Lucille was in the kitchen a moment later. She opened the back door and hurried to the car. Unfortunately, one of the few reporters who had remained at the Wander house saw her—and saw Chris. He came hurrying across the street, followed by his colleagues.

"Go away!" Lucille demanded, putting a protective arm around Chris.

"Just a few questions, Mrs. Wander!"

"Do you know anything about the blood at the old Gammel house?"

Chris swung around, her eyes huge.

"Blood?"

Eda stepped around her friends, flashing her badge quickly so no one could see it was from out-of-state.

"Back off!" she snapped as the other two women raced for the back door. "Or I'll have you in jail on harassment charges!"

"Freedom of the press, lady!"

"Up your freedom," Eda mumbled, entering Lucille's house.

"Blood?" Chris said again, as if she didn't understand the word. "What was he talking about?"

"They found fresh blood at the Gammel house," Eda told her. Chris gasped, and Eda held up a hand. "Mike doesn't think it's from the kids. For one thing, they found a woman's shoe that wasn't there a few days ago."

"Never mind that now," Lucille said. "Chris, we were worried sick about you! Tell us what you've been doing all morning!"

They brought Chris into the living room, where the drawn curtains gave them some privacy. Their friend's face was blotched red, her eyes shining. She looked from Eda to Lucille, then blurted:

"He set me up! My own brother set me up just to get money!"

Her friends sat to either side of her.

"Start at the beginning, Chris," Eda said.

"I wish you hadn't gone to see Harvey," Lucille said. "I knew he would upset you."

Chris shook her head.

"No, I'm glad I went," she said. "This is something that's been a dark hole inside of me for thirty years. At least now I have some answers."

She sniffled hard. Lucille found a box of tissues and handed them to her.

"You know how I've always been so down around the holidays?"

Both women nodded.

"Now I know why," Chris said. "Harvey told me everything. That night of your Hanukkah celebration, Eda, when he came to walk me home, it was really to lead me into a trap. He told me they were giving out free toys at the Salvation Army, but that was a lie. There was a man waiting in an alley for us. He'd told Harvey he'd pay my brother five hundred dollars for a little girl. He said there was a family who wanted to adopt me."

She sighed deeply.

"All the time," she said, "it was really the man who committed those murders, thirty years ago. Harvey told me so at the jail. But he wouldn't tell me the man's name. I tried to reason with him, but he's so much like my father. He started yelling and slammed his fist on the table so loudly the guard came and took him away."

The women gave themselves a few moments to absorb this new information. Then Lucille got up and announced she was going to make coffee.

"I need that," Chris said. "Thank you."

"Are you okay?" Eda asked. "I mean, about Harvey?"

"Not okay," Chris said, "but not surprised. I should have known he was up to something. After the party, I kept dreaming that Harvey was talking to someone. That person said I had seen too much. But I don't know what it is I saw! Only Irene Gammel with blood on her! Nothing more! What does it mean?"

Eda shifted position on the couch.

"We have some new information, Chris," she said. "We think the man who killed Brian and took the kids might be Teddy Gammel."

"Teddy!" Chris said in surprise. "You mean he's alive?"

"Yes," Eda said. "Mike called the doctor who's name was on the pad I found. He's one of her patients. He's been missing for a while."

"What about Adrian?"

"Adrian was put up for adoption," Eda said.

Chris turned toward the closed curtains and parted them just enough to look outside. Since her arrival back at Lucille's house, at least two more reporters had shown up.

"It's amazing how sick a family can be," she said, comparing her own nightmarish childhood to Teddy's and Adrian's. "Maybe Adrian was the lucky one. Maybe he got into a descent, loving family."

Lucille came back with coffee. Chris finished her cup and refilled it halfway before she, or anyone else, spoke again.

"If Teddy has come back to Aberdeen," she said, "then it was because someone told him to. That man who had been following me must have put Teddy up to this."

"If Teddy's that easily influenced," Eda said, "then he's more dangerous than we can imagine. Only a very unstable person would do the evil work of another man."

"It's almost as if the devil himself has come to Aberdeen," Lucille agreed with a shiver.

Chris turned and put her arms around her friend. Eda leaned close and embraced the other two. They hugged, gathering strength from each other as they had so many times before.

THIRTY-FIVE

▼

TEDDY GAMMEL WAS scared. Almost more scared than he had been that time when he and Adrian were kids. The sight of police cars around his old house shook him deeply. He stayed in the woods that wrapped behind the back three acres of his family's property, sometimes climbing up a tree to watch the activity. From that height, he could just barely make out the difference in the tall grass that indicated the trapdoor to the fallout shelter. He wished he could run to it, climb down inside and hide, the way Douglas had hidden him and Adrian so long ago. But then the police might see him, and they might take the kids away.

He knew the kids were the only way he was going to get Christy to come back to Washington with him. It would be just the way it had been with his mother and Douglas. They had gotten Daddy out of the way, and he had gotten Christy's husband out of the way. That was what Douglas had told him to do. Douglas had told him he didn't want Brian buying the old house, and had sent Teddy to Aberdeen to put a stop to it. Teddy had been nervous, but Douglas had said, "Just do as I would do. Just get rid of him."

Teddy knew the right way to get rid of people. When you took off someone's head, they never came back.

Mike hung up the phone after talking with the station manager of Cable 75 News. Tiffany Simmons had been due on the set at six A.M., but she hadn't arrived. The station manager had called her house, with no answer. Mike suggested she might have overslept, but the station manager adamantly disagreed. Tiffany was almost obsessive in her work, beyond professional in her punctuality and dedication. She would never oversleep. No, he believed she was sick, too ill to even answer the phone. He wanted to know why the sheriff was so interested, but Mike declined to reply. Instead, he drove to Tiffany's house to check for himself. Nobody answered his knock.

Mike had the impression that Tiffany would cry foul if she knew he'd gone into her house without a search warrant.

He didn't give a damn what she thought.

He worked the lock on the front door and went inside. Tiffany Simmons lived in a small Cape Cod, elegantly furnished in an ultramodern style. The interior was immaculate. Every knickknack seemed to have its place, every throw pillow was turned in a precise way and carefully fluffed. There were no newspapers scattered on the floor, no books left on the bed, no lipsticks or compacts out on the dresser. The place looked as if no one lived there at all.

Mike went into each room, picking up an item here and there. He found a huge trophy in the den, with the words LITTLE MISS NORTHWEST on it. There was a picture of Tiffany at a very young age near it; she was taking a bow in a frilly dress, showing off her new crown. Another trophy, only a foot high, sat on the mantel. It was an award for her work on Cable 75.

Pictures showed Tiffany with various celebrities, Tiffany with friends, Tiffany on the arm of a handsome man. Mike made a mental note to inquire about him. He was about to turn from the room when something jumped him from behind. A loud wail rang in his ears, and something sharp dug into his neck. He stumbled back against the fireplace, knocking down the big trophy. With lightning reflexes, he swung around as he pulled out his gun.

Then he laughed and holstered the weapon. His assailant was a cat. She rubbed herself around Mike's ankles, crying pitifully.

"You sound hungry," Mike said.

He went to the kitchen and saw that the cat had neither food nor water. If Tiffany was so conscientious about her job and her house, it was hard to believe she would have gone out without taking care of her pet.

Mike found some dry food and filled the animal's dish. As he poured water for her, worry about a new victim started to creep into his mind. He snapped off the water, cutting away the thought at the same time. Until all the evidence was presented (that is, until he saw a body), he wasn't going to waste time with speculation.

As he was setting the water dish on the floor, he noticed a scrap of paper. In this almost sterile environment, it stood out like a beacon. Mike picked it up and read:

"Property tax on Gammel place—Why was Wander paying it?"

So Tiffany knew about that. And if someone was aware that she knew, that person might have tried to stop her inquiry.

"Tiffany must have gone to the house to have a look for herself," he said. "She must have run into the suspect there."

He pocketed the note and left the house through the front door. Checking his watch, he noticed it was shortly after noon. Mike drove straight to the station, planning to work through lunch. Douglas Eastman had promised to come in from Washington to discuss his stepson, and Mike was hoping someone had heard from him. The man refused to come by plane, and Mike knew the trip would take nearly a day by car.

He was only a little surprised to see Eda in the records room, pouring over the files again.

"I couldn't stop thinking about the autopsies," she said. "Look, I've made some charts."

Mike came around behind her to study the papers. Eda had listed each characteristic of the killings in a column headed by the victim's name. Eda pointed to the descriptions of the wounds.

"Look at Darren Gammel," she said. "The wound was fairly clean. The coroner felt it was made by only a few sharp blows. But look at Basil Horton. His injury seems to have been made with a more sawing action. The edges are very ragged—in fact, they're downright sloppy. And he's the only one who took a blow to the back of the head. Brian Wander's wound is much like the first one, only there were bruises around his face to indicate he'd also been beaten. Other than a few scratches, Darren's injuries are concentrated on his neck."

Mike nodded.

"I remember," he said. "We all believed Darren had been attacked too quickly to put up a fight. Basil and Brian must have tried to stop the killer."

"But it seems Basil was hit from behind," Eda said. "The coroner stated he was bludgeoned first. He was probably dead before his head was taken off. And that's what bothers me. Why saw it off so haphazardly? Why not do it neatly, the way the first murder was done? A dead man wouldn't struggle."

"It's almost as if the killings were done by two different people," Mike said, reading Eda's mind. "But, remember, the equipment we had in the early sixties wasn't nearly as sophisticated as today's. Back then, all the evidence pointed to one person."

"You thought it was Irene Gammel at first," Eda recalled.

"We let her out after the second murder occurred," Mike said. "She had a good lawyer, who presented us with a writ of habeas corpus. We couldn't hold her without definite evidence, especially after the second body was found."

Eda thought for a moment.

"There were people who still believed she was guilty—" she said.

"We'll never know Irene's side, will we?" Mike interrupted. "But the very fact that this new crime occurred after she died could be a clue. Her husband should be here this afternoon, driving all the way from Washington. I'm hoping he can fill in a few clues."

Eda started to gather up the papers and return them to the files. "What do you know about this guy?" she asked.

"It seems Irene married him a few years after leaving Aberdeen," Mike said. "He's a rich and powerful fellow. Owns a huge trucking company."

"Rich and powerful enough to keep Irene away from the police all these years?"

"Maybe," Mike said. "We'll get more answers when he arrives. In the meantime, I have some questions about Tiffany Simmons. She's missing—didn't go to work this morning, and not at home."

Eda went to the cabinet and returned the files to their places. She was frowning when she turned around.

"I never liked her," she said, "but I'd never wish her real harm. I hope we don't have another victim, Mike."

"I don't let myself think about that," Mike said. "Because if I do, then I have to think about Chris's kids."

Chris stared at the soap opera playing on the television screen, but though the images were being fed to her eyes her brain wasn't really picking them up. Numbed by the things she'd experienced in the last days, she really wasn't seeing anything. Her mind was devoid of thought, but the red in her eyes and the paleness of her skin spoke of her torment.

She hadn't slept or eaten much, in spite of Lucille's efforts. She'd given herself time to pity the little girl who had been betrayed by her brother, but that tugging of her heart was quickly transferred to her own children. What were Josh and Vicki going through now? Did they think that their own mother had betrayed them because she hadn't come to their rescue? The idea was so disturbing she'd quickly shut it away. That effort, combined with exhaustion, had rendered her almost paralyzed.

A newsbreak came on between shows and the children's pictures were flashed on the screen. The newscaster told of the blood found around the old Gammel house and speculated on foul play.

"Police are not saying if Christine Wander is still a suspect," he said. "All efforts to reach the mother of these two missing children have failed. Our own Tiffany . . ."

Chris didn't hear the last of it. She started wailing, great tears pouring from her eyes, blurring the recorded image of the police at the Gammel house.

Hearing her friend's sobs, Lucille left her desk and hurried into the living room, snapping off the television. Without a word, she took Chris into her arms and held her until she calmed down.

"God, this has got to end soon," Lucille whispered.

In spite of the blanket thrown over it, the thing near the ladder looked like what it was: a person. There was no pretending it was a dummy or a robot. The blood that had caked on the shoeless leg was too real.

Vicki and Josh remained cuddled close together, not wanting to look at the body but unable to look away. Vicki thought it would get up and walk if they didn't watch it, and the thought of those cold fingers touching her neck kept her facing the hideous sight.

Josh looked at the ladder as he tried to plan their escape. Every few seconds, his eyes were drawn to the shrouded form, but he quickly averted them. This wasn't a video game, he told himself. You didn't win endless lives by entering the right secret code or picking up a certain number of gold pieces. Dead was forever, and dead didn't move.

But he still didn't want to go near that thing.

Dead didn't move.

He wondered how she'd gotten here in the first place.

Dead didn't move.

She sure as heck hadn't come down here on her own.

"I know!" he cried out, so suddenly that Vicki screamed. He frowned at her. "Be quiet."

"You scared me!"

"Sorry," he said. "I just thought of something."

"What?"

"Nothing."

"You said it was something!"

"It's none of your business!"

He didn't want to tell his little sister what he'd realized. Of course that woman hadn't come down here on her own. That creepy guy had brought her, the way he'd brought that extra food. Josh and Vicki hadn't noticed him because they'd been asleep at the time. Somehow, the guy knew when they were asleep.

"Josh, I'm hungry," Vicki whined. "And I want something to do. This is boring. I want my trolls and my toy pony and my play dishes and—"

"Quiet," Josh said. "I'm thinking. Go open a bag of chips and eat that."

Vicki made a worried face.

"It's okay," Josh said. "She can't hurt you. It's just a shell. There's no real person in there."

"The real person's gone to heaven?"

Josh shrugged.

"She isn't gonna get up and walk?"

"That's a really dopey idea."

Vicki got up slowly, never taking her eyes from the cloaked figure. She sidled over to the food shelves and reached back until she found a bag. It was cereal rather than chips but that was good enough. Still believing that woman would get up and chase her, she hurried back to the cot and plunked down. She crammed handfuls of cereal into her mouth.

"Cut that out," Josh said. "What the heck do you expect me to do if you choke?"

Vicki slowed down, but didn't stop eating. When she was finally satisfied, she started playing with the cereal that had spilled on the bed, making designs. She tried not to think about the lady under the blanket.

In the meantime, Josh was working out another plan. He had to trick that creep into thinking they were both asleep. Then, when the guy came down again, he'd be ready. He still thought throwing cans at him was a good idea. After all, there were no other weapons to use. Josh could hide a big can, then jump behind the jerk and let him have it.

The only trick was to stay awake long enough—and have the strength to fight.

THIRTY-SIX

JOSH TRIED VERY hard to stay awake. Long after Vicki had given in to fitful slumber, he remained alert, waiting. Josh wondered if the man had a hidden camera he used to watch them. Just in case he did, Josh kept his eyes closed. If the man looked now, he'd think both children had dropped off. But Josh kept himself awake, going over division facts in his head, thinking of all the tunes from his favorite video games, imagining seeing his mom again.

A vision of his father struggling with another man came to mind, but he snapped his eyes open to end it.

The blanket had fallen from the woman's body. Her eyes were staring at him. Josh was certain she could see him. In the strange light from overhead, her skin was a horrid gray color. Blood had caked around a wound in her shoulder and stained her blouse. Her mouth started working, her hand rose up slowly, pointing, accusing. . . .

She started to rise, moving ever so slowly, as if she was

in pain. One of her arms, cut nearly to the bone just above the elbow, hung at a strange angle.

Josh screamed.

And found himself sitting bolt upright on the cot.

"A nightmare," he whispered. "Just a nightmare."

He was shaking all over. He didn't want to look across the room, but forced himself. The body was still hidden under the blanket, unmoved and unmoving.

Josh got up on weak legs and hurried to use the rusted, dry toilet. When he came back, he grabbed hold of the end of Vicki's cot. He began dragging it towards the room that had been locked that first day, the empty closet. Vicki rolled onto her stomach and picked up her head, regarding him with bloodshot eyes.

"What're you doin'?"

"I don't want to be near her," Josh said. "We're moving into the other room."

"Oh, good," Vicki said, and dropped off to sleep again.

The cot was just a fraction of an inch narrower than the door, and it was a ten-minute struggle just to get it through. When he finally succeeded, he went back outside to pick up cans. Sometime while they were knocked out, their captor had gathered up their arsenal and had stacked the shelves neatly again. Josh gathered as many cans as possible and brought them into the room. He piled them around the bed, within ready reach. This time, that jerk wouldn't win.

Lucille was glad when Chris finally fell asleep. She left her friend lying on the couch, covered her with an afghan, and turned the dimmer switch until the room was bathed in a soft glow. Eda had gone back to the police station to work, and Lucille didn't expect her to return until very late. Lucille checked all the doors and windows before going to bed.

Some time later, unusual noises from the back of the house stirred Chris awake. She bunched the edge of the afghan in her hands and shifted position, trying to get back to sleep. But the noise was persistent. At last Chris pulled herself to her feet and padded back to the kitchen. She vaguely remembered Lucille saying Eda was working late at the police station. It was probably just her friend coming home.

Without thinking, she unlocked and opened the back door.

He stood there, her nemesis, her tormentor, her devil.

Ugly green eyes. A big, glimmering knife.

She opened her mouth to scream, but the sound froze in the back of her throat.

"I said I'd rip your face off if you told anyone," he hissed.

And the glimmering knife flashed forward, so quickly it seemed part of his hand, cutting, ripping. . . .

But she didn't feel anything.

She was lying on the couch in Lucille's living room. It had only been a horrible nightmare.

"Christy?" A whispered inquiry.

Chris gasped. He really *was* there! His eyes shone in the dim light, as evil as they'd been many years ago.

Oh, no, this is just another dream!

"Wake up! Wake me up!"

"You are awake, Christy! I've come back for you!"

Christy began to scream. She tried to get up, but the afghan was wrapped around her legs, tripping her. Malevolent laughter filled the room.

A knife flashed towards her. She rolled just in time, and the blade caught the cushion she'd been using as a pillow.

He tossed the cushion aside as Chris freed herself, stumbling towards the door.

"Lucille! *Lucille!*"

Why wasn't her friend answering?

Because it's only a dream!

"Christy! The game is over! I've come to finish you once and for all! You lose!"

He shot in front of her, blocking her exit.

"Please let me wake up!" Chris begged.

The sound of the kitchen door closing made both of them turn. Christy screamed as her assailant pushed her aside and ran for the front door. Lucille came running downstairs, her long, dark hair flying about the shoulders of her pink nightgown.

"Chris, what happened?" she cried.

Eda burst out of the kitchen.

"I heard her screaming," she said with concern.

Chris pointed to the front door.

"He was here! That man was here! He tried to kill me!"

Eda wasted no time. She shouted orders to Lucille to call the sheriff and took off after the man herself. Hidden in the shadows of night, and a few seconds behind him, she wasn't certain at first which way to go. But training and instinct took over, and somehow she knew to run towards the Gammel house.

She was only a block behind him as he reached the corner. He stopped, and even from a distance she could see his shoulders heaving up and down. The run had been an effort for him, and she was certain she would catch him. He seemed to hesitate, gazing down the street at the old house.

"Freeze!" Eda shouted. *"Police!"*

He took one look at her and bolted again. As she raced past the cross street, she saw a squad car, and seconds later heard the sirens blaring. Lucille's call had gone through.

The car pulled up alongside her, and the woman inside opened the door.

"Get in, Officer Crispin," Lieutenant Noreen Royston said. "My partner's waiting at the house in case he doubles back through the woods."

Eda caught her breath, then said:

"There's a recharge basin back there, right?" she asked. "He'd have to climb over barbed wire."

"That's what I'm hoping," Noreen said.

In seconds, they had passed the woods and come around the back of the sump. Another car came up from behind them, beacons flashing. Headlights, beacons, and moonlight illuminated the fence and made the recharge basin as bright as day. They fell upon a man struggling to free himself from the barbed wire. Eda got out of the car and watched as Mike Hewlett and his deputies took position with aimed firearms.

"This is the police," Mike boomed through his megaphone. "Come down from the fence, put your hands in the air, and turn around slowly."

Eda expected a struggle, but to her surprise the perp did as he was told. When he turned, she got a good view of him in the light, and gasped.

He was a frail old man, his eyes bugging out of his gaunt face. More alarming was his right hand, for there was no hand. The arm ended in a stump.

Mike and the others hurried to make the arrest. As the beacons swung around, Eda noticed something glistening up in the barbed wire. She walked over to the fence and looked up. Then she shouted for Mike and pointed:

"It's a prosthetic device," she said. "It must have worked loose when he got caught up there."

Noreen was reading the man his rights. Mike came to the fence and worked the device loose, then handed it to another deputy.

"Do we have our suspect, Mike, after thirty years?"

Mike shook his head. "I just can't know, Eda. He's only got one hand. How can a person with one hand commit three murders?"

"And it doesn't tell us where Teddy is," Eda agreed. Until they could interrogate the man, there would be no more answers.

The old man's head snapped up.

"Teddy saw too much! I shoulda killed that brat thirty years ago! I shoulda killed all of 'em!"

He began laughing maniacally. Mike gestured towards one of the cars, and the man was taken away.

"I'd better get back to Chris," Eda said. "You'll be wanting to talk to her. Do you want me to bring her down to the station?"

"I don't think that's necessary," Mike said. "She's been traumatized enough. I'll give you a ride and talk to her at Lucille's house."

At home, they found Lucille desperately trying to soothe Chris.

"We got him," Eda said. "We don't know who he is, but he's in custody."

When she saw Eda and Mike, Chris pulled away from Lucille's comforting embrace and ran to take her friend by the shoulders.

"It was that horrible man who chased me when I was a kid," she said. "Eda, I remembered something! I remembered something about the day Irene Gammel smeared blood on me!"

Lucille stood up. She'd dressed in a robe and had tied her hair back. Dark circles rimmed her eyes.

"She's been babbling ever since you left," Lucille said. "Maybe you can get some sense from her."

Eda took Chris by the arm and led her back to the

couch. Mike took another seat, pulled out a writing pad and sat ready to take notes.

"Do you know this man's name?" Mike asked. "Now that you've seen him up close, can you give us his identity?"

Chris gave Mike a quick glance, but looked directly at Eda when she answered the question.

"I don't know his name," she said. "But when I saw him tonight, when he grabbed me, I remembered! That day I rode my bike from your house, Eda, Irene came out all covered with blood. I always thought she was alone, and couldn't understand why that man was after me. Now I know why! *He* came out of the house and threatened to rip my face off if I told anyone what I saw!"

Lucille groaned.

"Did he have the metal hand?" Mike asked.

Chris nodded slowly, the memory of that horrible time coming back to her.

"He grabbed me and shoved that claw in my face," Chris said. "I thought for certain he really would gouge out my eyes."

"All those times you thought you saw a gleaming knife," Eda said, "it could have been that prosthesis."

"I think so, now," Chris said. "But there's something more. Irene was all covered with blood, but I'm sure that man didn't have any on him at all."

Nobody spoke for a few moments, each deep in thought. Finally, Lucille said:

"How come we never noticed him around town?" she asked. "I mean, other than when he was stalking Chris. How could a man with one hand remain unnoticed?"

"How could a man with one hand cut off someone's head?" Eda asked.

Mike leaned forward.

"Your theory about two people is beginning to gel," he said to Eda. "I don't think this man killed Darren Gammel. I wouldn't be surprised if Irene herself did it."

"But she was let go," Chris said, "because another murder took place while she was in jail."

Mike and Eda looked at each other, thinking of the differences in the autopsies.

"Irene killed her husband," Eda said, "but Basil Horton's wounds were sloppy. And it was a blow to the head that killed him. I think this man killed him, just to clear Irene's name."

Chris's eyes went round.

"Then he came back to kill my husband?" she asked, her voice rising. "Why? What did Brian ever do to him?"

Mike stood up. "I don't know," he said. "But I'm going to find out. They ought to be finished booking him by now. I've got to get back to the station."

Chris had been looking at Eda the whole time, but now she grabbed Mike's sleeve.

"No, don't go," she said. "There's more. That man threatened me another time, and it wasn't just when he was following me. My brother led me into a trap, and I think he wanted to hurt me."

"But you said you were unconscious through most of that," Eda reminded her.

Now Chris turned to her again.

"Through most of it," she said. "But bits and pieces keep coming back to me. And I remember something. I remember being carried down into a dark room. We had to climb a ladder."

She stopped, thoughtful.

"What else?" Lucille encouraged.

"I . . . I . . ." Chris said. "I'm sorry. It's starting to come back, but not fast enough. But I think that ladder and that room might be clues."

"There's a way to bring these memories out more fully," Mike said. "Would you consider hypnosis?"

Chris's reply was instant, firm.

"Hell yes," she said. "You know I'll do anything at all to get my kids back!"

THIRTY-SEVEN

▼

TEDDY LEANED AGAINST the chain-link fence that surrounded the recharge basin, his fingers entwined in the octagons. He had been roaming through the woods, waiting for a chance to get back to the fallout shelter, when he heard the sirens and saw the flashing red lights. Hidden in the shadows of the trees, he had watched the entire scene being played a few hundred yards away.

The police had arrested someone. He couldn't see the person's face very clearly, despite the light from the squad car beacons. But when he saw them freeing a metal device from the barbed wire he knew at once what had happened.

Somehow, Douglas had come looking for him. He must have learned how badly Teddy had messed up, and he had planned to teach him the right way to do things. Douglas was always teaching him the right way to do things.

Learning the right way hurt.

Teddy pulled away from the fence and tried to run back

into the woods. But his legs were as immobile as the surrounding trees. Only his knees moved, rapidly knocking together. He was dealing with more terror than he could handle: not only were the police after him, but his stepfather as well. There was no escaping the hurt.

If only Adrian had been there. Adrian was always nice to him. Even after those other people took him away, Adrian came back once in a while to visit his brother. Their parents tried to stop them from meeting, but the boys were too close. Teddy had loved Adrian so much.

Until he'd taken away Teddy's prize.

"Why did you steal Christy from me?" Teddy whispered aloud, sinking down into the dirt floor of the woods. "Douglas said Christy was for *me*."

Maybe if Adrian hadn't taken Christy it would have been okay.

He wondered where Adrian was now.

He wanted to tell him he forgave him, because Adrian had given up Christy after all. She'd married another man, some guy named Brian Wander.

Chris made herself comfortable in the big armchair near Lucille's bedroom window. Lucille had insisted on putting a blanket over her lap and a pillow behind her head. It was such a relaxing position that she had no trouble sinking into the depths of hypnosis as the psychiatrist spoke softly to her.

Mike Hewlett had explained the situation to Dr. Lloyd McKechnie, who had agreed to come to Lucille's house right away. When he introduced himself to Chris, he explained that he was good friends with the analyst who had helped Chris deal with her childhood. That immediately established a basis for trust. Chris was so eager to find out the truth she'd kept suppressed for years that she went under very easily.

Dr. McKechnie sat in a chair brought up from the kitchen, facing Chris. Lucille and Eda sat on the edge of Lucille's bed, and Mike was in a chair he'd borrowed from the twins' bedroom. In the quiet, dark safety of the bedroom, Chris began to go back in time.

And once more, she was Christy.

"Where are you now, Christy?" the doctor asked gently.

"Outside," Chris said in a higher voice. "The snow is so pretty."

Lucille turned to Eda with a surprised look on her face. Eda smiled reassuringly. She'd witnessed hypnosis before, and it didn't surprise her that Chris sounded very much like a seven-year-old.

"Tell me what you're doing," Dr. McKechnie urged.

"Walking with my brother," Chris said. "I was at Eda's party. It was so much fun! I have a new bracelet."

She held out her hand as if to show off the charm bracelet. Lucille found herself looking for it.

"But now you're going home," McKechnie said.

Chris shook her head.

"No, Harvey says they're giving away toys," she said. "We're going to get some."

"Christy, I want you to move ahead a little," McKechnie said. "You told me earlier that Harvey took you down a shortcut. What happened next?"

"We turned a corner and . . . Oh, no!"

Chris's face twisted up, and she began to wriggle in the chair.

"What do you see?"

"Oh, it's him! It's the bad man with those mean eyes!"

The psychiatrist gave her hand a squeeze.

"No one can hurt you," he said. "These are just memories. Tell us what happens next."

"He . . . he's pushing something yucky in my face," Chris said. "I—"

She stopped talking, her head dropping to her chest.

"What happened?" Mike whispered.

McKechnie held up a hand.

"Christy? Christy, come out of it, honey," he said.

Chris stirred again.

"I hear voices."

"What are they saying?"

"He says he's gong to take me to be with Teddy," Chris went on. "He says I saw, I know. But Harvey says it's a joke. Oh, no! He has a rope!"

"What is he doing with the rope? It's okay, Christy. The rope can't hurt you now."

Tears were streaming down Chris's face. She brought her hands up to her neck.

"He's tying me up," she said. "And .. ugh! . . . oh, he's putting me over his shoulder. I don't like hanging like this. Put me down!"

She wriggled in the chair.

"Christy, where is the man taking you?"

"Down a dark street," she said.

"Do you recognize it?"

Christy frowned, thoughtful.

"Oh, no," she whimpered. "He's taking me to that terrible house. To that house where the crazy lady put blood on me. My daddy beat me up because of that!"

Eda bit her lip to keep from making a comment.

"Go on," the doctor urged gently.

"We're walking across the yard," she said. "It's hard because the snow is so deep."

"Christy, why don't you yell for help?"

"Can't," Chris said. "He's got something around my mouth."

She paused for a few moments, her eyebrows furrowed.

"There's a funny door," she said. "A door in the ground! Why would there be a door in the ground?"

Another pause.

"He's pulling it open," she went on. "It makes a funny creaking noise. It's dark down there. I don't want to go down there!"

She began to wail. "Harvey! Harvey!"

"Christy! What is Harvey doing now?"

"He's fighting with the man. He's kicking him. Oh! Harvey just hit him really hard with a hubcap! The man fell down. Harvey's untying me. He's telling me to run, but I can't. I can't! I—"

Once more, she passed out.

"She must have fainted at that time when she was a kid," Eda guessed.

"You can bring her around, Dr. McKechnie," Mike said. "I've got my information."

Carefully, the psychiatrist helped Chris back to the present. She blinked and looked around at everyone's concerned faces.

"Is it okay now?" she asked. "Are we going to find my kids?"

Mike smiled at her. "You gave us a big clue."

"I don't understand," Lucille said.

Eda stood up and went to put a hand on Chris's shoulder.

"The door in the ground," she said. "That was 1962."

"So?" said Lucille.

"The Cuban Missile Crisis?" Eda prompted. "Lucille, Chris, there's a fallout shelter on that property!"

Mike was already heading for the door.

"And I would bet we're going to find your kids there," he said.

In her excitement, Chris stood up so quickly she became dizzy. Dr. McKechnie and Eda took either arm and steadied her.

"Easy," the doctor said. "Relax for a moment."

"No!" Chris said. "My babies might be trapped in a dark room underground! I'm not staying here!"

Eda looked at Mike, who nodded.

"Then come with us in the police car," Eda said. "Lucille?"

"You aren't leaving me behind," Lucille said emphatically.

After a quick thank-you to Dr. McKechnie, the foursome left. Lucille had found two working flashlights, and gave one to Chris. Mike found two more in his car. He radioed ahead for backup, in case Teddy was found. Within minutes, they were at the Gammel house again. As she stood looking up at the eerie old house, Eda remembered something.

"I heard voices the other day," she said. "I thought it was Josh, calling for help. But I couldn't find anything." She sighed, "If I had only known . . ."

To everyone's surprise, it was Chris who comforted her.

"You did the best you could," she said.

"Right," Mike agreed. "Now, let's finish it."

He called to the two officers who were on watch and explained his suspicions.

"This is a huge piece of property," Lucille said. "It could take us a long time to find that trapdoor."

"Not if each of us concentrates on a section," Mike said.

At his orders, they spread arm's distance from each other. They began to walk straight ahead, pushing aside tall grass that scratched at their arms and faces. Chris swatted at numerous mosquitoes, and Lucille mumbled worries about ticks.

"I have another idea," Eda called to Chris, who was standing about two feet from her. "Maybe we can get a good look at the whole property from the attic."

Mike had heard her. "Great idea. Why don't you run up there?"

"No," Chris said. "I want to go. If someone's going to find that door, I want it to be me."

Eda saw no point in arguing with that logic.

"Okay," she said. "But give us a call from that window when you get up there."

"What if Teddy's up there?" Lucille protested.

"He can't be," said one of the officers. "We would have seen him go into the house."

With a wave, Chris raced back to the house, entering via the kitchen door. The dark house smelled of must and mold, but it didn't frighten her now. Her mind was too full of determination to let fear creep in. Aiming the flashlight, she hurried up to the old attic.

The attic was so congested with summer heat that Chris found herself gasping for breath. Moonlight glowing through the window beckoned her, and she hurried to open it. But as she was reaching for the cobweb-strewn latch, someone grabbed her from behind.

There was no time to scream before he covered her mouth and pinned an arm behind her back.

"I can't wait for you any longer," the man whispered. "Adrian got to you first, but you were supposed to be mine. Douglas said you were mine!"

Chris knew that struggling would only make things worse. Somehow Teddy had managed to sneak back into the house, and had been hiding up here the whole time. She prayed she could reason with him, bring out the little boy who had been abused as much as she.

"Don't scream," he said.

She shook her head. Slowly, he pulled his hand away. When he was satisfied she'd keep quiet, he turned her around.

In the moonlight, his eyes were so much like Brian's that Chris had to bite her tongue to keep from crying out.

"Are . . . are you Teddy?" she asked. Her voice was even, gentle, but she was shaking inside.

"Uh-huh," Teddy said with a nod. He sniffled from the attic dust and ran a dirty hand under his nose. His cheeks were unshaven, nearly a week's growth of beard making him look like a ragged wino.

"Teddy, where are my children?"

"In a safe place," Teddy said. "I'm protecting them from the police. I know what the police will do. They'll take the kids away from us. But don't you worry. I won't let that happen. And I won't let them split the kids apart!"

"The way they split up you and Adrian?" Chris asked.

Eda, why haven't you come looking for me? I should have opened the window by now.

"Douglas made Adrian go away," Teddy said, his lips turning into a pout. On his unkempt face, the effect was grotesque. "He said Adrian was too little to help and he couldn't afford to feed him. He wanted me to go away, too, but Mommy said no. They had a big fight. Just like the one Mommy had with Daddy, only nobody got cut up this time."

Chris felt her heart pounding. Somehow, she had to bring out the truth.

"Teddy, what happened to your mother and father?" she asked, recalling the blood-soaked woman who had come running from the house.

Teddy licked his lips and stared up at the ceiling.

"They were fighting one day," he said. "I went to their door to listen. I was leaning against it. I didn't mean for it to happen! The door opened. The door opened and I made Mommy slip and she had an ax in her hand and I made her slip and she cut off Daddy's head and there was blood everywhere and she cut him again and again and I counted fifteen times . . . fifteen is an important number . . . I cut up that man named Brian fifteen times. . . ."

Chris let out a cry of dismay. Teddy went on babbling, seeming oblivious. Chris knew this was her chance to escape. She backed towards the wooden stairs, nearly stumbling over the top one. Then she turned and ran down, her heart pounding.

"You can't get away!" Teddy cried, lunging after her.

He caught her halfway down the stairs to the first floor. Chris screamed and struggled, but she couldn't break Teddy's iron grip.

"You can't have the kids until you say you'll be mine," he said. "Douglas said you were my prize. *Mine!* Adrian wasn't supposed to get you!"

Desperately, Chris blurted:

"But I married Brian! Not Adrian!"

"No! *No!* Adrian got you! It was Adrian!"

Chris screamed again, and her screams blended with Mike Hewlett's loud voice:

"Let her go!"

She stopped struggling and looked up to see Mike, as well as two deputies, pointing their guns. With a loud cry, Teddy let her go and sank down onto the stairs. Chris saw Lucille behind the officers and ran to her friend.

"He killed Brian!"

"I know," Lucille said. "Chris, we found the fallout shelter! They're trying to get it open now!"

As Mike dealt with Teddy, Lucille brought her friend out to the site. Eda and a deputy were busy trying to pry the door open.

"I couldn't believe how well hidden it was," Eda said. "If Lucille hadn't felt a strange rise in the ground, we would have gone right by it."

She looked up at Chris from her crouched position.

"You okay?" she asked. "I was worried about you when you didn't open the window."

"Teddy was up there," Chris said breathlessly. But she

didn't care about that right now. She only cared about getting that door open.

At last, the latch came free, and the door swung back with a loud clank. A soft glow rose from the room beneath them. The deputy looked at Eda.

"Someone's sitting down there," he said.

Eda looked into the hole. She saw a woman's bloody foot. Chris pushed next to her and leaned over, yelling:

"Josh! Vicki! Are you down there?"

And a few seconds later:

"Mommy? Josh, wake up! It's Mommy!"

The deputy unlatched the ladder and let it fall to the floor below. He led the way, followed by the women. At the sight of the shrouded body, Lucille cried out in horror. But Chris was oblivious to anything but the wonderful sight of her precious children. She ran towards them with opened arms, gathering them to her and covering them with kisses.

"I want to go home," Vicki said.

"Me, too," Josh said. "I've had enough of this action!"

Both children kept close to their mother as she led them to the ladder. Lucille helped them up, leaving Eda and the deputy to deal with the body.

Carefully, the deputy pulled off the blanket, revealing Tiffany Simmons. Her once beautiful face had begun to bloat, her skin was covered with ugly blotches of dried blood. Eda sighed.

"She must have run into Teddy," she said. "Damn!"

She couldn't help feeling a twinge of guilt for the hatred she'd expressed towards Tiffany. The woman had been her enemy, but no one should have had to suffer like this. She moved quickly to the ladder.

"I'll get Mike," she said, wanting to be away from the scene.

Blankets had been provided for the children, who

seemed chilled despite the July heat. They were led to a
police car, Chris carrying Vicki, Josh pressed close to her
side. The police half carried, half dragged a man out of the
Gammel house. The prisoner was trying to get away, but
the handcuffs he wore made it futile. At the sight of the
man, Josh suddenly shouted, "That's the man Dad had a
fight with! He came to our house and said that Dad had
taken Mom away from him! They had a big argument, and
then they started fighting!"

"Shh," Chris said. "You can tell all that to the police
later. Let's just get you home, okay?"

They piled into the back of Mike's car. The children
pressed as close to Chris as the seat belts would allow, as
if afraid she might disappear from their sight.

THIRTY-EIGHT

▼

IT WAS JUST a game," Douglas Eastman said.

"With Christine Burnett Wander as an unwilling player," Mike retorted.

They were sitting in a small interrogation room at the precinct, a table between them, and a guard outside the door. A tape recorder, on the table, whirred softly. Mike's gun was at the ready, tucked in his shoulder holster, but he didn't think he'd need to use it. This man wasn't going to cause any more trouble. He seemed too weak to even talk, but talking was what he was doing. A lot of talking.

He'd been read his Miranda rights, but had refused a lawyer. Douglas insisted he was smart enough to defend himself. He answered Mike's quietly insistent questions in a steady manner. It was the mark of a man with a cool head. Mike could easily see how he'd come to head up one of the largest trucking companies in the West.

Anyone looking at this frail man, with his sallow skin

and missing hand, initially would have felt pity. Mike, knowing his background, saw something profane in Eastman's eyes, the look of someone without morals. Chris had seen it, too. Even at seven, she'd known this man was evil.

"Tell me from the beginning," Mike said. "Tell me about the game."

Eastman smiled, and Mike resisted the urge to grab him and make him see this wasn't funny at all.

"What beginning?" he asked. "When I met Irene? When Teddy and Adrian came of age and got their inheritance? When—"

"I suppose meeting Irene Gammel was the start of it all," Mike prompted.

"I changed a tire for her," Eastman said. "She was leaning against this Rambler on a road in the middle of nowhere. She was crying her eyes out. Tiny, pretty little thing. Well, the parts that count were big. You know what I mean."

Mike kept a straight face and said nothing.

"Anyway, I stopped to help her," Eastman continued. "I was driving a truck from Spokane to Bozeman, and I was in a hurry. But she kept going on and on about how her new husband was gonna kill her. She was so sweet. Something got the better of me. I followed her home and made sure that bastard didn't lay a hand on her. But she was lucky. Or maybe I was the lucky one that day. He wasn't home. And she showed me her appreciation in a special way."

"Special way?"

The prisoner looked at the sheriff with disdain.

"We made love." He sneered, then mumbled: "Dumb hick."

Mike ignored the remark.

"Let's move ahead in time," Mike said. "Move ahead to the day Darren Gammel was murdered. Did you kill him?"

"Yes," was the simple reply. "He found out about Irene and me, and the kids, and—"

"What about the kids?" Mike interrupted.

"Adrian and Teddy," Douglas Eastman said. "They're mine. You can tell by looking at them that they're mine."

Mike sighed. This was becoming more and more complicated.

"All right," he said. "Go on."

"That day, Irene was gonna tell Darren the truth once and for all," Douglas said. "I went there just to be with her, but that bastard tried to kill her. It was self-defense. She was defending herself."

Mike's eyebrows went up.

"But you said you were the one who killed him," he reminded.

For a second, the calm demeanor seemed to melt away. But Eastman quickly regained his composure.

"That's what I said, all right," he insisted. "I killed him. But I mean ... well ... Irene didn't stop me or nothing. Anyway, I wasn't just defending her. It was the kids, too. *My* kids. I was sick of pretending they weren't mine. I was sick of hearing how that bastard beat up on 'em. It was time to put an end to that."

You sure as hell did that, Mike Hewlett thought.

"You know what Darren Gammel called me?" Eastman asked indignantly. "He called me a *Communist*. Me! A guy who lost his hand in the Korean War! Got a purple heart for that."

There was a great deal of pride behind that statement. Mike couldn't help wondering what kind of man he'd been during that war.

"What happened with the ax?" Mike asked.

"He tried to kill me," Eastman said. "But I got hold of

it, and I gave it to him. Irene got all messed up with blood, and she went running from the house like a crazy woman. That's when she ran into that little girl—into Christy Burnett. I saw her, too. I told her to keep her mouth shut."

"Chris says you threatened to rip off her face," Mike said.

The killer gestured as if to wave his hand, although there was no hand at the end of his arm.

"Right, right," he said. "I needed to make a big threat. Anyway, she ran off. I took the kids and hid with them. Irene was arrested. I didn't want her getting blamed for murdering Darren. I figured I could kill again to clear her name and get out of town quick enough. No one in Aberdeen knew about me. Sneaking around with a married woman taught me early how to lay low. I could clear Irene, and we could all be on our way. Got a farm in Washington. Plenty of room for us."

He began coughing suddenly, harshly. Mike signaled for the guard to bring him a glass of water. Eastman drank it all before speaking again.

"Can you go on?" Mike said. "Are you sick?"

"Sicker than you know," the pale man said, "but I want to tell everything."

"When did you come back to go after Christy Burnett?"

"I watched her right from the start," Eastman said. "When I got a load of that crazy mother of hers, and the way her father beat on her—"

"How could you know about that?"

"Takes an abused kid to know one," was the reply. "I could hear the screams and yells from that apartment when I was hanging around the street corner. I could see the kid's bruises. And I knew she wouldn't tell her folks about me. That's when I decided to make a game of it. I'd check up on her once in a while to make sure she wasn't talking

to anyone about what she'd seen. And when it was safe,
I'd take her, for my boys."

"What exactly did Christy see?"

"Irene with blood all over her!" Eastman snapped.
"Ain't you paying attention?"

"There was blood on you, too, wasn't there?"

"Well . . . well, of course . . ."

"You don't seem so sure about that."

"I'm sure! You want me to tell the story, or not?"

Mike nodded. "Go ahead. I want to hear everything."

With her arms firmly around the shoulders of Josh and
Vicki, Chris followed Lucille into the Brighams' house.
Eda stayed outside for a few moments to deal with the re-
porters who had come to talk to the newly reunited family.
Chris had spoken briefly with them, hoping that would
gain her some privacy for the next few days.

Josh, pressed against his mother's leg, had remained
quiet through the interview, but Vicki had charmed everyone with her straightforward recounting of their ordeal.
Although she understood her son's reserve, Chris was worried he might bottle up his feelings and hurt himself psy-
chologically. She remembered her own childhood secrets,
and how much they had hurt her.

Lucille seemed to understand Chris's worries. Inside the
house, she took Vicki upstairs to give her a bath. Chris sat
on the living room couch with Josh cuddled against her.
She kissed the top of his head, as she had kissed him hundreds of times since finding him.

"Are you ready to talk yet?" she asked gently.

"Vicki told everything that happened," Josh replied.

"But I want to hear your story," Chris said. "From what
Vicki said, it seems you were very brave. That was a smart
idea, using the cans as weapons."

"It didn't work."

"At least you tried," Chris said.

Josh sighed. Part of him wanted to forget what had happened, but part of him wanted to tell his mother everything. She had always told him that keeping bad things inside wasn't good. Dad had said it too.

Dad . . .

Josh fixed his eyes on a picture across the room, and began to retell the story of that horrible night.

"Someone rang the bell," he said. "Dad went to answer it. I heard him say 'I told you not to come here.' Then the other guy said, 'Daddy says it's time to end the game.' They got into a big fight. Vicki got scared and hid behind the couch, but I went to see. Dad punched the guy in the nose. Then the bad guy picked up the umbrella stand and hit Dad really hard. That made Dad fall down. There was a lot of yelling. The bad guy saw me, and I ran. He grabbed me and pushed this really gross-smelling stuff on my nose. That made me sleep."

"Then he took you to the fallout shelter," Chris said. "You . . . you didn't see what he did to your father?"

"He hit Daddy with the umbrella stand," Josh said. He turned to look at his mother. "I know he killed him."

It was such a matter-of-fact statement that Chris didn't know how to respond. She was only grateful that her children hadn't witnessed the way Teddy butchered their father.

Without another word, she took Josh into her arms and hugged him tightly.

The morning passed quietly, with Lucille fending off phone calls. Both children eagerly ate the pancakes Chris prepared. In the afternoon, Vicki took a nap without protest and Josh busied himself playing with Jerry's toys. Chris was enjoying a game of cards with Eda when the door bell rang.

Lucille escorted Mike Hewlett into the living room. For

the first time since she'd arrived from New York, Eda noticed just how much older Mike had gotten. Or was it the ordeal of the past few days that had put the dark circles under his eyes and the extra gray in his hair?

"I have some news," he said. "Eastman was more than willing to tell the whole story."

"Great," Lucille said. "Now we can find out the truth."

"I hope so," Mike said.

He took a seat and waved away Lucille's offer of a cup of coffee. As the women listened, he related the story he'd heard, beginning with the day the man had come home with Irene Gammel.

"So they conspired to murder Darren Gammel?" Eda guessed.

"That's right," Mike said. "It seems Darren was going to kill Eastman, but somehow Eastman got hold of the ax. He cut the guy to pieces. Teddy was hiding in the closet. He saw the whole thing, right down to knowing how many wounds the man had."

"That poor child," Lucille mumbled. Then she shook her head, remembering that the "poor child" had murdered her best friend's husband.

"No wonder the kid went crazy," Eda said.

They glanced at Chris, but she was sitting silently, staring at her wedding ring.

"Eastman hid the boys in the fallout shelter," Mike went on, "until it was safe to move them."

"I can't understand why you guys didn't find that thirty years ago," Eda said.

"Darren Gammel was terrified of Communist invasion," the sheriff said. "When he built that fallout shelter, he was careful to do it at night, so that no one would know about it but his family. He did such a good job replacing the sod over it that was virtually undetectable, even if you knew where to look, which we didn't." It was not an excuse, just an explanation. He turned over the cap he held in his hands, giving himself a moment to organize his thoughts.

"Eastman took the boys to a farm he owns in Washington State," Mike continued. "Irene caught up with them a few months later. Eastman's elderly mother had been taking care of the boys. She was very strict, probably even beat the kids. Teddy was submissive at this point, but Adrian was still young enough to be defiant. Eastman couldn't handle the kid, and forced Irene to give him up for adoption. Then he turned all his attentions to Teddy. He kept telling the boy about the pretty little girl in Aberdeen, the one who would be Teddy's when they both grew up. They were talking about you, Chris."

Chris nodded but still didn't speak.

"Well, unknown to their respective families, Teddy was sneaking off once in a while to visit with his little brother. Teddy told Adrian about this girl, too, and Adrian began to form his own fantasy about her. But neither boy saw her for twenty years.

"Darren Gammel had a will. He left all his possessions to his wife, but she couldn't collect on it until twenty years after the date of his death. It was iron-clad, and there was nothing Irene or Douglas could do to change it. The problem was, Irene was too sick by then to travel. The only way to collect the inheritance would be for either Douglas or one of the boys to come back to Aberdeen, and Douglas had a company to run and didn't have the time."

"But wait," Eda said. "If Teddy or Adrian came to check on their mother's inheritance, he would have had to explain where they'd been for twenty years."

Mike nodded. "Right. But Eastman was clever. He knew the right way to get around that problem. He couldn't send Teddy, but he could make contact with Adrian. Under the new name his adoptive parents had given him, Adrian could pretend to be a representative of the family. Douglas knew he would be loyal to his mother, and also he knew he was more easily trusted than Teddy."

"Teddy was probably in no state to handle legal matters," Lucille guessed.

"But he was jealous that Adrian was returning to their old home," Mike said. "He insisted on accompanying his brother. It was then that Eastman instructed him to begin stalking you, the way the man had when you were younger. The only difference was, Adrian was there, too. And Adrian had grown up to be a pretty nice guy. He didn't like what he saw his brother doing, and decided he had to rescue you."

Chris gasped, bringing her fingers up to her lips.

"I don't want to hear this," she murmured.

"But you want to know the truth, don't you?" Lucille said, coaxingly.

"I can guess," Chris said. "I've known it ever since I drew that picture. I know who Adrian grew up to be."

She looked Mike squarely in the eyes.

"His adoptive parents were the Wanders, right? They named him Brian."

Mike nodded. "Brian was his middle name. Douglas explained that Adrian—I mean, Brian—told Teddy he would stop his brother from hurting you no matter what it took. He really was in love with you, Chris. Love at first sight. No matter what else you learn about your husband, keep that in mind."

"I will," Chris said, almost to herself.

"He married you to keep Teddy away from you," Mike said. "And for a long time, it worked. Teddy became so much trouble after losing you that Irene and Douglas had him committed. But about a year ago, when Irene knew she was going to die, she begged Eastman to bring her son home, which he did. After Irene died, Douglas sent Teddy back to Aberdeen to finish what he'd started twelve years ago, when Chris and Brian married. You see, the house had passed from mother to sons. Eastman was afraid a search into the home's ownership would open up a new investigation. He sent Teddy down here to warn Brian to keep quiet."

"But that was a year ago," Eda said. "Why did Teddy wait so long . . ."

Mike waved a hand and shrugged. "I don't think Eastman meant for Teddy to kill his brother. But Teddy had been keeping secrets bottled up for so long that he snapped. I think he was trying to fix the problems of his own childhood by copying the crime that had killed his own father. I honestly don't think he would have killed the children, Chris."

Chris sighed, closing her eyes.

"That's little consolation," said Lucille.

Mike stood up.

"But at least we have a confession," he said. "Both men spoke to us, although Teddy's statement is questionable, considering his mental state. We know now, though, that Douglas Eastman killed both Darren Gammel and Basil Horton. And Teddy copied him by killing Brian."

"No!" Chris spoke so loudly that everyone turned to her.

"No, that isn't right," she insisted. "It isn't right at all. I *saw* them after the first murder. I . . . I remember that Irene had blood all over her. She did, but that horrible man with the metal claw didn't."

She looked up at Mike.

"If he used an ax on Darren, why didn't he have any blood on him?"

"Oh, my God," Eda said. "Mike, the theory about two killers . . ."

"The first was a clean wound," Mike said.

"Hardly something a man with one hand could accomplish."

"The second was ragged," Mike added, "and probably occurred after a blow to the head killed Basil Horton."

"Eastman killed Horton to clear Irene's name," Eda guessed. "She murdered her own husband."

Lucille whistled softly.

"And Teddy saw that," she said. "Can insanity be hereditary?"

"That's something for Teddy's lawyers to figure out," Mike said.

Chris looked worried.

"Does that mean he could be released on grounds of insanity?"

"Never," Mike said.

"You bet," Eda agreed. "Chris, I promise you, there's no way in hell either one of those men is going to get away with what they did."

Lucille put an arm across Chris's shoulder.

"They'll never hurt you again," she said. "You've got your two best friends here to make sure of that."

EPILOGUE

CHRIS WAS SURPRISED at how many people showed up for
Brian's funeral. Of course, reporters milled around the
church steps, waiting for photographs, but most of the at-
tendees were neighbors.

"See?" Eda whispered. "Everyone in town knew what a
nice guy Brian was."

Chris nodded in silent agreement. But she knew they
hadn't come only to mourn the loss of Brian Wander.
There was also pity for the little boy who had been kidnapped so long ago, for four-year-old Adrian Gammel.

The following day, Lucille, Chris and their children accompanied Eda to the airport. Mike Hewlett was there,
too, and as they waited for the flight to be boarded, he
watched the children with amazement. Josh and Jerry were
teasing Vicki, who in turn was flirting with the twins.

"It's as if nothing ever happened," he said. "How can
kids bounce back like that?"

"We just do," Chris said. "Somehow, we just do."

She smiled at her friends.

"But having the best friends in the world helps a lot," she added. "I don't know how I can ever thank you for what you've done."

"So you've said," Eda replied, "about a million times in the past few days."

"I'll keep saying it," Chris insisted. "You found my children, and you kept me sane, you and Lucille."

"Eda's detective work was really sharp," Mike Hewlett said. "Eda, why don't you stay in Aberdeen? You can be as good a cop here as in a big city like New York."

Eda smiled but shook her head.

"Believe it or not," she said, "I miss the city. And I miss my partner."

"Tim Becker?" Lucille asked. "Is there a romance brewing here?"

Eda clicked her tongue. "Tim's been my partner for years!"

"These things take time," Lucille said, casting a knowing glance at Chris.

Chris smiled back at her.

"I'm willing to travel for a wedding," she said.

"I'm not saying a word," Eda insisted, holding up both hands. "But don't hold your breath. I'll be too busy working on my detective shield."

"You'll get it, too," Mike said. "And you'll be the best cop New York City ever saw. Of course, if all those people get to be too much for you—"

Eda cut him off.

"I'll remember that," she said.

"But only if Tim comes with her," Lucille teased.

"Lucille!"

Everyone laughed, but only for a moment. An announcement invited passengers on Eda's flight to begin boarding. Quickly, Chris threw her arms around her friend. Tears welled in her eyes, but she didn't speak. As Eda had pointed out, she'd thanked her over and over already. But she couldn't stop thinking that, if it hadn't been for Eda and Lucille, the children might never have been found.

"You hurry back," Chris said. "We didn't really have a chance to visit this time."

Lucille came to hug Eda, too.

"I might visit my agent in New York this fall," she said. "I've got a great idea for a mystery series. Three women detectives."

"You can stay at my place," Eda suggested.

Lucille gave her another hug and stepped back. Mike kissed Eda on the forehead and took both her hands.

"I'm going to report your work on this case to the governor," he said. "You deserve some kind of commendation."

The children came running over to say good-bye. The twins simply shook hands with Eda, while Jerry shyly accepted a hug. But Josh and Vicki, knowing what Eda had done for them, trapped her in a bear hug.

"Oh, I love you guys so much!" Eda said, on her knees.

"We love you, Eda," Vicki replied.

"Yeah," was all Josh would say.

Eda looked past the two little heads and up at her friends.

"This is all the reward I'll ever need."

Then she stood up, waved her hand, and boarded the flight to New York.